NINE MONTH CONTRACT

a mountain man romance

AMY DAWS

AUTHOR NOTE

Please note that this book has subjects of traditional surrogacy included in it. I did a lot of thoughtful research on this subject matter and assigned multiple sensitivity readers to it including surrogates and people who work at surrogacy agencies. I even spoke in depth with a woman who did traditional surrogacy. And my own experiences of infertility and multiple miscarriages and years of considering our own options of surrogacy made me especially dedicated to making sure I got this story right. But ultimately, this is a work of fiction between two consenting adults and should be read with an open heart and mind. For full legal requirements on becoming a surrogate, please consult the 2024 guidelines issued by the American Society for Reproductive Medicine at asrm.org.

Dedicated to Jennifer: My busted hip sounding board.

NINE MONTH CONTRACT

PROLOGUE

Help Wanted: Grumpy Mountain Man seeks baby momma to grow his seed. Uterus a must. Ovaries negotiable. Boobs not required but a nice bonus. Job is an incubator position only. No parenting allowed. Surrogate must be impervious to grunting in the form of communication and impartial to goat droppings. Rustic mountain range housing available upon request. Interested parties can text 555-5456. Murderers need not apply. Expect sizable payment and signed legal contracts before insemination commences. Also, must be cool with brotherly neighbors…and no, that isn't code for Why Choose.

CHAPTER 1

PET GOATS: 1
ANNOYING BROTHERS: 3

Wyatt

"**Y**ou fucking fuckers!" I roar as I slam my foot on the brakes in front of my brother's cabin, sending a dust storm of gravel swirling around my truck. Jumping out of the driver's seat, I charge up the steps toward my two siblings sitting on Calder's front porch and come to a stop between them. I glare at their relaxed frames stretched out on a couple of wooden rocking chairs with tin cups of coffee in hand.

Like it's just a normal Saturday fucking morning.

I hold up the piece of paper in my hand. "Which one of you posted this at the bar?"

"Easy there, Wyatt…you don't want to hit your daily word quota all before lunch." Calder laughs and sets his cup down on the end table beside him and snaps his fingers. "Although I guess 'fuck' was redundant, so you have a few more words to burn."

Without warning, I reach out and grab his collar, yanking him out of his chair. I knew it was Calder. It's always fucking Calder. "Is my life some kind of joke to you?" I seethe, feeling every muscle in my arms flex as I hold my six-foot-three brother up on his tiptoes. I'm only an inch taller than him, so it's no easy task.

"How do you know it was me?" Calder's eyes dance with mirth. Mirth that I am two seconds away from punching off his smug face.

I glance over at Luke, the youngest of us, who seems perfectly at ease as he scratches his short beard and enjoys the show. I slant my gaze back to the most typical middle child on the face of this earth— never mind the fucker is thirty-five now. He was a pain in the ass when we were young, and he's a pain in the ass now. The only difference now is he has more disposable income and more "inspired" ideas for his shenanigans.

My voice is growly as I crumple the sheet between us. "'Impervious' was your word of the day last week, and you used it incorrectly for hours."

The corner of Calder's mouth tips up. "Pretty sure I got it right in that ad, though, didn't I, Papa Bear?"

Rage spikes in my veins now that he's confirmed his guilt. "I'm going to throw you off this mountain and burn your cabin down."

I drag Calder's floundering body down the front steps of his porch toward the lookout point in front of my cabin, ignoring his raucous laughter that echoes off the foothills. I spent weeks clearing trees from this mountain vista when I bought this land to create this view before I even built my home. I wanted a place to quiet my thoughts and bring me peace.

This is the opposite of peace.

"Whoa, whoa, whoa," Luke calls out, his boots crunching on the gravel as he jogs past me to press a hand to my chest. "It's way too early in the day for manslaughter and arson threats."

"No shit," Calder scoffs, extricating himself from my grip. He steps back and straightens his flannel, concealing the ink scrawled across his chest. "This violent behavior will make finding you a Momma Bear very difficult, Papa Bear."

"Stop calling me Papa Bear," I hiss, ruing the day I ever thought it'd be a good idea to have my brothers build on this secluded mountain with me.

I fist the ridiculous ad in my hand and glance up the hill at the three cabins we all built together almost ten years ago. Three brothers living on a mountaintop I bought in rural Colorado sounded like a dream back then. We all worked side by side to develop this stretch of land and build self-sustaining cabins to survive up here on minimal energy resources. Even in the snowiest of winters, we have everything we need to survive for days without contact from the outside world. Weeks even.

Sounds like fucking heaven.

Or it did…until something started to feel different for me. *As though some*thing *was missing.*

"This isn't a fucking joke," I grumble, running my hand over my short hair.

Calder's expression shifts from cocky to damn near somber as he pins me with a serious look. "I didn't make that ad as a joke, Wyatt. I made it because you're a damn fool for going back to that agency in Denver that's going to charge you six figures for a surrogate when there are decent women right here in Jamestown who will grow your baby for a fraction of the price."

"It's not about the cost, Calder," I boom for the hundredth time. "I'll pay whatever it takes to become a…" I hesitate to say the word out loud, my voice getting caught in my throat as the weight of it presses down on me.

Dad.

When will that word ever stop being difficult for me to say out loud? My eyes move over to the memorial bench Calder built and placed at the lookout point two years ago after our father passed unexpectedly. Our dad's favorite saying is inscribed on it: *"We're not here for a long time, we're here for a good time."*

Dad was the salt of the earth—hardworking, protective, and challenging in all the best ways. I can close my eyes and still feel his presence all around me—his signature scent of Brut cologne, his chastising tone when my brothers and I were late to a jobsite, his bark of a laugh, or the way he never sneezed just once. It was always an attack of eight sneezes in a row. Fuck, I miss him.

And let's not even think about how hard it's been for my mom, who was just about to celebrate their forty-fifth wedding anniversary before he passed. Now, she's a widow who still cries at family events.

Dad was the definition of patriarch, and when we lost him, we lost our guide, our anchor, our voice of reason. The world got a little darker.

Now, I want to bring some light back into our lives. I want to see my mom hold my kid for once instead of my niece or nephew. I'm proud of what my brothers and I have built on this mountain, and I want to share that with a child of my own.

And I'll be damned if I let Calder fuck with my plan.

Calder playfully hits me on the arm, snapping my attention back to him. "You know, I might have some babies toddling around the foothills and not even know it. You're welcome to one of those if you can find one."

My jaw clenches, and I can't tell if this comment is better or worse than the other things he's said. A few months ago, Calder suggested I use Tinder and just go out and randomly knock someone up. And I admit that in a drunken stupor, I began to consider that idea but then remembered nobody goes to Calder for advice. Unless you want the name of a good sex club, maybe.

I open my mouth to argue with him for the hundredth time, but an approaching car forces all our heads to turn. I own the entire mountain, so all visitors are here for one of the three of us. When our eldest brother Max's SUV appears on the horizon, we all murmur, "Fuck."

Max isn't a total asshole. He's just a different breed than us. And God love him, he can be a controlling, condescending fucker sometimes. He got even worse after Dad passed.

Back in the day, he worked construction for Dad's renovation business just like the rest of us, but Max always had different life goals. He broke off early, went to business school, and climbed the corporate ladder to eventually break out on his own. He owns his franchise development company and is likely the wealthiest man in Boulder, but I'm not doing too bad myself. I just choose to hide in the hills of Jamestown, the tiny community at the base of this mountain, rather than flaunt my money with a fancy house. I'm not Max rich by any means, but my land is worth a pretty penny, and the green cabins we've built up here make our lives very affordable.

Plus, flipping houses has been good to all of us. Our father taught us well, and we've managed to continue growing his business in his absence. Honestly, we're harder workers now than we ever were when he was here. His passing was a bit of a wake-up call. I only wish he was here to see it.

But the cash rolls the housing market has gifted to us for investments have been well taken care of the past decade, which is why I'm not concerned about how much it will cost for me to become a...

Dad.

Regardless of who has more money, Max likes to throw around that CEO boss energy everywhere he goes. And, well, we play by different rules on the mountain.

Like being able to cover up murder and arson relatively easily.

Max stands in front of the three of us and pulls his expensive sunglasses off his face to pinch the bridge of his nose. "Can someone please inform me why I just caught my teenage daughter making an Excel spreadsheet of viable candidates to be the baby momma for her uncle?" Max looks as confused as I feel.

"Oh yeah." Calder grips the back of his neck and looks uneasy for the first time all morning. He clears his throat and stares down at his boots. "I posted that bar ad on Craigslist a few days ago and directed all calls to Everly."

"You what?" Max roars, and I lunge for Calder, only to be grabbed around the shoulders by Luke, who I struggle to shake off. He's not the biggest of the four of us, but he's a wiry little shit.

Max blows past us, and just before his fist connects with our annoying brother's face, Calder bellows, "This was Everly's idea!"

"Dick." Luke scoffs, looking disappointed. "Way to throw your niece under the bus. Super brave of you."

"One of them is going to kill me if I don't tell the truth," Calder snaps back defensively and turns back to me and Max. "She was determined to do this and asked for my help. And you know I can't say no to Evie girl. I honestly didn't even know Craigslist was still a thing. Everly figured that out in all her research."

Max's stunned reaction causes him to pull back from Calder, his face cast in confusion. "Everly figured all this out?"

Calder straightens and tries to gain back an ounce of his manhood. "Yes."

Max, Luke, and I all gape at him, dumbfounded by this onslaught of new information. I had a long conversation with Everly several months ago about my plans to find a surrogate to carry my baby, but I had no idea she was this invested in the whole thing.

Max's voice is scathing as he turns accusing eyes at me. "You never should have told her, Wyatt. She's just a child. She doesn't even understand all this."

"She was relentless with her questions, Max," I argue, anxiety prickling the back of my neck at the possibility I did something that could have hurt her. "And she's eighteen—it's not like she doesn't know how babies are made. And hell, she's graduating from high school in a few months and moving overseas. If she's old enough to move away to a foreign country, she's old enough to understand all this." My tone is bitter.

"She's not moving away forever." Max's voice catches in his throat, revealing what we're all feeling as I look around to see the same sad, desperate look on our faces. The look we've all had since Everly told us she was going to Ireland for college several months ago.

Evie girl is leaving us.

Another set of approaching tires breaks through our shared moment of depression, and when I see the familiar white Jeep truck pull up the lane, my heart aches all over again.

Everly Fletcher…my eldest brother's first kid, the sweet little girl Max had with his college girlfriend before they even graduated, gets out of her truck and walks toward us all with a look of determination.

I was only twenty when she was born, still just a kid myself. Hell, Luke was barely a teenager. But the moment they placed that tiny pink bundle in my arms with a spray of fuzzy white hair and long, slender little fingers that wrapped around my calloused thumb...I became a man.

And when Max and his wife split up when Everly was just two, she became all our responsibility. This little girl would want for nothing in life, and it was Calder's, Luke's, and my job to make sure she felt no pain from that break. My brothers and I have doted on her for the past eighteen years. We still take turns taking her out on weekly uncle dates when her busy teen schedule allows it. She and my brother's other kid, Ethan, who's seven now, get plenty of quality time with us. They love it.

We love them.

Flashbacks of Everly as a little tyke with blond braids bouncing around this mountaintop, begging to bottle-feed my goat, Millie, flash through my mind's eye. She would sleep over at one of our cabins every chance she got, which wasn't as often as we liked after my brother got divorced. Shared custody was a bitch for all of us.

This is why I want to do this fatherhood thing with a professional. With a contract. With no strings attached at the end. I don't want to share my time with my kid. Ever.

I'm still tormented at the thought of my only niece moving away. If I could take Everly to court and sue to keep her right here in Colorado, I would. Our girl in another country without all of us there to look out for her is unthinkable to me. My body tenses at the idea of something bad happening to her. Or hell, even someone just hurting her feelings. I can't believe Max said yes to letting her go that far away to college when perfectly good colleges exist right here in the same state.

"Dad," Everly exclaims, her tall six-foot frame striding toward us. "Don't you go blaming them for this...it was all my idea!"

"That's what I said," Calder confirms with a guilty shrug toward Everly. "Sorry, kid, but one broken nose in my lifetime is enough."

"You're welcome for that," Luke says with a smug grin. "Hi, Evie girl."

"Hi, Uncle Luke," Everly says sweetly, then turns her attention to me, hitting me with those clear blue eyes I'd give my life for. "Uncle Wyatt...don't you be mad at Calder either. This was all me. You're not having any luck finding a surrogate in Denver. That agency clearly doesn't see you for all that you are, or you would have been matched by now, so I think it's time you tried a new plan."

"What plan?" I ask, feeling suddenly bone-tired at the idea of discussing this huge life-changing decision I've made with my entire family...*again*. I'm already exhausted by this process, and I only had to jack off into a cup once so far to ensure that my swimmers are good.

My boys are gold medal swimmers...or so that old fertility doctor told me. But what's not earning me any medals is having to deal with my family's fucking input during nearly every step of this process.

"I think I can find you a surrogate," Everly says, her jaw taut with determination. "Someone who's perfect for this job."

"Evie," I say, but she holds her hand up to shush me. So, I shush.

"Just give me one week," she says, her youthful eyes flaring with so much grit I can't help but root for her. "Next week is my spring break, and I will interview the viable candidates who reply to the ad and see if anyone might be a good fit for this project. I'm certain I can find you someone special you'll never be able to say no to."

I shake my head. "Everly, I have another appointment at that agency on Monday. I could find someone then."

"Then we'll cancel my plan, and this will all be for nothing. No biggie."

"Everly," Max expels under his breath. "Finding a surrogate for Uncle Wyatt is a very big deal. It's real life, which is why he's going through the proper channels and trying to hire a professional from an agency. You're too inexperienced to understand all this."

"Please, Dad." Everly scoffs casually. "I'm not even a virgin."

Calder screams. Literally screams. It echoes off the foothills, likely sending all the wildlife scrambling.

Luke stumbles and nearly drops to the ground, his shoulders rising and falling as he braces himself on his knees and pants heavily, a look of disgust smeared across his face.

Max's jaw drops with horror as he stammers with what to say back to that very unexpected bomb his only daughter just dropped.

And I remain frozen, begging for a time machine to take this moment away immediately. Or, better yet, go back in time to who-ever fucked my niece so I can kill that person before he has a chance to ever lay his eyes on her.

"Who is the fucker?" I rumble, my voice low and threatening. "Was it that Hilow prick who took you to prom last year? I thought you two broke up."

"We did," Everly exclaims defensively.

"Oh my God," Max groans, looking like he's going to be violently ill at any second.

"It was a one-night stand?" Calder coughs as he rakes his hands through his hair. "I knew I was a bad influence on you. I never should have hung out with you so much. I'm a dirty, filthy, disgusting, rotten pig. I'm never having sex again. This is my vow to—"

"Uncle Calder…get over yourself," Everly drawls, her eyes roll-ing to the back of her head. "All of you, get over yourselves. This isn't about me. It's about Uncle Wyatt, who has dedicated so much of his life to making sure I was happy and loved and protected. Now it's my turn to do something for him."

My body stills with the weight of her words. Goddammit, when did she get so mature? The little girl we all helped raise is gone, and I'm looking at a woman now. A strong, independent, headstrong woman who I am so proud of my heart could burst. I turn around so she can't see the tears forming in my eyes, my jaw clenching with humiliation over the power this teenager has over me. It will kill me not to see her whenever I want next year.

Her footsteps are soft as she comes close and wraps her tiny, man-icured hands around my arm and rests her head on my shoulder. She used to have to stand on my feet to dance with me. This is so fucked.

"I know I won't be able to find you love, Uncle Wyatt. You've made it crystal clear that's not what you want in life. But please, let me be a part of helping you become a dad before I go." She stands on her tip-toes to kiss me on the cheek and whispers in my ear, "Because I know you will make an amazing one."

Well, fuck.

CHAPTER 2

UNCLES IN NEED OF EPIC LOVE: 3

Everly

Operation Mountain Man Matchmaker is officially underway.

First order of business…find Uncle Wyatt a *wife*.

Wait…scratch that…*Baby Momma.* Just a baby momma. *For now.*

An evil laugh echoes in my head as I type up some notes on my Excel spreadsheet dedicated to my three single uncles.

Obviously, every evil plan needs a spreadsheet. That's just science.

Who cares about school!

Who cares about relationships!

Who cares about my upcoming senior prom that I still don't have a date for because I dumped my boyfriend of two years. I'm moving to Ireland at the end of summer, and I refuse to be tied down during that life-changing experience…

I'm going to find my uncle a match!

"Everlyyyy," Ethan whines. "I want to help."

I lower my screen to conceal my master plan and turn from the kitchen island to stare into the eyes of my seven-year-old little brother. "Ethan, this isn't really an age-appropriate activity for you."

"What makes it not appropriate?" He stumbles over the long word.

"Well…" I bite my lip and glance over at my stepmom for help.

Cozy doesn't know of my grand plan to find my uncles love. But she knows of the Craigslist ad and my eagerness to help Uncle Wyatt find a surrogate. She shrugs, clearly struggling with how to answer this question too.

"You're finding Uncle Wyatt a baby, right?" Ethan asks with big, curious eyes. Damn, that little kid is a silent ninja, always sneaking around and listening to the grown-up conversations. He marches over to the sink and tugs on Cozy's shirt. "Mom, how are babies made?"

Cozy's head jerks to me in panic. Honestly, I can't blame her. Ethan is far too young for the-birds-and-the-bees conversation. I think I was twelve when I finally learned about the mechanics of sex, and it was my lesbian mom who gave me the talk, so then there was a second talk about sex between two women and sex between two men and stuff about fluid sexuality, and, well…let's just say, it gave me a lot to think about.

Throwing my stepmom a lifeline, I answer, "Well, Ethan, a baby is made when two haploid cells fuse to form a single diploid cell that is also known as a zygote and that undergoes a lot of cellular division and development inside the uterus of a female over a period of nine months or so, resulting in a baby."

"Took the words right out of my mouth," Cozy adds with a laugh.

"Mommy, you said I came from your tummy." Ethan sticks his hand up her shirt to touch her belly, and Cozy squeals and backs up, pulling his hand away from her.

"Totally breastfed this kid too long," she murmurs under her breath, and I can't help but laugh. "Ethan, I'll tell you how babies are made when you're older…or better yet, I'll let your uncles tell you. Speaking of which, you better go find your shoes because Uncle Calder is taking you to the park in ten minutes."

"Yay! Caldie is my favorite!" Ethan yells as he runs off.

Cozy rolls her eyes and glances back at me. "He says that about all of them."

"Mm-hmm," I reply doubtfully, sitting back to think about all the different notes I have on my dad's brothers. They are all unique in their own right.

My dad is obviously the biggest standout of the four Fletcher brothers as he traded in his tool belt for a suit and tie years ago. And because he doesn't live on Fletcher Mountain with the rest of them, he's a bit of an outsider.

People in Boulder think it's weird my uncles all live on a little compound up in the sticks, but that's just because they haven't seen how magical it is up there. Especially in the winter during a snowstorm when all you have is a wood-burning fire and candles to keep you warm. It's like existing in another universe.

But my dad's still cool. Got even cooler when I managed to make him fall in love with Cozy, who happened to be my nanny at the time, which people also think is weird.

I guess the Fletcher family is good with weird!

Uncle Calder is a case in point. He's brother number three in the birth order and by far the craziest. He'd probably buy me booze if I gave him puppy dog eyes, which makes him wildly irresponsible, but man, he makes me laugh. Women seem to cycle in and out of his cabin every few weeks, but none stick around long enough for me to even have a conversation with. He's going to need a strong female to tame his wild ways.

And then there's sweet Uncle Luke. He's much more go with the flow and doesn't cause many waves. He's the closest to me in age, so he feels more in touch with the times. If I ever need to talk out my feelings about something, he's the first one I'll call. I still haven't figured out why he's so against relationships…but don't worry, I have months before I fly to Dublin. I'll figure him out.

And finally, Uncle Wyatt…the mysterious one. He doesn't talk much, but it feels important when he does. And when he's not speaking, he always looks worried, like he's trying to fix the world's problems. It's honestly why I want to help him so much. He'd never ask for it. And I've never seen him spend time with a woman. Does he even know how to date? He's made this huge, life-changing decision to have a baby on his own, which means he's finally ready to think about his future. And it's my job to make sure he's considering all the options.

Like having a baby with *someone he can fall in love with*.

Uncle Wyatt deserves a happily ever after like my dad and Momma Cozy. And I think this surrogacy thing could work out perfectly because he'll be forced to interact with a woman for more than a few weeks.

Which is why this baby momma needs to be incredible. Equally as incredible as my stepmom.

"Did you ever consider offering to have Uncle Wyatt's baby?" I ask, my thoughts spilling out before I could even stop them.

"Why do you ask?" Cozy asks, her jaw dropped.

I roll my eyes and elaborate. "Sorry, but I've been researching a lot, and family members make some of the best surrogates. I assume you'd need to do a donor egg, though, because I couldn't see you giving up rights to your own genetically linked child. You still tear up whenever I leave the house, and I'm not even your kid."

"You are too my freaking kid," she snaps, looking angrier than I think I've ever seen her in my life.

My eyes widen in horror as I realize my mistake. "OMG, I'm sorry! I seriously didn't mean it like that." I leap up and run around the kitchen island to hug this wild, crazy, amazing stepmother of mine who came into my life unexpectedly and made our whole family fall in love with her. Even my moms love her.

I wrap my arms around her neck and pull her into my chest. "That was a slip of the tongue, and I didn't mean it. I'm such a jerk." Jesus, you'd think with three mothers, I'd be more sensitive than this.

Her body shakes with laughter against me. "I used to hug you into my bosom, and now it's the other way around." She chuckles, pulling away to look up at me. "Good grief, this growth spurt of yours is done, right?"

"I think so." I shrug, pretty ambivalent about my height. I used to hate it, but my stepmom has taught me so much about loving the skin I'm in. She's the most stunning curvy woman I've ever seen. "I've been six feet since freshman year, so I imagine I'm all set."

"Thank God." She hugs me again and rubs my back soothingly. She really gives the best hugs. "And I know what you meant, but the fact that I'm so attached to you is exactly why I know I could never be a surrogate for your uncle…donor egg or not. It'd be too hard for me to go through a birth and give away the baby."

"What are we talking about?" My dad's voice interrupts as he walks in through the attached garage door into the kitchen. He smiles broadly when he sees us wrapped up in a hug.

Cozy releases me and throws me to the wolves. "Everly just asked me to have your brother's baby!"

"What?" my dad roars. "Everly, how many times are you trying to give me a heart attack this week?"

"It was just a theory I was exploring." I laugh and return to the counter, where I left my spreadsheet. I minimize my master plan and pull up the sheet of all the viable candidates who have replied to the Craigslist ad so far.

To be honest, I'm impressed by the amount of interest that crazy ad is generating. My phone has been buzzing off the hook with photos and bizarre résumés. Which is cool because I'm pretty sure Uncle Calder was trying to sabotage me by putting the most ridiculous things in that ad, but it clearly backfired because this might actually work in my favor.

My dad leans in to embrace his wife. "This kid is going to be the death of me."

She laughs and stands on her tiptoes to kiss him, instantly soothing his stress like always. Watching my dad and Cozy's relationship grow throughout the years has been inspiring. Gross, obviously. But it's couple goals, even if watching them make out makes me want to yak. It also shows me that I know what I'm talking about when it comes to true love.

If only I could apply it to myself.

When my dad is done rizzing my stepmother, he marches over to the kitchen counter and presses my laptop closed with that scowl he displays a lot these days.

"I'm working here," I say, scowling right back at him.

"We need to talk rules," he states ominously.

"Rules?" I pull my computer out from his splayed hand. "Dad, I'm eighteen. I'm old enough to handle this."

"You're still my kid," he hisses, and I can see a bit of fear in his eyes that makes me tuck away the defiant-teenager vibe and put on the soothing-daughter hat.

"Okay...what kind of rules?" I ask, my tone softening.

He inhales deeply. "You conduct all your interviews at my office. I'll clear the boardroom out for you this week so you can have plenty of space, but it will still be monitored."

"Okay..."

"And we will run background checks on everyone you want to interview before you interview them."

I nod thoughtfully. "That's actually a great idea, Dad. Thanks!"

"And we're getting you a new phone number once you're done with this whole fiasco."

"Why do I need a new phone number?"

"Because your number is on that Craigslist ad."

"Oh...no...Uncle Calder set it up under a Google number, so it forwards the calls and texts to me, but no one actually has my real number."

"That was Calder's idea?" My dad looks taken aback. "Didn't know he had it in him."

"Max," Cozy snaps from the kitchen. "Be nice to your brother."

"I'm exhausted by all my brothers these days. They've been pouty babies ever since she told them about Ireland."

I wince at the memory of my three uncles all staring back at me with devastated looks when I told them I got into the college I applied to in Dublin six months ago. The idea came to me after we went on that class trip for band, and I'm still pinching myself that it's really happening.

Yes, I'll miss my family, but they can be a little smothering sometimes. I feel like such a dick being ungrateful for a wholesome, supportive family that drops everything if I need them...but damn, my life has been too perfect. I need this adventure. And Grandpa always said we aren't here for a long time, we're here for a good time. This is my time!

And I'm kicking it off early with some Baby Momma Drama.

My dad's voice snaps me back to reality. "And when this plan of yours doesn't work…"

"When?" I begin to argue, but he holds his finger up.

"I want you to look me in the eyes and say…" He smiles gleefully, nay…evilly. He looks like a Disney villain as he leans close and adds, "Daddy, you were right. You're always right. I'm so sorry I doubted you."

Heavy, dramatic sigh.

This really has to work.

Because I am not admitting my dad was right on this.

Not. Happening.

CHAPTER 3

SURROGATES INTERVIEWED: 12

Wyatt

"Welcome, Mr. Fletcher." A woman in a pink lab coat points at a set of pale pink armchairs across from her desk as she lowers herself into her seat.

I fall into the plush fabric, my denim-clad legs practically under my chin as I shift uncomfortably. This chair is worse than those stupid Adirondack chairs that Calder built. No man over six feet enjoys sitting inches from the fucking ground. They were a waste of his time, but he was just getting into his custom furniture. His style has improved a lot since then.

I glance out the high-rise windows overlooking downtown Denver and wonder for the twentieth time why such a giant building has such tiny-ass seats.

"I don't believe we've met before. I'm Eva, the director of the agency, and I'll be conducting this appointment today. As you know, Reagan is out on maternity leave now. Triplets, can you imagine?" Eva looks at me with wide, hungry eyes. The women in this place are always a little too…eager.

Regardless, I appreciate the update on Reagan. I'm not sure if the babies are even hers or if she was a surrogate for someone. All I know is that every time I've come into this agency over the past few months, I've had to physically stop myself from offering her my arm.

The woman looked like she could tip over from the size of her swollen belly. I'm honestly a little relieved to hear that she's on maternity leave and doing okay. The female body is a fucking wonder.

Eva squirms in her seat, nervously ruffling through the papers in my file. Her cheeks are flushed, and her hands tremble slightly. I tend to have this effect on people just meeting me. And it's not just because I'm six foot four, tattooed, bearded, and all the typical things that make people feel on edge.

It's the silence.

The lack of chitchat.

It's my willful refusal to fill dead space with meaningless conversation because nothing irritates me more than fucking small talk. The less I say, the less they say, and the quicker we can get shit done, and I can heave myself out of this stupid doll-sized chair and get back to the construction site I left my brothers at in Boulder.

Eva offers me a weak smile as she scans a document in front of her. "I see you've conducted quite a number of these interviews."

I wince as I flash through the countless women I've met here in the past six months. "Is twelve considered a lot?"

"It's twice the average." Her lips purse together before she adds, "May I ask what the issues were with those you interviewed?"

I pause for a moment before answering. The truth is, I'm a gut person, just like my dad was, and my instincts rarely fail me. I knew pretty much at first sight that none of the women I interviewed were a good match. None were even close. Three of them basically stared at me like I was a piece of meat they wanted to devour. And the others all had husbands and kids already. And while I know that shows proof that they're good at making babies, it never sat right with me to think of my child hanging out, in utero, with another family.

Another man.

God, I'm fucked up.

"They just didn't feel right," I grunt, knowing there's no way in hell I can say that last part out loud. I can barely admit it to myself.

Eva clears her throat. "It could be because you're not our typical clientele..." My eyes flare at that comment before she blurts out,

"I mean, we get single candidates in here, but they're usually women. Some men...but they're typically..."

I silently finish her sentence. *Gay.* How does she know I'm not? *Way to be fucking inclusive, Eva.*

She splays her hands on her desk and asks, "Just so I fully understand, you are looking to become a single father? No partner in your life currently? We might be able to find a few more surrogate options if...well, if that *could* be the case. Many of our 'belly buddy babysitters' prefer to select more...complete families."

"No partner," I grind out, my gravelly voice at odds with the flowery word she used to describe surrogates. I've seen that "belly buddy babysitter" phrase in many of the books I've read, and it makes my nose wrinkle. This entire place and all the soft pink colors make my nose wrinkle too. God, how have I kept coming back here time after time? Especially because this is the fourth professional in this agency who I've had to reassure that I know what I'm signing up for.

Believe me, *I know.*

I've had to spend the past year reassuring my entire family that I'm not in the middle of some midlife crisis. Can you have a midlife crisis at thirty-eight? It seems a little premature, but try telling that to my three brothers, who insert their opinions at every opportunity. Or my niece, whose "interview process" bordered on TMI. Despite what Calder thinks, there are things uncles should never share with their nieces. *Like dating habits.* And Craigslist accounts...

Eva tilts her head and rakes her eyes over my whole body, like somehow my blue flannel shirt and faded blue jeans with a tear on the thigh will reveal something that will make this make sense to her. Maybe I should roll up my sleeves to show her the ink of my dead dad's favorite saying scrawled through the various ink on my forearm? Or prop my Timberland boots on her desk so she can get a good look at the lingering manure on the bottom? Let her really get a good mental image of the loner mountain man with a pet goat who's seeking a surrogate to fulfill his dream of becoming a father? Because clearly, she's having trouble digesting all of this...along with the rest of the fucking world.

"This is making a lot more sense now." Eva sighs, pushing my envelope to the side. I frown, wondering what she means by that, and she answers my unspoken question. "I'm afraid we've run out of qualified candidates for you at this time, Mr. Fletcher. Unless, perhaps, you have a family member who might be interested in helping you. A sister or sister-in-law? We could find you a donor egg for the process if there are genetic connections."

"No sisters," I bark back a touch too aggressively. I want this process to be as disconnected from someone as possible, so that idea is off the table. She looks taken aback by my tone, so I soften my voice. "Sorry, but I have enough trouble with my three brothers," I add dryly.

"There are three more like you?" Eva whispers this question to herself, her lips parting as her gaze drops down to my body once again. She catches herself and shakes her head. "Sorry…um…what I mean is…I'm afraid, at this time, you are unmatchable, and there is nothing we can do for you. But we'll keep your name on file and contact you if a new potential surrogate pops up who we think might be a good fit."

Great. What she really means is: *"But we'll keep your name on file and make sure we don't look for a potential surrogate for you."*

And that's when a startling truth takes form.

My future dream is now in the hands of my eighteen-year-old niece.

CHAPTER 4

POTENTIAL SURROGATES INTERVIEWED: 6
POTENTIAL SURROGATES DISMISSED: 6

Everly

"**S**o basically, I feel like if I get pregnant for money, then I can't get pregnant by accident again!" Savannah laughs and begins chewing her thumbnail once more.

That finger has barely been out of her mouth during this interview except for her to have one sip of the kombucha beverage she selected from the reception area minifridge before she proceeded to spray the contents of her mouth all over the floor and yell that it tasted like "cat piss."

I'm not a fan of kombucha either, but even I knew that was a red-flag moment.

Savannah looked so good on my spreadsheet, though! Twenty-five years old, which is a bit young for Uncle Wyatt, but there's an age gap between my dad and Cozy, and they worked out great. Her application indicated that she had a baby at eighteen that she placed with an adoptive family, and I took that as a positive. A woman who's been pregnant before and wasn't ready at the time, but maybe she'd be ready now…with the right man? It could work!

But the getting-pregnant-by-accident remark…it's going to be a no for me.

I excuse Savannah from the boardroom and let her know that I'll give her a call if we want to go to phase two of meeting Wyatt even though I know that call will never happen. She just didn't have the right vibe. I could overlook the cat-piss comment if she had that rizz about her. But she doesn't.

No one has.

I'm three days into these interviews and realizing with great regret that my spreadsheet is failing me.

Day one, there was Polly. A twenty-nine-year-old mother of two kids. Loves being pregnant because she doesn't have to have sex with her baby daddy, who she lives with. He thinks pregnancy is gross, but he likes money, so he supports her endeavors. Her most notable pregnancy craving was cottage cheese and Doritos, and she'd like that food supply noted in the contract.

Lives with baby daddy...hard pass.

Then there was Valerie. Divorced with three kids, who all piled into the boardroom with her for the interview. She has them full-time because her ex is behind on child support payments, and she can't afford childcare. My heart went out to her, and while there were no obvious red flags, I just don't think Uncle Wyatt could handle four kids all at once.

Twenty-six-year-old Morgan is currently in a "toxic situationship," and if selected to be a surrogate, she needs to have a C-section because she wants her vagina to remain high and tight.

Gulp.

And those all cleared the background checks!

Honestly, after three days of this, I'm exhausted. Apparently, Uncle Calder's ad is attracting the wrong kind of ladies, which is weird because based on my spreadsheet, I had some very promising prospects. I've never had a spreadsheet fail me before. Never. Spreadsheets are my thing. My dopamine high. When I put together a spreadsheet and see everything laid out all pretty and perfect...it's better than sex.

Then again...I've only had sex once, and it was...no bueno. Let's just say that I don't blame Uncle Wyatt for wanting to become a father in a nontraditional way. It's scary out there! This is like online dating, but my ulterior motives make this ten times more difficult.

And the sheer panic I feel over having to tell my father...my arrogant, know-it-all, bossy father, who popped his head in on a number of the interviews just to nod and smile gleefully, knowing that he was just days away from me telling him he was right.

It's too much.

And the pain of telling my uncle Wyatt that I failed him when he has literally given me so much…ugh, this sucks! I can't go to Ireland at the end of summer without finding my uncle true love.

At the very least, I need to find him a baby momma.

I pull open my phone and begin googling other options for finding a surrogate. There are definitely some websites out there dedicated to helping people connect for this sort of thing, but the problem is, I don't just want a surrogate. I want a single surrogate. A single surrogate who's pleasing to the naked eye and open to love from a grouchy mountain man with a pet goat named Millie and not a lot of girlfriend experience but clearly wants a life beyond mountain views and goat manure.

No offense to my girl Millie.

But this surrogate needs to see that he's more than his calloused, quiet exterior. He has a big heart with plenty of room to grow, especially if he's willing to become a single dad! That's obviously a man desperate to have his home filled with noise. The good kind of noise. The noise of a happy family.

"Ugh, these stupid ads are everywhere," I scoff to myself in the front seat of my truck when, yet again, that same Denver surrogacy agency ad pops up on my Instagram feed.

It's the agency my uncle goes to almost every month, searching for his baby momma. He said he felt like a bull in a Barbie house there, and thus far, they haven't been able to find him a match. They clearly don't know what they're doing.

I bet this agency has stopped offering him decent candidates to interview. He's such a good man, even if he's a little gruff on the outside. I'm sure they see him as an introverted loner, not a man ready to become a dad. If only Uncle Wyatt was a woman, because then—

My eyes lift to the windshield as an idea comes to mind. A sneaky smile lifts the corners of my mouth as I glance at myself in the rearview mirror. "Maybe it's time for a little drive to downtown Denver."

CHAPTER 5

SURROGACY AGENCY VISITS: 1

Everly

"**N**obody's gonna know...they're gonna know..." That trending TikTok sound echoes in my head as I slide my shades on and pull my hood up over my hair. I do my best to blend in while I scurry through a crosswalk around a group of corporate workers on a busy street in downtown Denver.

I come to a stop in front of the glossy high-rise building that my GPS led me to. This is where my uncle was when they informed him they could no longer help him. That he was "unmatchable."

Assholes.

How dare they dim that hope in my uncle's eyes. This place is crushing his spirit.

I'm going to burn it to the ground.

Okay, maybe that's a slight overreaction. I've probably been hanging out with my uncles too much.

But seriously, this place is supposed to help people grow families, and somehow my uncle is the exception? What the fuck is wrong with these people?

Yet...here I stand with a revised version of Calder's baby momma ad ready to stick to their window and poach some of their surrogates. Craigslist was a bad choice, and I only have a couple more days left of my spring break. Desperate times call for desperate measures.

I amble up to the window, pressing my face against the glass to see what's inside. There appears to be a security desk with a man in uniform talking to a couple of women. One is dressed in pink scrubs and the other in street clothes. Maybe a baby momma in the flesh! Beyond them is a large bank of elevators that I assume will take you up to the agency. Looks pretty fancy. Definitely not a place I could see Uncle Wyatt hanging out in.

The woman in street clothes flails her hands aggressively, her muffled voice rising in pitch as she storms toward the exit. My eyes fly wide, and I move to beeline past the door, but the ad gets stuck to my forehead. I struggle to peel the duct tape from my hairline when my body is jolted into another dimension as the door swings open right into my face.

A strange noise erupts from me as my nose and kneecap make friends with the glass. I bring my hands to my face to cup my nose in agony.

"Oh crap," the woman exclaims, rushing over to me. "Are you okay?"

"Am I bleeding?" I cry, confident that blood gushes violently from my nose.

"Um…no," the woman answers hesitantly.

I wait a beat and then ask, "How about now?" The sobs billowing up in my throat hurt really bad. Blood drips down my palms now, but I can't bring myself to look.

"Still no blood," she replies, her voice full of concern.

"Are you sure?" I ask again because, seriously, the stinging in my face must mean we're looking at an ambulance ride here.

"I know what blood looks like." Her tone ventures on less sympathetic and more impatient.

"Maybe it's internal?" I peek one eye open at her.

"An internal nosebleed?"

Terror washes over me. "Is that a thing?"

"I don't know. You're the one who suggested it!" She hunches down to get a better look at me.

I groan, my head throbbing now from the stress of having a potential internal nosebleed. That can't be good.

"You better come sit down." Soft hands wrap around me as I'm ushered to a nearby bench. "I think there are nurses inside this building who could come take a look at you if you want. Though, fair warning, they're complete assholes."

"I thought nurses were heroes." I squeeze my nose to try to stop the burning.

"Okay, not you too," the woman says flatly, lowering herself beside me.

"What?" I glance at her through my tear-filled eyes.

"Obviously, nurses, in general, are heroes, but that doesn't mean some aren't assholes."

"What?"

She stands and begins pacing in front of me, making me a little dizzy as she moves back and forth. She stops to thrust a finger back toward the building. "Trust me, those nurses were trained at the asshole academy."

"Why do you say that?" I ask as the burning in my nose lightens enough for me to be able to focus on the person standing in front of my slumped body. She's tall…maybe not quite as tall as me, but close. Her chestnut hair looks like it has natural curls, but it's balled up on top of her head in a messy bun, so I can't tell how long it is.

My eyes drift down her body…

Healthy hips…check.

Ample bosom…check.

Robust yet feminine physique that reminds me of my stepmom in a not-so-creepy way…check.

No sign of a wedding ring…talk about a sea of great check marks!

"Do you know you can't be a surrogate unless you have prior experience having a baby?" She props her hands on her curvy hips and glares up at the building.

"I didn't know that." I clear my throat and lower my hand to straighten a bit more, the pain lifting from my face as hope blooms in my chest.

"Apparently, they want *proof* that all your parts work." She gestures toward her groin area. "Pardon me for appreciating the scientific marvels of birth control. My God! I got off it three months ago, and I can assure you...I'm a sharp twenty-eight-day cycle. I even did those pee sticks that tell you when you ovulate. I'm as regular as they come. Also...did you know there's a weight limit for surrogates?"

"What?" I ask, shocked that it never came up in my research. And I researched a lot. Like, for example, there are basically two types of surrogates. A gestational surrogacy is when the surrogate does not supply the egg. The egg comes from a donor, and they go through the process of IVF to implant the fertilized egg into the surrogate. All very clinical, and it involves no genetic connection to the surrogate.

In traditional surrogacy, you artificially inseminate the surrogate so the baby is genetically linked to the female. That one only involves intrauterine insemination, which is still clinical but not as invasive as IVF. But the surrogate has to sign legal documents to terminate the rights of the birth mother at the time of delivery.

"Two hundred pounds is the weight limit!" the woman balks, snapping me out of my thoughts as her voice takes on a high-pitched note that probably has nearby dogs' heads turning. "Two hundred pounds is nothing these days. And they don't care how tall you are either. It's just about that number on the scale. Tons of women are over two hundred pounds and perfectly healthy."

"Did they say why?" I ask, genuinely curious.

"Something about my BMI being bad and obesity being high risk to pregnancies," she snarls and rolls her eyes dismissively. "But Jesus, anyone with a brain knows the BMI system is outdated and physiologically flawed. There is no allowance for the proportions of bone, muscle, and fat. Bone and muscle are far denser than fat. That's how some professional athletes find themselves registering on the BMI scale as overweight or obese. Tell me a man who runs a football field every day of the week for his job is unhealthy? I won't believe you."

"Yeah, that's fair," I reply, enraptured by this perfect stranger speaking so confidently about her size. She's inspiring.

"Check my labs." She smacks the veins on the crook of her arms. "I'm the healthiest fat person you'll ever meet. My cholesterol levels are incredible. How dare they. How *dare* they not even consider me.

The BMI system is just an insurance scam so they can charge higher premiums to fat people who are perfectly healthy, and the rich man just keeps getting richer."

She exhales heavily, and I take a moment to note her appearance a bit more. She's dressed in a pair of wide-leg jeans, and her top is a fitted sleeveless gray tank that shows off her full arms. They aren't flabby, but they aren't slender either. And every time she moves her arm, you can see a definition of muscle peek out. Either she loves lifting weights or does manual labor for a living. And considering she's in a pair of well-worn cowboy boots, I imagine she works hard for her money.

Honestly, she's beautiful. Powerful yet still feminine. I'd never call her obese, though. Yes, her hips, rear, and stomach might not be that perfect hourglass figure that all the magazines immortalize, but anyone with eyes has to see this woman is stunning.

A force of nature.

She stops glowering up at the building to lower her soft green eyes to me. "Like I said…assholes."

I can't help the smile that spreads across my face.

Spirited demeanor that could withstand the asshole-ish ways of my uncle…big fat check!

"Sorry, but I haven't weighed in onederland since high school, and that was because I was depressed, so this entire afternoon has been very triggering. Ask me how pregnancy and depression work together…I'm guessing not good. The fact that they have the audacity to point at me like I'm a giant plus-sized flaw is ludicrous. I've worked hard to appreciate my body. This is me at my healthiest, and no one will tell me otherwise."

"I'm on your side," I state firmly, feeling equal parts terrified of this woman and moved by her. "I think you're perfect."

"Thank you," she says distractedly and then shifts her focus to me again. "Sorry, did you need a hospital? I totally forgot about the door bashing you in the face."

"No…I'm fine." I gingerly touch my nose and wave her off. "I don't think I'm bleeding internally anymore."

She tilts her head curiously at me. "What are you doing outside that door anyway?" She glances at the paper in my hand. "Are you applying to be a surrogate too? My God, you're young. They have an age limit too, you know, so I hope you weren't banking on this opportunity. Dare not be too young, too old, or too chubby, or they will boot you out the door before you can even get up the elevator. It's like a weird mean girls club up there. It's gross."

"Yeah, I mean...no...I'm not trying to be a surrogate," I reply quickly, nerves swirling in my belly. "Just...passing by."

She nods and smiles politely. "Well, good. You sure you're okay?"

"Yep!" I reply brightly and flash her a smile as proof.

"Great." She winks at me, and it makes me feel warm and fuzzy inside. "Now that we're sure your nose isn't bleeding internally, I'll be on my way. Take it easy, girl."

She begins to walk away, and I watch her for a moment, feeling a gust of wind sweep up around me, practically pushing me in the direction she's going. I'm not really a spiritual person, but ever since my grandpa passed, I swear he's been guiding me in my life. Maybe he's trying to tell me something with that glass-plated door to the face, and I'm about to let that something walk away from me.

So...I shout what's in my heart. What I feel deep in my bones is destiny and spreadsheets and my pushy grandpa all aligning with my soul. "How do you feel about having my uncle's baby?"

CHAPTER 6

SURROGACY APPLICANT ACCEPTANCE: 0
CRAZY ENCOUNTERS ON THE STREET: 1

Trista

The hairs on the back of my neck rise as the young girl's words call out to me. The smart thing to do would be to pretend I didn't hear her. She is a stranger, after all, and this is by far one of the weirdest things I've ever had someone ask me…and I've been in some weird situations.

But intuition niggles, so I turn on my heel and eye the girl while glancing around cautiously. I slowly make my way back to the adorable blonde, who was a pretty good sport to listen to my tirade moments earlier. That wasn't my best first impression with a human, but I had to get those things off my chest, or I was going to explode. Life has been handing me a shitload of lemons lately, and no matter how hard I try, I can't seem to find a way to make some freaking juice.

When I reach the girl, I tuck my chin down and hush my voice. "Are you okay? Do you need help? Blink twice if you do."

The girl's brows pinch together. "What?"

"Shhhh." I pull her into a hug so I can whisper directly into her ear. Her body is as stiff as a board in my embrace, furthering my suspicions. "If you've been abducted and someone is forcing you to do this, just give me a tight squeeze. You don't have to say anything."

"What are you talking about?" She yanks away and looks at me like I'm crazy. Her face is screwed up in confusion as she asks, "Do you think I've been human trafficked?"

I look side to side. "Um…pretty much."

"I haven't," she exclaims, pushing the loose strands of blond hair out of her face. "I drove myself here from Boulder, where I live with my parents, to check out this agency for my uncle."

She gestures up to the high-rise, and I cock my head at her. "For your uncle?"

"Yes, I want a baby for my uncle." She repeats her phrase like it's the most normal thing in the world. *This is not normal.*

My stomach churns as reality sets in. "Sweetie, it is not okay for your uncle to want your baby. That's some backwoods mountain hill-billy shit—"

"My uncle doesn't want my baby," she shrieks, her face distraught with horror. "My uncle wants to be a single dad. He's looking for a surrogate, and I'm helping him."

I inspect her for a moment, noting she's clearly a little nuts. Then again, so am I, so I press on. "Why doesn't he just adopt?"

"A lot of adoption agencies won't give him the time of day because he's a single man." She fiddles nervously with the strings of her sweatshirt, and I wonder what kind of man would inspire this much devotion from a teenage girl. It's impressive.

My lips thin because his rejection sounds very familiar. "Adoption agencies can be just as bad as this surrogacy agency. Especially the private ones. Both are rackets trying to monetize on babies."

She nods and glances up at the surrogacy office with a forlorn look on her face. "And now this place is dumping him too. My uncle was just here yesterday, and they basically released him because they couldn't find him a good match."

"And you're sure nothing is wrong with him?" I can't help but ask. These surrogacy agencies aren't really in the business of turning away good money.

"Of course I'm sure," she replies defensively. "My uncle is the best, and you'd know that if you met him."

"If you say so," I murmur under my breath and shake my head at her. "But picking a random woman up off the street can't be a good plan for finding someone to carry his baby, right?"

"I'm just following my gut." She shrugs helplessly. "I have a good feeling about you, and, well, I think it sounds like you and my uncle both might need each other, so maybe there was a reason we met."

She looks down at the paper currently stuck to her sleeve and yanks it off to hand to me. It has a piece of duct tape stuck to the top of it, and I wonder briefly if she was planning on sticking this to the window of the agency. The thought of it makes me smile. The girl has balls, that's for sure.

> Thirty-eight-year-old single male seeks surrogate to carry his baby. Compensation will be market competitive. Applicants must sign a legal contract with agreed-upon terms and prepare to sign away all parental rights upon delivery of baby. Rural mountain housing outside of Boulder available upon request.

"Rural mountain housing," I hum, my heart rate doubling in speed at the mention of that. I look up at her with renewed interest. "What does that mean exactly?"

"My uncle lives on a mountain, and he has this barn with an apartment on the upper level. I know that doesn't sound real fancy, but it's nice and private and has running water. The view is so pretty. I've slept up there plenty of times."

"It sounds perfect," I whisper under my breath as my own housing issues come flooding to the forefront of my mind. I lick my lips nervously because regardless of my less-than-pleasant circumstances, this all sounds a bit too good to be true. "Okay, so how do I know your uncle's not a creep?"

She rolls her eyes and crosses her arms over her chest, looking more like a teenager every second. "Would a creep put together a slideshow of all our pictures and sync them to Taylor Swift songs for my sixteenth birthday?"

My face falls, and I turn to walk away...immediately.

She rushes over to chase me down. "Okay, out of context, maybe that sounds a bit creepy, but he concluded the slideshow to inform me that he bought Taylor Swift concert tickets for me and my friends...

but I ended up taking my uncles instead because they're honestly more fun than my friends."

"This all sounds made up," I reply, picking up speed to walk the two miles to the only free parking spot I could find.

"Why do you say that?" the girl asks, her long strides easily keeping up with me. Man, she's tall.

"Because no family gets along that well." I should know.

"Mine does," she says, her brows puckered with determination. This girl might be crazy, but she's also kind of charming. And persistent. How long is she going to walk with me? "And for your information, my grandpa had just died, and we all needed that time together. Taylor is extremely cathartic."

I stop walking and turn to face her, my brow quirked. "Show me some proof."

"Proof?"

"Pictures or videos. Something to see this family who goes to Taylor Swift together to grieve and enjoy each other's company."

"Oh!" She bites her lip and smiles as she pulls her phone out to search through her camera roll. I glance at her outfit, noting her expensive Lululemon activewear and fresh Nikes. The girl clearly comes from money. But the odds of having money and happiness?

Slim to none.

She holds her phone up to me and plays a video of them at the concert. Two bearded men in flannel sing every single lyric to "We Are Never Ever Getting Back Together." At one point, they press their backs to each other and join hands above their heads. It's intimate and hilarious, and I have to fight to hide my smile. This shit could go so viral.

The phone pans to show blondie here with tears in her eyes from laughing, and then she moves the camera to another bearded guy who's not singing along. In fact, I can't even tell if he's having fun.

Except for the fact that he's wearing a Taylor Swift Eras Tour concert tee and has a stack of bracelets running up his inked forearm.

Who the fuck are these people?

My mind shakes off the stupor of the hot bearded man being a Swiftie combo that I didn't know would rev my engine so much, and

I ask the girl, "So let's say you're serious and your uncle does want a surrogate. Why would you ask me to do it? You don't even know me."

"Well, you'd need to consent to a background check, of course. And I'll give you a background check on my uncle so you know he's not like a criminal or creep and stuff. But all this doesn't necessarily mean I'm offering you the job. I'm just asking for you two to meet. You guys have to choose each other from that point."

Her response is more mature than I gave her credit for, so I press further. "Why do you think I'd be a good fit for him?"

She hesitates for a moment before a coy smile tugs at the corners of her mouth. "What if I told you I'm a mastermind?"

I roll my eyes at her Taylor Swift lyric quote and frown hard to get a straight answer.

She sighs. "Because you've both been rejected recently, and my grandpa always said that rejection just means you're one step closer to finding your solution."

CHAPTER 7

SURROGATES HIRED: 0

Wyatt

"**C**ome here, Millie!" Everly calls out as the old girl bleats her hello and gingerly trots over to greet us at the pasture enclosure attached to my small red barn.

When I bought this mountain a decade ago, the barn was the only standing structure on the property. I lived in the shitty apartment above it while I cleared trees to prepare for the cabin build. Had to shower outside until I updated the apartment to allow for the tiny luxury of indoor plumbing. It was definitely rustic.

But I gave the barn a fresh coat of paint, revamped the apartment, and now it's not so bad. But my cabin was a definite upgrade when I moved into it. It's honestly probably what I'm most proud of in this life. That and old Millie here.

Millie bleats loudly as Everly's long legs scale the fence, and she squats down to hug my pet goat. Though she's more like a dog than a goat if that makes me any more manly.

I lift the latch and eye Everly dubiously for not just opening the gate. Some days, Everly seems so mature, and others, she's still the same bouncing kid who hemmed and hawed over what to name Millie when I first got her. It was between Millie and Selena Goatmez, so I think I got the lesser of two evils.

Millie's hooves stomp all over Everly's white jeans as she shoves her nose into her long blond hair to say hello. Watching these two grow up together has been surreal. Everly was just ten years old when I found Millie, a newborn Nigerian dwarf, abandoned in the snow on the side of a highway outside of Jamestown. Her caramel-colored fur was coated in mud, and she was trembling and barely able to hold her head up. I took her to a vet in Boulder in the middle of a snow-storm, and he sent me home with milk, a heat lamp, and everything else I needed. He said it would be a miracle if she survived the night.

I laid her in my bed and stayed up all damn night, terrified she'd die on me if I fell asleep. But she made it. In fact, I woke up the following morning to her licking my face and butting me in the neck, looking for a drink. It's been years now, and she's basically the dog I never wanted.

Everly pets the white patch of fur on Millie's crown and gives her a kiss before she asks me, "Have any veggies in your coat?"

I silently reach into my Carhartt and hand Everly a couple of car-rots. "Millie was bleating her demands at freaking six this morning, so I had to run to the Mercantile to pick up some produce. She's a pain in my ass."

"She's a woman who knows what she likes," Everly corrects, strok-ing Millie's ears as she offers her the carrot out of her mouth. God, my niece is a little weirdo sometimes.

She giggles when Millie gets close to her lips and pulls the veggie out of her mouth to give the rest before feeding her the next one. Everly glances up at me, and I notice her cheeks deepen in color.

"Out with it," I grumble, knowing it must be something big if she's nervous.

She hesitates before replying, "I think I found you a baby momma."

I tip my head, doubt casting a shadow over her bright mood. If the twelve vetted women I've already interviewed at the agency didn't work out, I don't have high hopes for whoever Everly found.

"You have to at least meet her," Everly demands, clearly noting my reluctant reaction. Millie notices Everly's intensity and stops eating the carrot to look at the two of us. "I've done a background check and read through her résumé and cross-checked a couple of things. Honestly, I think she's perfect, but it's not up to me. It's up to the two of you."

I sigh heavily, feeling foolish for entertaining this idea but also still desperate enough to at least meet the woman. What's one more "unlucky number thirteen" interview going to hurt? "What do I do next, then?"

Everly smiles triumphantly. "I made you a dinner reservation for tonight."

"Tonight?" I grumble, dreading the idea of driving into town. The longer I live out here in the wilderness, the less I like driving in traffic.

"I set it up at the Mercantile," she answers with a proud smile.

The Merc is basically in my backyard, so the idea doesn't sound quite as painful. "Do they even take reservations there?"

Everly smiles. "Judy likes me."

"Everyone likes you." I roll my eyes and exhale. "At least I can take the four-wheeler."

"You'll actually do it?" Her face lights up. "You'll show up tonight?"

"Yeah, I'll show up." The air is whooshed out of me when Everly jumps up and binds her arms around my neck in a big hug.

Millie bleats and jumps up, hoofing us both until we break apart and make room for her.

"I have a good feeling about her, Uncle Wyatt," she exclaims, dropping back down to pat Millie on her side.

"Just don't get your hopes up," I reply dryly, assuming I'll probably be able to get home before sundown.

She instantly stops smiling and nods seriously. "My hopes are in the dirt."

"Good."

"Under Millie's manure…which I'm going to go scoop out of her pen right now."

The corner of my mouth tips up. "You're a good kid."

"Uncle Wyatt, I'm a good *adult*. Remember? Eighteen? Going to college?" She flutters her eyelashes at me.

"Hmmm," I grunt.

She smiles and walks off, dangling a carrot as Millie excitedly pounces behind her like a puppy.

One dinner. And then it's back to the drawing board that is my life these days.

CHAPTER 8

SURROGATES INTERVIEWED: 13

Wyatt

Jamestown is a small foothills community where if you blink, you could miss it. It boasts a population of a whopping 260 people with little room for growth as the town rests snugly between steep canyon walls and thick forests. It cost me an arm and a leg to pave the private gravel drive up the mountain that overlooks the town. And because it's private, I can't get city snow removal in the winter, which means in a bad storm, my brothers and I have to leave our trucks at the bottom of the range and ride snowmobiles up until we can run my tractor plow through everything.

It's a bitch, but it's also very freeing to let your life go for a while because of old Mother Nature.

Because of the mining history here, the town has an old Western feel. Remnants of those gold rush days are scattered throughout. Like the old hotel that's now the fire department run by volunteers, two of which are my brothers. Then the dance hall that's now the post office, plus the parlor house that's the town's only bar called the Jamestown Mercantile. Their catchphrase is "where everyone is a little feral," and hell, it fits.

The Mercantile is more than just a bar, though. It serves decent grub, and its small grocery supply comes in handy during the winter when the weather gets bad. My brothers and I are regulars as we eat many of our meals here and grab beers after work a lot. It's about as small-town as you can get because I know literally everyone when I walk in. Something that took my brothers and me a bit of time to adjust to.

The first year after my brothers joined me on the mountain and built their cabins, we spent a lot of late nights at the Mercantile, making friends with the very limited single local ladies. Most of whom are long gone now. And truth be told…that's probably our fault.

The high of the mountain air and living off the land in our self-sustaining cabins was an intense aphrodisiac. So intense it nearly ruined everything my brothers and I were trying to build together. That was the first and last time we ever let a woman come between us.

Thankfully, that's ancient history now, and as a group, we all made a pact of sorts to choose mountain life over traditional lives. Women come and go, but mountain life and our brotherhood…it's forever. The three of us even do this annual Dark Night bonding tradition, which is meant to remind us of what is most important. Our pact seems even more meaningful now after the loss of our father.

"Here you go, Wyatt." A pilsner glass of amber liquid appears in front of me, and I glance up to see the owner, Judy, gazing out the large plate glass window through the Mercantile Café block text scrawled across the front. Her head nods toward the mountain, where you can see our three log cabins nestled up there like a postcard. "There's been a lot of traffic up your way this week."

"You're telling me," I grumble and tip my beer to her in silent thanks before taking a drink.

"Everly stopped in a few hours ago and asked if she could make a reservation." She barks out a smoky laugh and drops her hand on my shoulder for balance. "That slayed me."

"Yeah, she's kind of on a roll these days," I drawl before taking another sip of my beer.

"You be nice to her. That girl gives me a toothache she's so sweet." Judy smiles affectionately, then gets a nosy look in her eye. "Does this meeting have something to do with that surrogate ad Calder posted on my tagboard the other day? I thought that was a joke."

My hand tightens around my glass as my fingers twitch to wrap around my brother's neck. "It might."

Judy's brows lift as she takes a moment to digest this information. I would have liked to keep my plans to hire a surrogate quiet from the locals, but secrets spread like forest fires in a small town, especially with an obnoxious brother like Calder making it front-page fucking news for everyone to see. I'm sure they all think I'm crazy, but luckily, I don't give a shit what anyone thinks.

Judy pats me on the shoulder and shakes her head. "I hope you know what you're getting into, son."

"I guess we'll find out," I reply through clenched teeth.

She nods, seemingly appeased by that answer, and walks away without asking more questions. Judy always knows when to walk away. She also knows when to smack one of us Fletchers upside the head when we need it. Calder needs a smack more often than all of us.

I eye the other patrons scattered around me. They're drinking in small groups, and the acoustic guitar player performing in the corner tonight is pretty loud, so hopefully, no one will be able to eavesdrop.

I wonder what this gal I'm about to meet will think of this place. The Mercantile is dark and dilapidated in that perfect dive bar way. It's an old three-story building with the lower half all belonging to the bar. Judy lives upstairs, and I think there's one other vacant apartment on the third level.

She's got some rustic charm here, with the walls covered in wainscoting and mismatched tables and chairs scattered throughout. The artwork is all old pictures from the '50s that match the retro tassel chandeliers that hang in random spots. I have to duck to avoid knocking my head into them. Plus, there's a cabinet chock-full of old vinyl records that Judy has to yell at people not to touch when they've been drinking too much.

Out front, some Edison lights hang over the small patio area, where a lot of road bicyclists stop to refuel themselves in the summer. And in the back is a beer garden with picnic tables and a gazebo that gets pretty busy in the summer. We don't get tourists through here much. It's usually just neighboring townspeople looking for a change of scenery or the 4-wheeler crowd out here to enjoy the unpaved min-ing roads. Frankly, Jamestown is like this perfect uncut gem of a com-munity that I'm happy to call home…even if they all love to gossip.

If this potential surrogate isn't at least marginally impressed by the splendors of this place, then she's not fit to carry my baby, just like all the others I've met.

The bell chiming above the door has me glancing over to see a woman walking in, looking flustered and out of sorts. I don't know for sure that it's my girl, but every head turning to gape at the outsider makes it pretty fucking likely that it is.

Her face is covered by her hair as she digs inside the large tote bag hanging from her shoulder. I use this moment to take a physical assessment of unlucky number thirteen.

The setting sun slices through her long, curly chestnut hair. The frizzy, wild strands are kind of a perfect match to the frenzied energy she just brought into the bar as she continues to curse under her breath and struggle with something in her bag.

She's a decent height…maybe five foot ten or better—hard to tell if those cowboy boots she has on are heeled or not. I have to admit that the fact that she's wearing boots is intriguing on its own. None of the other ladies I interviewed looked like this one. They looked like women dressed for a job interview, so at the very least, I like that this one is different. Even down to her body, which…well, I wouldn't call her small, but I wouldn't call her big either. She's sturdy.

I like sturdy.

Jesus Christ, what's wrong with me? You'd think I'm picking out a prized heifer at the Boulder County Fair. I've been on this surro-gacy hunt way too fucking long. My brain is short-circuiting. If this woman is to carry my child, I should *not* be looking at her like I want to ride her.

I shake off my inappropriate thoughts and force myself to stop gawking and get up to say hello, my knees cracking as I rise. My boots are heavy on the scuffed wood floor as I approach. "Are you Trista?"

"Yes," she chirps, her head snapping up like she's been caught tex-ting in class.

When our eyes connect, a rush of adrenaline surges through me—through my gut, specifically. I swallow the lump in my throat and reach my hand out to her. "Wyatt."

Her hand is currently tucked deep inside her bag, so she offers me her opposite hand, making for a very awkward handshake. She rustles around with something that sounds like a wrapper in her bag and winces.

When we disconnect, her round eyes venture unabashedly down my body, her lips parting as she takes in my frame. The bag drops off her shoulder, and I hear a strange yip come from her before she begins coughing violently and whacking her chest.

"Excuse me," she says, her voice gruff from the cough attack as she points at her throat and repositions the bag back on her shoulder. "I sucked some spit into the back of my throat, and it went down the wrong pipe."

My brows furrow as I gesture to my table over by the stone fireplace. "Can I get you a drink?"

"A drink would be great," she replies desperately, and I watch as she storms past me to the spot, carefully tucking her bag alongside the chair like she's carrying a million dollars in cash.

I hesitantly take the seat across from her and gesture to Judy, who comes over in a hurry, likely sensing the awkwardness.

"I'll have what he's having," she says, pointing at my beer with a wink. "Not knocked up yet, right?"

"Coming right up." Judy shoots me a curious look and takes off for the bar. *That'll get the rumors flying.*

Still distracted by her bag, I decide to take the lead on this meeting…which I fucking hate. The beauty of the agency was that they managed all these meet and greets.

"I hear you met my niece," I offer stiffly.

Trista laughs at that and finally gives me her full attention. Her smile is actually pretty captivating. Her upper lip curls at the top in an interesting way. "Yes, I certainly did."

"Hopefully, she wasn't a total pain in the ass," I state with a sigh, leaning back in my chair. "And for what it's worth, I'm sorry about all this. She was very persistent about helping me, and I'm not good at saying no to her. Ever."

"There's no need to be sorry." Trista's brows knit together as her eyes sweep across my face in a way that feels disarming. "She seems like a sweet kid. And she didn't force me to come here. I'm interested in the potential behind this arrangement."

"That's...good," I reply stiffly, my hands finding my beard out of nervous habit. This is so much more awkward not having a moderator.

"I heard you've interviewed a lot of candidates," Trista offers, drumming her long fingers softly on the beat-up wood table.

"Yeah, I'm afraid so," I reply with a huff. "And they always seem to feel like..."

"Like you're picking out a livestock animal?" she offers with her brows arched.

My eyes widen at how she basically repeated my earlier thoughts. "Bingo."

"I get it," she says with a shrug. "I've researched a lot about surrogacy stuff on the lesbian blogs, so I know how hard it is to find someone you can trust with something so important."

Judy returns and sets a fresh couple of beers in front of us, lingering a bit longer than necessary as we both take a fortifying sip. I drink my beer slowly and ponder Trista's lesbian comment. I shouldn't give a fuck what her sexuality is because this isn't a date, and I'm not going to sleep with this woman. But I just...I don't know...something about that realization feels disappointing.

I swallow the knot in my throat before asking the most embarrassingly obvious question on the planet. "So have you and your girlfriend or...wife...done surrogacy stuff before?"

Confusion twists her features. "Oh, I'm not gay. I just realized through my research that the lesbians know their shit when it comes to getting knocked up by a man's sperm without having to do the actual deed."

"Oh." I lower my eyes so she can't see the relief painted over my stupid face. *Man the fuck up, Wyatt.*

She misinterprets my discomfort and reaches out to touch my

arm. "If it's any consolation, I think the fact that it's been so hard for you to find a match means you're taking this very seriously, and that's a good thing."

I glance down at her hand on me as an odd prickling sensation rolls through my veins that I haven't felt in a long time. Not many people touch me. I mean...don't get me wrong, I'm obviously not unfamiliar with women. I'm a single man, after all, and the bearded-mountain-man vibe seems to work out well for me. But in professional settings like this, I'm used to people being too intimidated to ever feel comfortable enough to embrace me in a casual manner. My gut is telling me this is a good fucking thing. A thing I should not shy away from.

"Well, what else do you need to know about me?" she asks, taking a sip of her beer. "I assume you need to know stuff you can't discover in a background check or résumé. Where do I start? I'm twenty-eight years old and a Scorpio, so I'm a little crazy and intense...but also fiercely loyal. I have a full-time job at a dog rescue facility. I never went to college because I could never figure out the whole student loan thing. And I also think college is a waste of money. But I'm not dumb. I am a great researcher. Anything I'm ever curious about, I go to the library and read all the books and obsess over the topic until I'm an expert. Last year, I learned a freakish amount of information on the Amish that sent me down a rabbit hole of reading Amish romances for a solid year. I love the outdoors and think air-conditioning is making us all weak. I have one sister who lives in Hawaii. I am a meat eater—"

I hold up a hand to pause her, shifting myself forward to prop my elbows on the table and eye the woman who might possibly make me a dad.

Dad.

It suddenly doesn't feel as scary to say to myself as it did yesterday.

"There's one big question I would love to ask." My voice is calm, but my eyes are probing, noting every single feature on her face as I mentally catalog the distinct beauty marks that decorate her pale skin. "Why do you want to do this? The no-bullshit answer."

She seems disarmed by my directness but also invigorated by it. Her coppery-green eyes glitter with challenge as she pulls her thick lower lip between her teeth. "You good with a truth bomb, Mr. Mountain Man?"

I inhale through my nose and ignore the nickname she's just given me. "Bombs away."

She exhales heavily and says without a second's pause, "I want to open a wildlife rescue facility. Not for dogs and cats but for all sorts of animals. Farm animals, injured birds, squirrels…all of it. I've seen countless animals turned away from my shelter because they're not equipped to handle other types of species, and it's something I'm passionate about. I don't come from money, and I know I need a fair amount of startup funds to open a facility. Surrogacy ads started popping up on Facebook after I started googling how to work two jobs at once, and before I knew it, I was begging the surrogacy agency in Denver to give me a chance even though I'm technically too fat by their prehistoric standards and have no birth history yet."

I sit back, noting her flushed cheeks and wild eyes. She's hard to look away from as she reveals her inner truths to me. And the craziest part is she's not done.

"I know I don't have experience being pregnant, but I think I'd be good at this because I've tracked my cycles and know exactly when I ovulate. And I'm not a baby person…never have been. Babies kind of freak me out. Every time someone says, 'Look at the cute baby,' I always think the baby's face looks weird and squished up. Don't get me wrong, I'm not against the creation of life. I just don't want the responsibility of raising said life. Fur babies are my life's passion. Or snakes… which…as you know, have no fur. Give me a baby doe or a guinea pig and I'm mother of the friggin' year."

Trista smiles sweetly and goes for broke. "Also, I have a foster puppy in my tote bag that I'm pretty sure peed in there because the side of my shirt is soaking wet."

CHAPTER 9

MONTHS OFF BIRTH CONTROL: 4

Trista

You blew it, Trista. You were sitting across from a ridiculously hot mountain man who wants to pay someone to grow his baby that you wouldn't have to take care of, and you just told him you're covered in dog piss. Prepare to be fired.

I've been let go from my fair share of jobs on account of being Latey McLateface. Seriously, if I could teleport, I'd probably still be late for everything. But I've never been fired before even getting the job. I'm usually quite the charmer! It's easy for me to connect with people. But this time, I may have just topped my pathetic self.

"The puppy piss comment was too much, wasn't it?" I state, choosing to be candid rather than walk out of this place, wondering if he'll call.

"No," he answers, and a tiny glimpse of a smile toys with his lips. He doesn't look like a guy who smiles much, so maybe this is a good sign. "But I'd honestly prefer it if you took it out of the tote. Dogs are welcome here, and I don't like the idea of that little guy sitting in its own piss."

I exhale a sigh of relief and quickly grab the little black mixed Lab the shelter guessed to be about four months old. She shakes in my hands and desperately starts licking my face as I hold her to my chest.

"This is Queenie," I say, introducing her to the man who may, in fact, be impregnating me very soon. "She was dropped off at the rescue center an hour ago. I'm sure she'll get adopted in a few days—puppies usually go pretty quick—but she hated the kennel, and I didn't want to leave her there overnight."

"I see," Wyatt replies dismissively, making no move to pet the adorable creature in my hand.

"Not an animal guy?" I ask, watching his body language carefully.

He wrinkles his nose and shakes his head, and this is the first red flag he's thrown me so far. I thought he seemed normal and level-headed. His niece really sold me on this whole "happy family" situation. But I can't understand humans who don't love animals. Maybe this surrogacy gig won't work out after all.

Then again…it's not like that Denver agency is banging down my door.

"Oh, my goodness!" the server from earlier squeals as she comes over to pet the little gal in my hand. "Can I hold the precious puppy wuppy?"

I arch a pointed brow at the giant mountain man across the table and make my reply real big and exaggerated. "Absolutely you can hold da puppy wuppy lovee dovee. Who doesn't love to hold a puppy?"

The woman cradles Queenie in her arms, and instantly, she's assaulted with licks all over her face, to the woman's absolute delight.

"Actually, do you have a bowl and some water I could give her?" I ask, thinking it's been an hour since she's had anything.

"I sure do," the woman coos. "Mind if I take her out back? My grandson is out there, and he'd love to play with her. I'll let her go potty and bring her back once she's stretched her legs a bit."

"Oh my God, that would be so amazing. Thank you!" I watch in delight as the kind woman squeals and scurries off with the puppy. I can't help but eye Wyatt dubiously as I point at where they've disappeared out the back door. "That's the normal reaction to puppies."

He grunts at me.

Literally grunts.

Okay, this is too much. "What kind of man who wants a baby doesn't like puppies?"

He shrugs and leans forward, hitting me with those stunning light blue eyes that are a gorgeous contrast to his light brown hair and beard, which has flecks of gray in it. "You've met my niece, right?"

"Yeah."

He quirks his head and adds, "She's better than puppies."

"Okay, that's fair," I reply with a laugh at that simple but effective response. "So, what's your deal? You love your niece and want one of your own?"

"I suppose that's part of it. She's going to college in Ireland at the end of the summer, and that's messed all of us up quite a bit," he replies with a thoughtful look. "But I'm ready to be more than an uncle. And while I know I want to be a dad, I don't want to be a husband. And I realize I don't have to be married to have a baby, but I don't want to co-parent with someone. The idea of splitting time with my own blood the way my brother has to with Everly…it looks painful to me." He pauses for a moment as his hand grips the pilsner glass firmly in his hand. His eyes darken when he adds, "I can be kind of possessive when it comes to those I love."

A flush rushes up to my cheeks, and the carnal reaction my body has to that last sentence is something I did not expect. I mean, look, I'd have to be blind not to find the tall, bearded lumberjack sitting before me attractive. But I'm someone who can normally keep my cool with guys. Mostly because I'm not a relationship girlie. My tendency to be late annoys most men until they give up on me, and my focus truly has always migrated more toward animals than humans. I don't even have many close friends for all those reasons. And I'm cool with that. Rejection fucks with my head, so it's easier to just expect nothing when it comes to people. But this guy…Mr. Mountain Man Wyatt? I'm going to need to keep my shit together if this works out.

My body shivers as I take a second to inspect him and try to figure out what I find so alluring about him. He isn't one of those classically handsome Disney prince guys who are a dime a dozen in Denver. He has a rough-around-the-edges look to him. His beard is short and trim but crawls down his neck like he doesn't do any sort of shaping to it. His brown hair is scruffy and sticking out every which way, like it was shoved under a hat all day. And his nose slopes slightly more off to one side. I wonder if he's ever broken it. And his eyes. Damn, they are penetrating. They are narrow and intense, almost animalistic in nature. That's what it is. I'm attracted to him because he looks like a wolf, ready to attack. Typical me.

It isn't until he sits back to take a drink of his beer that I realize I'm staring at his thick neck, completely slack-jawed, as he swallows the foamy liquid.

I shake off my hormonal daze and shrug casually, my mind snapping me back to reality as I realize he was the last one to speak, and now it's my turn. "Possessive or protective…both are good qualities in a future father. I'll accept that answer."

"Is this a test for me as well?" he asks, arching one thick eyebrow at me.

"A little," I reply honestly. "Can we continue the truth bombs?"

"By all means." He crosses his arms in front of him, and I can't help but eye the way his bicep pulls against the flannel of his shirt.

"Well," I start, clearing my throat for the next bit, "I am about to be a little bit…homeless." His brows furrow with concern, and I hold my hands up defensively. "But not in the 'I don't know how to pay my bills' sort of way. I mean, I am low-key poor, but I manage my money just fine. The problem is…I got busted with a potbellied pig in my apartment last week, and my landlord is kicking me out, even though I told him I got all the stains out of the carpet."

"Did you say a potbellied pig?" His tone is not impressed.

"Yeah."

"Are you about to pull a pig out of your bag next?"

"No…Jesus, he's a hefty bastard! I can barely lift him into my car." I stretch my back at the memory of that pain. "Reginald is at the pet facility I work at, but they are not equipped for farm animals, and it's actually illegal for him to be there, so I have to get him out of there ASAP."

"I see," Wyatt replies, looking a bit confused.

"Your niece said you had some lodging options for the potential surrogate you hire?" I offer hopefully. "Something about a barn on your property. And, well, if I'm about to move next door to a man to have his baby…I need to make sure he's not a crazy person and that this is a safe situation for me. So yeah…this is a test for you as much as it is for me."

"That's fair," he replies stiffly.

"But a barn sounds amazing for Reginald," I say wistfully, dreaming about him having more room to root around than my apartment complex parking lot.

"So…the barn is an option for housing," he replies dubiously. "But…"

"But what?"

He glances sideways, looking uncomfortable for a moment before turning a firm look at me. "I'm not sure my goat will like a pig in the barn with her."

"You have a goat?" I exclaim, my voice rising much higher than I intended. Everyone in the bar turns to stare at me, so I lower my voice and try to wipe the delighted smile off my face. "I'm sorry…Mr. Animal Hater has a *goat*?"

"It's no big deal," he drawls.

My brows furrow as a thought strikes me. "Do you just have the one goat?"

"Yes…why?"

"Well, goats typically don't do well in captivity alone. They need a friend. How long have you had this goat?"

"Going on ten years, and I've had her since she was a kid. She's been perfectly fine on her own all these years," he replies defensively, his hard look turning damn near angry. "Millie is a very happy, well-adjusted goat."

He flinches at his last sentence, almost like he can't believe he said it out loud, and my hands fly to my mouth as I cover my smirk. "Her name is Millie?"

"Don't mock my goat. Remember what I said about how I feel about those I love?"

"I am not mocking!" I hold my hands up in surrender, smiling like a cat who got the cream. "I'm just really happy to discover you're not a puppy hater. You simply only love your *own* animals. It's really sweet, actually."

Wyatt rolls his eyes, and his face softens a bit. Damn, I think this might be going well. I think this whole crazy plan of that blond girl Everly, who's been texting me nonstop since I left her on that Denver street corner last week, might actually work.

I grab my beer and take a victorious sip before holding it up to him. "So what now, Wyatt? What's our next move with this crazy modern family you're trying to build?"

He frowns for a moment and then says something I never would have expected. "Do you want to meet my goat?"

CHAPTER 10

ANIMALS ON THE MOUNTAIN: 2

Trista

Queenie rears back on her hind legs to playfully attack Millie the goat's legs. Millie bleats her encouragement, nudging the little gal softly, clearly enjoying the company. I distract her by feeding her a stalk of celery provided by Mr. Grumpy Puppy Hater over here and pet the old girl on the ribs, turning a satisfied smile up to the mountain man.

"I hate to say it, but Millie seems like she might enjoy a new friend."

His eyes narrow on the pair as they frolic away from where I'm squatted in the dirt. They're inside the small, enclosed pasture connected to the red barn, and Queenie could easily slip out through the horizontal whiteboards, but right now, she doesn't look like she's going to leave that goat's side.

A mountain man with a goat…what an odd combination.

Then again, a lot has surprised me about Mr. Mountain Man today. Everly might actually have been telling the truth about her uncle. He might be a decent human.

"Millie likes this puppy because she's basically a puppy herself."

I scoff. "If she likes Queenie, she'll love Reginald."

"Why did you name him Reginald?" Wyatt asks, and I try not to stare at the veins running up his forearms as he props himself on the white-painted fence.

He took his jacket off earlier and draped it over the fence, and the view of him basking in the golden sun against the backdrop of pine trees with a piece of straw hanging out of his mouth was intense. I had to physically stop myself from going into heat like a farm animal.

Being attracted to the man who could be the ticket to opening my own animal sanctuary would make things tricky. But I have a degree from the school of hard knocks, so detaching from my emotions is easy peasy.

"It was either that or Piggie Smalls," I answer with a shrug and rise up from the ground, brushing off my pant legs as I do. "And Sir Reginald just felt right. He has a stately look about him. Wait until I get him up here. You'll see."

"Get him up here?" Wyatt's eyes drift down my body as I continue wiping the dust off my jeans. "Did I miss the part where we decided we're doing this for sure? Pretty sure we have some details to iron out first."

"Well, yeah, but that's all semantics." I wave him off and move toward the enclosure, smiling politely when Wyatt opens the gate for me. I join him at the fence, keeping a close eye on Queenie as she nips at Millie's hooves. "I already have your niece's approval, and I gather that counts for a lot around here."

Not to mention, he let me meet his pet goat.

"Hmm," he hums, fingering the piece of straw in his hand, a thoughtful look clouding his eyes.

"Can I ask what the reasons were that you refused all the other surrogates?" I ask, watching his eyebrows pop in surprise at my question.

"All twelve?" he replies with a disappointed huff.

"Twelve?" My eyes widen. Maybe this isn't a done deal after all.

After a long pause, he shrugs and says, "They all had the same answer of 'I want to use my gift to help others,' and while I think it's really noble, I guess it just never landed right with me. Maybe I'm a cynic, but who really likes to help a stranger that much? Especially for something as big as having a baby for someone. It was a hard answer to believe. I just wanted someone different. Someone to be real with me, like you were at the bar. Hearts-and-flowers answers aren't my thing. And considering this whole ordeal will involve a sizable exchange of money, I want to be certain I pick someone I can trust."

I nod thoughtfully at his answer. This surrogacy decision he's made is a big deal, and I think it's a good sign he's been so choosy. And I low-key respect the fact that he wants to become a single parent, even if it's not something I ever want for myself. That takes some balls.

And sperm.

And an egg and uterus, which I am pretty certain I have ready and available.

"If it's honesty you like, I should confess that I'm a little scared," I offer, turning around and pressing my back to the fence to gaze out at the stunning mountain vista that this man built with his bare hands. "I've never been pregnant before, and I am fully aware there are no guarantees it'll work and a lot of ways that things could go wrong. Also, I'm sure people will think I'm crazy for trying to make money this way."

"Well, when you put it like that," he says and shocks me when a warm smile spreads across his face. Damn, he doesn't pass those out for free, and I'll admit, having it directed toward me causes a rush of heat to surge through my belly.

I inhale a cleansing breath and turn to focus back on the view. "But life is nothing if not a game, and I'm almost thirty, so I need to start playing. Being frugal and safe all these years hasn't got me very far. This feels like something that could help me get ahead, and I might actually be made for it."

I can feel his eyes on me as my gaze moves up the hill to register his home again. He calls it a cabin, but it's anything but. It's an architectural dream with sharp angles and giant windows that showcase the views yet somehow fits perfectly among the pine forest. He put some serious time and money into this estate.

The two additional cabins farther up the hill are more modest log cabins but still really beautiful. Wyatt told me earlier that they belonged to his brothers. Three grown-ass men who are related to each other and choosing to live communally like this is so bizarre. Especially when my only sister couldn't move farther away from me. Then again, my upbringing isn't anything to write home about, so who am I to judge?

Is it crazy to move up onto a mountain with three men?

Definitely.

Do I have any other appealing options that allow for me and my potbellied pig?

Negative.

Did I double-check the locks on the barn apartment upstairs when he gave me a tour?

You bet your sweet ass I did.

And while this commune living might seem like a giant red flag... Wyatt Fletcher is a man full of beige flags...all the way down to the hunk of celery he had in his coat pocket for Millie. Like he knew he'd stop out here to see her before bed.

That one might even be a green flag.

I inhale the fresh mountain air and eye the mature trees everywhere. I could definitely get used to this view. Growing up in Denver, we never got out to the mountains. We never got out of anywhere. We lived in a tiny two-bedroom apartment, and I remember my friends in school talking about family vacations on actual airplanes, which seemed like such a fantasy to me.

Look at me now.

This is definitely a huge step up from my shitty apartment in a sketchy neighborhood. Those neighbors weren't exactly making me feel safe either. How bad can these mountain men brothers be?

Truth be told, there's something about this whole place that just feels like the life I was meant to have. The only bummer is that this is really just a nine-month contract. After that...I'm on my own again.

But if I can get my certifications done while I'm pregnant, then I'd be ready to move on. To start my life. To complete my dream of opening up my rescue facility, maybe on a property like this someday.

With renewed determination, I turn to face the grumpy mountain man and get right down to business. "As I mentioned, I've read a lot on the lesbian blogs."

"Sorry?"

"The lesbian blogs…for how to get me knocked up without us actually having to roll in the hay. The lesbians know their shit."

Wyatt looks taken aback. "Wouldn't we use a fertility clinic with a donor egg? That's usually the way these things go."

"Is that what you want?"

He blinks back at me in confusion. "I'm not sure what I want matters."

Beige-flag answer.

"Well, I can tell you from my research that if we do IVF and a donor egg, it will involve way more work on my part. We're talking multiple trips per week to the clinic, daily intramuscular shots, bajingo suppositories—"

"What's a bajingo?"

"My vagina, obviously," I answer emphatically. "Not to mention oral medications, supplements, ultrasounds. Good God, the expense of that alone will be insane, especially because my health insurance does not cover fertility treatments. And most fertility clinics are booked out for months. So really, I think the farm way is best."

"The farm way?" Wyatt looks like I'm speaking a foreign language. God, he's cute when he's flustered.

"You know…inseminate me like a cow." I make a squeezing motion with my fingers. "Turkey baster style. You can buy the kits on Amazon. Or if you have like a children's medicine syringe, that could work too. Like for kids' Tylenol? Lots of ladies getting knocked up that way. Just pull the semen up into the syringe and shoot it up my bajingo. We would make sure it's sanitary, of course."

"Jesus." Wyatt runs a hand through his hair and looks wildly uncomfortable. You'd think interviewing twelve women for this job would have made him less precious about all this by now.

"I'm sorry, I just don't know you well enough to sleep with you. And I think it would feel kind of awkward afterward, don't you? Especially if I'm going to live up here."

"I wasn't suggesting…" He stumbles over his words, and I have to admit, I love watching him squirm.

"You're going to jizz in a cup either way, so I really prefer to try it the traditional surrogate way, if you don't mind. And if you're worried about me feeling too connected to the baby because of the genetic link…don't. I met with a counselor while I was researching becoming a surrogate, and I know what it takes emotionally. And the way I see it, I'm just wasting my eggs every month as it is. Why not donate one to you? Hopefully just one. God…I really hope I don't get pregnant with more than one?" I gasp and hitch my voice as I state in a mock tone, "Triplets for the mountain men! You and your brothers can all take one!"

"Can we slow down?" Wyatt's Adam's apple slides down his throat as he struggles to process everything. He stares out at the pasture with a panic-stricken look, and I get a sense that I've gone too far again.

My voice is softer when I reply, "We can go as slow as you want, but I have two weeks left before I'm homeless, so the sooner we decide, the better."

Wyatt's nostrils flare as he drums his fist on the fence for a moment, clearly having a full-blown conversation with himself for the second time. He nods firmly and looks at me with wide, electric-blue eyes. "Let's get the contract part negotiated first, make sure we agree on all the terms, and then we'll go from there. Work for you?"

The corner of my mouth tips up victoriously, but I try to remain calm and professional. "You're the boss, Mr. Mountain Man."

He eyes me flatly. "And maybe we can negotiate a new nickname."

CHAPTER 11

SURROGATES HIRED: 1
IRRITATING BROTHERS: 3

Wyatt

"**N**o fucking way."

"No fucking way!"

"No fucking way."

All three of my brothers repeat the same three stupid words as they stand on my front porch way too early for a Saturday morning, gaping at me like three circus monkeys. *I'm beginning to hate Saturday mornings.*

"You signed a contract with a surrogate?" Max asks, and his stern tone echoes in off the foothills. He hits me with those concerned-dad eyes that he usually reserves for Everly and Ethan.

I let the screen door slam behind me as I lean on my log cabin and button up the flannel I tossed on before coming outside. My three brothers are staggered on my front porch in various positions of angst, looking at odds with the peaceful mountain view behind them.

Calder is hunched over the log railing, shirtless and obviously hungover. Luke's sitting at the bottom of my steps, looking like he wants no part of whatever meeting Max must have called after I sent out a group text an hour ago informing my bros of the news. And

Max…good old Max…he looks so much like our dad it hurts to look at him sometimes.

I shrug, refusing to answer a question Max already knows the answer to, so he marches up the steps toward me, his eyebrows furrowed with concern. "Wyatt…you've done some crazy shit," he says, shaking his head and gesturing all around him. "I mean…buying this mountain property that you can't even drive out of in the middle of Colorado winters, for one…"

"That rarely happens," Calder drawls, running his hand over his inked arms as the brisk morning air bites at his bare skin.

Max huffs, clearly not accepting that answer. "Letting these two morons build up here so the three of you can live out in some crazy hillbilly-mountain-man cult is crazy shit number two…"

I glance up the hill at their cabins, noticing how beautiful they look today. Much better than they did a few weeks ago when I was going to burn them down.

"You're just mad you didn't build on Fletcher Mountain," Luke murmurs loud enough for all of us to hear.

"I didn't want to build on Fletcher Mountain," Max bellows over his shoulder at Luke before turning back to me. "And now you're actually going to raise a baby up here like it's some sort of Three Mountain Men and a Baby movie?"

"Hey…I never signed up to raise this baby," Calder snaps, pointing an accusing finger at me. "I don't do diapers. Didn't do it for Everly or Ethan, and I won't do it for your offspring."

Max releases an exasperated laugh, like he can't believe the one argument Calder has right now is over diapers. "I thought the fact that you were rejecting all those candidates at the agency meant you weren't going to go through with this. Now you decided to select a surrogate that my kid found you?"

My jaw clenches, and Max's face softens when he sees I'm not changing my mind on this. With a heavy sigh, he says, "At least let my lawyer look over the contract before you guys…do it." Max looks uncomfortable with the last couple of words, and I internally guffaw. What a child.

"I hired my own lawyer, Max. I'm good. The papers are already signed, and we're doing this."

"What happens next?" Luke asks, his eyes full of genuine curiosity. He's got different energy about all of this than Max, and it's very much appreciated.

"She's moving into the barn today."

"What?" all three of my brothers bellow in unison. Jesus, they should start a boy band.

"Lodging was a request of hers, and she needs the barn for her own animal, so this was necessary."

"What about our mountain pact?" Calder grunts, looking far more awake now and very unimpressed by this tiny detail I left out of my group text.

"You're the moron who put rural housing available upon request in your ad!"

"I didn't think that would actually work," he murmurs, blinking back his disbelief as his eyes flash over to the barn. "The last time we had a woman living up here—"

"That won't happen again," I snap, my temper flaring instantly as memories of the past try to flood my vision. I shake them away to the dark corners of my mind, where they've been living for the better part of a decade. "This is business, not personal. Our pact remains. You guys don't even need to interact with her."

"You didn't think you needed to run any of this by us first?" Luke asks, his voice showing his anxiety.

"No." I move down the steps to get some space before I decide to remind them that I own this land and they live here by my invitation. Not that I'd ever kick them out. Honestly, it would kill me to lose them. I picture us all up here until we're old and gray. But I need them to see the bigger picture here. "Do you guys really care more about the past than my future? I'm trying to start a family here."

"We just know how hard it was after everything that went down with Robyn." Max sighs heavily. "You took it the hardest."

"Don't say her fucking name," I grind out, my entire body radiating anger at the fact that my older brother feels entitled to remind me of the past. It's impossible to forget. And I took it the hardest because I was the one who lost the most.

But that's ancient history now. Robyn might as well be Lord fucking Voldemort because I do not speak her name. Ever.

"Trista is different. You guys will see. She's not like other women," I state honestly. Not that I need their approval. I'm doing this, and my brothers need to get right with it, or we'll have problems. "This is essentially a nine-month contract. We can handle a female on the mountain for nine months."

Calder and Luke look doubtful, but honestly, I don't care. This feels right. It felt right the moment I laid eyes on Trista, and it's felt right every day since. As weird as it might be to have my niece find me a baby momma, I think her crazy fucking plan just might work. Shit, I could be expecting a baby by the end of the month, maybe.

Calder interrupts my thoughts. "Well, if she's going to live so close, maybe you should make this baby the old-fashioned way? Lay out some candles...play a little music."

"If you don't have anything respectful to say about all of this, then please shut the fuck up." My tone is flat, knowing I've reached my daily quota on word allowance all before breakfast. Damn these big life changes are fucking with my silent-mountain-man vibes.

Calder laughs and leans back on the log railing, murmuring, "Not even a dad yet, and already sounding like our father. Way to go, Papa Bear."

I growl my wordless response to Calder about having sex with Trista, knowing full well I'm not going to tell any of my brothers how we're making this baby. It's none of their damn business. It's mine and Trista's, and no one needs to know exactly how this is all going down.

I fight back a smile as I recall how Trista's face scrunched up when she made the squeezing motion with her hand to gesticulate the insemination. It was horrifying at first, but now, every time I think about it, I can't help but laugh.

"You know...inseminate me like a cow. Turkey baster style. You can

buy the kits on Amazon. Just pull the semen up into the syringe and shoot it up my bajingo."

She certainly has a way with words.

In the end, I agreed with her. The contract states that Trista and I will try to do it the "farm way," as she requested, though it was outlined more scientifically in black and white with mentions of an at-home insemination kit. If we don't have success in the first month, the contract allows us to try for two more months, and after that, we'll attempt three cycles of IUI with a clinic. If there's no success in six months, we both part ways—Trista with a small stipend and me with…well…nothing. But that's life, I guess. There are no guarantees.

It's even outlined in the contract what happens if there are any health issues with this baby that are genetically linked to Trista, and, well, she has a say in that decision. Rightfully so. But whatever it is and whatever she decides, I'll handle it. I'll devote my life to handling it. I'll make sure this baby has every need met, even if that means moving off the mountain.

This is my priority now. Nothing else matters. Not even my brothers. I'm ready to become a father. And Trista Matthews is my hope to get there.

This past week, I did a deep dive on her social media to ensure that I made the right choice with her. I had my doubts at first because the girl looks damn near feral in all her Instagram photos. Messy hair, smudged makeup, always some animal in her hands. So many animals, I know she can't own them all. But oddly enough, that made me feel like I got it right. Like of all the women I interviewed, none were like her—*genuine*…real—and maybe she was the one I'd been waiting for.

And if we're successful at this…I will owe my niece big-time.

My phone pings with a text from Everly…as if she could tell I was thinking about her.

> Everly: Don't let my dad cause you to doubt this decision. Trista is perfect, and I have a really good feeling about all of this, Uncle Wyatt. <3
>
> Me: Me too, Evie girl. Me too.

Luke steps forward and slaps me on the back. "I'm excited for you, Wyatt. This is exciting."

I exhale heavily and look up at Max, who wears a rare proud smile. "I can't believe I'm saying this, but...I'm excited for you too. I hope this all works out."

"Is our baby intervention over now?" Calder drawls, rolling his eyes. "I have a girl in my cabin and would like to do some baby dancing of my own." He pauses and holds up his finger. "But hold the baby, please."

CHAPTER 12

OVULATION TEST STRIPS USED: 6

Trista

"**Y**ou said all of that, and he still hired you? You must have been dressed real slutty," my sister, Vada, drawls as I drive the shelter van through the winding roads north of Boulder toward Jamestown.

The van is stuffed to the gills with most of my belongings, and my boss, Earl, said I needed to get his vehicle back no later than 2:00 p.m. today because he has a litter of kittens to pick up in Nebraska. It took me longer than expected to load everything up on my own, so I'm for sure going to be late, which will infuriate Earl. This means he'll do his gruff, chastising speech about time management and threaten to fire me for the tenth time.

Thankfully, he's all talk because my life is not conducive to punctuality. When you have to do everything on your own, the last thing I remember to do is look at the clock.

But I will need to work on my tardiness now that I'll have about an hour commute to work every day, or Earl could put his money where his mouth is and drop me. The drive to the shelter isn't ideal, but I knew after laying eyes on that barn, there was no way I wouldn't want to live on Fletcher Mountain.

"Fletcher Mountain," I say to myself with a laugh. What a lame name for a peak. I realize that's their family name, but couldn't he have created something more inspired? Like…Three Brothers Peak, or heck, he could have named it after his goat.

Mount Millie!

Now, that has a nice ring to it and would look super cute on some custom T-shirts. I might suggest that…you know…after I get knocked up and feel secure in actually staying there.

And the barn apartment is a dream come true for an animal lover like me. Frankly, that big barn is wasted on his single pet goat. So many empty stables that could be filled with all sorts of critters. I love the idea of a full barn below me as I sleep. And I didn't tell Wyatt this, but the apartment is nicer than the place I just moved out of. It's a converted hayloft with vaulted ceilings, all-natural timber, and exposed beams. Refurbished barnwood floors with southwestern-style rugs laid out everywhere. It's a studio style that flows effortlessly from the kitchen into a living and dining area, with a queen bed beneath salvaged windows. It has a rustic charm that HGTV could never pull off. Throw in the enclosed bathroom and a mountain view—what more could a girl want?

Although I will admit, when I saw the outdoor shower on the side of the barn, it sparked my curiosity about how often Wyatt might need to use that. There's a perfect view of it from my bathroom window, and something tells me that man gets dirty out here on the mountain during the hot summer months.

Do not have indecent thoughts about the mountain man whose baby you're going to carry, Trista!

"Trista?" Vada echoes in my ear, snapping me out of my thoughts. "Did you hear my question? I asked what you were wearing. You must have looked skanky for him to hire you after you told him you owned a potbellied pig."

"I didn't look skanky," I state flatly. "Actually, my clothes had puppy pee on them."

"He has to be crazy. Totally fucking crazy," she replies, and I know she's being serious but not serious enough to be genuinely concerned about my well-being. "What's the next step, then?"

"Well, I suppose we do the insemination song and dance, then wait to see if it worked."

"This is totally crazy!" she squeals into the line, and I really wish she could come up with another word to describe this because she's wearing on my last nerve. "I think it's weird you're going to donate your own egg. You're going to give your baby to this mountain man and never see it ever again?"

"I'm not giving him my baby. I'm giving him my egg. It doesn't become a baby without his...sperm." I cringe at that thought.

"And your uterus."

"Obviously."

"But seriously, you don't think you're going to give birth to this baby that's yours and feel any type of way?"

Not when I know it will go to a man who truly wants it. It's already blatantly obvious this child will be loved. Cherished. And I will be one hundred percent okay with that. "No, Vada, trust me...the lawyer had me do a full psychology workup and a couple of sessions with a counselor, plus some medical testing on both of us. I'm like...bulletproof. Honestly, I got the impression the psychologist thinks I might be a sociopath." Because heaven forbid a woman not want to be a mother.

"Oh, that's comforting."

"And by donating my egg to him, I make another twenty grand."

"Twenty grand on top of the fifty-five grand plus free housing? Holy shit, this sounds too good to be true!"

"Well, cutting out the surrogacy agency saved him a considerable amount of money, and rather than keeping all of it, he's giving a lot of it to me. He's been super generous through all the negotiations. I get the impression he's just happy not to have to go back to that agency, and I don't blame him. I did not get good vibes when I was there either. I seriously owe so much to his niece for approaching me. I wonder if I could send her a kitten!"

"This is all so *crazy*. Then again, I *never* want to be pregnant, so I can't even understand people who do."

Her tone is full of disgust, and my hands instinctively tighten on the wheel. I mean, I get it. Our upbringing wasn't exactly the cozy family vibes the Fletchers seemingly have going on. Our parents acted like they loved us, but they loved themselves more.

Oftentimes, we'd go days without seeing them. I remember when we'd get low on food, Vada would stand outside our apartment complex, waiting for a random delivery vehicle to show up. She'd rush to the car and say her mom sent her down to grab it, and the pizza guy would just hand it over. My sister was always so brave and resilient. I admired her for that.

And it wasn't even drugs or booze that took my parents away from us. I think if it was addiction, I could understand their neglect better. It was just selfishness. They were always between jobs and looking for that next big thing that would turn their life around.

And somehow, that was our fault. *"If we didn't have you girls, we'd be in a much better place. If I hadn't had kids, I could have gotten that job. Kids can't come to places we want to go."* And when you get told that year after year, you can't help but hear *"I wish I'd never had you. Then I'd be happy."*

It was traumatizing and not exactly something that inspired me to want a family of my own. And even though I know I'm a better person than both my parents put together, I can't get past the fear of hurting a child the way my parents so easily hurt me. Which is why animals are the safer bet.

However, a strange part of me still wants to know what it would feel like to have something growing inside me. To have something that I create with my own body. Will it feel like a mini alien trying to kick its way through my ribs? Will this even work, and I'll get the chance to know? Something in me feels like my strange upbringing might make me uniquely good at this.

Either way, maybe telling my sister was a bad idea. Our relationship is strained at best. She moved to Hawaii with her boyfriend, Kai, when I was just sixteen and hasn't returned to Denver once. Meanwhile, I'm still here…living alone in the same place we grew up in and trying to make a life for myself. It's hard not to feel like everyone left me behind.

A knot forms in my throat as the image of me standing in our empty family apartment flashes through my mind. I thought I'd feel relieved when I left earlier today…like I was finally getting out. But honestly, I just felt sad. Like all my childhood had to show for itself was a dingy, worn-down two-bedroom with potbellied pig stains on the carpet.

"How does this dude have this kind of money on hand? Is he loaded?"

My sister interrupts my inner musings, and I lift my shoulders. "He and his brothers build houses. They make a lot of green homes with eco-friendly and recycled materials. I guess they're in high demand."

My mind ruminates over him mentioning in one of our meetings that his own cabin is self-sustainable. I was equal parts impressed and fascinated. I've never met someone like Wyatt Fletcher. Someone who puts the world before himself. *Certainly not my parents.*

"Our deal required him to show me bank statements to prove his worth, and the salary he's going to pay me is all in an escrow account that the lawyer will make monthly payments to me from. I've already got my first deposit, so I'm just trusting it."

"Money before you're even knocked up. This is crazy."

The sign for Jamestown comes into view, and the turn for Fletcher Mountain is just after it, so I use that as an excuse to get off this regrettable phone call.

"Hey, I'm headed up the mountain now, so I'm going to lose you."

"Okay…call me when you're preggo!"

"Okay, bye." I hang up and sigh. I won't call her when I'm knocked up. And she probably won't notice I didn't call her either. That's the extent of our relationship. And it's sad, but she's the only family member I still talk to, so I tolerate it.

My somber mood instantly lifts as I traverse the final bend through towering pine trees, and the big red barn comes into view. It's the first building you see when you get to the top of the hill, and Millie the goat is out in her pasture, munching on some hay like a damn postcard. I park in front of the barn entrance, and she comes trotting over to the gate to greet me just as my phone pings with a notification.

Everly: Happy move-in day!

> Me: Thanks, kid. Millie says hi.

I hold my phone up and send a quick pic of the goat that she hearts right away.

> Everly: One final warning before you begin this great adventure...Uncle Wyatt has a heart of gold, but he occasionally treads the fine line between sweet and psycho. Nothing to be afraid of...I promise it's always sweet, and I know you're tough enough to put him in his place. Just keep that in mind if you ever want to stab him in the gut with a pitchfork, okay?

My eyes bulge out of my head at that last sentence. Okay, maybe my sister was right. This is crazy.

CHAPTER 13

WEEKS PREGNANT: 0
ANIMALS ON MOUNTAIN: 2

Trista

"**H**ow many animals are in that thing?" a deep voice rumbles from behind me.

I turn to find Wyatt standing at the entrance to the barn. It's a classic Dutch door with the top section open while the bottom is closed, and I can't help but think it's another postcard moment. No psycho vibes so far, thank goodness.

I smile brightly. "Just Reginald in there. Queenie was adopted by a lovely elderly couple. She's going to give them a run for their money. But I borrowed the van from work to haul the rest of my stuff. It holds more than my car."

Wyatt eyes me warily. "Didn't our contract include moving expenses?"

"I used some of the money to move out," I reply with a shrug, thinking about the teenage neighbor boys who were more than happy to take twenty dollars each to haul my shitty furniture and mattress to the curb. I put a "free" sign on it, along with some other odds and ends, and the stuff was gone before we even loaded the rest of my van.

It's not blind optimism that made me purge all my old shit. More so, it was a conscious decision to use this opportunity for a fresh start. It's entirely possible I won't get pregnant and have to leave sooner than

I thought. But I still don't want to go back to the past. Not that apartment and certainly not that dumpy sofa.

This is my chance to leave that all behind, and since Wyatt's barn apartment came fully furnished, there was no reason not to put all my ovarian eggs and pig in this basket.

Plus, I have some serious confidence in this gruff mountain man. *Even if he does supposedly tread the line between sweet and psycho.*

Wyatt swings out the lower gate to come striding over to where I've opened the van door to reveal my entire life jam-packed into various dog-sized kennels. Kind of a depressing sight.

Reginald spouts out a series of short grunts from his place in the bottom-row kennel. "Welcome to your new home, Reggie!" I coo and reach my hand into the metal fence to touch his stubby snout. "This is Mr. Mountain Man." Reggie grunts only once, and my brows lift. "Yikes."

"What?" Wyatt asks, frowning at the pig like he's diseased. The dick.

"I don't think Reginald likes you," I tsk while grabbing the long wooden board I use as a ramp to help Reggie out of the vehicle. I open the gate, and he stands there, staring out at me as if he's saying, *"Who's this fucker?"*

Just kidding, I don't know what he's saying, but I often narrate Sir Reginald's thoughts in my mind, and that's the vibe I'm picking up.

I press my hand to Wyatt's chest. "Can you maybe go hide behind the van?"

"Hide behind the van?" Wyatt's tone makes you think I'd just asked him to go to war.

"Yes," I exclaim with my hands on my hips. "Reg doesn't know you, and he just made it very clear that he doesn't like you. If I want him to come out of the kennel, then we'll need a little space."

Wyatt does that grunting thing he does sometimes but thankfully does as I say. With a little verbal encouragement, I manage to get Reg out of the van and into the barn that's honestly way too nice to be called a barn. It's got a large alleyway with multiple big, beautiful horse-sized stalls on each side. So many animals could fit in here. And Reggie's freshly washed pink body with sleek black spots and coarse white hair looks fantastic in this space. This home is perfect for the king he is.

"I laid some straw in that pen on the far-right corner," Wyatt says, following me into the barn and pointing at the enclosure beside me.

Reggie huffs and shuffles over to hide behind my legs, rubbing his coarse skin back and forth along my jeans to soothe himself. Wyatt said a couple of weeks ago that Millie was like a dog. Well, Reggie boy here is like a cat. Moody and starved for attention and food but only on his terms.

I frown as I look into the very nice pen set up with two concrete troughs, fresh straw, and a closed drop door that leads out to the pasture. "Are you getting another goat?"

Wyatt frowns. "No…why?"

"Who is the pen for?"

"Your pig."

My eyes widen. "You expect Reginald to sleep in the barn?"

"Where else would he sleep?"

"In his sleeping quarters upstairs next to me, obviously."

"Come again?" Wyatt is loud in the quietness of the peaceful barn.

"Reggie is a rescue, Wyatt! He came from a horrible situation where the owners neglected him. He had hoof rot and couldn't freaking walk. I had to give him daily doses of antibiotics and hand-feed him, or they were going to put him down!"

"Jesus Christ," Wyatt murmurs under his breath, looking away in obvious agitation.

"Sir Reginald sleeps on a nice little crib mattress I bought second-hand. He even has a special blanket and likes to sleep in most mornings."

Wyatt's head snaps as he points at the open wooden stairs leading to the apartment. "How are you going to get him up the stairs every day? Those legs don't look long enough to climb stairs."

"I'll carry him." I shrug.

The mountain man's eyebrows shoot to the moon as he points an accusing finger at Reggie. "He's got to weigh at least fifty pounds."

"Sixty-five, actually, but my vet friend, Avery, just put us on a low-calorie feed even though I think Reggie is beautiful just the way he is."

"For fuck's sake," Wyatt growls and jams a hand through the top of his hair. "You aren't going to be able to carry him up those stairs when you're pregnant, Trista."

"Well, I'm not pregnant yet." I scoff, my chin cocking up to meet his as he looms over me with his giant mountain-man stature.

He pauses for a second as his eyes rove over my face. His voice is deep and husky when he replies, "*Yet.*"

Goose bumps erupt over my flesh as one of the tiniest words in the English language just had a massive impact on my not-so-tiny body. I realize we're not doing this pregnancy thing the old-fashioned way, but it's been a while since I've been laid, and with that one little word, my traitorous mind wandered to a reality where we did it the old-fashioned way. *And I liked that thought.*

I swallow slowly, desperate to get control of myself. I glance down at our chests, which are nearly brushing each other. When did we get so close? His scent of pine trees, woodchips, and hay is intoxicating.

Wyatt's eyes flick down to my lips as I wonder what the hell are we actually arguing about? I want to be pregnant. And I suppose he's right…I shouldn't be lifting sixty-plus pounds once I have a baby growing inside me. I guess Reginald's sleeping quarters never came up in all our lawyer negotiating.

And why is he looking at me like that? And why does my body feel the way it feels right now? I'm hot and agitated having him so close to me and telling me what to do. *I like it, and I loathe it. I like to loathe it! Gasp! This is the sweet-and-psycho bit that Everly warned me about.*

The voices of men outside force us to pull away from each other just as they walk into the barn with armloads of my stuff.

"Trista, these are my brothers Calder and Luke." Wyatt's voice is strained as he avoids eye contact with me. Oh, he's mad mad.

The two giant men in flannel stop talking and gape at me for a moment. The heavily tattooed one with devilish eyes tips his chin up and says, "What's up, MB?"

Wyatt glowers at his brother. "Calder…"

The slightly smaller one (although none of them are small, honestly…I'm in a barn full of flannelled giants) with floppy blond hair laughs boyishly, clearly enjoying the tension between his two brothers.

"What's MB mean?" I ask curiously.

"Don't ask," another voice echoes from behind them.

Calder and Luke spread apart to reveal what I can only assume to be another brother. "Wait…there are four of you? I thought there were only three."

"This is my eldest brother, Max," Wyatt explains with a wave of his hand. "He's Everly's dad. He lives in Boulder, not here on the mountain."

My brows lift knowingly as I come face-to-face with the man who raised the girl with bigger balls than me. "Didn't want to join in on the *Seven Brides for Seven Brothers* remake up here?"

Max stares blankly at me, clearly not as up-to-date on his classic musicals as he should be. Honestly, I love that film, even if it is highly problematic. It's about a bunch of bros who look like the retro Brawny paper towel man dressed in skintight buckskin and tassels. They sing and dance when they're not busy kidnapping young women and trapping them up on their mountain with an avalanche until they develop Stockholm syndrome and fall in love with them.

It's a cinematic masterpiece.

I stare slack-jawed at the men blessing me with all their beautiful hides and feel thankful I am up here of my own free will. If not for work, then for the beautiful views.

Wyatt is the thicker of the four, pulling off that "I work hard, but I still like to eat" look. Calder, the one with all the ink, definitely looks like he clocks some serious time at the gym. And Luke, the smaller but not-small brother, is still fit but not nearly as bulky as his brothers. Hell, even Max, the non-flannel-wearing one, looks like he'd stretch some plaid if given the chance.

"You want this stuff upstairs, I assume?" Luke asks and makes a move toward the steps.

"Yes, but just leave it at the bottom here. I can carry it up."

I hear a low rumble from Wyatt, and my eyes fly wide. Seriously… I'm not pregnant yet. I can carry as much as I want to carry until we do this insemination, I pee on a stick, and we make this arrangement official.

I move to take the stuff out of Luke's hands, and he shakes his head and offers me a sweet smile. "I got it, MB. Give us an hour, and we'll knock out that whole van."

Slightly irritated, I back up as the three of them stomp their way up the steps, making light work of a task that I expected to take me the better part of the day to accomplish.

"Is there a way to make them stop?" I ask Wyatt, who is currently staring at Reginald, whose snout is pressing into the crack of the doorway that leads out into the pasture. "I planned on moving my own stuff. Your brothers don't even know me. Moving my stuff is asking way too much."

"You didn't ask." Wyatt shrugs. "And they're doing it for me as much as they're doing it for you."

I frown at that simple response, feeling a bit stunned by the generosity of everyone, and I've barely been here for five minutes. Don't get me wrong, it's not like I've never met someone who's been kind to me. But these are literal strangers. Hell, Wyatt is still a stranger.

And he made Reggie a pigpen.

Heavy green flag, definitely sweet-not-psycho sigh.

"I suppose we can try the pen out tonight, but I can't promise Reggie will be okay with it."

Relief washes over Wyatt's face. "You can put the crib mattress in there if it makes you feel better."

I nod. That certainly makes me feel something.

The next forty-five minutes are a flurry of mountain men lugging stuff up to my apartment. At one point, his brother Max started opening up a wardrobe box and was going to hang my clothes for me, but I begged him to stop. If a pair of my granny panties tumbled out in front of these four beefy men, I would die of humiliation.

Once I've shooed the big, tall men out of my space, I make my way down the stairs to take the van back to Earl. He'll be so impressed that I'm on time for once!

I find Wyatt leaning over the pen, watching my pig, so I move over to join him. "I suggest we introduce Millie and Reggie tomorrow. Tonight, we just let them get used to having another animal in the same building."

"That sounds good," Wyatt replies with a thoughtful nod. "If they don't get along, I already worked out a way for me to partition off the pasture so Reginald can have his own space and Millie can have hers. My brothers can help me run some new fence lines. It should be easy enough to pop up within an hour."

"You boys get a lot of stuff done in an hour, don't you?" I reply with a smirk.

He shrugs. Real chatty, this guy.

"Anyway, I have to go, or I'm going to be late to return the van." I slap my hands on the fence and make my way out of the barn, turning on my heel at the door to let Wyatt know one more very important fact. "Oh, by the way…I'm ovulating right now, so I say we get this show on the road tonight."

"Tonight?" Wyatt blurts out, his eyes the size of saucers. His Adam's apple slides down his throat before he asks, "Are you sure?"

"Yep." I smile and shoot him a wink. "I should be back by sundown, so I'll come up to your place then. Toodles!"

As soon as I'm out of the barn, I cringe, my face scrunching up so much I can't even see where I'm walking. Did I really just say to the mountain man whose sperm I'm about to inject into my vagina… *toodles?*

I think I might actually be the psycho on this mountain.

CHAPTER 14

SURROGATES CURRENTLY OVULATING: 1
ANIMALS ON THE MOUNTAIN: 2

Wyatt

The sun is just beginning to disappear behind the hill when I see Trista finally return to Fletcher Mountain in her tiny, beat-up Honda Civic.

"Fuck," I murmur as I glance at the tires on her car. They look like they've seen better days. It's spring now, so they should be fine, but if she gets pregnant, that means she will be here for the winter...which also means that the car will not do for the duration of this.

Yet another aspect of this arrangement we didn't take into consideration. Along with the pig, who looked quite happy in his pen this afternoon.

Dammit anyway.

I make a mental note to talk to my brothers about loaning me one of the work trucks for Trista. We have a couple that sit at our shop, so I'm sure we could spare one for her to drive when the snow comes.

Provided she actually gets pregnant with my baby, which apparently could happen sooner rather than later based on the bomb she dropped on me before she left to return the van to her boss.

"By the way...I'm ovulating right now, so I say we get this show on the road tonight."

She sped off in her van, leaving me in a wake of nerves and anxiety.

I wore a path in my recycled wood floor, pacing my house and waiting for her to return. I knew this day was coming. I just didn't know exactly when. And now that it's here...I'm not sure how to prepare for it.

A knock interrupts my obsessive thoughts, and I realize it's her.

Time to make a baby.

I open the door and stupidly grunt out, "I went to the Mercantile and picked up pizza."

She holds up two brown bags in her hand. "I picked up booze."

She kicks off her beat-up cowboy boots and marches past me, dropping her purse on my small farm table like she's been in my place a million times...which she hasn't. I watch her curiously as she props her hands on her hips and assesses the space for a second before making her way toward the kitchen, giving no outward reaction to the home I built with my bare hands.

Not that I need her approval on this house, but I guess I just...I don't know what I want. A baby. That's what I want. That should be all that I want from this woman.

She sets the brown bags on my butcher-block island and pulls out two bottles of white wine. Without pause, she twists the cap off one and takes a swig straight from the bottle.

My brows lift. *It's going to be that kind of night.*

"These were two for seven bucks at the gas station, and it tastes like it." She coughs and winces at the taste.

"Do you want something else?" I offer, making a move to my refrigerator. "I only have beer."

"No," she mutters and takes another quick sip. "I'm not a very big drinker, but I'm nervous as shit, and lots of people get pregnant drunk, so...science. How are you doing?"

Her candid response is more comforting than she realizes. I haven't known Trista for long, but I like that she calls a spade a spade. I move to stand next to her at the island, noticing how much smaller she is out of her boots.

I point at the second bottle. "Is that other one for me?"

She silently slides it over, and I twist the cap off and join her in the wine-bottle-chugging experience. I shudder at the horrible taste because I'm not a wine drinker…but I will be tonight. I want her to feel supported through this, and if that means choking down a disgusting bottle of cheap wine, I'll do it.

"Pizza?" I point at the box on the other side of her.

She nods and helps herself, mindlessly chomping down on a bite.

"I checked on Millie and Reginald before I came in here, and they both looked very content in their pens," she says around a mouthful. "That was really sweet of you to buy those troughs for Reggie. Sorry if I was a bitch about the pen thing." She takes another swig.

"You weren't a bitch." I take another swig, eyeing her baggy T-shirt that's covered in Millie hoof prints and a substance I can only assume is from the pig.

It's odd to have Trista in my house. All of our meetings thus far have been pretty professional. And this whole concept of me hiring a surrogate felt like something that was never actually going to happen. It feels more real now that we're here, face-to-face, without a lawyer talking for us. More personal. Like we're letting our guards down.

Probably because you're about to put your cum inside her, my inner voice adds with a dirty sneer. I take a big drink.

I reach across her for a slice of pizza, murmuring around a mouthful of pepperoni, "I, um…didn't get one of those insemination kits you mentioned. Did you?"

"I meant to get one from my vet friend, Avery, but I forgot." She reaches into her brown bag to pull out a white drugstore bag. Inside it is a box that contains a bottle of liquid children's Tylenol and a plastic-wrapped syringe. "If it's good enough for the lesbians…"

My brows lift. "What do I…dispense into?" *Swig.*

"Fuck," she murmurs around a mouthful. *Swig, swig, swig.*

An idea comes to mind, so I reach down and touch her hip to move her back a little bit to access the drawer in front of her.

"Are those disposable salad dressing cups?" she asks, her brows pinched together in genuine curiosity.

"Yeah, I use them for ranch in my lunches." *Chug, chug, chug.* "Could they work?"

She shrugs, finally lowering the bottle. "Will they be big enough?"

I swallow nervously. "I guess I don't know." I move to take another drink and then realize my bottle is empty. *Shit.*

I walk over to the fridge and grab two bottles of beer. I don't know if I envisioned doing this drunk, but the more I drink, the less awkward this feels, so I'm good with this if she is. At least for this first time.

"Listen, Wyatt, if this doesn't work…" Trista's eyes are wide and wary as she turns to face me and moves to take another drink.

"It'll be fine," I soothe, not enjoying the stress lines forming between her brows. I pat her shoulder encouragingly and then pull my hand away because my touching her is definitely the booze talking. "We'll figure it out."

Her eyes blink rapidly. "It's like…even though I know that I ovulate, I don't know that I can actually get pregnant. Some people try for years to get pregnant, and it never happens."

"I know. Life isn't a guarantee. That's why we have some backup plans in place."

"Sorry, I guess I'm just now suddenly feeling a lot of pressure."

"You're feeling pressure?" My eyes widen as I glance at the wine bottle that I emptied in like fifteen minutes. "I'm the one who has to…" I make a lewd hand gesture that's not intended to be perverted…just… literal. "Perform."

Her eyes glance down to my groin, and my cock twitches with just that tiny bit of attention. "Do you sometimes have trouble finishing?"

"Fuck no," I bark out, then instantly feel weird about being so defensive. "Sorry…but no. I've never had that problem. I've just also never…well…tried to make a baby before."

"Right, but you've gone in a cup before at the clinic, haven't you?" She licks her lips as she stares thoughtfully up at me.

"Once…but it wasn't in a ranch cup." I glance down at the pink children's Tylenol and the plastic sauce container laid out on the counter and feel extremely stupid for not being better prepared for this.

"Can you imagine if you mistook this for your lunch ranch?" Trista spews out a drunken laugh, and I realize we might be getting a little carried away with the booze.

I take the wine bottle from her hand, and she gazes at it with a forlorn look. "Probably for the best."

She glances up at me nervously, her head hitting just below my chin in her socked feet. I like how tall she is. I wonder if this baby will be tall too? Or will it have her beauty marks that decorate various areas of her face? They're not freckles—freckles are lighter and collect all in one area. Trista's moles are unique. They're really striking when you look at her up close like this.

"So there's one more thing I haven't told you yet," she says, and her cheeks deepen to a crimson color, showing a moment of embarrassment that I have yet to see on Trista Matthews.

"You have an alpaca in the trunk of your car, don't you?" I deadpan, trying to lighten the mood.

She bursts out laughing and falls into my chest. Her long fingers grip the flannel on my arms, and I can't help but lean down and breathe in the smell of her shampoo. It smells like roses. I fight the urge to take her hair clip out so I can watch it fall down her back. Like it was the day we met. Down and wild.

Shit…definitely too much booze.

When she's done with her fit of giggles, she leans on the counter and looks gravely up at me. "So on the blogs, I read that if the surrogate orgasms with the semen in her bajingo, there's a higher chance of success for pregnancy."

My eyes flash with that new bit of information. "Are you suggesting we have…"

"Sex? Good God, no," she exclaims, the thought of it clearly horrifying her. "They just masturbate after they inject it."

"Oh," I reply and inwardly cringe at the sense of disappointment I feel. Fuck, I'm an idiot for getting my hopes up, but I haven't properly fucked a woman since I got on this surrogacy track, and my cock doesn't enjoy my hand nearly as much as the heat of a woman. I steel myself to be calm and collected when I add, "Well, you should probably do that, then. The fewer times we have to do this, the better, right?"

She nods slowly. "That's what I thought."

"I'm going to…you know…into that ranch cup, and you're going to take it back to the barn and…"

She winces. "They said the sooner you get it in you, the better. I think walking it all the way back to the barn first is probably not a good idea. Too much chance of contaminating it. And it kind of said I should sleep with it in me if I can. At least for the first night."

"You can have my bed," I blurt out, then wince. "Sorry, is that creepy?"

She shakes her head. "No, not creepy. I don't even have my bed made up yet…so…that works for me."

"It's logical." *Totally logical to have the woman you're impregnating through insemination sleep in your bed after orgasming.*

"Yeah." She licks her lips nervously. "Where will you sleep?"

I shrug dismissively. "There are two bedrooms upstairs, but my couch is also really comfortable."

She nods and chews her lips. "Are you…ready?"

My heartbeat thunders in my chest as my gaze zeros in on her mouth, noticing the beauty mark on the edge of her upper lip. I missed that one before. "I'm ready."

She glances down, and I feel my cock thickening in my jeans. Fuck, this is weird. I don't know if it's the booze talking or some caveman fantasy coming to life, but I just know that if she gave me the green light, I'd throw her up on this counter and fuck her till she was pregnant. And I'd like it. I'd like it a lot.

Her voice comes out hoarser than before as her lashes flutter up to look at me. "Do you, like…need to watch porn or something?"

And now I'm hard.

The idea of watching porn isn't what did it. The thought of her watching porn is what did it. Imagining Trista in my house, watching an erotic video. Her body squirming on my sofa as things get heated. Picturing her rubbing her thighs together to stop herself from pressing her fingers to her clit but eventually succumbing to the hormones coursing through her body.

Fuuuck.

"I don't think I'll need to watch anything tonight," I croak, my voice gravelly.

"You're just...good?"

"Yeah, I'm good." My voice is soft when I add, "What about you?"

"What about me?"

"How are you going to...?"

"How?" she asks, her eyes wide, pupils dilated.

I clear my throat. "Do you need to watch porn to finish?"

Her cheeks deepen again, and I have to fight the urge to reach out and drag my finger along her face just to feel the heat under her skin. Her throat contracts with a heavy swallow. "I threw my vibrator in my purse. Works like a charm."

I nod slowly. "That's good."

Her gaze moves as she grabs something off the counter. She holds up the plastic ranch cup between us and says, "You first."

CHAPTER 15

RANCH CUPS FULL OF SEMEN: 1

Wyatt

Blood rushes between my ears as I pump my cock in the bathroom attached to my bedroom. Thank fuck for tight jeans because if my jeans were loose, Trista would have seen just how rock fucking hard I was in front of her moments ago.

I close my eyes and picture the last girl I fucked. Was it Lacey? Or Tracey? Hell, maybe it was Macey? She had big tits and a big ass...just my style. I met her at a dive bar outside of Denver, and it took all of ten minutes for her to drag me into the women's bathroom.

I don't make a habit of fucking in public, but the idea of not having to go back to her place and awkwardly excuse myself afterward was an offer too tempting to pass up.

My cock chafes in my calloused hand, so I release my grip to spit on my palm, slicking my saliva along my shaft. Macey isn't doing it for me. Performance anxiety has truly never been an issue. Then again, I've never jizzed in a fucking ranch cup while a woman stood outside the door with a Tylenol syringe in hand, waiting to inject it into her body.

"Why is it so fucking hot in here?" I growl and release my dick to yank my flannel over my head. I glance at myself in the mirror and don't know if it's the wine or the pressure of what tonight could mean, but I feel like I'm looking at a stranger. An animal even. The veins in my neck protrude and run down into my hairy chest. My pecs and abs

are popped like I haven't eaten in days…every part of my body partic-
ipating in this act like it's a team fucking sport.

My face looks red and blotchy, the hollows of my eyes dark, like
I'm an addict going into detox. Like I'm seconds away from yanking
out a needle and injecting myself with heroin just for the sweet nectar
that will bring me oblivion.

I want to end this torture. Grunting, I can already feel the tingles
of ecstasy creeping up my spine just thinking about my release.

I inhale sharply as the image of Trista assaults me. Instantly, my
hand reaches back down, and I grip my dick harder. Punishingly hard.
So hard, it fucking hurts, and I hiss through the adrenaline surge that
ratchets to an unbearable level.

I pinch the head of my cock and watch with satisfaction as a dab
of precum seeps out the tip. Rolling my thumb over it, I use the bit of
liquid as lubrication, the tiny smear making my shaft sticky with friction as my forearm flexes with every pump.

The image of Trista is back again. Her legs spread wide on my
white sheets, that baggy T-shirt still on her but riding up just enough
so I can get a look at her lush curves. The bottom swell of her breast
tortures me like the stickiness around my cock.

I like her body. I've barely seen it, and I can already tell I want
to fucking touch every supple inch of it. I want to spread my seed all
over her.

"Fuck," I croak softly as my mind shows me her fingers teasing
the slits of her cunt. Her chestnut hair is loose around her shoulders,
one strand covering that beauty mark on her upper lip as she throws
her head back. I can almost hear the moans she would be making as
her hips arch up while her fingers work over her needy clit. Her digits
would be shiny with arousal, making my mouth water.

God, I bet she tastes good. Dirty and naughty and all the fucking
things that make sex so fucking worth it. But the image of her playing
with herself isn't enough. I can't come. I'm still not ready. As hot as it
is to picture her…something still stops me from coming.

Christ, I shouldn't even be thinking of her at all. She's essentially
an employee. A surrogate. A "belly buddy babysitter" human incubator

with just one purpose of carrying my offspring. My thoughts are inappropriate as fuck.

"*Blow it in me, Wyatt,*" her hoarse voice echoes in my head, and I feel the veins in my shaft bulge beneath my palm. "*I want your cum inside me.*"

"No," I bark and slam a fist into the wood-paneled wall next to my mirror. *You will not fucking picture blowing your cum inside your surrogate. You creepy fuck.*

But a dark voice tells me it's not creepy. It's natural. It's primal. It's the way it should be.

"Oh God," I moan, unable to control my mind a second longer. My head sags back, and my fist gyrates fast over and over as I close my eyes and picture my long, thick cock sinking into her tight, dripping-wet pussy. She's coming already. One thrust of my cock has her vibrating all over me as she screams my name, begging for my cum, begging for me to put a baby inside her, begging for me to make her mine.

My balls ache with wanting to give her what she asks for, so with a roar, I blow every shred of my being into her—my manhood, my sanity, my hopes and dreams. My semen. Nothing matters when I'm balls deep in her. It's all hers.

I pull out and watch my cum drip down her center, but she pulls me back in, desperate not to lose a single drop of my seed, milking me hard and fast with the quivering channels of her cunt, her walls clenching me to hold every bit inside.

Reality crashes in on me, and with trembling legs, I snap myself out of my stupor and stumble over to the sink to grab the plastic cup. With a growl, I spurt my release inside it, coating my knuckles white as warm semen spills over the edges of the container.

And my dark fucking mind takes over one more time as I stare at the excess climax on my hand and whisper out loud, "All for her."

CHAPTER 16

SYRINGE FULL OF SEMEN: 1

Trista

"Oh my God," I exclaim as I look down and see that I've finished the entire large pizza that Wyatt bought for us. When the hell did that happen?

I grab the box and look around nervously for a place to stash the evidence of my stress eating. I am not eating for two yet, and I'll be damned if I let Wyatt see this.

I hustle out the back door located off the kitchen to see if there's a trash bin out there. A large deck overlooks acres of forestry, but no trash in sight. Just several giant solar panels and a compost bin. If I had anything left to compost, I'd do it.

Unfortunately, it's all in my belly.

Frustrated, I abandon the pizza box on the table outside and make my way back to the cabin for some water. I seriously need to sober up. This is a job...a unique job...but a job, nonetheless. Be a professional, Trista.

I look around Wyatt's home, inspecting the space a bit more than when I got here, and he was all brooding and full of sperm and making it hard for me to focus. I could barely think, let alone admire his taste in decor. But now that I've had a little distance from him, I can really admire what he's done with the space.

The headline for this home would be: RUSTIC MOUNTAIN MEETS MODERN MINIMALISM.

The main floor is an open floor plan except for the giant river-rock chimney with a double-sided fireplace that sits right in the middle of all three rooms and carries all the way up to the vaulted ceiling. I drag my fingers along the stone, wondering if he foraged for these rocks himself. He looks like a forager.

A flight of stairs off the kitchen leads up to a second level, but I know the primary bedroom is on this main floor because that's where Wyatt took off to nearly ten minutes ago...to jack off.

To rattle the snake.

To wrestle the rooster.

To massage the one-eyed ostrich.

Or my personal favorite...make the bald man cry.

I'm thinking Mountain Man wouldn't love any of those terms. He's far too...*manly*.

I giggle to myself and meander into the living area to admire the massive angular windows that expand up to the vaulted ceilings and flank the main-floor living and dining area. The view looks directly down the mountain, where you can glimpse Jamestown through the pine trees. Off to the left is a nice shot of the big red barn, and I realize just how easily he can watch me from this point of view.

Then again, if he can watch me...I can watch him.

I shake off the tremor that runs up my spine at that thought and make my way over to the walnut dining table that looks custom-made. I picture Wyatt feeding a baby in a high chair, and I must admit, it's a cute sight to behold. Not that I'll ever likely see it for myself. We discussed having contact after the delivery, and while he was open to keeping me updated on the child's life, I requested no contact. From all my research in the forums, it's just easier to detach fully from the sperm donor or, in my case, the surrogate. This job isn't going to change my thoughts on babies. It's just a temporary position that will hopefully set me up to move on and do bigger and better things.

Provided I can actually get pregnant.

I wander back into the kitchen and spot Everly's senior photo pinned on the refrigerator. She's sitting on the edge of a pool, her feet in the water, blond hair off to one side, smiling like she doesn't have a care in the world. Probably because she doesn't. Although she seems awfully invested in her uncle's well-being if she was willing to hit the streets and find me. That's sweet, I suppose. Not psycho.

The photo beside hers is of a little brunet boy who can't be more than eight. This must be his brother Max's other kid, but I'd swear I was looking at a mini Wyatt. Same dark lashes and blue eyes, same sullen, moody expression. It's uncanny. I wonder if some version of this is what we'll possibly be making tonight? Kind of a crazy idea to think about.

But I'm not going to think about it.

I'm an incubator and nothing more. I'm like an artificially insem-inated cow. My body is meant to house this human for another and nothing more. I can't care what this child will look like. I just need to focus on getting this child created because this job doesn't exist with-out me getting knocked up.

Let's get this farm animal knocked up!

A throat clears from behind me, causing me to jump out of my skin. I twirl on my heels to find Wyatt standing awkwardly in the kitchen with a sheepish look.

"It's done," he murmurs, his cheeks looking flush under his trim beard as he struggles to make eye contact with me.

"Great! Where's the syringe?" A strong sense of light-headedness engulfs me as I walk over and hold my hand out expectantly. Maybe it's the wine. Yeah, we can blame the wine. Not the overwhelming panic that this is actually all fucking happening.

"Um…it's still in the bathroom." He grips the back of his neck and shoots me an uneasy look. "I didn't…you know…transport it into the thingy yet."

"Do you expect me to suck it in there?" I exclaim, my voice high-pitched and accusing.

"I don't know," he answers with a growl, his entire body radiating discomfort. "I didn't want to touch anything you might have to touch…"

"Good Lord," I grumble and push my way past Wyatt to find

whatever mess he has going on back there. "The sooner we get this inside me, the better."

I can't believe I just said that out loud, but it's the truth. The quicker, the better because this whole evening feels like an out-of-body experience, and I need it to come to fruition. This is the climax we've been waiting for.

I giggle at my inner joke, hearing his boots heavy on the wood floor as he follows me down the hall and into his bedroom. My eyes widen briefly as I take in the large king bed with a white bedspread. Knotty wood accent tables decorate the space, and I note that he manages to pull off that contemporary-rustic vibe nicely in here as well. I wonder if he had a designer because this place screams, "Woman's touch."

"What the hell is that?" I ask, stopping dead in my tracks at the foot of his bed to point at the weird little window above his headboard with weeds stuffed inside it.

He harrumphs as he barrels into my back, his hands grabbing me around my waist for balance before he yanks them away. "It's called a truth window."

"A what?" I turn and wonder for the first time if I've perhaps read this man all wrong. "Is that like some sort of sex thing? Like a glory hole? What the hell do you do with it?"

"It's not a sex thing," he snaps back, his jaw taut with anger over my accusation. "It's a design thing. It reveals that the walls have straw bale insulation. It keeps the sleeping temperature in here comfortable year-round. It's eco-friendly. This whole house is built with recycled and sustainable products."

I exhale with relief. It's not a sex thing. In fact, it's possibly one of the unsexiest things he could have made up. I smirk and elbow him playfully. "We really are doing this the 'farm way,' aren't we? Should I let out a loud moo when I inseminate myself?" I laugh nervously, wishing I could just shut my mouth.

Wyatt doesn't laugh.

Wyatt looks grumpy.

Poor Mountain Man.

Unbothered by his surly demeanor, I march into his bathroom and discover the ranch cup on the counter. Filled to the brim.

Gross.

Lips pursed with determination, I unwrap the sterile plastic syringe and hover over the pearly liquid.

You've washed rescue dogs with mange before, Trista. One even had a sore with maggots crawling in it. This is nothing!

I pull the fluid into the syringe until I can't get any more in it. My body shudders when it touches the tube's plastic to find it still warm. I swallow the lump in my throat. "That there's a fresh batch, ain't it?"

"Jesus Christ," he expels, unable to look at me.

He's kind of cute when he's mortified.

I carefully make my way back into his bedroom, holding the syringe in my hands like it's a grenade with the pin pulled. "Guess I'll just...oh, fuck!" I exclaim when a thought hits me.

"Jesus, what? Did you drop it?" Wyatt stomps over to me like a giant lurch.

"No, no. I forgot my um...my vibrator." I bite my lip nervously. "It's in my purse. Do you think you can go get it?"

Without a word, Wyatt turns on his heel and practically runs out of the room to go get my toy. He looked almost relieved to finally have something to do other than grunt and turn beet red.

When he returns, I have to bite back a laugh because I didn't expect him to actually grab my vibrator out of my purse. I thought he'd just bring me my whole bag.

He's a mess.

His giant hand dwarfs my tiny pink vibrator as he holds it in front of him like another grenade with no pin.

And there we both stand, face-to-face, staring at each other with bombs in our hands and no fucking idea what we're about to get ourselves into.

"Bombs away," I reply and take the vibrator from him, noticing it's now warm from his touch.

"Here's to lucky thirteen," he states with a wobbly smile and turns to walk out the door.

"Thirteen?" I call out.

He turns and leans on the doorframe with a shrug. "You were my thirteenth interview, and, well…thirteen has always been my lucky number."

I feel oddly jarred by that sweet remark, but those warm fuzzies disappear entirely when the door clicks closed, and I'm left alone with his big, ominous bed. Should I get under the covers, or is that weird and creepy? I mean, since I'm going to sleep here the first night, I guess it's expected I'll use the blankets.

And what if some of his semen leaks out? Should I lie on a towel? I mean, it's his jizz, so I don't think he'd mind a little spillage. But what if he thinks it's from me? What if he thinks I get so hot and horny in here I spray the walls with my horniness?

Oh my God, I'm drunk.

"Just get your shit together, Trista. You're a cow. You're a cow, you're a cow, you're a cow."

Setting the vibrator and syringe on the nightstand, I peel back the covers and undress quickly from the waist down, grateful for my big T-shirt because it serves as a good nightgown.

Doing as the blogs instructed, I lie on my back with my knees bent and legs shoulder width apart.

"Just like inserting a tampon," I tell myself as my hand trembles while grabbing the warm splooge.

I stare up at the creepy truth window and cringe as I inch the hard plastic vessel between my lower lips, pushing past the small wall of muscle down there because I'm tensed like a motherfucker. All the blogs said my cervix is way too high to poke, so I should be able to insert up to my fingers, but Jesus, what if it gets lost inside me? Good God, can you imagine?

Patient enters ER with lost Tylenol syringe full of stranger's semen. I must have missed that episode of *Grey's Anatomy.*

With one horrifying quiver, I quickly depress the plunger like I'm a fucking Hostess cupcake and recoil as the warm liquid fills my center. A slurping noise echoes in the quiet room as I pull it out and stare at it, pearly liquid dripping off the tip and onto my shirt.

I feel it sliding out of my vagina already, so I quickly twist to grab my vibrator. The buzzing noise is deafening, and I picture Wyatt sitting in his living room, hearing the sound like it's on a megaphone speaker.

God, this is awful.

But as the suction cup vibrator works over my clit, I begin to have other thoughts...ones that don't feel quite so horrifying.

What if Wyatt wasn't disgusted by me masturbating in here? What if he was turned on by it? What if he imagined me in this position while he came? What if I opened the door and let him watch me?

I prop my head up and look at the closed door, allowing my lust-filled imagination to see his large frame standing there. He's propped his arm on the frame in that way that only big, strong men can pull off. He's leaning against it, his eyes trained on me and what I'm doing to myself.

I bet Wyatt is a dirty talker. I bet that man of few words doesn't know how to shut up in the bedroom. I bet he would tell me to use that syringe with a little dab of semen left inside it and rub it over my clit for lubrication.

Shamelessly, my free hand reaches back to grab the discarded syringe, and in horror, I do as my filthy mind begs me to do. I smear the remaining seed over my throbbing clit and debate shoving the syringe back up inside me to fuck myself with it while picturing Wyatt's cock.

I bet he's bigger.

I noticed his package in the kitchen earlier, and something tells me Wyatt has plenty to work with. I drop the syringe and press the suction tip over my clit again. My eyes go back to the door and picture Wyatt standing there, his dick hard in his jeans as he rubs himself over the denim, the veins in his forearms bulging as he shows me what watching me does to him.

God, would he like this? Would he like me? Would I be someone he'd fuck in real life? Could we have done this the old-fashioned way and not the farm way? Was this a completely missed opportunity?

The image of his cock plunging inside my semen-drenched center causes a groan to echo from my lips. *Fuck, that was loud.* Too loud. I'm sure he heard it. Then again, he knows what I'm doing in here...

it's not a secret. The jig is up…I'm masturbating! What do I care if he hears me? At least he knows I'm giving it my all. Maybe he made some noises when he jerked off too. I should have listened at the door instead of shoving a whole-ass pizza in my mouth.

I like the idea of him hearing me. The thought makes my inner muscles clench around his spent cum. I can feel myself growing wetter at the thought of him in the other room, listening to every breathy moan I expel, a feral, animalistic look on his face like a caged animal.

A wicked smile teases my lips, and I decide to throw my manners and professionalism and insecurities out the window. I decide to give Mr. Mountain Man an aural delight.

I let myself completely go, not holding back a single breath, moan, groan, or gasp. I rattle the fucking creepy truth window with my climactic cry because, dammit, I'm feeling lucky tonight.

CHAPTER 17

INSEMINATIONS: 4

Wyatt

"Sundown," Trista says as she waltzes into my house one week later.

"Sundown," I repeat stiffly and head to the drawer in my kitchen where my ranch cups are stored. "Give me five."

She lets out a soft laugh. "Only five minutes? Took you ten the other night."

I cross my arms and prop myself on the counter to glower at her before stating through clenched teeth, "I told you I was stressed at work that day."

"And today was a good day?" Her eyes wander down my body before snapping back up to my face.

She's been doing that a lot lately...*inspecting me*. I swear it's like she's waiting for me to run out of sperm or something. Or maybe she can read my dirty thoughts and is going to call me out for being a creep any fucking second.

The first night we did this, I was untethered and completely out of control. I let myself get off to fantasies of the woman I hired to carry my child. The woman I'm clearly obsessing over.

Even after she closed the bedroom door to do her thing, I still couldn't get control of myself. I felt my cock getting hard again just at the idea of hearing her vibrator. Then she started moaning. She started gasping and making these little fucking noises like she was having a goddamn party in my bed.

And I wasn't there.

A flash of me opening the door and offering to make her scream even louder meant that I had to go for a walk in the woods.

Immediately.

Before my horny, buzzed thoughts had me doing exactly that.

I ended up at the natural spring that flows through the mountain. I was fully dressed and did a cold plunge on my aching balls that had already emptied themselves more than I'd ever seen before. I came back to my cabin soaking wet to find her fast asleep and curled into a ball, her knees at her chest, her hair cascading over my pillow. I covered her up and stared with jealousy at the vibrator on top of my duvet.

I was losing it.

I was an unbridled, horned-up animal that couldn't get the sounds of Trista's raspy moans out of my fucking head. And smelling her on my sheets every night this week after she waddles her way back to the barn with her vibrator in hand and my seed in her cunt hasn't helped with my obsession.

She always smells like roses.

I keep telling myself it's the thought of her carrying my child I find so unbelievably attractive. And I do…but a small part of me wonders if this fixation I have on her is more than that.

Let's just say I've been doing a lot of cold plunges this week.

We've been doing this insemination song and dance every other day for the past week now, and I've been trying to play it cool. Be detached. Aloof. But the more she invades my space, the more she invades my thoughts.

It's becoming a problem.

Thankfully, the blogs say one week is all you need to cover your bases. After that, it's up to the human body to finish the job. Her human body. *And what a body it is.*

My eyes wander shamelessly over to her, eating up her full figure that's always covered in way too many fucking clothes. She's dressed in her standard boots, loose T-shirt, and baggy, ripped jeans. Most women buy their jeans with holes…Trista seems to make those holes herself because if I've learned anything about her this past week, it's that there is nothing this woman won't do on her own.

The other morning, I heard Millie bleating like a banshee before the sun was even up, which was unusual for her. I slipped into my boots to figure out the problem, only to discover that Millie had gotten her head caught in the metal fence that runs the forest line on the backside of the pasture.

Trista had beaten me down there and was in the process of freeing her when I approached. The force of Millie yanking her head out caused Trista's jeans to snag on the metal fence. I had to stand behind her to help tear the denim loose, and the process of it revealed a good deal of her leg to me.

Legs I should not be looking at.

Her thigh was bleeding, and I tried to help her out. Begged her to come back to my house so I could clean it up, but she just waved me off and headed back toward her apartment. It fucking pissed me off, honestly. It was my damn goat. She didn't need to be rescuing it in the dark when God knows what other animals could be lurking outside.

She's been driving me fucking crazy doing the absolute bare minimum.

I was fucked.

The mountain was a hell of a lot quieter before she arrived. For example, the other morning, Trista must have been running late for work because I came out early to do chores for Millie, and she barreled into me with the barn door. She had one boot on her foot, a donut in her mouth, and a jacket half on her body. Her wild curls swung loose, but she was too quick for me to get a good long look at it.

Irritating as fuck.

And I don't know when the woman sleeps. She has to leave the mountain by six in the morning every day to have even a chance of making it to Denver in time for her work at the rescue center. And she doesn't get back until damn near dark and doesn't shut her lights off in the barn until nearly midnight. She's burning the candle at both ends, and I don't like it. Should I have included sleeping hours in my contract with her? Surviving on less than six hours of sleep isn't healthy.

She's this untamed, wild little creature that I just can't seem to get out of my head...or my cock. And she's only been on my mountain a week.

"What made today such a good day for Mr. Mountain Man?" she asks again, blinking her green eyes at me like a puppy dog.

Ignoring that unimpressive nickname, I answer, "We sold a smart house on a new development we're working on, and hopefully, it's the first of many more to come."

She might not notice it, but there's pride in my voice. These energy-efficient houses have been a passion project of mine for the past couple of years, and it took some convincing to get my brothers on board with it. We're the first ones doing it in the Boulder area, and I think it's going to be huge for us and the environment.

Trista frowns at me. "Why don't you seem happier about that?"

My body tenses. "I am happy. What do you mean?"

"You seem sad to me," she says as she watches me thoughtfully.

How the hell does she see that? I wonder as I struggle with how to respond. The truth is, she's not wrong. Trista's more perceptive than I give her credit for. But I shouldn't be sad. My life is pretty damn perfect, despite my idiot brothers, but on days like today, when we achieve something amazing, I miss seeing the look of pride in my father's eyes. I miss hearing him grumble over the missteps. I miss hearing his pride...when I was out of earshot.

And even though I don't generally share too much of myself with anyone outside of my family, it almost feels...important...to share this with her. Like she deserves it after everything we're going through together.

I slide my hands into my pockets and sigh heavily. "I guess I'm a little sad my dad isn't here to see this."

Her face softens. "How long has he been gone now?"

"A little over two years."

"Do you mind if I ask how he died?"

My lips thin as I refuse to replay the course of that awful day. "Heart attack."

Trista nods. "Would he have been proud of you for selling this smart house?"

"Not outwardly." I huff with a knowing laugh. "He would have bitched that this development was more work than it was worth, and the old way of building houses was just fine. But then I'd catch him bragging to his friends about it." I can still picture his knowing smile, sitting in his favorite chair in the barn we frequented after work.

My chest aches as it always does when I think of him.

"That's odd." Trista's brows furrow. "Why wouldn't he want you to know he's proud of you?"

I smile and glance out the window at the mountains. "My dad was the king of being the devil's advocate. He always challenged our ideas and pushed us to make sure we knew what we were getting into. But he never stopped us. I think he just wanted to make sure we considered all the angles. His voice lives rent-free in my mind all the time."

Trista bites her lip thoughtfully before she asks, "So were you guys super close?"

My lips press together for a moment before I answer. "He was our boss, our coworker, our best friend, and our dad. I'm not sure we could have gotten any closer."

Trista gets a strange look in her eye that I want to ask about, but she distracts me when she says, "What would he think about what you're doing with me? With this surrogacy stuff?"

"Shockingly, I think he'd love it." I pause as a pang of sadness hits me in the chest that I'll never get to talk to him about it all. "He always hated that my brothers and I chose mountain life over traditional family life. And I thought when I bought the mountain, that would be my passion. I killed myself working the land, setting up a sustainable water source from the creek, installing solar panels, and mining the forest for stones for my fireplace. It was an obsession for years."

"So what changed your mind?" she asks, her eyes piercing into me in a way that makes me want to bare my soul to her.

I hesitate for a moment as the memory of holding my mom in the hospital after they told us our father had died hits me like a ton of bricks. The memories of that day still cause my stomach to churn. Luke's face...especially Luke's face.

"I think in the back of my mind, I always wanted to be a father. When my brother Max had Ethan, everyone talked about how much he looked like me. It's probably vain or narcissistic, but it made me feel proud in some weird way. And once my dad died, I started to think about my own legacy and how I don't want this mountain to end with me. Deep down, I'm still trying to make him proud...even in my own nontraditional way."

A smile lights up Trista's face, and my eyes zero in on her upper lip as it curls. A flash of wondering what it'd be like to kiss her right there invades my thoughts, and I feel my mind going to a place it should definitely not be going.

"Well, I should have brought you a cake or something to celebrate your big sale," she says brightly, snapping me out of my fantasizing.

My brows lift. "Cake? Is this a children's birthday party?"

"I don't know. Do they serve cake at those?" she asks, and nothing in her expression tells me she's joking.

I frown curiously. "Have you never had a birthday party?"

"None worth mentioning," she replies dismissively and heads over to the windows to stare out at the view.

The change in her energy is as obvious as the twenty-foot fireplace in the middle of my home. Our interactions this past week have been brief and mostly all business, which felt imperative to my sanity. I mean, shit, all she's done today is ask me about my dad, yet one little smile from her and my dirty thoughts have come tumbling back into my mind. But this goes well beyond my attraction. I want to know this part of her, even if she doesn't want me to.

"Why didn't you have any good birthday parties?" I ask, watching her shoulders rise slightly.

"My parents were just really flakey." She sighs. "They were either always working or trying to find jobs or caught up in their own personal stuff. They were messy. Birthdays and holidays were the last thing on their minds. And you kind of need money to have birthday parties."

Guilt darkens my vision as I process the struggle Trista just described because it's completely foreign to me. My family didn't have a ton of money, but we wanted for nothing, and my parents never missed an important event in my life. Even with four active sons, they would divide and conquer so one of them was always at our hockey games, school concerts, birthdays. Everything. I hate that Trista didn't have that. Maybe that's why she seems to think she needs to work all those hours at the rescue facility. Maybe I need to pay her more to let her feel like she doesn't have to stretch herself so thin.

"Is your upbringing the reason you work so many hours at your job?" I can't help but ask.

Trista cocks her head, her eyes blinking curiously at me. "Why do you ask?"

I wince and grip the back of my neck, knowing I'm probably crossing a line here but unable to not feel protective over her. "I just noticed you're getting back kind of late most nights, considering how early you leave in the morning. I hope your boss isn't taking advantage of your work ethic."

"Who, Earl?" She scoffs and waves me off. "He's an ass, but he's not the one keeping me out late."

"Who is?" I brace myself as I consider that it might be a social thing keeping her out. Maybe she's about to tell me about an ex-boyfriend that she's recently reconnected with. I swear to God, if another man's vehicle starts parking outside of the barn on a regular basis, I'll need to board up my windows to survive this.

"My vet friend, Avery," she replies cheerily. "The one who takes care of Reggie. I assist on some of the large-animal house calls in rural areas. It's a good learning opportunity that will give me great experience with all types of animals for when I start my own rescue center."

"Oh," I reply with a forced smile as I try to mask the relief that washes over me when she confirms that she's not off with some guy every day. She's just helping animals with her girlfriend.

She's an ambitious workaholic, and I'm pathetic.

With one last lingering look, I shake my head and take my cup down the hall into my bathroom, feeling somehow worse than I did the first night I did this fucking act. The more I know of Trista, the more she gets under my skin. But tonight is our last sundown session. Then it's probably best to get some space until we find out if we've accomplished our goal...or if we have to do this song and dance again.

God help me.

CHAPTER 18

INSEMINATIONS: 5

Trista

"**C**rap," I shriek and chuck the fourth negative pregnancy test into the trash can with the others as a heavy weight settles in my stomach. "Crap, crap, crap."

I flip my two middle fingers off at them, feeling like a child as I pace inside the small bathroom in my new barn apartment. I've been here two weeks, and I'm nowhere near unpacked, but it's already starting to feel like home, and I don't want to leave. Which means *I need to get knocked up.*

I grip my soft belly with two hands, trying to manifest that stress ball inside me into life. This is what I'm here for. This is my big idea that's supposed to help get me ahead. If I can't get pregnant, then I'm not just going to be out of a job, but I'm going to be out of a place to live. And apartment shopping with a potbellied pig is not easy. Plus, I'll be back trying to figure out what the hell I'm doing with my life.

Quitting the shelter is probably the first thing. The pay sucks, and there's no chance of making more because we operate mostly on donations and volunteers. The problem is, I love the work and am lucky to be one of very few paid staff members. But ten years of my life there and still only making thirty-five grand annually doesn't help me make any big life moves. That's why this surrogacy thing appealed to me so much. It's an incredible opportunity to continue to do what I love but in my own way.

But I can't "be the cow" if I don't get pregnant first. With a heavy breath, I stare at myself in the vanity mirror.

"I look tired," I say out loud, my eyes sliding over the various beauty marks on my face. I used to hate them as a child, but as I've grown older, I've come to like them. They make me stand out in a world that likes to forget about me.

My dad had these too, and I briefly wonder if I get pregnant, could the baby inherit them? Would Wyatt like that? I mean, he did pick me to do this, so he must not think I'm completely horrid-looking.

I'd been mildly happy when he seemed concerned about my long hours the other week. It was nice to have someone other than Reginald care. Do I burn the candle at both ends? Quite likely. But I've never been one to be idle. *And you've never been one to be vain either, so stop gawking at yourself in the mirror.*

But today is just not my day. My chestnut hair is piled on top of my head, and I have dark circles under my eyes from my sleepless nights after stressing over these negative tests. The pressure is real. How many cycles of this turkey-basting process will Wyatt allow? I know our contract allows for more chances, but at what point will he consider me more of a burden than a working cow? *Especially if I'm not actually a working cow.*

I turn to the side and stick out my belly, trying to picture a big round bump. It feels impossible, so I shove the hand towel under there to get a better visual, and the reflection staring back at me is just… bizarre.

Becoming a mother has never been something I wanted. As a kid, while other girls in my class would talk about getting married and starting a family, I could never relate. I knew by age eleven I never wanted to become a mom. The nagging fear of turning out like my own parents worried me to the point I didn't even like boys for a long time.

That changed as I got older, obviously, but the moment a guy would get serious, I'd find a reason to pull away. It was easier than having the "I don't want children" talk.

Besides, I'm better off on my own. I can accomplish a lot if I put my mind to it, and no one will disappoint me if it's just me.

I stare at myself, wondering how it will feel with an alien growing inside me. Even the thought is foreign for me, and I imagine the feel of a baby cow moving around. Cringing, I scrap the entire image, thinking about hooves punching me from the inside, and rip the towel out from under my shirt.

Maybe I won't be good at this after all.

I glance out the window at Wyatt's cabin, illuminated in the darkness. It looks so beautiful with the twinkling starry sky above it and mountain trees all around. The life Wyatt has built up here for himself with his brothers right next door is like a dream come true. No way will his baby go hungry. All sorts of people around here are checking in and making sure it's okay.

Is that what Wyatt wished for when he bought this land? Solitude within beauty? *Within family?* It's impressive he actually did it.

What I wish for still seems so out of reach, yet being here on this mountain strangely feels like it's where dreams could come true. I can't lose hope yet. And if it doesn't work this month, all this means is I get to spend more nights walking up the hill to see my burly, dangerously hot mountain man.

Well, not *mine* mine. That's a dream even this magical mountain couldn't provide. But my insides warm as I think of his steely blue eyes on me every time I came into his house for one of our sessions. He looked at me like he was happy to see me. Like I was a sight for sore eyes.

That's a feeling I could get used to.

But I need to get myself pregnant to do that.

Maybe it's time for a backup plan.

CHAPTER 19

ANIMALS ON THE MOUNTAIN: 2
UNNECESSARY SOLO SESSIONS: 5

Wyatt

"**W**hen do you guys start, like…trying to get her pregnant or whatever? Or have you already started?" Luke asks from the back seat of the truck as Calder drives us back home after a ten-hour workday.

"None of your business," I reply, staring out the window and not offering them a shred of detail.

"Oh, come on," Calder exclaims with a laugh. "I've seen her walk up to your cabin from the barn multiple times this past week."

"You have?" Luke asks, leaning over the bench seat as he swats me on the arm. "Damn, I can't see anything from my cabin. Does this mean you guys are, like…doing it already? How does it work?"

"I said it's none of your business," I growl and turn murderous eyes on Calder. "And stop staring out your window at her. Both of you just leave her the hell alone. I mean it. Don't go in the barn, don't talk to her, and don't look at her. Don't do anything with her."

Luke's brows furrow, obviously hurt by my harsh words. "We would never *do* anything with her. Surely you know that, Wyatt."

I swallow the lump in my throat at that loaded remark and refuse to let my brain walk down memory lane. "I just don't want her to feel pressured," I offer, trying to soften my tone. It's been fourteen days since we started trying, and she should be able to take a pregnancy test any day now. My anxiety is at an all-time high, as I wonder if it worked or not. This crazy plan of mine might become a reality.

Holy shit.

But I shouldn't get my hopes up. We never even got a chance to try with that official Mosie Baby at-home insemination kit that arrived several days too late. The odds that a Tylenol syringe and plastic dressing cups worked are slim to none. We can try again next month.

My phone pings with an incoming text, and I swipe it open to see a text from my mom. Luke reads over my shoulder and laughs. "She wants to meet Trista?"

"Yes," I groan and rub my hand aggressively over my hair. "She's pissed at me because I won't let her come up to the mountain and give Trista a welcome gift. She's been bugging me all week."

"You're not going to be able to hide her forever," Calder says, eyeing me seriously.

"You know our family," I grind out. "This whole thing is stressful enough without comments from the peanut gallery."

Calder scoffs as he turns off the road and up Fletcher Mountain. My heart rate instantly increases when I see Trista's car parked outside. She's usually not home before us, so I can't help but wonder if she's home early because she has news.

"Drop me at the barn," I demand and ignore the look Calder and Luke shoot each other. As I slide out of the truck, I point my finger at them. "I'm serious. Don't go near Trista."

Calder pounds his fists on the steering wheel and mimics the voice of a caveman. "Me no touch Wyatt's toy or make Wyatt angry like demon dragon."

My eyes narrow on him, and he just laughs before taking off and kicking rocks all over as he heads up the lane toward his and Luke's places.

As soon as I walk into the barn, Trista's head pops up out of Reginald's pen. "My boobs aren't sore!" she blurts out while tossing a pile of muck into a wheelbarrow.

"What?" My brow furrows in confusion as I make my way over to her.

Trista stops working and props her hand on top of the gate, using the back of her hand to push her loose curls that have fallen out of her messy bun off her face. "All the baby-making forums say my tits should be sore by now. Or I should have some implantation spotting. I got nothing. I feel the same, and all the early response pregnancy tests I've taken the past few days are negative."

Disappointment shudders down around me, but I steel myself to remain calm. "Then we try again."

Trista studies me. "You're not mad?"

"Why would I be mad?" I mirror her stance on the fence, my hands inches from hers, noticing her long, elegant fingers for the first time.

She digs her fingernail into the wood and kicks at the gate. "So much for your lucky number."

I harrumph as my mind rushes back to our first night of insemination. It feels like a million years ago. I barely remember half the things I grunted out in a horned-up daze that night. "Don't give that another thought."

She swallows nervously, picking at a nailhead sticking out of the wood. "I know, but I want this to work for you. For both of us."

"We'll try again," I repeat with a shrug. Yes, I'm disappointed it didn't work on the first try, but I'm not concerned about having to do our whole process again. It got a little easier every time we did it. At least for me. All it took was thinking about my cum inside her and I was hard.

Trying again is no problem, but I am bothered by her defeated attitude right now.

"Trista, it's okay," I state firmly and reach out to tuck my finger under her chin to force her to look at me. Her sad copper-green eyes are like a gut punch, and I resist the urge to hug her to my chest. She looks so young right now. "We try again next month. Simple as that. We were prepared for this."

Her eyes glint with something I can't quite decipher before she shocks the hell out of me with her reply. "Maybe we need to do it the regular way. Like actually have sex with each other."

My heart explodes in my chest as my emotions swing from

disappointment to raging arousal in a flash. "Have sex?" I repeat to make sure my hormones aren't hearing things.

She nods, her brows furrowed as she looks forward and ponders this suggestion. "I know I'm probably not your type, but we can shut the lights off and just—"

"We wouldn't need to shut the lights off," I bark, my voice firm and way too aggressive for the quiet stillness of the barn. The idea of me fucking her and not *seeing* her is more painful than the disappointment of this first month not working.

Her head jerks back as she gapes at me, her eyes curious and alive. She inspects my entire face as if looking for something in my expression. Does she think I'm lying? Does she think I'd need to shut the lights off to fuck her? Is she fucking crazy?

She pulls her lower lip into her mouth, and it's like I can see the fantasy playing out in her mind, and my cock stirs at the thought of that. At the thought of her picturing me the way I imagine her. I feel myself drawing closer, like my body can't help itself, and I briefly wonder if we're not going to try this baby-making dance right here, right now—in Reginald's fucking pigpen.

It's not even sundown yet.

She barks out a nervous laugh and yanks herself away from the fence, away from me and my thickening cock. "Well, we've got time before I ovulate again to consider that option. Let's just give it some serious thought, and we can meet and discuss it again next week?"

Right. Ovulation. She needs to ovulate before we do this. Obviously, I knew that.

I nod and watch her curiously as she goes back to cleaning out the pen like she didn't just suggest I fuck her to get her pregnant. That will certainly complicate things. But if she's up for it, so am I. I'm more than up for it.

With a deep, cleansing breath, I turn to do my own chores, knowing full well what I'll be doing to myself at sundown tonight, baby making or not.

CHAPTER 20

DAYS PAST OVULATION: 16
ANIMALS ON MOUNTAIN: 2

Wyatt

"Millie," I holler from the pasture enclosure. Millie stops walking to jerk her head in my direction. She wiggles her ears but then resumes her stroll with the pig, clearly not giving a shit about her human companions anymore.

"I feel so rejected!" Everly states with a laugh.

I shake my head as my goat and the pig continue walking the fence line together like they've known each other for years, not two weeks. "They like to walk together a lot. It's the damnedest thing."

Everly's face lights up with amusement. "The cutest thing, you mean. Millie finally has a friend."

I harrumph, not nearly as impressed by the sight as Everly.

"Is there any exciting news you want to tell me about, Uncle Wyatt?" Everly elbows me, waggling her brows excitedly.

"No," I grunt out awkwardly. It's really fucking weird to talk about knocking up my surrogate with my eighteen-year-old niece. Then again, she found Trista for me, so I guess we've probably already far surpassed normal.

Her lip juts out in disappointment. "Bummer."

"These things take time," I state with a shrug, feeling like a fucking creeper for being somewhat grateful that it didn't work the first time because month two of trying to knock her up is fixing to be a lot more interesting than month one. *Bring on sundown.*

"Are they ignoring you again?" Trista cuts in, and I turn around to see her walking out of the barn toward us.

My heart hammers in my chest at the sight of her. She wears a pair of Carhartt coveralls with dried paint spattered all over them and her hair in its standard topknot. She looks fucking good.

"Trista!" Everly shrieks and runs over to greet the woman who just offered to have sex with me five days ago.

"Hey, crazy kid," Trista replies, returning Everly's overly eager hug. "Nice to see you again."

"You too," she replies with a smirk, wrapping her arm around Trista's as she drags her toward me. "How do you like living in the barn?"

"Um…I low-key love it," Trista says unabashedly, flashing me a warm smile and a wink that goes right to my cock. "You weren't lying that the views are spectacular."

"I told you!" Everly beams proudly. "Uncle Wyatt does good work."

My eyes connect with Trista's, and we hold each other's gaze for a moment. I haven't seen her since our chat in the barn the other day, and something about her seems…different. Her presence always inflicts a feeling of restlessness in me, but seeing her now, it's like every cell in my body is being electrified.

And it doesn't take a genius to know why.

Trista put sex on the table. And in the blink of an eye, I went from likely never seeing her naked to possibly fucking her very soon. I'm too old to be this excited by the prospect of sex, but lucky number thirteen isn't just some chick I picked up at a bar. To think I might be able to take her in my bed, with her arms held above her head and her legs spread wide, dripping wet and ready for my—

"Reginald is so adorable," Everly says, snapping me out of my dirty thoughts. "He's even cuter than the pictures you texted me."

Trista nods. "And he loves the barn life. Who woulda thought?"

"I would have," I grumble softly. They both stare at me with accusing eyes, and I shrug. "He's a pig. Pigs belong in barns, not apartments."

Trista rolls her eyes. "He only likes it because he has Millie. Do you see how they stroll together? I swear it's like they're out there dishing on all the hot gossip."

"I always begged Uncle Wyatt to get more animals out here, but he told me no."

"I didn't know he was capable of telling you no," Trista says with a laugh. "I got the impression you have your uncles all wrapped around your finger."

"Oh, I totally do." Everly laughs. "Speaking of uncles, how's it going with them? Are they driving you crazy? They can be a lot sometimes."

"I weirdly haven't seen much of them," Trista answers with a shrug. "I suppose between the commute to work and the extra hours I put in with my vet friend, I haven't had a chance to really hang out with the whole family."

"Count yourself lucky," I murmur under my breath.

Everly elbows me, and then I notice her smile drop as Millie and Reginald approach us. "What is Millie chewing on?"

"Oh my God," Trista exclaims and moves to jump over the fence.

"What is it?" I ask, terrified that Millie could have gotten into something. I've had to rush her to the vet one other time when she ripped open a bag of feed and overate. Her stomach was bloated, and the vet had to literally fucking stab her behind the ribs to release the air buildup. It was one of the most terrifying days of my life.

I open the gate and drop down on my knees to pull out the shit in her mouth. "Give it here, girl. What did you get into?"

"Millie, spit it out!" Trista cries, her voice shrill. She shoves me over and swipes her fingers right in Millie's mouth, causing her to gag and bleat in a way I've never heard before. "Shit!"

"What is it?" I demand again, my tone angry because it seems an awful lot like Trista gave my goat something bad for her. "What did you do to my girl?"

"I didn't do anything to her!" she snaps at me as she continues thrusting her finger in her mouth. "God, why do goats have to eat everything?"

Finally, a big chunk of plastic falls out of her mouth and lands in the dirt. I stare down, my eyes seeing double for a second as I reach down and pick up the familiar-looking object. I turn it over and see on the other side a little control window that says the word PREGNANT.

"Reggie, get out of there!" Trista snaps, sitting on the ground to block her pig from eating the scraps that just came from my goat's mouth.

"What is it?" Everly asks, and I struggle to find my own voice to tell her.

"It's a pregnancy test," Trista answers, flustered and out of breath as she sits crisscross in the dirt, hugging her sixty-pound pig to her body. "I'm pregnant."

"Oh my God!" Everly exclaims, leaping over the fence to join the chaos all around me. She squats beside me and takes the plastic chunk out of my hand to inspect it herself. "Uncle Wyatt, you're having a baby!"

I remain frozen, my eyes fixed off in the distance as I adjust to this life-changing bit of information.

"I attached the pregnancy test to Millie's halter to reveal the news, but she must have gotten it off somehow." She grabs Reggie's snout to pull his face to hers. "Reginald, did you pull it off Millie's collar, you naughty boy?"

A series of grunts indicates God knows what because I don't speak fucking pig. I'm not sure I even speak English right now. *Holy. Fuck. She's pregnant?*

My eyes finally find Trista's, and I can't hide the catch in my voice as I whisper, "It actually worked?"

She smiles warmly at me, and it feels so fucking good it makes my eyes sting. Her voice is soft and knowing as she replies, "Finally popped up positive this morning. Ranch cups and children's Tylenol defied the laws of science. Who woulda thought?"

"What?" Everly asks, her head snapping back and forth between mine and Trista's in confusion.

Without thinking, I leap to my feet and grab Trista, yanking her off the ground and away from her squealing pig. I wrap my arms around her and crush her body to mine in a tight hug as I spin her in a circle. My entire chest vibrates with overwhelming emotion that I can't put into words.

Words have never been my thing.

"Someone is certainly happy!" she exclaims with a laugh as I set her down. She holds on to my arms and locks eyes with me before she says, "Congratulations, Wyatt."

My brows furrow at that response. It's very cordial. And professional. And if I'm being honest…a little distant. I know being a single father is what I wanted, but this didn't happen on my own. I couldn't have done this without the woman in my arms.

"Thank you, Trista." My voice is gravelly and full of confusion, happiness, and a million other emotions someone might feel when they've just found out their whole life is about to change.

We pull apart, and I glance to see Everly watching us with a knowing look. She bounds over, wrapping us both in a hug, and murmurs against my shoulder, "I'm so happy for you guys!"

And it's at that moment that I realize there isn't a "you guys." This is just me. Yes, Trista's role in this is vital and necessary and still highly important for the next nine months. But I'm the only one whose life will change after all this. And that's a staggering realization.

CHAPTER 21

WEEKS PREGNANT: 5
ANIMALS ON MOUNTAIN: 2

Trista

My stomach churns as I muck out Reginald's pen while he goes to town on some leftover watermelon rinds that I dumped into his trough. I'm usually not such a marshmallow about the smell of manure, so I don't quite understand why I'm struggling so much today. Honestly, cleaning out a stable is a hell of a lot easier than the litter box with the side cut out that I trained Reggie to eliminate in at my old apartment. That was always a mess, so I wasn't surprised when the landlord gave me the boot.

When I'm all done, I glance around the barn and feel a sense of relief that I get to continue calling this place my home for the foreseeable future. The anxiety I had last week over not knowing if I was pregnant or not was next-level. I must have peed on ten tests in total that week. And I know the contract said we could try for several months, but Wyatt doesn't exactly strike me as a patient man. And like it or not, I kind of need this job. And this barn.

My phone pings in my pocket, and I pull it out to see a text from Avery.

> Avery: Hey, I'm going to be vaccinating a herd of lambs tomorrow. Wanna join?
>
> Me: Ewe know I do. ;)

> Avery: I'll text you the time when I get it confirmed. How are you feeling?
>
> Me: Can morning sickness happen at only five weeks pregnant?

I watch the dots bounce on my phone as I impatiently await the reply. Avery was the first person I texted after the pregnancy test came back positive. I wanted to make sure I wasn't seeing two lines by mistake, which prompted me to go to the store and get one of those foolproof tests that say the actual words: Pregnant or Not Pregnant. They are way more expensive, but the stakes are high. I needed more proof that the Tylenol syringe actually freaking worked.

Although I have been doing my fair share of fantasizing about doing the deed the old-fashioned way. I kind of blurted out that idea in the barn and was pleasantly surprised when Wyatt seemed down for it. In fact, I think I even felt a tiny pang of disappointment when the test turned positive because now I have no excuse to see the mountain man naked.

What a missed opportunity.

But obviously, that's for the best. Sex with him would be so messy. And stupid. And just…a bad, bad idea. I don't know what came over me that day, but I do know that neither of us has ever spoken of it since. *Thank God.*

I'm blaming that suggestion on pregnancy hormones. Hormones are my get-out-of-jail-free card, and I will use them as an excuse liberally for the next nine months.

> Avery: I would guess it's normal, but I'm an animal doctor, not a human one. You should ask your own doctor. When do you get your first scan done?
>
> Me: In a couple of weeks.
>
> Avery: Did they confirm the pregnancy with blood work?
>
> Me: Yes
>
> Avery: Then I'm sure it's just hormonal fluctuations. But if you're worried, don't be afraid to call your doctor. Or do something crazy like read a baby book.

My nose wrinkles at that. I tried to read a baby book at the library the other day, and it made me feel weird. It was clearly written for a woman who's keeping her baby and embracing the life growing inside her, and that is not the headspace I want to entertain.

I want to stay as detached as possible. What's happening inside me is science, and that's how I will continue to look at it for the next nine months. *I'm an inseminated cow.*

Although I will admit, getting picked up and spun around in the pasture by Wyatt was a bit of a butterfly-inducing moment. Mostly because I was shocked he could lift me without causing himself physical harm. But also because he seems so certain about all this. There is no doubt in his mind that he wants this baby all on his own. Which I guess is good because it's too late to turn back now.

I grab my phone to reply to Avery.

> Me: The baby books all suck. They're all written for mothers planning to keep their kids.
>
> Avery: Maybe you should join a surrogacy support group?
>
> Me: Do those exist?
>
> Avery: If not in person, then surely they do online.

I consider that idea. It'd be nice to have someone to talk to about this pregnancy stuff, but the thought of opening up to a bunch of strangers sounds awful. And unfortunately, I don't have any close friends who I'd feel cool with talking about this crazy surrogacy journey I'm on. I pretty much grew apart from my old high school friends once they all went off to college, and other than meeting up for an odd drink to catch up here and there, we don't really keep in touch.

Plus, I work too damn much to find a local support group. The only reason my friendship with Avery even exists is because of the work we do together.

I just need to get through this first ultrasound and confirm this baby actually exists before I go spilling my guts to my doctor about how I feel like yakking every time I catch a whiff of something unpleasant. Gotta stay strong.

CHAPTER 22

WEEKS PREGNANT: 7
ANIMALS ON MOUNTAIN: 2

Trista

"**F**ucking fuck," Wyatt's deep voice growls softly as he grabs the crook of my arm and yanks me back toward him.

I'm assaulted by his scent as I stumble into his chest, my eyes closing in pain because no man has the right to smell as good as he does. I always thought the soaps labeled "mountain rain" were complete bullshit. How could any lab ever fully capture the aroma of mountain rain? And now that I've lived on a mountain for over a month, I'm convinced they are bullshit. Because no soap can fully capture the natural scent of Wyatt Fletcher. He's all the things... clean and fresh and rugged and woodsy. Which is why I take far longer than I should to extract myself from his embrace.

I look up, hating how tall he is when we stand face-to-face. As a tall girlie, tall guys are always these elusive creatures. They're usually only seen on television or coupled up with some tiny five-foot-nothing girl because big guys like tiny girls. That's just a sad fact of life.

I bet Wyatt likes tiny women—a little slip of a thing that he could completely annihilate in the bedroom.

And why the hell am I thinking about Wyatt Fletcher in the bedroom? That is a thought I have painstakingly tried to avoid since that first night in his bed, and re-invoking that image as we walk into the clinic for our first ultrasound appointment is not good. What if there's something on the machine that can show the tech that I'm horny? Like some sort of dilated ovary or something.

Good God, pregnancy makes me stupid.

Which is why I need to keep reminding myself that Wyatt Fletcher likes tiny girls with tiny asses and tiny vaginas. And I'm here with my plus-sized birthing hips to give him a baby. Nothing more.

"I told her not to come," Wyatt hisses, his jaw muscle twitching beneath his freshly trimmed beard, making the little flecks of gray in it harder to see when it's short like this.

"Told who not to come?" I ask, noting how the hospital fluorescents cast ominous shadows on his face, but he still manages to look hot. Bastard.

I bet I look like a witch in this lighting.

"Wyatt!" an older female coos from behind him, and I see his eyes roll to the back of his head before he grumbles and turns around to face her.

An attractive female with a short blond bob who looks about in her sixties comes charging out of the clinic waiting area to greet us by the elevator we just stepped out of.

"Mom," he bites out through clenched teeth as his eyes narrow on her.

"Your mom is here?" I slap my hand over my mouth because I tend to laugh when I'm nervous, and right now, I am highly uncomfortable.

"You must be Trista the Surrogate." The woman, who's a good five inches shorter than me, pulls me into a hug, crushing the cellophane-wrapped bouquet she's holding between us. "I'm Johanna, and it is so nice to finally meet you."

I crouch down to return her hug and am assaulted with a wave of expensive perfume. Wyatt shared some stuff about his late father but not much about his mom, so I don't know how to react.

"I think you are so special," she says as she pulls back, and I notice her eyes are welled with tears. "Doing this for my boy. I mean, don't get me wrong, I was shocked when he told me about all this. But if this is how I get more grandchildren, I am Team Trista the Surrogate."

"There are no teams, Mom," Wyatt murmurs under his breath, his tone exasperated. "What are you doing here?"

"I wanted to meet Trista the—"

"You can just call me Trista," I interject, desperate not to hear the full label she's pegged me with.

"Trista," she repeats and smiles warmly at me as her eyes assess my face. "Gosh, you're pretty."

"Mom," Wyatt groans and pinches the bridge of his nose.

"What?" she snaps at him in a chastising, motherly tone that only a woman who's raised four boys can pull off. "You didn't mention how pretty she was. Can't I notice how pretty you are?"

"I love it when people tell me I'm pretty," I reply with a shrug. My God, this is weird, but watching Wyatt squirm makes this awkwardness incredibly worth it.

Johanna reaches up and tucks a piece of my loose hair behind my ear. It's overly affectionate but kind of amazing, and I turn into her embrace.

"Wyatt rarely invites me up to the mountain, so I had to come here to see you for myself."

"I see you in town every week, Mom," Wyatt says gently and then looks at me. "She brings me and my brothers lunch at our jobsites at least twice a week."

"That's so nice." My jaw drops, and I murmur, "My mom never even made me breakfast."

Johanna's face falls. "Oh, honey, that's awful."

I cringe as I realize I've said too much. "Oh, don't worry. I made my own breakfast." I offer a wink that doesn't seem to soothe her obvious disappointment.

Her brows are pinched together as she watches me for a moment before thrusting the bouquet into my hands. "These are for you. There's a little gift card in there from my favorite bakery in town too."

"Oh, wow." I inhale sharply as I stare at the expensive bouquet in awe. I don't think I've ever received flowers from anyone in my life, and the fact that she bought these for me without even knowing me is low-key bizarre. My own mother would never. She doesn't even call me on my birthday.

If this is the type of love these Fletcher boys grew up with, then this baby will be in great hands.

"Thank you. These are beautiful."

"You're welcome," she says, looking pleased. "I would have delivered them up to the mountain where you're living, but Wyatt told me I couldn't."

Wyatt growls under his breath. "Because we haven't even had our first ultrasound, Mom. I didn't want Trista to feel pressured."

I glance over at Wyatt and am shocked when I notice his entire body radiates protectiveness. I thought he was uncomfortable because his mom was here, which felt weird to me because she seems wonderful. But now I understand—he's just looking out for me.

His words from our first interview replay in my mind: "*I can be kind of possessive when it comes to those I love.*"

I shake that thought away because, *obviously*, he doesn't love me. He doesn't know the full extent of my crazy yet. It's this baby I'm growing inside me he's protecting. But right now, I'll take this as a sign that of all the people I could have become a surrogate for, I might have gotten lucky with Wyatt. He's definitely sweet...not psycho.

"I'm not trying to pressure anyone." Johanna clutches her hands to her chest defensively. "We've met, and now I'll leave. I hope to see you again soon—"

"Is there a Trista Matthews here?" a voice calls down the hallway, and we all turn to face the nurse dressed in pink scrubs. "We're looking for Trista Matthews."

"I'm Trista." I hold my hand up and wave around Wyatt's mom.

"Great!" The nurse bustles over to us with a warm smile and a clipboard in hand. Her eyes move to Wyatt and his mother. "We're ready for you back there. Is everyone here coming back for the ultrasound?"

"No," Wyatt snaps as he reaches out to grab my hand and pull me down the hallway.

I glance over my shoulder and see Johanna's eyes go from wildly hopeful to crushing disappointment. It's heartbreaking. And I'm still fascinated by a mother caring so much that she just shows up to her son's first ultrasound appointment.

The tech leads us down the hallway, and I stop, forcing Wyatt and the nurse to stop with me. All their eyes settle on me before I glance over my shoulder and say, "Johanna, would you like to join us?"

"Really?" Johanna jumps up and down with joy.

Wyatt immediately pulls me in close, so close I can smell his mountain-man musk again. "Trista, you really don't have to do this."

My eyes slide over to his mom, who's looking at the nurse with so much hope and excitement I can't help but want to continue watching this show…whatever it is. I turn my gaze to the grumpy mountain man in front of me and whisper, "I just have to see what this looks like."

Wyatt's face twists in confusion, but I shake him off. Now isn't the time to unpack my baggage with my intended baby daddy.

"Truth bomb?" I murmur quietly to Wyatt, who's standing beside me on the exam bed. I awkwardly shift on top of the white paper that I can feel sticking to my ass as my nerves cause my body to sweat. I lean up to his ear and whisper, "I didn't realize I'd have to take my pants off when I said your mom could join us."

"Do you want me to ask her to leave?" Wyatt's eyes are wide and urgent. "Just say the word and—"

He motions with his thumb like he's going to bounce his tiny mother out of the room, so I grab his hand and lower it. "Chillax, Mr. Mountain Man. I'll be fine. I'm covered…mostly." I reach back and attempt to make sure the top of my ass crack is still covered by the blue cloth the tech gave me before she cheerfully told me to undress from the waist down.

Walking out of the attached bathroom and clutching the sheet to my back because it wouldn't wrap all the way around me was bad enough. But making eye contact with Wyatt's tiny mother as I shifted on the exam table to peel the white paper off my butt cheek was a moment of humiliation I wish I never experienced.

Damn nervous giggles.

And fuck these lady clinics. Honestly, what's so hard about having some extra-large sheets on hand? As a full-figure female, this is a problem I encounter more times than I care to admit, and our society needs to evolve past that. And the ridiculous BMI scale.

Hotels are horrible about that too. Those towels are a joke. I'm lucky to get them wrapped around half of my lower body. My ass, hips, and thighs require some extra material. And I've got a little pouch of a belly situation that's always giving "is she pregnant or just bloated" vibes...you know...before I actually got pregnant.

When the ultrasound tech returns, I get the nervous snickers again because we must look about as awkward as can be right now. Wyatt's mom stands under the giant television set hanging on the wall, unwrapping a roll of breath mints, and Wyatt is low-key staring at his feet, muttering obscenities.

"Looks like the gang's all ready!" the tech declares as she sits in the roller chair and squirts gel over a long probe covered in a condom. She smiles warmly down at me and says in a thick Minnesota accent, "I get so excited to do these surrogate scans because it's just such a special gift you're giving to someone. A real-life belly buddy babysitter. Go, you!"

"Thanks." I force a smile that doesn't reach my eyes and wonder if I can one-star review this baby-talking, hearts-and-flowers nurse who really just needs to say less.

"Where does that thing go?" Wyatt blurts out, his eyes wide and fixed on the object in her hand.

In her bubbly, singsongy voice, the nurse replies, "Well, at seven weeks pregnant, the little guy or gal in there is about the size of a jelly bean. Much too small for us to see through the belly. Which means we do a vaginal ultrasound, so this special tool will go in her vagina." She waves the giant dildo toward a stunned-looking Wyatt. "Next week, your little baby will be the size of a popcorn kernel and then a gumball and a tater tot, and by the time you get to the size of a Reese's cup, we'll be able to do belly scans! Yummy, right?"

"Yummy!" Johanna cheers as she pops a mint into her mouth.

Wyatt's face morphs into a look of disgust as his eyes flick from his mother's and back to the tech. I have to bite my lip not to laugh. I get the impression he's not disgusted by the vagina wand. I think he's disgusted by the tech's food analogies. She clearly doesn't speak mountain man. He would have better understood her if she replied in grunts or used bits of nature to describe the size of this baby.

Acorn. Pine nut. Goat turd! Those are analogies this man can respect. I wonder how far along I'll be when the baby is the size of a goat turd?

"Okay, I'm going to need you to scooch all the way down to the edge of the table so we can get a look at your belly buddy."

The exam table makes a painful screeching noise as I shift down-ward. I don't know what's more cringey, the sound of my skin ripping off this vinyl or the nickname she just gave this baby. Surely, we can do better than "belly buddy," right? I mean, we haven't even seen this baby on a scan yet. Aren't we getting the cart ahead of the horse here?

Although, I will say my body already *feels* different, so the hormone thing that Avery mentioned might actually be legiti-mate. The nausea seems to be getting worse, and my aching tits are next-freaking-level. Do you know how hard it is to carry dogs at the center with nipples that feel like a light breeze will set them on fire?

Not fun.

But I'm not complaining about any of it because it's just all the comfort I need to know that things are still…developing in there. Bring on the ultrasound.

The nurse pats my leg and looks under the blue drop cloth. "Keep scooching."

The paper is agonizingly loud as it peels off my ass when I scooch some more.

"Come on now, don't be shy," she says as she continues staring at me under the blanket. "Scooch, scooch, scooch!"

I swallow nervously and shift down more. Does she have to gaze at my bajingo so enthusiastically while I do this?

"Almost there."

"My feet are going to fall out of these stirrups if I keep going," I snap, sitting up on my elbows to look at her with fury.

"Yeah, hasn't she scooched enough?" Wyatt's deep voice booms in the room, making no mistake that he's just as irritated as I am.

Or was. I'm suddenly less irritated after hearing Wyatt use the word "scooch." He looks at me and scowls, clearly wondering why my belly is shaking with silent laughter.

"That should do it," the lady says, and before I know it, she's shoved that damn wand up inside me without any warning.

This is happening! I currently have a giant dildo-like wand up my bajingo with my baby daddy and his mom breathing the same air. *This is totally normal.*

"Based on your last menstrual cycle, you're about seven weeks and four days along." She clicks on the screen and then points at what she's measuring. "And that's right where you're measuring! Congratulations…" She pauses as her eyes move off me and to Wyatt. "…Dad!"

Wyatt blinks back at her, his face completely unreadable. He moves closer to me, his eyes glued to the screen. "Is that…?"

"The baby? Yep!" She moves the wand inside me as if zooming in for a close-up. "That's your little jelly bean (goat turd), and the M&M-looking thing right next to it is a yolk sac (smaller goat turd). The baby feeds on that until the placenta is formed."

"Jelly bean and M&M," he repeats, surprising me yet again with words I wouldn't expect him to utter.

"Let's see how the heartbeat sounds." The tech zooms in further on a tiny little fluttering happening inside the jelly bean and then turns a knob on her computer to suddenly fill the room with the sound of a thundering beat.

"That sounds fast," I blurt out, feeling an unexpected wave of anxiety hit me all at once. I need this to go perfectly for myself and the people in the room whose eyes suddenly feel heavy on me.

"Let's just see how fast it is," she replies, looking completely unbothered when I am very fully bothered. My heart rate doesn't get that high even when I'm forced to run, which I never do. "We're sitting right at 132 bpm. Perfect for this gestational age."

I sigh with relief and hear a strange noise come from Wyatt.

"Oh, sweetie." Wyatt's mother moves over to put her arm around her son's waist. Her hand strokes his side in a soothing way, and I watch the embrace like a complicated movie with subtitles. She whispers in his ear, "That's your baby right there."

Wyatt clears his throat, and the two of them embrace for a moment, the sounds of his mother's sniffles fighting with the racing heartbeat on the speaker.

"I wish your dad was here to see this," she croaks into his chest, and I feel a heaviness in my stomach.

"Me too, Mom." He lifts his head, and I have to look away because the sight of an emotional Wyatt is too much for me to bear. Seeing this happy family unit is honestly too much for me to handle. I thought it would be interesting to watch…like I could learn something…but it just makes me feel yucky inside.

My family existed like ships passing in the night. No hugs, no meals, no attending appointments together. Certainly no sharing in big life experiences.

I remember making the honor roll in middle school and my mom telling me she'd try to make it. I stood with the other students to accept my medal and stared out into the audience for her. I even deluded myself into thinking my dad might show up and surprise me. Like one of those military parents who return home from war, and everyone tears up as they watch him embrace his kid.

But not my family.

No one showed.

My medal wasn't spoken of, even after I left it on the kitchen table, hoping someone might at least want to congratulate me.

The tech prints off ultrasound pictures and hands them to Wyatt and his mom. They gush over the photos and begin talking about the nursery plans. I disassociate from them to stare up at the goat turd on the screen.

There it is. The thing making my breasts feel like foreign objects. Hard to believe something so small can make such an impact on so many. Not everyone gets lucky enough to have a family who cares about them before they're born. But it looks like this kid growing inside me will.

Good for little goat turd.

All that matters to me is that I did the job I was hired to do. I have a little more job security today than yesterday, and I'm one step closer to my happily ever after with animals…not babies.

CHAPTER 23

WEEKS PREGNANT: 9
ANIMALS ON MOUNTAIN: 2

Wyatt

The next couple of weeks are odd. None of the prep work I did for this surrogacy situation equipped me for what it would be like to have my surrogate living on my property. And I realize it's not uncommon for intended parents to pay for surrogate housing, but most don't have them live literally next door to them. So yeah, this is an unusual situation. But when the only woman who came into your life and felt right for the job of being a surrogate happens to have a potbellied pig, I guess it called for an unusual answer.

And I've really grown to hate the word "surrogate." Ever since my mom said it in the hospital, I started loathing the term. It feels so impersonal and medical. The woman living in my barn is anything but "Trista the Surrogate" or a "belly buddy babysitter." She's happy, easygoing, and has this odd way of existing in my life like she's always been here.

With that said, she can also be maddening as fuck. She doesn't let me do anything for her. Like anything. I can't fill Reginald's water trough or muck out his pen. I can't pick up food for her, even when I text her to let her know I'm picking up food for myself. She's keeping a safe distance between the two of us, and after how fucked up my brain was during our sundown sessions, maybe that's for the best.

But when she demanded to drive her own car to the hospital in Boulder for our first ultrasound, that's when she went too damn far. The economic inefficiency of both of us driving to and from the same place made me see fucking red. And then, she let my mom come into the exam room. Where the fuck did that come from?

Like I said…maddening.

Although admittedly, my irritation with her disappeared the moment that baby's heartbeat erupted in the room like a galloping horse, and I saw the look on my mom's face. Her grief has been hard for me and my brothers to manage. We all miss Dad, but no one more than her. The gift Trista gave her of having that special moment with me was something I didn't expect but will forever be grateful for. I just wish Trista was better at letting me show my appreciation.

"Yo!" Calder interrupts my thoughts as his pickup stops in front of my house. "Let's roll, Papa Bear."

I jog down my porch steps with my lunch box and coffee in hand, but my eyes drift over as I notice Trista's vehicle parked in front of the barn. It's after nine. She's usually long gone for work by now.

"What's your deal?" Luke calls over from the passenger seat as I pause in front of the driver's door, resting my elbow on the open window to look for any signs of life above the barn.

"Trista is still here," I state with a frown.

"So what?" Calder shrugs.

"I wonder if she's sick or something."

Luke makes a peculiar noise from inside the truck. "Bro, you are level-ten stalking that girl now."

"No, I'm not," I growl, turning my lethal eyes on him. Luke was over the other night and giving me shit for how often I glanced out at the barn. "I just keep an eye on her. She's a single woman driving to Denver every day for work. She doesn't talk about any boyfriends or friends, except her girlfriend Avery, who she often helps out after work. But I have no clue if anyone is actually looking out for her. And she's carrying precious cargo these days, so I'll fucking watch her if I want to watch her."

"Holy fuck," Calder gapes at me, his stupid face looking really punchable this morning. "That's the most words I've heard you say consecutively in, like…my whole damn life. Maybe you're the one who's sick." He reaches out to put the back of his hand on my forehead, and I swat him away.

"Why don't you guys go on ahead," I say, making my way toward the barn. "I'll meet you at the jobsite later."

"You hate driving two cars into town," Calder argues, looking seriously disturbed. "You say it's bad for the environment. You literally started a Fletcher Mountain Google calendar for our schedules so we could combine as many trips to town as possible."

"Will you get fucked?" I hiss and kick rocks at his truck wheel.

He laughs and shakes his head before pulling away. I don't care what they say—it's normal for me to look out for her. She's living on my property, carrying my baby. This isn't stalking. This is caring. I'm like a protective father of sorts.

But I do not look at Trista like she's my daughter.

If I'm ever fatherly to her, it sure as fuck better be in a sexy daddy sort of way.

I make my way through the barn and glance into the pig's pen to notice he still hasn't been fed. That's definitely not like Trista. She usually feeds him before I get down to feed Millie, even if the lazy bastard doesn't crawl off his mattress until damn near eleven most days.

Anxiety spikes in my veins as I take the wooden steps two at a time up to her apartment door. I knock loudly and call out to her. When there's no answer for several minutes, I try the door and sigh with relief when I find it unlocked. Slowly, I open it, calling her name as I head inside. I haven't been up here since she moved in, doing my best to give her space like she clearly wants.

Glancing around, I can't help but notice it's kind of a mess. There are dirty dishes in the sink, half-unpacked boxes everywhere, and am I seeing things, or did a fucking rabbit just scamper across the living room and burrow under her bed?

"Trista, are you in here?" I call out a bit more forcefully. I hear a groan come from the bathroom door, which is wide open, so I charge over, and my chest contracts when I find her hunched over the toilet. "Fuck, are you okay?"

I drop down on my knees beside her, and my hands hover around her body, wanting to touch her but also wanting to respect her space.

"No," she whines, resting her forehead on her arms surrounding the toilet bowl. "Morning sickness isn't just something they made up for the movies. Can you believe that shit?"

"Are you sure you don't have the flu or something?" I ask, still feeling useless as I sit beside her on the wood floor, my hands balled into tight fists.

"Yeah." She sniffs loudly and lifts her head. Makeup is smeared across her face, and her eyes and cheeks are sunken. "I talked to the nurse a few days ago after I threw up in my car."

"You threw up in your car?" I repeat, my head tilting as immediate frustration hits me hard and fast. Why is this the first I'm hearing of that?

She nods sadly. "Literally just vommed in my Dunkin' Donuts bag. An egg sandwich was a bad life choice."

"Why didn't you tell me?" I hiss through clenched teeth, my hands itching to touch her because she looks so weak and pathetic, and it makes me feel weak and pathetic to sit here and do nothing.

"They can give me meds if it gets bad enough, but they said it's better for the baby not to take anything. I've been trying to make these ginger smoothies, but they taste like ass."

"If you need the meds, you need the meds. Being this miserable can't be good for you or the baby." My chest swells when I say the word "baby." It still doesn't feel real sometimes, but seeing this woman pregnant with my child and sick as a dog feels painfully real.

"I know, I know. I'll call Earl to let him know I'm not coming in and—"

Her voice cuts off as she sits up and begins dry heaving, her whole body tensing and contracting with the act. I reach out and grab her hair, holding it at the nape of her neck as she retches over the toilet, unable to vomit up even liquid at this point. Her stomach must be empty.

"You could be dehydrated. We're calling the nurse," I state firmly, using one hand to hold her hair back. "I'm getting you some fucking drugs."

"Let me just go lie down in my bed for a minute, and I bet I'll be fine," she groans and moves to stand.

As soon as she's on her feet, I bend over and scoop her into my arms.

"What are you doing?" she squeals, her arm wrapping around my neck as she attempts to wiggle her way out.

"I'm carrying you to your bed."

"No, you are not!" she bellows, and I feel a moment of relief that she still has enough energy to argue with me.

"This isn't up for debate, Lucky," I grumble, my boots loud on the floor as I stomp toward the bed under the recycled windows I installed.

"Lucky." She grumbles back the nickname I've just given her and moves her hand to pinch my ribs. "Put me down before your luck changes and you throw your back out."

I hiss at the sharp bite of pain that shoots up my side. "If you keep pinching me, I'm going to drop you."

"Then put me down!"

"You are so maddening. Why do you have to make everything so damn difficult?" I growl.

"Because I'm plus-sized. Difficult is my way of life," she bites back and makes a squeaky noise as I drop her on the bed.

I exhale heavily as I prop my hands on my hips and glare at her.

She points at my chest. "You wouldn't be out of breath if you had let me walk."

I lean over and press my hands onto the mattress to glower at her. "I'm only out of breath because you fought me the whole damn way."

"Oh, please." She scoffs and tucks her feet under the covers. "I'm sure you're used to tiny women you can throw over your shoulder. It must have been quite a shock hefting up all of me...pregnant or not."

I tilt my head and eye her with wicked challenge. Even sick and depleted, she still has a good amount of fight in her. It's alarming how much I like that. My voice is deep and promising when I reply, "Trust me, I can handle each bit of you every day of the week and twice on

Sundays." Her lush lips part as she stares up at me, stunned into a rare silence, so I take the opportunity to add, "I'm calling the nurse."

An hour later, I return to the mountain from Boulder with a pharmacy bag of meds the doctor called in for us, a sack full of Gatorades, ginger ale, and Pedialyte, and some fresh croissants I picked up from the Mercantile.

I knock and let myself in again, grateful to find Trista where I left her. Sitting on the edge of her bed, I watch her carefully as she swallows the pills with a Gatorade and accepts the flakey croissant. After she takes a few bites, she looks up at me with mirth dancing in her eyes. "Remember that time you carried me from my bathroom to my bed?"

I frown and glance over at the bathroom door just ten feet away from us. "It just happened. Of course I remember."

"That was really impressive," she says with a giggle, and I feel the heaviness in my chest lift as the light returns to her eyes. Her voice hitches low when she adds, "You are strong like a bull."

I rub the spot where she pinched me, certain a bruise is already forming. "You're pretty strong yourself."

"Sorry about that, but I'm not a delicate female used to being manhandled, Mr. Mountain Man." Her sleepy eyes look stunning in the light streaming in from the large windows above the bed.

"You were weak and could barely stand from the floor. What did you expect me to do? Just watch you struggle?"

She shrugs as she nibbles on her bread. "This croissant is delicious."

"It's from the Mercantile," I reply with a satisfied nod. "They get them fresh from a bakery in Boulder every morning. I'll bring you one every day if you think it'll help."

Her eyes blink rapidly with confusion. "Are you for real?"

"Yes, I'm for real," I state firmly, staring down at her in frustration. "I want to help, Trista. I've been giving you space these past couple of weeks, but I hate that you were sick and struggling on your own. This baby and what it's doing to your body is as much my responsibility as it is yours."

She sets her food down and moves to sit up, so I quickly move the pillow until it rests behind her.

"Wyatt, I'm used to taking care of myself," she offers, clearly trying to be polite, but she's giving off a coldness that I don't like. "Getting my meds and all this was kind of you, but eventually, I could have made it to town and got this all myself."

"But why would you want to when I'm literally right there?" I point toward the direction of my cabin.

Her eyes fixate on the bread in her hands. "Because I don't like people taking care of me."

"Why not?"

"I'm a strong girl." Her brows knit together as she shrugs dismissively. "And I've been taking care of myself since I was sixteen. And I was making my own breakfasts long before that. No offense, but…I don't need you."

My heart stops as I absorb the words she just shared. There's no question Trista is fucking strong. It's what I like most about her. It's what made me feel so confident about doing this surrogacy thing with her. But that glimpse she's given me into her past pains me. I can't imagine not having a parent make me breakfast. It's such a simple, basic thing that should be a given. Literally the bare minimum.

I inspect the lines on Trista's face a bit more, as if they'll reveal more about her. Perhaps this has to do with why she never wants children of her own? Maybe there's more to her story than her love of animals.

And I get that Trista doesn't need me. But what does she expect? I jizz in a cup, she gets pregnant with my baby, and that's it? I see her in nine months to collect my purchase? That's not how I want this to go. Not now that I've gotten to know her a bit. I want her to feel supported through all this…especially after what she shared with me.

I eye her warily. "Just so you know, I'm famously not good at doing nothing."

"I'm gathering that." Her lips press off to one side. "But you tending to me like this wasn't a part of our contract."

"Neither were ranch cups nor Tylenol syringes, so I guess I thought we were making up our own rules here." My voice ventures on a little desperate, so I try to soften my approach. "Living next door to each other doesn't mean we only need to see each other during appointments or in passing at the barn. If you need me, all you have to do is ask. You're never going to feel like a burden to me."

Her head tilts as she stares up at me with shock and awe all over her face, and I swear her eyes redden around the edges like she's fighting off tears. Has no one really ever tried to help her like this before?

My voice is soft when I add, "It's my hope that maybe we can become friends through all of this."

She swipes quickly at her eyes as her lips twitch with a poorly concealed smirk. "I don't have any friends who look like you."

"What is that supposed to mean?" I ask, feeling oddly offended.

"Tall, tattooed, bearded, and hotter than the Fourth of July?" Her gaze drifts down my body, and she shudders slightly. "Yeah, no...I don't have friends like you, Wyatt."

The rush of satisfaction that surges through me at the fact that she just told me she's attracted to me is embarrassing. I'm pushing forty years old. I should not be having some sort of prepubescent jolt of giddiness zap through me when I realize the hot girl at school likes me back. I am not in grade school, and having a crush on my surrogate is out of the question...even if I do hate that fucking name for her.

The problem is, Trista has been a hard one for me to get a read on. When I go out to bars with my brothers, I know instantly if a girl wants to fuck me. The eye contact, the body positioning. It's almost scientific how easy it is for me to tell if a girl is interested, even if she's trying to play it cool. It's a game that I play well.

But Trista keeps her cards close to her chest. She doesn't show emotion easily, so up until this moment, I couldn't tell if she liked me or hated me or, even worse....was indifferent to me. I was pretty sure my most appealing asset to her was the fact that I had a barn for her pig to live in.

She'd probably kill it at our poker nights.

"So you think I'm hot?" I ask, my voice low and dripping with a more flirtatious tone than I have any business delivering to the woman pregnant with my baby.

"Don't be dense, Mountain Man," she replies with a little scoff.

"You've got a vibe about you that works. Don't pretend you're unaware of it."

"I'm not unaware of it." My eyes drift down and linger on the beauty mark just above her lip. "I just didn't know you were aware of it. Didn't think you looked at me like that."

"Every woman within a fifty-foot radius would look at you like that. And it's annoying because Reggie does *not* appreciate the competition for being the hottest in the barn."

"Oh, and Millie does?" I retort, arching a challenging brow at the stunning woman before me.

"What are you talking about?" Her brows pinch together in the middle.

"You heard my mom. You're not exactly a pain in the ass to look at." I eye her in the bed, looking sick and depleted, knowing full well I would fuck her if she gave me the green light. *God, I'm sick.*

"Oh, please." Trista huffs, cheeks flush, showing a rare sign of insecurity. Confidence isn't something I've ever noticed this woman lacking, so this has me wildly fascinated.

"I'm serious." I gesture toward the steps that lead down to the barn. "My brothers basically had to roll their tongues into their mouths when they helped move you into this space. It's why I told them to keep their distance from you while you lived here. I don't want them to make you feel uncomfortable."

"Uncomfortable?" She barks out a laugh and shakes her head. "You think I can't handle the attention of a few mountain men?"

"Do you want to handle their attention?" I ask, my jaw taut as I steel myself for her answer that I might not like.

She stares back at me, her eyes flicking back and forth between mine. "One mountain man is plenty for me, thanks."

A rush of heat surges down to my cock at the glint in her eye. God, I was just finally starting to shake off my obsession with her. Now, she's stoking the fucking fire, and that is not a good thing.

Inhaling slowly, I decide to get back to the subject at hand. "Since we've determined it's not my face making you violently ill, maybe that means we can be more than just a surrogate and intended parent." I gesture to her and then to me. "Maybe we can be friends?"

"Friends." She repeats the word like she's never said it before, her eyes roving over my face for a long moment before a soft smile lights up her eyes. "I guess we can try it."

My brows lift in satisfaction at how easy that was for her to agree to. Then again, I'm pretty sure she's dehydrated and probably doesn't have her normal fight in her, but I'll take the win.

"Well, as your new friend, I have to ask…did I see a rabbit in here earlier this morning?"

Trista's eyes widen as she presses her lips together. Timidly, she reaches under the covers and pulls out an orange-and-white rabbit. She clutches it to her chest as her fingers stroke its floppy ears. "This is Strudel."

"Come again?" I grind out, pulling away from her and the living fuzzball in her hands.

"She's an English lop rabbit and was turned over at the rescue facility two days ago. Earl said she couldn't stay there because they didn't have the space."

"What is she doing here?" I ask, shaking my head back and forth.

Trista smiles. "I thought she could live here with me?"

"You know how I feel about pets in the apartment."

"I thought that was just pigs," she says, her teeth sinking into her lower lip. "But she's too little to be down in the barn with Reginald, and she's really well-behaved. She sleeps in a cage at night. And just *feel* how soft her fur is."

"I do not—" My voice is cut off when Trista starts dragging the rabbit along my cheek. The warm little furball makes a weird squeaky noise as its coat catches on my beard.

"Soft, right?" Her eyes are bright and hopeful as she waits for my reaction.

"Can you please stop booping the rabbit on my nose?" I pull her arm away from my face. "I don't want animals up here."

She sighs heavily. "Fine, I'll get rid of her."

"Thank you."

I stand to make my way toward the door and hear her say, "I'm sure someone will adopt her just to turn her into lucky rabbit-foot key chains. Lucky for them…not for poor Strudel."

I pause, my eyes rolling to the ceiling.

"Or maybe they'll turn her into a hearty rabbit stew," she adds, her voice cracking. "Never mind that she was the only one who snuggled me when I was puking my guts out this week because of this precious baby inside me."

I turn and eye her warily. "I know what you're doing."

Her nose wrinkles. "It's fine. I don't need that kind of comfort these next nine months. It wasn't a part of the contract, and we're not friends or anything, so…" Her voice trails off as she clutches the tiny animal to her cheek, dropping soft kisses on its long ears while hitting me with puppy dog eyes. My mind briefly flashes to the sight of a little girl with her eyes, begging me for a puppy.

The baby could have her eyes.

I drop my head and aggressively rub my hand over it, trying to put those thoughts well away. With a heavy sigh, I begrudgingly murmur, "Okay, friend, the rabbit can stay."

She gasps. "Did you hear that, Strudel? The mountain man said you get to live! Thank you, Wyatt. You're a great friend."

I grumble and walk out of her apartment, eyeing the mess of dishes in the sink. If she gets what she wants, then that means I can get what I want…and I want a few things for my maddening new friend here.

CHAPTER 24

WEEKS PREGNANT: 9 ½
ANIMALS ON THE MOUNTAIN: 3

Trista

O ver the next few days, I'm greeted by a brown Mercantile bag in front of my door. Every day, come rain or shine, before I head out for work at six o'clock, there's a buttery, flakey, gooey croissant waiting for me. One day, it had chocolate in it. Another day, a side of jam. Today's looks like some sort of donut/croissant combination, and I practically orgasm when I take a bite of it.

When I hoof it down the steps, I pause in stuffing my face as I spot Wyatt in Reginald's pen, filling his trough up with feed.

"What are you doing?" I ask, glancing inside the stall to see that this mountain man has mucked it and filled it with fresh water as well. Reggie is still passed out cold. Not even food will wake my fat boy up. A king needs his beauty sleep.

"Good morning to you too," Wyatt huffs as he steps out of Reggie's pen. He closes the gate and eyes me carefully, his gaze sweeping over my entire body in a way that makes my veins hum. "How are you feeling?"

I struggle to breathe normally as I stand in front of him. Something about him telling me I was attractive a few days ago has made things feel different between us. Almost…naughty, which I know sounds fucking weird because I'm not a child, but I feel guilty looking at him the way I do these days.

Today, I can't help but notice the flecks of gray in his beard and temples. He's not George Clooney–level gray by any means, but he's got a little salt mixed with that pepper, and it's not a bad look on a guy pushing forty.

And those frown lines he's rocking are totally self-induced. I swear he's always in a state of perpetual scowl. You'd think the potential of being a soon-to-be single father would have made him smile more often.

"I'm feeling fine," I state casually, tearing my eyes away from his body.

"What about the nausea?"

My stomach roils a little with just the mention of it. "It's still there, but it's getting better." Honestly, his breakfast deliveries help, but I'm not about to tell him that.

"Are you doing my chores?" I ask, wiping a bit of donut off the corner of my mouth.

Wyatt shrugs and moves over to Millie's pen next. "It's no trouble."

"Um…yes, it is. It's big trouble," I reply, following him as he heads outside to fill the bucket of water from the hydrant by the outdoor shower. "And I assume you're the one leaving me the baked goods every morning?"

He nods and smiles. "A croinut was today's special. It's a croissant/donut combination. Do you like it?"

"I love it, but it has to stop."

"Why?"

"Because I leave at the butt crack of dawn every day."

"So?"

"You don't need to wake up early, drive down the mountain, buy me fresh bakery items, and drive it back up here. That's crazy."

"I'm just being friendly," Wyatt says, placing a hand on my arm to move me out of the way so he can get back inside the barn.

I frown as I follow him down the alley, hating how I liked the heat of his palm on me. "But my body needs more than buttery, flakey, gooey goodness."

He pours the water into Millie's tank and nods. "Got it."

"You do?" My brows lift as I watch him.

"Yeah, I hear you." He nods stoically.

"Okay then," I reply with a sigh and then point at Reginald's pen. "And I do my own chores."

He pauses, his brows lifting at that response. "Is that right?"

"Yes," I reply, hating the way his eyes are burrowing into me right now. God, it feels hot in this barn.

He licks his lips slowly as his gaze travels down my body. "Hearing you loud and clear, friend."

I sigh heavily and turn to leave the barn to go to work. That was easy enough. Everly was right. Wyatt is just sweet and not at all psycho.

CHAPTER 25

WEEKS PREGNANT: 10
ANIMALS ON MOUNTAIN: 3

Trista

My phone buzzes in my back pocket as I walk the fence line with Millie and Reginald. I smile as Millie nudges my butt, trying to find the source of the foreign sound.

> Everly: Hey Trista, how are you doing? I heard you weren't feeling well. ☹

I roll my eyes at that comment, not at all surprised that my bout of morning sickness made its way back to Everly. If she texts me weekly, I'm guessing she texts her uncle even more.

> Me: Hey crazy kid, I'm doing a little better now, thanks.

The meds haven't completely healed me, but I notice that if I try to snack more often, the nausea doesn't get quite so intense.

> Everly: Great because Uncle Wyatt told me I could invite you to my graduation party! It's in a couple of weeks, and it would mean so much to me to have you there. Can I send you an invitation?

I frown at this surprising invitation. The truth is, I would love to go because my bank account has never looked better, and I owe it all to this kid. But this past week, I've been a little overwhelmed by her uncle.

I thought the daily breakfast deliveries would stop. They didn't.

He just started giving me more of a variety. One day, it was a couple of boiled eggs. Another day, it was fruit and a protein bar.

Then the HelloFresh grocery box appeared on my doorstep, and the label said it was catered to healthy eating while pregnant.

Real subtle, Wyatt.

And as if things couldn't get any more intense, Wanda the cleaning lady showed up yesterday. When I refused to let her come inside, she looked like she was about to cry. Apparently, Wyatt had prepaid her to come here weekly for the next several months, and if I refused her, then she was going to have to give him the money back. And she needed the cash to fix the foundation on her house, or it was literally going to crumble to the ground.

I freaking let Wanda come in and clean.

I've never had a cleaning lady in my life, though, so I couldn't just sit back and watch her clean my mess that had seriously gotten away from me. I rolled up my sleeves and scrubbed the tub right alongside her. She cuddled Strudel, and we watched *The Real Housewives of Salt Lake City* on my iPad while we worked. Honestly, it was kind of a lovely evening. Jen Shaw is crazy, and I was happy to have someone to chat with about it.

And I swear my car was almost on empty last night, and this morning, the gas tank was magically full.

My eyes fly wide when I see a large delivery vehicle parked in front of the barn. "What in the world is that now?" I ask out loud to Millie and Reggie, who just ignore me.

I shoot a quick text back to Everly that I'll RSVP soon and scurry my way through the muddy pasture. When I walk into the barn, I see two men hauling a giant memory foam mattress up my apartment steps.

"Can I help you guys?" I ask, my voice rising in pitch as they struggle to make their way up the steps. "I think you maybe got the wrong place because I didn't order a new bed."

"Our instructions say it goes in the apartment above the barn," the old guy at the bottom says as he squat lifts. "And there are no other barns on this mountain."

"Okay, but I didn't order this," I repeat again, nervous that I'm going to get slapped with a big bill that I absolutely will not be able to pay.

"The order is under a Wyatt Fletcher," the younger delivery guy at the top says. "It's all paid for."

My head lowers in submission. Of course it's from psycho Wyatt. I'm actually shocked it didn't come with a new sofa and end tables.

"We already got the base set up and fully operating, so we'll be out of your hair real soon."

"Fully operating?" I growl in frustration as I follow them up into my apartment and watch as they finish setting up the giant monstrosity that looks crazy expensive. Which is why this mountain man has officially lost his damn mind if he thinks this is how friends interact.

When the deliverymen leave, I hear a crack of wood splitting off in the distance and decide it's time for me to have another chat with my new "friend."

I trudge my way through the mud up toward Wyatt's house. It's rained a lot this past week, which would normally depress me if I were still living in the city. But rain on the mountain? It's too beautiful to hate. It stirs up something special in the atmosphere, so maybe it's stirred up something in him, and that's why he's acting like a maniac with the gifts.

Another crack of wood echoes, and I spot Wyatt up the hill behind his house. He's dressed in his standard flannel and jeans, chopping wood like it's his job. *And I hate how good he looks doing that job.*

My breath quickens as I take a moment to admire the view. Clearly, I'm extremely hormonal because that's the only excuse that makes sense for me not having more self-control than this. Because while my mind is raging mad at him, my body just wants a hug from him. But like… the vagina kind of hug. I want his mountain-rain scent all over me.

His large hands grip the ax as his broad shoulders twist and rotate to descend upon the unsuspecting wood. My God, how did this man ever doubt that I found him attractive? What I wouldn't do to be that tree stump right now.

A twig snaps under my foot, and Wyatt looks up from the pieces of wood that have just dropped to the ground to find me approaching. "Hey," he calls out, slightly out of breath while tossing the wood into a wheelbarrow.

"Hey," I repeat sharply, telling my hormones and crotch hugs to get lost as I come to a stop on the other side of his wood-chopping station.

"You feeling okay? Need anything?" Concern is etched in his eyebrows as he inspects every part of my body. He's been doing that a lot this past week. Watching me. And he has an uncanny way of making me feel uneasy and turned on all at the same time.

Fuck you, hormones!

"I feel great, and I need nothing," I state firmly for the fifth time this week, wishing like hell he didn't have to see me praying to the porcelain gods because it's clearly unearthed some sort of caveman protection mode that I cannot seem to turn off.

"Good." Wyatt nods and rests the sharp part of his ax on the stump while lazily propping his elbow on it.

I tear my eyes away from his body and add, "I especially don't need that expensive-looking bed that just got delivered to my apartment."

"Oh, it came?" Wyatt squints down the mountain toward the barn and nods like he hasn't been the biggest pain in my ass lately. "Good. It's adjustable, so if they didn't get it hooked up right, let me know, and I'll come take a look."

"I don't need an adjustable bed."

"Why not?"

"Because I'm not geriatric, for one!"

He frowns. "It's supposed to be great for pregnancy. Once you get further along, I think you'll really like it. You know you're not supposed to sleep on your back, right?"

"Wyatt," I hiss, my hands firm on my hips. "People have been pregnant for centuries without memory foam hydraulic-lift mattresses. Women had babies in caves, for God's sake."

"I know, but all the baby books say that sleep is important in the first trimester, and that mattress up there is old. It needed an upgrade."

"You could have bought a mattress from Goodwill, and it still would have been the nicest thing I ever slept on!"

He scowls at that response.

"And your daily breakfast deliveries have to stop. We talked about this." I press my hands to my belly, which is definitely more carbs than baby at only ten weeks pregnant. The changes in my body aren't yet obvious to the naked eye, except for the intense veins in my engorged boobs. Those puppies are practically pornographic. "I am perfectly capable of feeding myself." My voice is venturing on shrill because I'm sad to see the food delivery stop, but it's necessary for my sanity.

"I thought about it, and the breakfast is nonnegotiable," he answers stiffly, his gaze lingering on where my hand is on my stomach before snapping up to meet my eyes. "If you want something specific, just let me know because I'm going to continue dropping breakfast off at your door every morning until that baby is born."

"But I don't want it."

"I don't care. I'll try to stop everything else, but I'm not stopping that."

My jaw drops as I stare at this psychopath trying to force-feed me breakfast every day. "Wyatt, none of this was in our contract."

"I know, but we're friends now." He states it like that's the most obvious answer in the world.

I slice my hands through my hair, feeling completely out of control, which is a rare thing for me, and another thought occurs to me. "Did you fill my gas tank up last night?"

"I had extra gasoline for the mower, so..."

"Wyatt!"

"What?"

"You're like...dad bombing me!"

"I'm what?"

"Like love bombing but in the weird mountain-man surrogate-dad sort of way. You have to stop. I'm feeling better now, and I have everything I need. Can you be a little less friendly for a hot minute? I actually like taking care of Reginald."

"I know, but I'm already doing chores for Millie," he says, swinging the sharp edge of his ax into the log so his hands are free to pick up the loose pieces of wood and toss them over to his wheelbarrow. "I'm just being practical."

I open my mouth to argue but am distracted by his ass in those faded jeans as he bends over. Coming up here was a bad idea. I should have just called him. Watching him do this makes it hard to remember that I'm mad at him. But I am mad at him.

I tear my eyes off his biceps, which are stretching his flannel sleeves, and force a deep, cleansing breath before I add, "I'm not some weak thing that needs to be taken care of. And I don't like feeling indebted to people. It makes me uncomfortable."

"These are gifts, Trista." Wyatt stares back at me, looking mortally wounded. "You're not indebted to me in any way. I hate that you'd think that."

His words should make me feel better, but they don't. They make me feel worse. Like I'm broken because I can't accept someone doing something nice for me.

And truth be told, I love everything he's given me. The groceries, the baked goods…I'm sure that thousand-plus-dollar bed is going to feel like heaven. God, I love it all. But I know what getting comfortable with people means. What counting on those you love means.

It means it hurts ten times worse when they leave.

"Can you just try to back off a little bit on the helping?" I ask, swallowing the knot in my throat to add, "It's important for me to be independent."

He nods slowly as he watches me. The furrow in his brow clearly indicates he doesn't fully understand me, and frankly, I don't even understand myself. I don't even hang out with my coworkers or Avery when they ask. I just like my independence. It's natural for Wyatt to be helpful and involved, but it's foreign to me. I've been on my own for so long that I don't know what it's like to be part of a team.

Deciding to change the subject and lighten the mood so I don't spiral into a depressive, self-loathing episode, I gesture to his pile of logs. "What is it you're even doing here?"

Wyatt frowns at the obvious display. "Chopping wood."

"What for, though?" I ask, realizing I've always wondered

why those hot guys on TikTok do all that wood chopping. "Like where's all that wood going? Is it for an actual purpose, or is it just a mountain-man-aesthetic thing?"

"Mountain-man-aesthetic thing?" He scowls, clearly not liking my suggestion that he would chop wood for anything other than some meaningful purpose. "I chop for wildfire mitigation. I have to constantly keep a clear zone around my house to prevent it from igniting in the event of a catastrophic fire. Because I have to chop so much, I built a masonry heater in my home. It burns wood and traps the heat in the brick chambers to distribute slowly. Goes through way less wood than a wood-burning furnace and causes a lot less pollution, which makes for improved air quality up here."

My mood shifts as I feel oddly proud of this overbearing, over-generous, eco-savvy guy I let knock me up with his ranch cup sperm. "Definitely not for TikTok, then."

"I don't even have TikTok," Wyatt huffs. He sounds funny when he says "TikTok." He sounds funny when he says anything outside of grunts and basic conversation he's forced into by me. "Chopping wood is kind of like my therapy. It's meditative. My mind stops racing when I'm here."

"Does your mind race a lot?" I watch him carefully because I haven't even begun to scratch the surface on this guy yet, and I'm curious about what makes him tick. What causes that nearly permanent glower on his face most days? And how did us becoming friends turn into him going nuts and dad bombing me?

"I guess so." He pulls his ax out of the stump as he sets a fresh log up on his chopping station. "My dad always called me a 'five minutes from now' person. Always stressing about the future and what's to come."

"Sounds exhausting."

"It is…which is why I love chopping wood." He takes a swing, and a satisfying snap of wood draws my eyes to the log he split with just one cut. He frowns and juts his bearded chin toward me. "What about you?"

"What about me?"

"Are you a now person or a 'five minutes from now' person?"

My brows lift as I ponder that question. "I think I'm more of a 'five minutes late' person. Especially because I'm supposed to be helping Avery this afternoon, and I should have left ten minutes ago."

He laughs and nods, and I get little butterflies in my belly at the sight of it. It's not easy to make this man smile, but I feel like a million bucks when I do.

"What's in the bag?" Wyatt asks as I turn to walk away.

"Oh gosh, I got so distracted by all this hard wood that I forgot I grabbed this." I trudge back over to Wyatt and hand him the bag, our fingers brushing as it exchanges hands. Heat floods my face as I add, "Just a little 'congrats on becoming a dad' present. It just arrived yesterday."

"You didn't have to get me a present."

"I know, but maybe you can consider this a cease-fire request for your overly kind gestures."

He harrumphs and pulls out a monogrammed coffee mug I ordered for him.

"Dad Era?" He shoots a puzzled look my way.

I smile brightly. "Because you're such a huge fan of Taylor Swift."

Wyatt's face falls. "What?"

"You're a Swiftie, right?" I point coyly at him. "It sure seemed like it in that video of you at the concert with Everly and your brothers. Man, how many bracelets did you trade with people? Your arm was stacked."

"Alright, who showed you that?" Wyatt loses all good humor on his face. "Was it Calder? I told him to leave you the fuck alone." His jaw clenches as he looks up the mountain where his brother's cabin rests.

His barely contained fury over being outed as a Swiftie has me erupting into a fit of giggles. "It was Everly."

His demeanor instantly shifts. "Well, fuck."

"Yeah, take it easy, Mr. Mountain Man. That's your niece."

He grumbles something under his breath I can't quite hear.

"Speaking of your niece, she invited me to her graduation party in a couple of weeks."

Wyatt's knowing blue eyes find mine, looking a touch more green in the forest.

"She said it was your idea?"

He shrugs. "Seems like a *friend* thing to do."

Heat floods my body because the way he just said *friend* felt a lot friendlier than it should. But maybe that's just my hormones talking.

"It wouldn't be weird for you if I went?"

"Why would it be weird?" Wyatt props his hand on his ax and eyes me seriously.

"Well, I'm assuming a lot of your friends and family will be there, and I'm not sure how many people know about this situation or if you even want to talk about it. Surely, they'll wonder who I am."

"Trista, this may come as a shock to you, but I don't give a fuck what most people think." His eyes are lethal on mine, and a rush of heat moves through me, settling heavily in my groin. He's hot when he's threatening. "The only people who really know about what we're doing here are my family. As far as I'm concerned, it's no one else's business."

A slow smile spreads across my face. "Sounds good to me. And I already have a gift in mind for Everly. I'm going to have a mug made that says Cousin Era on it. Think she would like that?"

"Definitely," he replies, and affection blooms on his face as if it's the first time he's considered the fact that he's giving his niece a cousin.

"Okay, then I'll come." I nod and smile.

"You'll come," he repeats and smiles back.

Our eyes hold each other for a moment, and I swallow the lump in my throat at the way he's looking at me. My face feels hot when I give an awkward little wave and turn to leave, only to hear Wyatt call out, "Plan on riding with me and my brothers to the graduation party and to our twelve-week scan coming up. It's more fuel efficient, okay?"

I pause and exhale heavily. I came up here to give him a piece of my mind about being overly friendly, and now I have a new mattress, a guaranteed daily breakfast delivery, and a couple of rides to town. Something tells me this mountain man isn't used to being told no. If I want to survive on Mount Millie for a full nine months, I'll need to make sure he realizes that I know how to get what I want as well.

CHAPTER 26

WEEKS PREGNANT: 12
ANIMALS ON THE MOUNTAIN: 3

Wyatt

"We're just going to tuck this right under here," the ultrasound tech says as she rolls a towel over Trista's jeans and pulls the fabric so low I can see the curves of her groin.

My hands ball into fists as I turn away from the exam table, trying my damnedest not to ogle the skin on full display in front of me. Jesus Christ, her body is something else. It's soft and curved in all the right places. And I've shamelessly noticed the change in her breasts these past several weeks too. They're practically bursting through the fabric of the cropped tank she's wearing today. She usually doesn't dress so revealing, so I'm ashamed to admit how many times I've caught myself looking.

It's no secret that I've always preferred curvy women. When my brothers and I do our boys' nights in Denver, we can all depend on not being attracted to the same girl based on our types. I like women with curves who can handle a good romp in the bedroom. Calder likes feisty women who act like they hate him until they're fucking like animals in the car. And Luke gravitates toward the quiet girls… the ones who look too innocent to have a one-night stand but make an exception just for him.

We don't overlap on our taste in women…except for one time. And ever since then, we've learned to stay in our fucking lanes.

Trista Matthews is definitely in my lane, and if I think too much about why I picked her to be my surrogate, I start to feel really uncomfortable.

"Wyatt, don't be so awkward." Trista reaches out and grabs my wrist to pull me toward the bed. The sensation of her skin on mine sends shivers up my arm.

"Just trying to give you privacy." I scowl at the tech, who's watching our interaction with rapt fascination.

"What is there to see? The fact that my jeans don't button quite as good as they used to?" She laughs as she props her hand behind her head. "Our contract says you get to be in the room when I give birth, so no need to be bashful now."

"You guys are cute," the tech says as she readies the ultrasound machine. "Were you friends before you agreed to be his surrogate?"

"We're still figuring out the friends part," Trista cajoles, and my brows furrow at that response.

I've tried really hard the past week to back off on the gifts, even though everything I've given her seems like valuable things anyone growing a human in their body would appreciate.

She doesn't get how impressed I am by her. The fact that she used a fucking Tylenol syringe of my sperm and now there's life growing inside her is a miracle of science. I want to make sure she's taken care of during this nine-month contract. She deserves at least that much, and I get the sense that no one has ever really done that for her.

Although I'll admit putting gas in her car was a bit much. But at least I canceled the appointment I made to buy her new tires at Tire Depot in Boulder. That would have sent her over the edge, for sure. I can maybe try that once we're in the second trimester. Spread my "dad bombing" out a bit.

I watch the tech squirt gel all over Trista's stomach, which looks pretty flat still to me. There's a slight rounding happening below her belly button, but I can't tell if that's baby or not. She looks great to me either way.

"It appears someone's awake," the tech coos, and I glance up at the screen to see the video image of my baby dancing.

"Holy shit," I rumble, my voice hoarse as I gawk at how much it's changed.

"From a jelly bean to a plum!" the tech confirms with a big, toothy smile. "It'll be hard to get the measurements with all the movement, but everything looks really great at first glance, Dad."

Her dad reference causes a rush of emotion to swell in my chest, and I watch in awe as the baby wiggles and dances on the screen. Something about this little digital bundle looking like an actual baby now has made this all a thousand times more real.

I blink through the burn in my eyes as the baby's hand moves up toward its mouth. My voice is deep and garbled when I ask, "Is it true they can suck their thumb at this gestation? That's what one of the baby books says."

"You've been reading baby books?" the tech asks, her voice full of shock.

I shrug because it's like the bare fucking minimum effort. "After Trista got really bad morning sickness, I wanted to make sure I knew what else might be coming for her. You know...so I can help out more."

"Oh, he loves helping," Trista murmurs with a laugh and pats my arm teasingly.

I frown once again as the tech replies to my earlier question. "Well, you're correct. They can suck their thumb at this point in the pregnancy. They are also fully formed now...all their fingers, toes, and organs are present and accounted for. The teeth are even beginning to develop."

"Teeth?" Trista cringes. "Is this a *Twilight* baby? I didn't know babies were born with teeth."

The tech laughs. "Just the buds. Although babies can actually be born with teeth. It's really rare, though."

I can't help the smile that grows on my face. The baby isn't here yet, and I am already proud of it.

"Measurements are all good, and the due date is on track. Can't quite see the gender yet, though. You'll find that out at your next ultrasound around twenty-week gestation…that is…if you want to know. Maybe you want to be surprised?"

The tech looks at me, and I feel a surge of anxiety. For someone who constantly stresses about the future, how had this thought escaped me? How have I not even wondered what sex of a baby I'm having? Surely I need to figure out the baby room before the baby is here. Pink? Blue? Maybe green so the baby can decide what color it likes. Or go gender-neutral with yellow and then be surprised? Can I really wait that long?

Trista appears to be waiting for my answer too, so I mumble, "I'll, um…need to give that some more thought."

The tech winks at me, and my mind races through the follow-up appointment with the OB. So much has changed in the past few months. A new person living on the mountain, a new future to look forward to—a totally different future. I'm going to need to get a baby room ready. I'm going to have to figure out paternity leave and childcare. Maybe start researching schools and shit.

Jesus Christ, I'm really doing this. I'm actually going to be a dad.

There's not a lot I've accomplished in life to be proud of. In fact, Calder and Luke and I have fucked up more times than we care to talk about this past decade. It was always a source of stress for my dad because we didn't care about the family business. All we cared about was mountain life and fucking our way through half of Denver. I hate that it took him dying for me to finally get my shit together.

But this…this feels right. It feels important. This feels like something my dad would be proud of.

I just wish he was here to see it.

Trista

"For the love of God, am I going to have to buy new bras?" I exclaim as I sit across from Wyatt at the Mercantile and glance down at my quad-boob situation. After we met with the OB-GYN, he asked if I wanted to have dinner, and since I was too tired to cook, it sounded like a great idea to do with my new friend.

But my bra situation is very unfortunate, especially with this tighter top I chose to wear today. With a heavy sigh, I tug at the top of my bra to try to get my girls back in their jail cells. I used to be a solid D-cup, but whatever is happening to my chesticles now is most definitely not fitting in my D-cup bras. I hold my hand to the side of my mouth and use my best flight attendant voice as I add, "Ladies, please return to your assigned seats."

I smile and glance up at Wyatt, expecting to get a chuckle out of him, but all he does is grab his glass of beer and take a long chug, downing half of it in one go. Lame friend.

He turns his scowl to the patrons watching us curiously. They've been staring ever since we walked in and ordered our food. It felt like one of those record-scratching moments when the city slicker walks into a biker bar. Jamestown sure is an interesting place. I haven't really gotten to see much of it with my crazy work schedule, unfortunately. And the last time I stepped into the Mercantile was my first meeting with Wyatt, which feels like a lifetime ago now.

I lean forward to murmur under my breath, "Why does it feel like everyone is watching us?"

"Probably because you just talked to your breasts," Wyatt deadpans.

I glare over at him and state the obvious. "They've been staring at us long before my titty talk. I just decided to give 'em a little show."

Wyatt scowls as he lazily surveys the crowd, shooting daggers at anyone who doesn't immediately look away. "I suppose they're not used to seeing me with a woman."

"Huh?"

His lips purse together as he rests his elbows on the table. "I don't date, really, so seeing you here with me not once but twice is probably why everyone is rubbernecking. Just ignore them. Our situation is none of their business."

Wyatt's eyes glance down at my belly, and I can't help but notice a tiny glint to his gaze that wasn't there before our appointment today. I think the grumpy mountain man might actually be happy today. And he should be. Today was a big milestone for us both. All the baby books say that once you're out of the first trimester, the morning sickness subsides, and the risk of miscarriage goes down a lot, so this is getting real now. And I have the peek-a-boobs to prove it.

Aside from the shitty morning sickness, I feel like I'm doing pretty good at this pregnancy stuff so far. I'm keeping my mind detached from the emotions of it and focusing on being the cow. And that stupid bed Wyatt bought me gives me the best sleep of my life. I swear it was crafted out of the foreskin of newborn babies it's so comfortable. Not that foreskin is comfortable. I wouldn't know, I guess. But I venture to bet it's soft. Adult penis skin is crazy soft. At least what I remember of it. It's been a while since I've touched a penis. *Boy, this analogy is really getting away from me.*

"Here you guys go," the female bartender says, forcing me to tear my eyes off the happy mountain man as she places two plates of food in front of us.

"Thanks, Judy," Wyatt says, ready to tuck into the hot roast beef he ordered.

"I'm Trista." I offer my hand to introduce myself. If people are going to stare, they might as well know who they're staring at.

"The one with the puppy from a few months back, right?" Judy asks as she shakes my hand. "Whatever happened to that sweetheart?"

"She was adopted!"

"Oh, that makes me really happy." Judy's eyes dart from me to Wyatt and back to me. "So are you the one who…" She gestures back and forth between us with a knowing look.

"Just friends," Wyatt harrumphs as he shoves a forkful of beef into his mouth.

"And neighbors," I add with a much warmer smile than Wyatt offers. "I'm living in the apartment above the barn on his property."

"Oh, you're living up there?" Judy's eyes are saucers as she glances back at Wyatt. "I'd heard some rumblings around town about someone else driving up there a lot. How are you handling those crazy Fletcher boys?"

I cover a laugh. "I really only see this crazy one. He keeps me pretty well hidden, I guess."

Wyatt grunts in response to that.

Judy lifts her brows and leans in close. "Well, you let me know if they get to be too much for you, okay? I've known them a long time now and seen them through some crazy stuff."

Wyatt clears his throat and stops eating to eye Judy with a know-ing look. She stops herself and pats Wyatt on the shoulder.

"Oh, I'm sure you'll be fine," she says with a warm smile. "They're good boys…these days, at least. And it's high time that mountain had a woman up there again." She pauses to gesture to our plates. "Anyway, you two enjoy your food. Let me know if I can get you anything else."

My eyes are wide and blinking as she walks away like she didn't just drop a little bomb on our meal here. I turn a curious look at Wyatt. "What woman is she referring to?"

He shakes his head dismissively. "It's nothing."

"Doesn't sound like nothing," I pry because it sounds like the exact opposite of nothing. It sounds juicy. "You just said you don't date, so was it one of your brothers' girlfriends who lived up there?"

Wyatt looks visibly uncomfortable as he struggles to eat.

"Was it someone you had relations with? Like of the sexual variety?"

His eyes snap to mine, full of warning, but I will not be deterred.

"My interest is piqued. Maybe I'll go get the dirt from Judy or one of the locals. They're much chattier than you." I move to get up, and he sets his fork down and reaches out to grab my hand, halting me in my tracks. His hand is warm, and I love the contrast of it against my skin so much that I have to fight the urge to turn my palm up and thread my fingers in his.

When I sit back down, his brow furrows as he quickly releases his hold on me. "There was a woman who lived in the barn apartment. She was new to town and a bartender here at the Mercantile. She needed a place to live, and, well…it was convenient."

"Kind of like me," I offer cheerily.

"She was nothing like you," he nearly growls, and I get the distinct impression this woman wasn't just a local needing a place to live. She was something much more.

"Anyway, don't worry about her. I gutted the apartment after she split. It's much nicer now than when she lived there."

I nod slowly, wanting to pry further, but I gather that I've pushed this mountain man to his limit, so I should stop.

Wyatt eyes me thoughtfully for a moment, the muscle in his jaw twitching as he chews his food and swallows. "What about you?"

"What about me?" I grab a french fry and pop it into my mouth.

"What's your dating situation?" There's an intensity in Wyatt's eyes that wasn't there a second ago. He probably thinks if I refuse to share my dating life story, then he's in the clear, but the joke's on him because I'm an open book.

"Well, I'm not a monk, but I don't date much." I sigh heavily and prop my chin on my hand. "I've never even had a boyfriend, so there's nothing good to really even share."

Wyatt's brows furrow as he tilts his head. "Never?"

"Nope," I reply with a shrug. "Guys I've hooked up with just seem to slowly stop talking to me. I pretty much always assume it's because I'm fat."

Wyatt drops his fork on his plate, and the undiluted rage I see in his eyes is alarming. "You aren't fat."

I laugh and shake my head. "Wyatt, it's okay. I like myself just fine. And I can admit that I'm fat. I'm okay with it."

"You're beautiful."

"Well, thank you, but you can be beautiful and fat, you know?" I wink and kind of want to punch him.

"I didn't say you can't."

My brows lift knowingly. "Are we fighting again?"

"No, we're not. I just…" Wyatt presses his hands together in front of him, clearly frustrated with this line of conversation. "You said guys stop talking to you because you're fat. Therefore, you put being fat in a negative light. That's what I'm questioning."

My head jerks back as he targets me with my own internalized fatphobia that I didn't even realize I had. I don't dislike my size. I like my body. I've always been big, so I've embraced it. I look in the mirror and tell myself I'm beautiful on a pretty regular basis. Even more beautiful now. My body is doing this pregnancy thing extraordinarily well, so I dare say my body is the shit.

But when it comes to romantic partners, I suppose I haven't been giving myself the same respect.

"You're right," I offer simply because deep down, the fat thing is just the excuse I use for why I don't let men get close enough to me to be more than sex. The real reason is much more intense and would probably take years of therapy to unpack.

Wyatt nods firmly. "I just think confidence and independence are two qualities that some men find hard to handle in a woman, and you just haven't found a guy strong enough not to be afraid of it."

My lips part in shock at this normally very quiet mountain man's astute observation. I feel overwhelmed with the sense of wanting to fall head over heels in love with him or crawl across the table and fuck him in front of everyone staring at us right now. Maybe I want both.

Fuck you, hormones!

I steel myself to get my thoughts back on track. To not paint a picture of myself as this needy, insecure girl because I am not. I am woman, hear me roar.

"The real reason is that I'm too selfish, I guess. I like just taking care of myself and my animals. Plus, not wanting kids can be a deal breaker for a lot of guys. If I have my animals, what more do I need in life?"

Wyatt watches me thoughtfully for a moment, and I can't help but see the mischievous glint flicker in his eyes. His voice is low and breathy when he asks, "What do you do if you have…needs? Besides your trusty pink vibrator, obviously."

The corner of his mouth tugs up into a teasing smirk as heat instantly floods my cheeks. God, this man can go from grumpy stick-in-the-mud know-it-all to wicked challenging sex on a stick in the blink of an eye. Those sundown sessions feel like ages ago now, but one little look from Wyatt, and I'm right back on his bed, getting myself off with his scent all around me.

My voice is coy when I give him my answer. "I have some non-battery-operated options. Sort of a no-strings-attached roster that I access whenever I feel the *need*." I pause to breathe because it suddenly feels very hot in this room. "My friend Avery calls it my bullpen."

And if I'm honest, as much as I've enjoyed that *bullpen* on and off over the years, and despite how horny these pregnancy hormones are making me, I haven't once thought to hit them up.

The brooding man in front of me obviously has nothing to do with that.

Wyatt nods, watching me seriously, but says nothing. I really hate when he does that. Usually, I can tell what he's thinking, but tonight, the look in his eye makes me wish he'd say the quiet part out loud.

I stare back at him as our eyes play a game of chicken for who will look away first. I'm very competitive, so without blinking, I ask, "What about you? Do you have a bullpen of your own?"

He watches me thoughtfully for a moment, his eyes dropping to my lips before he replies, "I haven't felt the need to access it lately."

My lips purse together curiously. "Why is that?"

A low rumble vibrates his chest as I watch his square jaw slide from side to side. "Because I might be focusing too much on getting into someone else's bullpen."

With that simple reply, there's a shift in the atmosphere. Suddenly, the air feels heavy and dense, like the calm before a really bad storm. Our food goes cold, and the gawkers around us disappear from my periphery. Right now, it's just me and this bearded man staring at each other for what feels like a lifetime and a split second all at the same time.

I open my mouth to ask what he means by that exactly when a glass shatters from somewhere behind the bar. It causes Wyatt to break eye contact with me, and I take that reprieve to drag in a deep, cleansing breath. *Jesus Christ, I need to get control of these hormones.*

We're quiet and contemplative for the rest of dinner, and when Wyatt parks in front of the barn to drop me off and do his nightly check on Millie, I wonder what his answer would have been if I'd asked him what I nearly asked him: *Whose bullpen is he trying to get into?*

I'm just about to do the smart thing and say good night when he shocks me in the alley of the barn by pulling me into him. All the air escapes my lungs as my hands splay out on his chest and he wraps his arms around my shoulders. He presses his face down into my neck and holds me for a moment in the quiet of the barn.

Wyatt and I don't touch a lot...in fact, it's probably a bad idea for him to make a habit of it because I was painfully reminded at dinner tonight that it's been a while since I've felt the heat of a man. And if I'm not careful, I'll misinterpret that naughty look in Wyatt's eye tonight and think it's my bullpen he's set his sights on.

But gosh, he feels too good to pull away from.

His hot breath sends shivers down my neck as he says, "In case I don't say this enough...thank you."

"For what exactly?" I murmur, my fingers flexing on his sculpted chest as I inhale deeply and relish in his woodsy, mountain-rain scent.

"For having a baby for me," he replies simply, and his hand moves up to comb his fingers into my hair. It feels so good and so comforting my knees wobble, my body wanting to just fall into him like I fall into that expensive mattress every night. "I hope you know how much this means to me."

He releases me but stays close, his hands rubbing my arms as his blue eyes stare down at my face with so much reverence my heart thunders in my chest.

I offer a wobbly smile and croak out, "Don't mention it, Mountain Man."

A devastating smile lights up his face as he releases me to head up to my little apartment above the barn. As my shaky, lust-laden legs climb the stairs, I have one single, solitary thought on my mind... something this mountain needs more than anything. Even more than me getting laid...

CHAPTER 27

WEEKS PREGNANT: 13
ANIMALS ON THE MOUNTAIN: 4

Wyatt

"Abso-fuckin'-lutely not," I growl as I park in front of the barn and stare at the mini horse Trista is currently preparing to lead off a trailer. I step out of my truck and stomp over to her, shaking my head adamantly.

"Wyatt!" She draws out my name with a big, toothy smile from inside the trailer. "You're home early."

"What the hell is going on?" My teeth are clenched as I come eye to eye with a horse whose tongue is hanging out of its mouth.

"This is Handsome!" She wraps her arm around his neck and gives him a hug. "Ain't he a beaut?"

"What the fuck is wrong with him?" I ask when I notice his tongue just sort of hangs there permanently.

"Nothing!" She swerves an accusing glare at me. "He's perfect just the way he is."

"Well, that's not technically true," a male voice corrects, and I glance past Trista to see a guy stepping out from behind the gate inside the trailer. He drops a bag of feed on the trailer floor and lays a hand on the back of the chestnut mini horse. "He has a neuromuscular disease that caused the relaxed-tongue issue. I'm afraid it's untreatable. Just be sure any buckets or feeders you use with him don't have any sharp edges, and make sure he doesn't start chewing on your wooden fence out there. Lacerations are kind of common with this issue."

He looks at me like he's giving me these instructions. Like this horse is now my responsibility. "I'm sorry, but who the fuck are you?" I snap, my temper getting the best of me as I stare at the guy who looks about my age but several inches shorter than me. Hell, I think he might even be shorter than Trista.

"Wyatt, this is Avery." Trista smiles and places her hand on his shoulder. "He's the large-animal vet in Denver who I help. I've mentioned him to you before. We've been friends for years."

Avery's a man? Her best friend…is a dude?

"Gosh, how long has it been?" He scratches the back of his neck as he squints at Trista. "Ten years?"

"I was nineteen when I started at my first shelter, so that must be about right." Trista smiles brightly. "Avery and I met when we were both asked to be guest judges for a golden retriever talent show—"

"At the downtown library," he says, finishing her sentence. "God, that was such a weird event."

"Weirdly awesome," Trista exclaims, laughing and looking back at me. "This one contestant just lay on the ground and had his golden eat treats out of his mouth. Not at all a talent, but it was still fantastic. Honestly the best Sunday afternoon I can remember in a long time."

"Jesus, you were only nineteen back then?" Avery asks, frowning over at the woman currently pregnant with my child. The way his eyes twinkle at her irritates the fuck out of me. "I thought you were older. You seemed older."

Trista's jaw drops as she whacks him on the arm. "You better not be saying I looked old!"

"No, no, no." Avery laughs and clutches Trista's hand to his arm. "You looked beautiful. You just seemed so mature for that age."

"I'm an old soul." Trista smiles over at him and bats her eyes.

I clear my throat to snap their attention back to me. I have yet to meet a single person in Trista's life, and the fact that it's this guy Avery who Trista spends an obscene amount of time with…*unpaid*, doesn't sit well with me. Especially because I thought Avery was a girl until two fucking minutes ago.

"Thought you were a chick." The intrusive thought spills out through my clenched teeth.

Avery laughs a boyish laugh that I hate. "Not last time I checked."

"It's just that Trista spends a lot of time with you," I add, shoving the sleeves of my flannel up to reveal my ink. It's a douchebag move that I'm not proud of, but I'm highly agitated at the moment. "She spends a lot of hours *volunteering* for you. I take it your vet clinic is for charity?"

"Gosh, no." Trista laughs nervously, her head snapping back to Avery. "I told you he's training me, Wyatt."

Avery's eyes narrow on me like a bull getting ready to charge. "She's got big goals, and I'm trying to help her achieve them, that's all. I think Trista is capable of great things."

"You don't have to tell me that," I reply curtly, stepping closer to the trailer, my eyes locked on his, the horse's floppy tongue lolling in the corner of my eye. "Just hard to make those dreams a reality when she's always working for free."

"Wyatt," Trista snaps, her voice echoing inside the small trailer and spooking the animal.

"Lucky she found such a great situation here with you, then." Avery offers me a tight smile that doesn't reach his eyes. "Definitely an interesting way to start a family."

His tone is very clearly judgmental, and I feel slightly betrayed when my eyes move to Trista. What has she told him about me? About us? How is she framing this?

Ignoring her frustrated glare, I glance at the animal in Trista's hands. "What's the plan here for *Handsome?*" I feel stupid the instant that name comes out of my mouth, but now I'm committed. "Just paying Millie, Reginald, and Strudel a quick visit?" *Seriously, these fucking names are not helping me be intimidating right now.* "And then getting right back in that trailer to return to where he came from?"

Trista smiles politely as she hands the halter off to her "friend" and walks toward me. I reach out to help her down off the trailer, and she doesn't miss a beat when she hits the ground and drags me by the arm toward the barn, out of earshot from the vet with that annoyingly perfect smile and cocky glint in his eye.

As we stand facing each other inside the barn, my eyes wander down to her thirteen-week belly. She's dressed in her Carhartt overalls, and I think I can see a bump starting to form, though if you didn't see her on a regular basis, you might not notice it.

Either way, she looks perfect.

And the baby growing inside her is perfect too. I've been on a high since our appointment last week. The baby wiggled and danced all over the screen, and I'm not ashamed to admit I showed my whole damn family the photos from that day.

And Trista and I seem to be getting along better than ever too. Her morning sickness has subsided, and she hasn't complained about the snacks I leave around the barn to help keep her comfortable. Life has been good here on the mountain...until this fucking Avery guy showed up.

"Wyatt, you're being crazy rude to my friend." She seethes, tucking back some curly strands that have fallen out of her topknot.

"Friend," I scoff and shake my head. "You could have mentioned it was a dude."

"What difference does it make?"

I jut my head toward her, my eyes dancing over the freckles on her face. "Just feels like you kept it from me on purpose. Why would you do that?"

"I kept nothing from you on purpose," she exclaims, hugging her thumbs onto her overalls. God, have her breasts gotten even bigger since last week? "You probably just didn't listen."

"All I do is listen," I retort, feeling the veins in my neck bulge as I tower over her. I listened very intently when she told me she has a roster of men she can call to fuck anytime. That little sentence has played on repeat in my mind ever since, haunting my every waking moment. My voice is low when I add, "You never mentioned Avery was a guy. Is that because he's a part of your bullpen?"

Her eyes are lasers as she stares up at me. "And what if he is?"

My nostrils flare as my eyes drop to her lips. "Then he's taking advantage of you in more ways than one."

"Here we go." Trista rolls her eyes to the heavens. "You thought my boss, Earl, was taking advantage of me too. Do you want to know if he's in my bullpen too?"

"Well," I snap back, my hands flexing at my sides as I fight the urge to touch her. "These men occupy a lot of your time."

"What do you think you're doing?" She gestures to her belly to confirm her point, and I sag back, feeling wounded, but she steps into my space, her finger sharp as she pops it into my chest. "People like me have to work a lot to get anywhere in life, Wyatt. Stuff isn't just handed to me. I didn't inherit a job under my father's business that allowed me to buy a big mountain and pay someone to have my baby and shower her with gifts and cleaning ladies and food deliveries. I may be your lucky number, but I'm still waiting for my own lotto numbers to be drawn because when this is all over, I have a life to get back to that I'm still figuring out."

"Trista, I—"

"No," she bites. "I'm not going to have you mansplain my situation to me. I know exactly what I'm doing and who I'm spending my time with."

"Fine," I grind out through clenched teeth, not liking her on-point assessment of me.

"Fine," she volleys back, not missing a beat. "Then let's get back to the real issue here. Avery rescued Handsome from a meat truck that was headed up to Canada. The previous owners kept him at a youth camp, but once he started having his neurological issues, they wanted to dump him because he began to frighten the kids."

My throat rumbles because a rabbit upstairs tells me exactly where this is going.

She sighs heavily before she continues. "Can Handsome stay here while I look for a new home for him? Avery doesn't have the facilities to board him, and I'm certain I can find someone who will love him. But I just need a little time. I'll do all the chores myself. I'll even feed Millie for you."

"I don't need you to feed my goat," I bark, my hands finding my hips as my body tenses with irritation. I feel out of control right now, and I'll be damned if she takes away my goat responsibilities on top of everything else.

My eyes move to the pasture entrance, where Millie and Reginald are standing, staring at us like they know they're about to get a new fucking playmate. Jesus Christ, my brothers will think I'm letting this woman turn Fletcher Mountain into Old McDonald's farm. But after the dickish things I just said to this fucking vet, I don't really have a leg to stand on.

"What if Millie doesn't like the horse?" I grumble under my breath, feeling pouty and annoyed that everything on my property is changing way too fast these days.

"I will take my time introducing them," she replies swiftly. "Millie adjusted great to Reggie. I'm sure she'll be the same for Handsome in there. And Handsome will be fine with her because he was around a lot of other animals at the camp. Even chickens."

"No fucking chickens, Trista," I beg, my hands forming tight fists at my sides.

"No chickens." She holds her hands up, her eyes softening now that she's got me right where she wants me. "Does that mean Handsome can stay?"

I close my eyes and shake my head while congruently saying yes out loud because, truth be told, I don't know if I'm capable of saying no to this woman. Ever.

Her entire face lights up, and she wraps her arms around my neck without warning. The scent of roses envelops me as her hand cups the back of my head, her fingers teasing the short strands of my hair. I can't help but wrap my arms around her waist and squeeze her body to mine. The pressure of her hug feels like a balm I need after the tongue-lashing I just endured. And rightfully so.

It's becoming clearer and clearer to me that Trista and I grew up in two very different situations, and while I might not like this vet douche, it doesn't mean I don't respect the hell out of her hustle. Truth be told, I think she's incredible. And every time I touch her, my body aches for more. It's becoming a bit of a problem.

The hug lasts longer than is appropriate, and when we break apart, the flush in Trista's cheeks and the pulsing in my jeans are unmistakable. Her tongue flicks out to wet her lips as she stands on her tiptoes and presses a soft kiss to my cheek, lingering there for a moment. Her delicate hand cups my cheek as her warm breath pushes heat straight to my core.

It's a damn good thing her hand is holding me in place because the urge I have to turn my head and make contact with her soft lips is at an all-time high.

Seemingly out of breath, she pulls back and stares at me for a brief indescribable moment before running off to rejoin Avery the fucking vet, who is, in fact, a dude. *Who Trista did* not *deny was part of her bullpen.*

At that moment, I realize that I am completely consumed by lucky number thirteen, and I have no idea how I will survive the next several months with her and, even worse, the months afterward without her.

CHAPTER 28

WEEKS PREGNANT: 14
ANIMALS ON THE MOUNTAIN: 4

Trista

I roll the window down from the back seat of Wyatt's brother's truck, enjoying the summer breeze as we make our way down the mountain to Everly's graduation party. The family apparently all attended the ceremony a few weeks ago, and today is the reception at Everly's dad's house, which should be very interesting.

All of Wyatt's friends and extended family will likely be there, so I should be fretting over what I'm going to say if someone asks who I am. But the only thing on my mind is what kind of food they'll be serving because dammit, I'm ravenous these days. Wyatt has a stash of snacks in the barn that I keep eating, hoping he doesn't notice, but I'm sure he's noticing. He's just too polite to say anything. He's been too polite to say much to me this past week. Grumpy is always kind of his vibe, but ever since Handsome moved into the barn, he's been downright testy. He snapped at me the other day when I was carrying a bucket of water into Reginald's pen. He said he hooked up a hose so I wouldn't have to lift buckets, and he'd appreciate it if I took care of myself better.

Fine, I'll use the freaking hose, psycho.

At first, I thought it was Handsome he was extra sour about because I pretty much manipulated him into letting him stay, but the other day, I saw him giving the mini horse some carrots from his coat pocket, so I don't think that's the issue here.

The truck is quiet as I look from Calder in the driver's seat to Wyatt in the passenger seat and Luke in the back next to me. They're all staring out their prospective windows, acting like it's normal for me to hang out with them when we've barely exchanged three words since I moved up here. I think it's high time I get to know my neighbors, grumpy Wyatt be damned.

"What do you guys do for fun?" I singsong in an obvious way as I try to break the ice.

Calder's eyes find mine in the rearview mirror, but he says nothing, nervously glancing at Wyatt and then back to the road. I turn to Luke, who shifts his body away from me, focusing really hard on the great outdoors. *Strange.*

Maybe they have weird hobbies and don't want to divulge what they get up to in their free time. Judy at the Merc did kind of make me wonder about them.

I'll try something a little easier.

"It's crazy how much cooler it is up in the mountains than it is in the city," I offer, thinking the weather is always a safe topic. "How hot will it get on Fletcher Mountain when summer peaks?"

Other than a heavy sigh from Wyatt, I'm again greeted with silence. What's the deal with these guys? Did they run out of Brawny paper towels? Do they need to kidnap some future brides and take them up to the mountain to get laid? You could cut the tension in here with a knife.

"I like your shirt, Luke," I offer, staring at the red-and-black checked print. "It's very...lumberjacky."

Luke makes an odd noise in his throat as he turns and finally makes eye contact with me. "He told us not to talk to you."

"What?" My brows furrow in confusion, and I move to Wyatt, who looks positively raged. "Wyatt said you can't talk to me?"

"I think his exact words were 'Talk to her, and you die.'" Calder imitates Wyatt's deep monotone perfectly, and my mouth drops open in shock when Calder adds, "Murder Wyatt is scary."

Wyatt slides a flat look at his brother in the driver's seat that clearly says *you're lucky you're driving, or you'd be dead right now.*

"Wyatt, did you really threaten their lives?" I ask, sliding to the edge of my seat to see his face better.

He ignores me, and that will not friggin' do. "Alright, one of you better start talking, or I'm going to start singing, and trust me, no one wants to hear that."

With a deep grumble, Wyatt turns around to eye me seriously. "You don't know them like I do. They don't get out much. They've lived on the mountain too long and don't know how to communicate without offending people. They're construction guys, and it shows. Frankly, they're fucking animals, and they should live out in the barn with Millie and Reggie."

"Don't forget about *Handsome.*" Luke hitches his voice high and covers his mouth when a girlish giggle billows out of him.

The car swerves, and I fall back as Wyatt reaches back to punch Luke on the thigh.

"Fuck!" Luke howls, gripping his denim-clad leg as he slides farther away from his brother so he can't get another swing in.

Calder's shoulders shake with silent laughter, and then he cowers under Wyatt's murderous glance. "I didn't mock the mini horse!" he exclaims defensively. "I think he *is* rather handsome, gross tongue and all. The bunny, on the other hand—"

"How did you find out about the rabbit?" Wyatt looks at him accusingly, his eyes twitching with rage. "Have you been in the apartment?"

"No. Calm the fuck down, Papa Bear." Calder grips the steering wheel nervously. "I saw her giving the little furball a scrub in the outdoor shower the other day."

"You shouldn't be looking at her at all," Wyatt bites out, and my mouth drops open when I realize he's dead serious.

"Wyatt!"

"What?" he barks, turning his anger right at me. When our eyes lock, he quickly snaps out of his crazy trance and blinks sheepishly. "Sorry."

Luke whines, rubbing the spot his brother punched him. "We pass the barn every time we leave the mountain, bro. It's impossible not to lay eyes on her."

"Okay, you guys are all friggin' nuts. Wyatt, please let your brothers speak to me. This graduation party will be awkward enough for me as it is. I know nobody."

"You know me," Wyatt grumbles, the muscle in his jaw flexing as he faces forward and watches the road. He looks mad, but I can't figure out why exactly. His brothers can't be any worse than him.

"I'll risk murder and talk to you," Calder says, wagging his eyebrows at me in the rearview mirror. He glances at Wyatt and hesitates a bit before asking, "So tell me, MB…how exactly did you get knocked up with my brother's baby? I want all the dirty deets. He won't share, and it's driving me crazy."

Wyatt groans as he covers his face with his hands in surrender. Okay…maybe they are animals, but luckily, animals are my specialty. I waggle my brows at Calder in the rearview mirror and reply, "Tell me what MB stands for, and I'll give you the whole juicy story."

Wyatt's head snaps to look back at me with a silent warning while Calder glances at Luke, who both grin like they've just won the lottery.

"MB stands for Momma Bear," Calder answers with a leer and then points at Wyatt. "Papa Bear. Momma Bear."

I frown, disappointed at that label because I won't be this child's mother when all is said and done, and the less I think about that fact, the better. I'm a mere cow.

"Your turn," Calder urges, glancing back at me.

They asked for it.

Biting my lip, I lean forward and drape my arms over the back of Calder's seat. If Wyatt is going to be a grouchy dick this week, then it's high time I make some new friends. I feel Wyatt's eyes trained on me as I whisper breathily into his brother's ear loud enough for everyone to hear, "It was late at night, and I was out by the barn, tending to the animals…the wild, *hungry* animals. There was a cool chill in the air, and a heavy spring rain had just begun, soaking my clothes all the way through. I ran under the overhang for protection. The sound of rain pounding on the tin roof was deafening when suddenly, Wyatt came up behind me, pressed me up against the barn, and ripped my drenched bodice off my breasts before he lifted my skirt and…fucked… my…brains out."

I sit back with a Cheshire cat grin as the truck goes completely silent, all three men too afraid to breathe, let alone speak. Luke shifts in his seat, trying to get farther away from me, and Calder's brows are furrowed with confusion as he stares down the highway.

I giggle quietly, relishing that with all the testosterone in this truck, I still managed to command the space. Who's the king of the mountain now?

I feel on top of the world until I spot the heated look in Wyatt's eyes—a look that isn't angry or grumpy or sour. It's a look that sends a frenzy of butterflies through my entire body. A look that would incinerate me if he directed it my way.

And I'd be happy to burn.

CHAPTER 29

WEEKS PREGNANT: 14
ANIMALS ON THE MOUNTAIN: 4

Trista

Wyatt's brother is rich rich. Not the kind of rich that Wyatt looks like where he doesn't necessarily drive fancy cars, but you can tell he has plenty of money. Max Fletcher is the kind of rich that means not one family member is working in the kitchen at this graduation party. They have staff taking care of everything.

This means that when I follow the guys through the exquisite house bustling with people and we enter the backyard where the full party is, my jaw drops like I've never seen civilization before.

First of all...the yard itself is bananas. A giant swimming pool with floating lights, a guesthouse, and a creek runs along the back end of the property. It's not gorgeous mountainside, but they are surely rocking their little oasis back here. And the Boulder housing market is even more insane than Denver, so I know this house is worth at least a couple of million.

The party decorations are next-level too. Skirted high-top tables are scattered throughout the pool deck area topped with fancy floral arrangements. There's a DJ booth with a slideshow of Everly playing on a giant screen, an outdoor buffet with bacon-wrapped shrimp, steak... *holy shit, is that an ice cream truck?*

I count not one but two open bars. What kind of high school graduation party has open bars?

Everly Fletcher's, I guess.

And the worst part is that...the girl is so sweet, I can't even hate her.

"Trista, you came!" Everly calls out from the other side of the pool and waves enthusiastically. She extracts herself from a group of teenagers to come running toward us. I can't imagine how I look right now, flanked by three plaid-covered mountain men and dressed in a clearance JCPenney dress.

Everly wraps her arms around me and squeals into my hair. "I'm so glad you're here."

She pulls away and moves on to greet her uncles. I gaze longingly at her outfit. It's an elegant blue jumpsuit that manages to look expensive and laid-back at the same time. Everly has one of those bodies that can wear whatever she wants, and it'll look great on her, whereas I am constantly dressing to accentuate my curves because if I wear a shapeless dress, I look like a potato.

I tug nervously on my floral wrap dress. It cinches at the waist and makes me feel womanly, a step up from my standard jeans and baggy T-shirts. Though admittedly, I've been wearing some of my more revealing tank tops lately because I like how it makes Wyatt act all weird and twitchy. He's normally so stoic, but one day, I had a dash of abdomen showing, and he was suddenly very interested in the color of the sky.

This means when I came out in my dress and saw his reaction, I felt like a million bucks. All three of the Fletcher brothers did a double take. Probably because this dress is giving more titty than it did prior to me getting knocked up, but it's still graduation-appropriate cleavage.

"Nice to see you guys dressed up for the occasion," Wyatt's brother Max chastises as he joins our little group. Max dons a perfectly tailored gray suit, and his tie even matches his daughter's jumpsuit. He turns and offers me a kind smile. "Trista, you are excused from that dig. You look lovely."

"Oh...thanks." I glance at the guys and curse myself for not telling them to wear something other than jeans. Clearly, they need some womanly guidance on that mountain.

"Max, be nice to your brothers," a dark, curvy brunette says, coming over to greet us. She's dressed a bit more casually but equally as cute as Everly. See, why can I look at this plus-sized female and see that she looks amazing, but my intrusive thoughts have to be such a dick to me? God, being a woman is such a bitch sometimes.

"Trista, I am so excited to finally meet you," she says, reaching out to shake my hand. "I'm Cozy, Wyatt's sister-in-law. I'm married to the bossy brother."

"Nice to meet you." I laugh as Max rolls his eyes. If Max is the bossy one, what the hell does that make Wyatt?

"How are you feeling?" she asks as her gaze flashes to my stomach.

"Great, thanks." I fight the urge to cover myself. It's strange how pregnancy sort of makes your body a part of casual conversation. Like is there anything else that happens to a human body that makes it normal for people to ask, *"How are your innards, Trista?"*

"I heard you had some bad morning sickness." Cozy's eyes move to Wyatt. "I had that with my youngest, Ethan. It's awful."

I frown over at my mountain man, wondering if there's a family newsletter or a group chat he sends out to update everyone on me. I know it's his baby inside me, but I sincerely hope the ranch cups and Tylenol syringes didn't make any headlines.

"I feel amazing now," I reply with a polite smile. "No issues eating these days."

"Oh God, I remember that. Once you get past that horrible morning sickness, your body wants to make up for lost time and eat everything in sight."

"That's exactly how it feels." I laugh and feel oddly comforted by hearing another woman relate to this experience. It's not a support group, but it feels pretty good. "My vet friend says it's normal to be on full feed after the first trimester, but admittedly, his pregnancy knowledge doesn't extend much beyond farm animals."

Cozy laughs, and I open my mouth to continue chatting with her, but Wyatt steps between us, causing our eyes to look up at him. "Let's get you some food."

My brows furrow as I try to wave him off. "The full-feed thing was a joke, Wyatt…kind of."

"Come on," he commands and puts his hand on my lower back, swiftly ushering me away from everyone.

I offer a polite smile to Wyatt's family, who are all staring at us in rapt fascination. Once we're out of earshot, I shake his hand off my back. "I don't need to be led to the trough like a farm animal," I snipe, turning to shoot daggers at him. "I said the Avery comment was a joke."

"I don't like that guy."

"You met him for two seconds."

"Two seconds too long," he murmurs, his eyes narrowing and fixating on me. "What did you tell him about me? He obviously knows about our situation."

"Of course he knows. He's my friend. Plus, I was getting sick at some of our house calls together."

Wyatt's nostrils flare. "Did you tell him you were sick before me?"

My head jerks back. "He's my friend."

"I know, but that's my baby inside you, so I have a right to know before him." He licks his lips and glowers at my lips. "Before anybody, for that matter."

My eyes flash with barely concealed rage because it's all making a lot more sense now. It's not the mini horse bothering him or the pig or the rabbit. It's Avery. And the fact that Avery has a penis.

Mountain Man is…*jealous.*

The thrill that shoots through me over that realization is almost as messed up as his behavior. It's certainly as messed up as the warmth that spreads to the area between my legs over the thought of him claiming me in some strange way. I shouldn't like these thoughts. I should hate that he's trying to mark his territory because I have literally shot his sperm up into my vagina and am carrying his genetic child. What more does this crazy man need?

I close my eyes before I let myself finish those thoughts.

I lean up close to whisper my reply into his ear, "You better watch your tone with me, Wyatt, because last I checked, me telling you stuff wasn't a part of our contract. It was a gift I gave you as a friend. This is my body, and no one will tell me who I can talk to about it. Got it?"

Wyatt's expression morphs from anger to horror in the blink of an eye. He steps back as if mortified by what he's just said. "Will you please just eat? I know you haven't eaten in a while."

"How do you know that?"

"Because you were in the barn with me earlier and didn't touch the snacks."

I frown at that comment. "Well, I wasn't hungry, and they're not my snacks, so why would I touch them?"

He looks at me like he knows I'm lying. Which is true. I wanted to grab one of those granola bars on the counter in the barn, but Wyatt was standing right there watching me, so I couldn't.

Finally, I shove him out of my way and fix a plate because dammit, I am hungry. Wyatt watches, and I frown over at him. "Aren't you going to eat?"

He shakes his head. "What do you want to drink? I'll go get it."

"I can get my own drink."

He closes his eyes for a moment, clearly frustrated. The veins in his neck are bulging, and his hands flex at his sides like he doesn't know what to do with himself.

"I'll have a cranberry juice," I say with a heavy sigh, taking pity on the poor guy. He's being a dick, but I know he hates himself for it, and that sort of neurotic behavior makes me feel kind of bad for him in a strange, dysfunctional sort of way.

I find a high-top table by the pool away from the crowd and am just about to murder a bacon-wrapped shrimp when a tall blonde comes bounding over to me.

"How's it going on Fletcher Mountain?" Everly asks, propping her elbow on the table and watching me with wide puppy dog eyes.

"Oh, it's going," I mumble around a bite and quickly dab at my lips with a napkin, careful not to wipe off all the lipstick I carefully put on tonight. "Although your uncle is definitely treading that fine line between sweet and psycho."

"Oh no, what did he do?" Everly groans and turns her full attention to me.

"His mood swings are insane. We're trying to be friends through this whole thing, and he's not making it easy."

Everly chews her lower lip nervously. "Well, in fairness, I don't think my uncle is used to having female friends."

"It shows," I huff out indignantly.

"But he's a great brother and an exceptional uncle, so just be patient with him. He's really a sweetie pie when you get to know him. He loves to take care of people."

I can't help but soften as I watch him stand in line at the bar to get my drink for me. There is a sweetness to Wyatt buried under that gruff exterior of his, and I will do my best to find it before this baby is born.

I nudge Everly with my elbow. "You're really cool for a kid, you know that?"

"Well, I am eighteen, so I'm technically an adult." She beams proudly.

"When do you leave for Ireland?" I ask before biting into another succulent shrimp.

"End of August." She inhales deeply and runs her fingers through her hair. "Just a couple more months. I'm so nervous and so jacked at the same time. I hope I'll be able to come back when the baby is born, though! Can we maybe video chat occasionally so I can see your belly growing?"

My brows lift at that thought. "That's weird, but sure. Why the hell not?" She smiles happily, and I add, "Oh, did you hear there's a mini horse in the barn as well now?"

"What?" Everly practically screams, and all the guests around us turn to gawk.

I laugh and nod. "His name is Handsome. You should come up and see him before you leave. He's a hoot."

"Um…obviously!" Everly takes a deep breath to adjust to the news. "How did you get Uncle Wyatt to let that happen?"

I shrug and pop another shrimp into my mouth. "I just asked him."

Everly's brows furrow at that. "I've asked him for more animals on that farm ever since I was little, and he wouldn't even consider it! He always said Millie was a lone wolf like him."

I giggle at that comparison. "It may have helped that I asked him after the animal was already on the property. That lessened the barrier of entry, I suppose."

"Or maybe my uncle likes you," she coos, her eyes twinkling.

I pause before taking a bite of the salad as his face at the Mercantile a couple of weeks ago replays in my head: *I might be focusing too much on getting into someone else's bullpen.*

I shake off that lust-worthy thought. "Well, I like your uncle too, some of the time. That's part of the whole friends thing."

"But do you think he's cute?" Everly eyes me curiously.

My brows shoot upward. "Yeah, he's cute, but I don't like him like that."

"Why not?"

"Because he's about to be a single dad, and kids aren't my thing," I state simply because it's an easy truth to use as an excuse.

Everly looks taken aback. "Why don't you like kids?"

"It's not that I don't like them. I just don't want any of my own. Life can still be very fulfilling without children as well."

I can't help but notice the crestfallen look on Everly's face. She looks like I just told her Santa Claus isn't real, the poor thing. She needs to see more life experiences and broaden her horizons. Ireland will be good for her.

"But it's not just the kid thing," I add, feeling like I need to give her more of an explanation. "I have career aspirations, and it's going to take the right kind of partner to be cool with my crazy ideas."

"Everly," Max calls from behind me, interrupting our conversation. "Grandma Eleanor has just arrived. She's over by the ice cream truck and asking to see you."

"Grandma E!" Everly exclaims and bounds off like the good kid she probably always was.

"That girl is something else." I turn to Max as he sets his drink down on the table beside me and assesses the party for a moment.

"You're telling me." He huffs, and I can't help but notice a shift in his demeanor. "We're all really going to struggle when she leaves for college. She's kind of our family cheerleader. She keeps the whole gang together."

"Dad!" a young boy shouts from the other side of the pool, and Max's head snaps over to look at him. He starts unbuttoning his dress shirt and bellows, "I'm going swimming!"

"No, you're not," Max yells back at him, standing at attention. "Ethan, we talked about this. Ethan!"

The dark-haired little boy has stripped out of his shirt and is about to jump in the water when his mom appears, fishhooking his arm and catching him midjump. Cozy holds her hand up to Max. "I got him!"

"Jesus Christ," Max grumbles and loosens the tie around his neck as he points at the scene on the other side of the pool. "My youngest is the exact opposite of Everly. He's going to be the death of me."

I laugh as I watch Cozy struggle to get Ethan's shirt back on him, all while they argue about his desire to swim.

"That's what Wyatt has to look forward to," Max states, pointing at his son with a laugh. "We all stupidly thought Everly was how most kids were. Easygoing, a good listener, and sweet down to her very core. Ethan was quite the wake-up call."

I glance over to see the little boy walk away from his mother and stand in the grass, unbutton his pants, and start peeing. The guests nearby all begin laughing, and Cozy shakes her head and throws her hands up in the air.

Max pinches the bridge of his nose. "And I hate to say it, but Wyatt was just like him."

"Liked to pee in the grass?"

"Yes," Max laughs and shakes his head. "He always did exactly what he wanted, when he wanted, didn't matter what anyone else said."

"Why does that not surprise me?" I laugh knowingly. I've only known the guy for four months, but he didn't take long to figure out.

Affection blooms on Max's face. "It's going to be really fun watching him become a dad."

I watch Max for a moment, noting how serious he is. "Man, you guys are like the closest family I've ever met."

"Are you not close with yours?" he asks, turning his focus back to me now that Cozy seems to have the wild child under control.

"Not even a little bit," I answer with a shudder. "My sister lives really far away, and we talk maybe a couple of times a year. And my parents, well…they're just not in the picture. And I don't know any of my extended family. I never even had a graduation party. Honestly, I'm lucky I graduated from high school at all."

"Interesting." Max frowns at my confession. "Wyatt made it seem like you had big career aspirations. Something about opening your own rescue center?"

I can't help but laugh. There must be a family newsletter. "That's my hope after this baby is born. There are so many pet facilities in the Denver area, but the amount of wildlife and farm animals that get abandoned or slaughtered because people can't take care of them is atrocious. I plan to use the money I make doing this to invest in a space suitable for a wildlife sanctuary. I don't have much in terms of equity, so I need all the capital I can get."

"Aren't there grants available for that?"

"Yeah, there is some, but not enough to lease property with. And I'm getting ready to apply for a 501(c)(3) so I can operate as a charity, which will help make applying for those grants a possibility."

"That's great. I hope you're considering contacting potential investors." He reaches into his pocket and pulls out his business card. "My company takes applications from charities all the time. When you get a 501(c)(3), give me a call. We'd be willing to donate. You're helping my brother out. It seems only natural for my company to help you out."

"Seriously?" I exclaim. Dropping the shrimp from my hand, I look at his expensive-looking business card like he's just handed me a million dollars. "Oh my God, that would be amazing!"

"It's not a hard process to apply," Max waves me off dismissively. "Just reach out as soon as you're ready, and we'll make it happen."

He harrumphs when I shock him with an unexpected hug. My mind reels at this new possibility.

I feel like I'm in shock. In my life, it's not easy to make contacts like Max Fletcher, an affluent man who seems to have it all. He's someone I would never have even crossed paths with had I not met his daughter on the street. To know he's willing to help me get my life goal started means my dream is now closer to becoming a reality.

Wyatt

"Wyatt, you have to chill out," Luke drawls, grabbing my shoulder and turning me to face him. "You're going to freak her the fuck out."

"I'm not doing anything." I shrug out of his grip and glance back to where Trista is talking with Everly at one of the tables by the pool. She looks so fucking good in that dress tonight. And that red lipstick she's wearing. God, I am struggling to function normally.

Luke shoves his blond hair off his forehead and pins me with a serious look. "You're being a moody, bossy asshole even more than usual. You said you guys agreed to be friends…so just be fucking nice."

"I am being fucking nice," I growl as we step up to the bar and I order her drink.

"What now?" Calder asks, joining in on our conversation. "You told me at work the other day that you actually liked that tongue-flopping horse."

"It's not the horse," I grumble under my breath.

"Then what is it?" Luke's eyes are trained on me, awaiting my answer.

I exhale heavily. "She is driving me crazy. She has this really maddening way of getting under my skin." And ever since she told me she likes casual sex, all I can think about is having sex with her. It's becoming a problem.

"So then have sex with her," Calder drawls as he takes the words right out of my head. Goddammit, we've lived on that mountain together for too long now. Sex is our answer for everything. He accepts a beer from the female bartender and shoots her a wink.

"I'm not sure that's a good idea," I mutter as the other bartender hands me Trista's cranberry juice.

"Sex is Mother Nature's cough medicine," Calder says with a dopey smile. "You got a little tickle in the back of your throat? A good bang session will make that pain disappear, guaranteed."

"We're supposed to be friends."

"Maybe it's not a friend she needs. Maybe she needs a good dickin' just as bad as you because, if I'm not mistaken, our Dark Night was the last time you got your dick wet."

"Shut up," I hiss under my breath. "Our Dark Night is *not* something we should discuss in public, especially at our niece's graduation party."

Calder and Luke both stare at each other with knowing looks. Yes, it's been a while since I've been laid, but I've had bigger things on my mind this past year. Like becoming a father.

But I guess now that I've figured that out, maybe Calder is right, and I should get out there again, at least before the baby is born.

God, that still feels weird to say.

A heaviness presses down on me as I consider going to a bar and picking up some random girl. Or calling one of the numbers in my phone of women I've been with in the past who are good with casual. The problem is, I don't want to fuck just anyone.

I want to fuck lucky number thirteen.

Calder leans in close and glances around to ensure no one is listening. "You heard her in the truck. That woman has fantasies you could offer to make realities, Papa Bear."

"She's my surrogate," I grind out and cringe at the idea of blurring that line. "It's like ten kinds of fucked up."

"Not when you're both consenting adults," Calder volleys back with a shrug. "And if you don't satisfy her needs, someone else will."

Red floods my eyesight as I imagine the vet or some other random fuck she picks up at the Mercantile going up into her apartment and laying her out naked on that bed. The bed I bought for her. My hand tightens on the glass as I picture a stranger fucking Trista... fucking what's mine.

Mine.

Except she isn't mine. She'll never be mine. We have a contract basically guaranteeing that once this baby is born, we never speak to each other again.

But the idea of another man's dick pounding into her with my baby inside her? It's a horror I didn't realize would gut me so much.

I shift my jaw from side to side, hating myself for acting like I haven't been considering fucking her since the first night we did the insemination song and dance. I didn't want to jizz into a cup. I wanted to jizz into her. I wanted it so bad I was actually disappointed when I found out she was pregnant. It meant I couldn't take her up on her offer of doing it the old-fashioned way, and that would have been so fucking worth it.

My eyes are hard when I glance over at my brothers and ask, "But what if—"

"She's nothing like her," Luke says with a serious expression. "And we've all changed since then."

I nod slowly because he's right. The three of us are closer than ever, and I trust them for the most part. But with Trista, I feel overly protective on some strange level. I've never met anyone like her before. She's a total enigma.

Calder elbows me gently. "If she's into casual and she'll be moving out and moving on after she has the baby, you'd be a fool not to go for it."

I consider that idea as I turn and see that Trista is in a conversation with my brother Max now. It looks kind of serious, based on her pensive expression. Paranoia prickles over what he might be talking to her about, so I nod to Calder and Luke to make my way over there. My heart thunders when Trista squeals and reaches out to hug him.

"What's going on?" I ask as I set the glass of juice in front of Trista and turn hard eyes on my older brother.

"Nothing yet," Max replies, pulling away with a laugh. "I just let Trista know that if she opens up her wildlife facility, my company would be happy to donate."

"Isn't that amazing?" she exclaims with a big smile like he's just gifted her the world.

My jaw clenches, and I force out a noncommittal "Sure."

Trista frowns curiously at me, and I feel my brother's judgmental stare weighing down on me. "You good?" Max asks, his voice deep and knowing.

"I'm great," I reply crisply, turning on my heel. "I'll leave you two to it."

I take off for the bar, ignoring the curious looks of my brothers as I struggle to control my temper. Fucking Max is always trying to do too much. I don't need him to step in and save the woman I hired to have my baby, just like I didn't need his lawyer to arrange this whole thing. Trista doesn't need his corporate money either. She's a trailblazer, a nontraditional thinker. She's figuring her life out on her own terms... just like I am. Or so I thought.

Now I have to wonder why it seems so easy for her to accept something from my brother when I get pushback for trying to buy her a damn bed? Or bring her breakfast. Or fill her car up with gas one time. Or ask her if Avery is taking advantage of her. She makes no fucking sense.

I decide that keeping my distance from Trista for the rest of this party is key to my sanity because I'm not in a partying mood. And it's not just because Max offered money to Trista. It's because this party is just a painful reminder that Everly is moving away in a couple of months, and our dad isn't here to celebrate her. Our family is getting smaller by the minute.

"Wyatt, honey, is Trista still here?" my mom asks, interrupting my solitary poolside brooding.

"She's over there." I point at where I've been watching her for the better part of an hour. It's dark now, and the sun has all but vanished behind the foothills. The DJ lights cast a colorful glow on Trista's face as they spin around the patio. She looks like she's entertaining the hell out of Everly's friends, all of them erupting into fits of giggles every five seconds. She was worried about not knowing anyone here tonight, but she seems to be fitting in just fine. And I hate how much that bugs me. I wanted her to have fun. I wanted her to cut loose and relax. What is my fucking problem?

"I want to give her this quilt I made." My mom turns to head toward her with a gift bag in hand.

"You shouldn't give that to her," I call out before she gets too far away. "She doesn't like gifts."

My mom's brows furrow as she turns to look back at me. "What?"

"She was unhappy about the bed I bought her, so I'm sure she won't like that quilt." I sip the warm beer I've been nursing.

My mom looks crestfallen. "I've been working on this since your first ultrasound."

I shrug dismissively. "I don't know what to tell you."

Her eyes narrow as she marches over to me. "Wyatt Anthony Fletcher, whatever the hell is the matter with you...get over it."

I open my mouth to argue, but she holds her hand up to silence me.

"I don't want to hear it," she snaps, her tone lethal. "I'm a grieving widow who's spent hours making this quilt for the woman carrying my future grandchild, and I will not be told I can't give it to her. I will play the dead husband card until I'm also dead and cold in the ground beside him. You hear me?"

Blood rushes in my ears as I realize what a complete fucking asshole I just was to my own mother. My mother! I open my mouth to apologize but am interrupted by Trista. "Everything okay over here?"

My mom's face morphs from rage-filled momma-bear mode to sweet, kind Johanna in the blink of an eye. She turns on her heel and coos softly, "There you are, Trista! Here, honey. This is just a little something to show my appreciation for letting me be a part of your first ultrasound. That was such a special day for me."

"Oh, wow, you didn't have to do that." Trista reaches inside the gift bag and gasps at the intricately made quilt. Her lips part in shock. "Wait, this is incredible. Are you sure you don't want to keep this for the baby?"

"No, silly, it's for you." My mom rubs Trista's arm affectionately, proud of a creation I'm sure she's worked around the clock on.

She's quilted for as long as I can remember. After my dad died, she made all of us quilts from his old T-shirts. It was really thoughtful, but sadly, mine sits in a closet upstairs because it's still too hard for me to look at.

"I know it's summertime, but nights are cold up on the mountain, and this will make you feel nice and cozy up there."

"Wow…this is so kind of you," Trista says with a soft smile. "Thank you."

"You're welcome, sweetie." My mom arches a knowing brow at me. "I just want you to know how much we appreciate you. I put my phone number in the gift bag, and I want you to use it if you ever need to talk. I've been pregnant a time or two."

Trista looks touched, and they hug for a moment while my mom shoots daggers at me before excusing herself.

The pool lights glow through Trista's curls as she approaches me, a nervous glint in her eye that I don't like. "Do you know if an Uber will take me back up the mountain?"

My brows furrow. "Why would you take an Uber?"

"Because I'm exhausted, and we drove here with your brothers, and I don't want to make you guys feel like you have to leave."

"I'll drive you." I set my unfinished beer on the table and heave myself off the pool chair.

"What will your brothers do?" she asks, glancing over at the two of them sitting at the bar with a bunch of Max's Boulder friends. They look like they're several beers in and in no position to drive home anyway.

"They'll probably crash here at Max's or call me for a ride later. It's fine, I'll go get the keys."

I make my way over to Calder and spot him at the edge of the bar in the middle of what looks like a tense discussion with Cozy's best friend, Dakota. As far as I knew, these two hated each other. Ever since Calder fucked up Dakota's house renovation years ago.

And as I draw nearer, I discover that is likely still the case because I hear Dakota say, "Go fuck yourself, Calder," before she storms away, nearly knocking me over on her way by.

I slide my eyes to Calder. "What are you even doing? Isn't she married?"

Calder smiles devilishly, his eyes following Dakota's hasty exit. "Recently divorced, actually."

"But doesn't she hate you?"

"Loathes me." Calder's eyes lower, and he sucks in a sharp breath. "I think I'm in love."

"Snap out of it," I bark, hitting my brother on the shoulder. "I need the truck keys. Trista is ready to go. I'll come back for you guys later."

"No problem." Calder waggles his eyebrows suggestively as he hands them over. "At least one of us is getting lucky."

"Wrong," I growl, shaking my head in defeat. "It's not happening. And knowing Trista, it will never happen."

Calder looks at me in confusion as I grab the keys and skulk off, admitting that I've read this maddening woman all wrong. It's not that she doesn't like receiving gifts. It's that she doesn't like receiving them from me. And that kind of rejection stirs up old wounds that I'd rather not dig into.

CHAPTER 30

WEEKS PREGNANT: 14
ANIMALS ON THE MOUNTAIN: 4

Trista

The car ride back to the mountain is quiet and charged with something I can't quite put my finger on. It isn't until Wyatt parks in front of the barn that I finally get the balls to ask, "Will you just tell me what the hell is wrong with you?"

The muscle in Wyatt's jaw twitches under the dashboard lights before he reaches forward and shuts the truck off, still not answering me.

"Clearly, something is wrong," I urge, turning to face him fully. The silence in the truck is stifling. "Wyatt." I shove him gently on his shoulder, trying to poke the bear because I want to get this over with... whatever it is. "Just say what's on your mind."

He turns to face me, and the yellow outdoor light from the barn casts shadows on his face, making him even more handsome. "I just couldn't help but notice tonight that you're fine accepting gifts from everyone but me."

Without waiting for my reply, he gets out of the truck and makes his way into the barn to check on Millie. I usually find it really sweet, but his comment makes it a lot less cute.

Sweet and psycho.

I slide out of the truck to argue with him but pause outside the barn when a text comes in on my phone.

Avery: Cow in distressed labor at a farm just west of Denver. Quick drive for you if you want to join.

I hesitate in the doorway, chewing my lip as I debate this. Maybe it'd be better for me to get away from Wyatt and not stir things up any more than I already have.

"What is it?" Wyatt asks as he steps out of Millie's pen and closes the gate.

I exhale heavily and slide my phone back into my purse. "Avery is treating a cow nearby. I might go help him."

Wyatt's brows lift. "You said you were exhausted."

"I was," I reply as I dig into my purse for my car keys. "But this is work."

"It's not work," he barks, marching over to me. His nostrils flare as he glowers down at me. "It's voluntary. You don't have to say yes."

"Maybe I want to say yes," I exclaim, propping my hands on my hips.

Wyatt reaches down and shocks me when he yanks the keys out of my hand. "It's too late for you to drive to Denver."

My jaw drops as I stare at him, holding my keys. The absolute fucking nerve of this guy. "Give me my keys back." I grind the words out slowly, my teeth cracking as I move closer to reach for them.

"No," Wyatt responds, pulling them back out of my grasp. "You're not going."

"Are you kidding me?" I bellow, my entire body vibrating with barely concealed rage. "Why on earth do you think you have any right to dictate what I do?"

"Because I'm looking out for you," his voice booms in the quiet barn as he fingers my keys in his big hand. "You're mine to take care of."

I stop attempting to grab them, my body frozen with that claiming statement he just made. It's what he's been silently saying for the past several weeks with the gifts and the demands, but now he's saying the crazy part out loud. "You realize how nuts you sound, right?"

"You work too much, Trista." His voice cracks, showing a rare glimpse of emotion as the veins in his neck bulge. "You've been on your feet all day, and you need to take some time for yourself. Just this once, you should not go and help Avery."

"You're not my dad, Wyatt!" I argue and jam a finger into his big, meaty chest. "You're not even my daddy. You don't get to control what I do even though it's clear that's exactly what you're trying to do."

"How am I trying to control you?" Wyatt snaps, his brows furrowed in anger.

"Oh, let me think," I state dramatically, holding my fingers up to count down my list. "You keep your brothers from me, you barely let me talk to Everly's stepmom earlier today, you ruined a potential donor situation with Max because he could clearly tell you didn't like what he offered, and now you're going to tell me I can't go help my friend?"

"A friend who wants to fuck you," Wyatt snaps, irritation evident in the tremble of his body. "If Avery isn't a part of your bullpen, he sure as hell wants to be."

"So what?" I cry out, my body exhausted at the mind games this guy is playing with me. "If I need to be fucked, then why shouldn't it be Avery? Nothing in our contract said I had to be celibate and in complete solitude for these next several months, so if I want to fuck Avery, I should be free to do that. It's not like I can get pregnant again."

"God, you are so frustrating!" He turns on his heel and marches down the alley of the barn. Millie's head pops up as she presses her hooves to the top of the gate to watch the show.

Reginald's snout sticks out from beneath his pen door, clearly pissed about his shitty seats, and Handsome's view isn't much better. This barn is equipped for real-sized animals, not this pick-a-mix batch we have going on here.

"You want to talk about frustrating?" I stomp over to the counter and slam my purse down so I can grab a fistful of granola bars. "Stop laying these barn snacks out. I know you're doing it just for me. You're not subtle, Wyatt."

He turns on his heel and scoffs. "Oh, you don't like those?"

"I love them!" I retort.

"Then what is the issue?" he begs, his hands stretched out in confusion.

"I don't know!" I cry out with exasperation, and Millie bleats her agreement. Or maybe her disagreement. I suppose she's Team Wyatt since he saved her damn life, the traitor. I rake my hands through my hair and damn near sob, "I just want to feel like I can breathe again. Like I can take a full breath without feeling your presence all around me. I'm used to being on my own, and you are smothering me."

His blue eyes darken as he stares at me from across the barn, watching my chest rise and fall with the emotion of my confession. It feels weird to accept so much from one person. It feels wrong and worrisome, and I want clearer boundaries.

Because if I've learned anything over the past twenty-eight years, it's that nothing comes without a cost.

Relationships don't last.

People leave.

You're stronger on your own. You know this.

But why am I tempted to allow Wyatt to look after me?

With a pop of his jaw, he pushes off the stall and stalks toward me. I shift, feeling like I should be running for the hills from this crazy man who's just trapped me up on a mountain alone with him. But I don't run. I stand my ground as he moves into my personal space, enveloping me in his scent. My ass presses up against the butcher-block counter as he bows over me and dips his head so he can meet my eyes straight on.

"Or maybe, just maybe..." his deep voice rumbles, causing my entire body to tremble. "You're not being smothered enough."

I struggle to meet his eyes as he looms over me in all his giant, flannel-wearing glory. "What is that supposed to mean?"

"I mean, maybe if I just kissed you right now...maybe if I stuck my tongue down your throat and laid you down in one of these stalls and fucked your brains out like the fantasy you described in the truck, we could both finally breathe a little bit easier."

Holy tits on a bull, Wyatt is saying all the crazy parts out loud now.

His face is deathly serious as he utters words I had merely fantasized about until now. But the reality of this man saying those words and looking at me like that...has far surpassed my wildest imagination.

"I don't give a fuck if you help out Avery, talk to my brothers and my sister-in-law, or accept gifts from my mother," he states. "So long as you quit keeping me at arm's length when it's clear as fucking day that all you want is for me to touch you everywhere."

My body shudders with desire, my hormones raging at what this man has just laid out on the table. Surely, I haven't been that obvious. Clearly, I've had moments of wanting him, but I've kept my cool with him…haven't I?

Then again, it's been ages since I've had sex. An embarrassing amount of time. Couple that with my hormones, and I've probably been walking around this mountain like a farm animal in heat.

But does he really mean what he's saying? Or is he just nuts and possessive of this baby inside me? Never mind the fact that it's wildly inappropriate to have sex with a man who's paying me to have his baby. He's all talk, surely.

I'm going to call his bluff.

I tilt my head and step into his space, my breasts pebbling as they brush just below his pecs. Jutting my chin up defiantly, I reply, "I wish you would fuck me. Maybe if you got off, then your grumpy mood would be slightly more tolerable."

His nostrils flare as the corner of his mouth tugs up into a smirk. "Don't tease me, Lucky."

"Don't patronize me, Mountain Man." I swallow the lump in my throat as the pressure building in my chest, in my groin, in every part of my fucking body reaches its boiling point. I feel like I could burst at any moment, and this man hasn't even laid a finger on me.

He noisily sets my keys down and watches me for a moment, his brows lifting expectantly as he waits for me to grab them. When I don't, he lifts his hand, and his warm, calloused fingers grip my neck. I inhale sharply as his thumb brushes over my chin and jaw as I lean back and allow him to command me because there's not much else you can do when a man has you by the throat. The smell of him coats me, and I have to fight to catch my breath, my chest heaving with over-whelming need.

His voice is dark and wicked when he says, "I'm not patronizing you, Trista. I would love nothing more than to take care of your *every* need, so if you want to be fucked, just say the word."

A garbled laugh erupts from my mouth as I turn my head to the side, feeling turned on and enraged all at the same time.

Fuck, now he's calling my bluff.

He pushes himself against me, his groin flush against my belly, and I gasp when I realize just how serious he is right now. His other hand slides around my waist to pull me closer, like any speck of space between us is offensive to him.

"But if we do this," he adds, his voice drenched with desire, "if you let me fuck you, then you need to know that means I will own your body. Every particle on your skin will be mine for the taking. Do you understand?"

A soft moan escapes my lips, revealing the depths of his effect on me. *Fuck you, hormones!*

A wicked glint lights up his eyes as he stares down at my cleavage. My tits are practically bursting out of my dress with every heave of air I drag into my lungs. They feel heavy and swollen, and my nipples ache with just the pressure of his body against mine.

But my God, I want that pain.

He leans in and whispers into my ear as his hand releases my jaw and moves to the back of my neck. "You thought I was controlling before? You haven't seen anything until I sink my cock deep inside you. Then you'll really be mine."

I pull in a jagged breath as goose bumps spread across my body. My hands tremble at my sides, and it takes everything in me not to reach out and grab him.

I should be grabbing my keys instead and running. Or I should grab a pitchfork and impale this man who is obviously completely insane. I should shove him away and tear out of this barn to call the cops. This is psycho, not sweet.

But my body craves his crazy…I've quite possibly never craved anyone more in my entire life.

"How would it work?" I croak, my voice thick with arousal, my belly swirling with butterflies. "If we have sex…then what? Just forget about it the next day? Act like it never happened?"

Wyatt tilts his head and eyes me seriously, his face appearing as though he's having a full-blown conversation with himself before he replies, "Or…we fuck as much as we want whenever we want until your due date…" His fingers glide delicately over the swell of my breast, sending a flurry of flames through me as he flattens his warm palm to my belly and adds, "And when *this* is over…so are we."

I inhale sharply, fully absorbing what he's just suggested: sex for the remainder of this pregnancy and nothing more. Which means *I'm finally going to sleep with the man who knocked me up.*

It sounds crazy but also logical at the same time. I mean, I've already had his semen inside me. I'm already stuck with him for the next several months. I'm already planning to cut and run when this is all over. What's the worst that could happen?

And hell, maybe if I finally fuck him, I can keep him in a box instead of this damn push and pull we both struggle to navigate.

Swallowing the lump in my throat, I grab his hand and shift it from my belly to between my legs. His eyes flash when his fingers graze my warm center over my dress. I lean up on my tiptoes and whisper against his lips, "What are you waiting for, Mountain Man?"

Wyatt

A low growl erupts from my throat as I push the fabric of her dress into her lower lips and feel how wet she is already as the fabric dampens. Good God, she's ready, and I've barely touched her.

Lucky me, lucky number thirteen.

I shift my hand down and ruck up her dress, desperate to feel her skin on mine. Enough talking, enough arguing, enough acting like we don't both want this. It's been clear from the start, and I'm done playing the dutiful intended parent.

Right now, we are just a man and a woman alone on a mountain.

Except for Millie…and Reginald…and Handsome…and I guess
Strudel upstairs. And my fucking brothers whenever they get their
dumb asses home. I better get my ass moving.

Her belly is soft against my rough hands as I tease the edge of her
panties, watching her reaction with rapt fascination. "You want me to
touch you, Trista?" I ask, dipping my hand into her underwear and
delicately grazing over her smooth mound.

"Yes," she cries out, her voice hoarse with need. "Wyatt, don't fucking tease me."

"Why not?" I ask, my finger grazing the very top of her slit.

"Because I won't live through it," she pants, her voice fraught with
need.

"I told you I wanted to take care of you," I murmur, my lips brushing against her neck, desperate to kiss her but knowing I want to kiss
something else first. "So let me."

I drop down in front of her and hook my fingers into the waist-
band of her panties, yanking them down to her ankles. She steadies
herself on the counter and shakily steps out of them. I take a moment
to admire her creamy thighs as I slide my hand up one leg, watching
in appreciation as her skin dimples under my firm touch. There's no
greater sight than soft flesh being punished.

"Wyatt," she croaks, her hands shoving into my hair. "What are
you doing?"

"I'm going to taste you at last." I splay a hand against her belly as
I toss one of her legs over my shoulder, and without waiting for her
encouragement, I press my lips to her center and growl in appreciation when I taste her arousal.

She's soaked, and the feel of her on my lips stirs a frenzy in me as
I shove my face into her, rutting like a wild fucking animal. I flatten
my tongue and lick and stroke and thrust as deep as I can, only paus-
ing so I can tip my head and suck greedily on her clit.

My cock throbs with need as her thighs tighten around my ears,
muting the sexy noises she's making so all I can hear is my racing heart
and the breath struggling to escape my mouth as I refuse to come up
for air. All the fantasies I've had about this woman are finally coming

to fruition, and I'm not going to let a little thing like oxygen get in the way of enjoying myself.

My hand leaves her thigh, fingers aching from where I must have been gripping her harshly. From beneath her ass, I pull back from her and hook my finger before pushing it up into her wet channel, reaching for her G-spot.

"Holy shit," she mewls, sounding unhinged as I finger-fuck her, dragging over the tight ridges inside her as I watch her belly expand and contract with every gasp, every noise, every cry. Her breath is high-pitched when she squeaks out, "I'm going to—"

A noise vibrates my chest as I descend on her clit, flicking my tongue violently over the hardened nub. She tenses around my digit, her fingers squeezing so hard on my traps I'm sure there will be bruises tomorrow. Her body bends, her frame falling down on top of me, and I yank my finger out and plunge my tongue into her center to feel her erupt on my face.

God, yes, I think as she quakes and ruptures over me, her wetness sliding along my stubble as she grinds down on me, fucking my mouth like it's my cock.

If you'd walked into this barn right now, you'd see me in some ungodly position that I didn't even know my body was capable of squatting in. But I'll contort myself in whatever way I must to swallow this woman's release. I'm milking her for once instead of the other way around, and I couldn't be more grateful.

"Holy shit," she repeats as I extract myself from her grip and stand in front of her. Her eyes are wide and horrified as she drags her palm along my lips and chin, wiping her arousal off me. "That's so embarrassing."

"Shut up." I grab behind her knees and hoist her up on the counter with a bit of effort.

Her brows pinch together as she shoves my shoulders. "Did you just tell me to shut up?"

"Yes."

Her red-stained lips part, her cheeks flushed, her hair a mess, and her stunning eyes fill with disagreement once again. "You can't—"

"Yes, I can." I reach down to pull my belt out of my jeans. My cock is numb from being constrained for so long, and I ache to release it from its denim prison. I grip her chin, my eyes zeroing in on her pouty mouth, which is two seconds away from telling me off. "Don't ever feel shame for feeling pleasure. You apologize for coming on my face ever again, and we'll have problems."

Her lips do a good impression of a fish out of water as she struggles with how to reply to that, so I decide to respond for her and cover her mouth with mine, thrusting my tongue deep into her so she can taste the deliciousness of what I just devoured.

In my time on the mountain, I've learned to let go of what society thinks is dirty or wrong...if it feels good and isn't illegal and no one gets hurt, it's fucking mine for the taking. If there's one thing I can send Trista home with after this pregnancy is over...it's the ability to let go of those inhibitions of hers.

And when her legs wrap around my waist and her fingers slice into my hair as her tongue meets my own, thrusting into my mouth, I have a feeling she will be a quick study.

"Fuck me in the stall like you promised," she gasps as she pulls away from me and slides off the counter.

My brows lift in appreciation. Can a student surpass a teacher on the first day of class?

She drags me into the open stall, pulling me into her body, her hand sliding over my denim-constrained cock. I hate it. It fucking hurts and makes everything in my body twitch with irritation.

"Stop fucking with it and pull it out," I growl, gripping the back of her hair before my lips descend onto her throat to drag my tongue up to her jaw.

"God, you are demanding." She huffs as she undoes my jeans, and my vision blurs as her fingers grip my bare shaft with frustration. Her head tips back, and I feel her warm breath on my neck as she sighs. "Better?"

"Uh-huh," I groan, my balance swaying as I reach out and brace myself on the gate. "Oh God, I don't know what I want more, your mouth or your cunt."

"Why not both?" she says, dropping to her knees. Without hesitation, she wraps her lush lips around me, causing my vision to blur.

"Fuuuck," I croon out, trying to regain focus.

She takes me as deep as she can, but it's not nearly deep enough. Her tongue laves over my tip with every bob, and it isn't until I feel the drag of her teeth over my crown that I start to wonder how long I'll be able to last.

"Get up," I command, gripping her arm and pulling her up.

"I was just getting started."

"I don't want to come down your throat," I hiss and turn her around, cascading my hands greedily over her breasts, which are still concealed under this fucking dress that's been torturing me all night.

"Where do you want to come?" she says, her face turning into my neck as her hand reaches back to fork through my hair.

My mind wars with itself as I grind into her ass because I already know the answer, but I shouldn't tell her. I should go get a fucking condom out of my truck and come in it like I have with every other woman I've ever fucked.

But my hand drops from her breast to her belly, and a possessiveness roars inside me as I feel a small bump there. The word "mine" comes into play again. This baby is mine, this woman is mine, this cunt…I want it to be mine.

No fucking shame.

My voice is hoarse as I grind into her ear. "I want to come inside you."

Her breath hitches as my hands roam over her body, memorizing all the supple peaks and valleys. We've both been tested. My semen has already been inside her. In the grand scheme of things, this isn't that big of an ask.

But I can feel her uncertainty, so I elaborate, "I want to watch my seed drip out of your greedy little cunt after I give you another orgasm." I exhale heavily, my nose gliding over the shell of her ear. "But if that's too much for you, just say the word, and I'll go get a condom right now."

Her voice is soft when she asks, "Have you slept with anyone since we were tested?"

My brows furrow. Has my brain stopped thinking of this woman long enough for me to even notice another woman? Fuck no. The answer is fuck no.

"No," I state firmly, my arms tightening around her as I ask a question I am terrified of the answer to. "You?"

Her belly tightens beneath me as she laughs. "Just my vibrator."

I growl again and grind my cock against her rear, pulling her dress up so she can feel my skin on her ass. "Lucky vibrator."

With my cock thrusting down between her ass cheeks, I skate my hand around to her front, teasing her clit, which is still wet from my tongue. When I thrust a finger into her, I groan at her tight wetness. I've never had a woman this wet before. God, I want to cry at the thought of it. So much I've been missing. "What do you want, Lucky? It's your call. No shame in saying no."

When I push a second finger inside her, she buckles over, her hands splaying out on the panel of the stall, nails biting into the chipped wood. She rocks back into my hand, her greedy pussy eating me up, begging for more. When she flips her hair and looks over her shoulder at me, her eyes are burning with need, cheeks red, lips parted as she cries, "Come in me, Wyatt. Give it to me bare. I want to feel you dripping out of me just like I did in your bed."

My thin line of control snaps at that visual that I've been fantasizing about since the second I smelled her scent in my sheets weeks ago. And the unhinged response I have to her words is a fucking blur.

It's me shoving her dress up above her waist. It's me gripping her hips as she braces herself on the giant empty feeder. It's me using one hand to guide myself into her wet heat. It's me careening like a fucking moose during mating season. It's me realizing I've never gone bare inside a woman before, and it's going to fucking suck when I promise myself to never do it with anyone else. It's me groaning as I watch her ass bounce against my groin as I rock into her over and fucking over again. It's me accidentally making eye contact with fucking Handsome and his stupid paralyzed tongue and still not losing an ounce of my erection. It's me feeling slick with sweat as I grind deeper into her tight channel. It's me making a core memory of Trista screaming my name in the quiet of the barn as she comes harder than she did on my face.

And it's me exploding inside her like a fucking cannon, pulling my cock out to watch it seep out before I thrust back in so she doesn't lose a drop.

"All for you," I rumble, blanketing my body over hers and shuddering against the quiver of her sex gripping me. "All for you."

CHAPTER 31

WEEKS PREGNANT: 14
ANIMALS ON THE MOUNTAIN: 4

Trista

The sound of tires on gravel stirs me awake, and I flex my arms above my head as I squint against the daylight pouring in through the windows. A delectable ache radiates between my legs as I squeeze my thighs together. I don't remember feeling sore down there…like…ever. None of the men I've slept with in the past have ever been big enough to cause a physical reaction in my body the next day. But Wyatt Fletcher?

Ouch.

The smile that teases my lips over that realization makes me kick my legs like a silly girl. People are referring to this when they talk about a good kind of pain. I could get used to this kind of pain.

I crawl out of bed and make my way to the bathroom, doing my best not to walk funny as I recall the pressure of Wyatt thrusting into me last night. I brace my hands on the bathroom sink as the memory of him ratchets through me like a spark of electricity. God, last night was crazy. It was otherworldly. It was one of those out-of-body experiences that I would think was a dream if I didn't have the lasting physical effects on my body.

I look at my reflection in the bathroom mirror, and I can see the proof there too. My brown hair is a wild mess of frizz, and the makeup

I wore to the party is smudged with mascara flecks all over my cheeks. Faded red lipstick is smeared around my lips, and I swear I have faint signs of a whisker burn down the side of my neck.

But above it all, there's also a glow about me that I have never noticed before. Is this a pregnancy glow or an "I just had amazing sex" glow? Either way, if I could turn this into a cream and bottle it up, I'd be rich. I'd call the magical elixir *Rode Hard and Put Away Wet.*

I strip and step into the shower, and as hot water cascades over my shoulders, a flash of how wet I was last night hits me as well. The look of his face with my arousal all over it. Ugh! Fucking hot and horrifying in the most hilarious way. It helped his massive dick slide right in without much preamble, that's for sure. My giggle echoes off the glass shower door as I try to recall if I've ever lost control with a man so much that I just drenched his face?

"What's so funny?" Wyatt's deep voice echoes, causing me to shriek and turn my back to the glass door.

"What the hell, Wyatt?" I bellow, my voice loud and obnoxious as this crazy mountain man just ripped me out of some serious reminiscing.

His large frame comes into focus through the foggy glass as he steps into my bathroom. "What's the matter?" he asks like it's totally normal for him to just come traipsing in.

"What are you doing in here?" I grab a loofah and attempt to cover my butt, which is certainly fully visible to him right now because the loofah is no match for the globes of my ass.

"Breakfast, obviously," he answers nonchalantly, and I have to squint over my shoulder to see that he's just pulled his shirt off over his head.

"Why are you taking your clothes off?" I turn around and wipe the glass to confirm that this crazy mountain man is now unbuckling his jeans.

"I'm coming in," he says as he pulls open the shower door, and I stupidly bounce my loofah from my groin to my breast and back to my groin, unsure which part of me I want to cover.

"No, you're not." I toss the only weapon I have at him.

He frowns and grips the sudsy pink object against his hairy pectoral. His eyes drift down my body and flare in appreciation. "Try to stop me."

"Wyatt!" I squeal and cover my breasts with one arm and my privates with another.

"No shame." He sighs as if annoyed and steps into the small shower, which is most definitely not built for two people. When he pulls the door shut behind him and turns back to tower over me, his semi-hard dick brushes against my leg.

"This isn't about shame," I exclaim breathlessly as I look up at him, my mouth opening and closing as I struggle to think straight in his presence. "This is about privacy. You can't just let yourself into my apartment whenever you want just because we had sex once."

His brows knit together as he tilts his head and stares at me like I'm making no sense. "We discussed this already."

"What did we discuss?" I ask, my mind replaying the moments after he came inside me last night.

My damn hormones are only interested in replaying the dirty stuff. I focus past the orgasms for a moment, but I'm pretty sure we ended things with him lowering my dress, patting me on the butt, and saying, "Sleep well, Lucky."

Wyatt presses into me, forcing my back onto the cool fiberglass as our fronts connect in all sorts of indecent spaces. My nipples pebble against his ribs as his hands drift down my sides, resting squarely on my hips like we've showered together a million times already.

Water cascades over his large shoulders as he replies, "As much as we want…whenever we want."

He dips his head like he's going to kiss me, and I press my hand to his mouth. "Okay, but two people have to want it!"

He frowns against my palm and murmurs, "You don't want it?" He gently thrusts his dick, which is now fully erect, into my belly. Either this man is into dubious consent, or he's just horny all the time.

I struggle with how to answer this question when literally every part of my body wants it. I want him in my mouth, between my legs, and in my ass. Honestly, I would take him in my ears if it was a thing.

It's not a thing…I've checked. I should probably speak with a therapist about those intrusive thoughts, too, because they are ten shades of fucked up.

The "wanting" is not the issue here. It's the lack-of-boundaries thing that he still seems to be unable to comprehend.

I swallow my arousal down to the depths of my belly and push my hands onto his chest to get a little space. He steps back, his hard cock bobbing between us like a lifeline pulling me in. "I want it, but remember that smothering thing I said you were doing before?"

"I thought you liked that part." His lips thin speculatively. "If you just let go of control a little bit, you might actually discover you're enjoying yourself."

My jaw drops. "You think *I'm* controlling?"

"Yes."

"You're the one who took my keys last night!"

"You're the one who let me." He tilts his head to the side and eyes me firmly. "I told you if I fucked you, every part of you would belong to me. Did you think I was joking?"

"Do you realize how crazy that sounds?"

"Didn't seem like you minded last night."

I scoff and shake my head. "My God, you are like a long-lost caveman who's never operated in normal society."

"I just don't live with fucking shame," Wyatt growls back at me, his face deathly serious. He leans forward and splays his hand on the shower wall by my face as he adds, "If there's something I want, I'm not going to pussyfoot around and act like I don't want it just to be cool or play games. I want you. I've been thinking about you since the moment I woke up. I want to be inside you again so I can see your face when you come this time. I lay awake half the night, regretting the fact that I didn't get to see your fuckable lips part when you came on my cock."

His eyes drift angrily down to my lips as my entire body begins to quake with anxiety. Or is that desire? Probably a bit of both.

"Would you like to come for me again, Lucky?" His voice is low and almost threatening. I like it way too much.

"Yes," I whimper, my head dropping back onto the shower wall as my hormones take over once again.

"Good," Wyatt replies and steps away from me to reach for my shampoo bottle. He squirts some into his palm and hits me with his stunning blue eyes. "Then let me get you clean before I take you to bed and make you dirty with my cum."

And that's when the mountain man begins to wash me.

Yes...wash me.

He starts with my hair, using his nails on my scalp in a way that makes my knees wobble. When he massages conditioner into my head, I wonder if I could orgasm from scalp stimulation. When the loofah comes into the mix, then I know what he's after. He grinds the tex-tured sponge over my clit repeatedly while his other free hand moves the bubbles around my breasts.

"Ow," I croak when he pinches lightly on my nipples.

"Does that hurt?" Wyatt asks, his husky voice deep with longing as he instantly releases them and cups my breasts gently.

I nod slowly. "My nipples are like little pain buttons since the pregnancy."

"I never want to hurt you," Wyatt says, moving me back under the stream so the water can cascade the bubbles down my body. "Just tell me if anything ever gets to be too much."

He proceeds to massage my entire body under the water, running small circles over my traps and my shoulder blades, his fingers glid-ing delicately over the swells of my ass as he rubs my lower back in a kneading sensation. He takes his time, never once turning the wash session into sex, which I appreciate.

Shower sex for bigger girls is so not a thing. First of all, water is a horrible form of lubrication. But mostly, it's the fact that I'm not light enough for Wyatt to pick up and rock me up and down on his cock. It's one thing for him to carry my sick body across the room to drop me on my bed or hoist me up onto a counter. But for him to hold me against a shower wall for sex...without a good base under my ass, big boy or not...forget about it.

But I gather that this shower is intentional in other ways beyond sex. It's about exploration, which we didn't really make time for last night. Wyatt's hands flatten over my belly as he rubs his rough palm against my flesh.

"What does it feel like?" he asks, his voice deep in my ear.

I wince against the contact, my body recoiling at the feeling of someone paying such close attention to a space I consider the problem area on my body. I guess I have a handful of problem areas if I were to compare myself to magazine covers or shine a light on the places where I have stretch marks and cellulite. But I've done some serious self-love reflections in the past decade to accept my body for what it is and be grateful for it for housing my organs and giving me life. And giving this baby life, for that matter.

It's a good body, even if it's not what society might see as perfect. It's perfect for me. And if this crazy mountain man wants to feel the life growing inside it, I won't let annoying insecurities get in my way of enjoying some good old human contact.

I'm a cow, I'm a cow, I'm a cow…

"It doesn't feel like much at this point." My shoulders lift as I remind myself this feeling of him touching me means nothing to me. "Aside from my sore nipples, I honestly forget I'm pregnant sometimes."

The corners of Wyatt's mouth turn down as he nods. "That's wild."

"I can't suck it in anymore, though," I add with a huff. "My stomach just goes nowhere."

The corner of his mouth tips up. He likes that answer. God, I bet he'll be obsessed when I start showing more. I might need to turn my cow mantra into a poem or haiku. Something a bit lengthier to get through the upcoming months if we're going to continue to be up close and personal.

When I started this surrogacy job, I never imagined seeing him this much. I thought it'd be doctor's appointments and maybe occasionally in the barn. Now, this man has somehow barreled his way into my shower.

By the time the water turns cold, my body is limp, and all my muscles that were sore before are completely healed from his tender caresses.

The nozzle squeaks as he shuts off the tap, and I struggle to keep my eyes open as he begins to towel dry me. I glance down and see he's still fully erect, his cock straining at the tip so much it looks angry, but his face looks completely content.

With the towel wrapped around me, he brushes through my hair, taking care to go slowly over the snarls. I briefly wonder how the hell he knows how to brush a woman's hair so well, and then a flash of his niece comes into mind.

"Your hair looks funny straight," his deep voice rumbles as he combs out the last few messy strands.

I frown at him in the mirror and then glance at my slicked-down hair. "Well, stop looking, then."

His heated eyes meet mine. "I like it like this, but I like your curls better." A tender look flicks across his face as he returns his attention to my head. "They suit you."

"God, you're weird," I reply with a laugh, shattering the moment. He glares at me, so I elaborate. "On the outside, you're this rugged, scary guy offering dirty orgasms, but on the inside, you're total mush, aren't you?"

The corner of his mouth tugs up, and the wicked look in his eye has my insides swirling. He leans close, his bearded chin teasing the shell of my ear as he replies, "Just don't tell anyone." His brows lift lasciviously. "How am I supposed to remain the mysterious, grumpy brother if word gets out I'm a softy?"

"And a Swiftie," I add with a grin.

He grips my sides with a wicked glint to his eye. "I'm going to fuck you for that."

"Now, don't go threatening me with a good time," I singsong, and a squeal erupts from my throat as he aggressively yanks the towel off my body and drags me out of the bathroom butt-ass naked.

My smile feels permanent as I fall back onto my rumpled white bed. I grab my wet hair to fan it above me, knowing full well it'll be a mess when we're done here, but I have better things to focus on than hair product because Wyatt stands at the side of my bed, and he just dropped his towel.

There's that big dick again.

I have a feeling today will hurt even more than yesterday. And my weird body simmers with excitement over that potential.

"Don't push my buttons," Wyatt says, standing between my bent legs and grazing his fingers up my calves. "I want to take my time with you this morning, and when you irritate me, I just want to fuck you hard and fast."

My brows lift because the hard-and-fast bit worked pretty damn well last night. But I let him do it his way instead because he's right— it's freeing to let go of control. With all the other men I've slept with, I've been in my head the whole time. Not necessarily in the driver's seat, but fretting over body position and length of time I should be doing oral versus how loud my moans are and are they believable or can they tell I'm faking it. It's a deep, insecure part of me that I don't even like to admit to myself. But magically, I'm not pretending anything with Wyatt Fletcher. He basically stopped me in my tracks when he saw me try to wipe my cum off his face. He's apparently a perceptive caveman.

Wyatt moves his fingers to my clit, teasing it as he pumps his thick, veined cock in his fist. He presses one finger deep inside me, groaning when he sees how wet I am.

Welcome to pregnancy hormones, my friends! I'm wetter than the Niagara Falls during a rainstorm these days. The dumb pregnancy books recommend wearing panty liners or packing extra underwear when you're away from home for longer periods of time. But I kind of think this mountain man might be a better solution.

I reach down and grip Wyatt's hand between my legs. "I don't want your fingers."

"What do you want, Lucky?" he asks, a look of intrigue in his eyes as he stands to full height and continues pumping himself.

My eyes drop, and I see a tiny bit of precum leak out of his tip, so I sit up on my elbows and reach for him, sliding my finger over the warm liquid before pressing it to my clit.

"I want you inside me," I reply breathlessly.

His eyes squint as if in pain, the veins in his neck taut. "Are you still good with no condom?"

I nod, unable to find words anymore, elated by the idea that I am seconds away from feeling that fullness that I ache for again. I want that throb back. I miss it.

The bed dips as he comes down over me, his body like a delicious, heated blanket as he holds himself on top of me. I reach down and position him where he needs to be, and a low growl vibrates in his chest as he pushes slowly into me, watching my body take him inch by glorious inch.

A burn lights up my insides as he stretches me to capacity, and a bark of a laugh escapes my lips when I think about his dick being good prep work for childbirth.

"Something funny about my cock inside you?" Wyatt asks, looking amused and not at all offended as he thrusts even deeper into me.

I gasp, my body at odds with the intense feeling between my legs and the ridiculous thoughts going on in my head. "My thoughts are insane. Just ignore me."

"Tell me," he commands, dropping his chin to eye me carefully. "No shame."

"Maybe a little shame," I reply with a wince and splay my hands on his chest as I muster up the bravery to say the crazy part out loud. "I was just thinking about how your gargantuan dick should make childbirth a little bit easier."

He frowns, clearly not understanding my thought process.

I bob my head up at him. "Because you're stretching me out."

He processes my reply, biting his lip and moving inside me again, sending shock waves through my limbs. His voice is deep and boyish when he asks, "So I'm the biggest you've had?"

"Yes." I snort laugh.

His smile is swoony. "And the best?"

"Okay, let's not get carried away."

That response made Mountain Man angry as the muscle in his jaw twitches. "Tell me," he barks, his body tense as he thrusts deep into me again.

My limbs jitter with need as my fingers dig into his muscled arms. I glance down at where we're connected. "This is literally the second time you've been inside me, so I haven't had enough time to fully assess your skill level."

I lie. I lie through my fucking teeth because I'm a lying liarson.

A wicked grin spreads across his face, and I realize I've never seen this man smile so much. Sex makes grumpy Mountain Man happy. His voice is deep and rumbling when he replies, "Oh, you really shouldn't have said that."

And his smile falls right before he sits up on his knees and tosses my legs up on top of his shoulders. He yanks me toward him and begins thrusting into me, taking my breath and my voice in one fell swoop. The punishing grind is so intense I see stars, and I lose complete track of time as I experience a spontaneous fucking orgasm.

But, like, not just any orgasm. It's one that won't quit.

Most orgasms in my life could be compared to going down a long slide. That little flip you get in your belly? That's what my climaxes have felt like. Intense and good for a second…but then over.

This orgasm?

It's like the biggest roller coaster in the entire world. It's like a roller coaster with no breaks, just loop-de-loops and drops and spins and swirls. It's so long-lasting time ceases to exist, and I start to wonder if it's one orgasm or a series of orgasms on top of others.

Jesus…what must that baby goat turd be thinking inside me?

By the time Wyatt comes, I'm completely spent. I barely even register him between my thighs, watching his semen drip out of me before he thrusts his semi-hard erection back inside me.

This is clearly a thing for him, and I'm not sure when it became a thing for me too, but I think it might have happened during one of our many sundown sessions.

God, this is fucked on so many levels.

I'm a paid surrogate having sex with the intended parent. This is going to get so damn messy if I don't get control of this situation.

After I go to the bathroom and clean myself up, I'm starfished on my bed, covered in a sheet, struggling to find the words I know I need to have with this crazy man crawling back in bed with me.

My head flops over to look at him, and he quirks an eyebrow, clearly waiting for something.

I groan and say in a huff, "Fine, you're the best and biggest I've ever had."

"I know." A victorious grin lights up his face as he rolls onto his back and props his hands on his chest casually. He looks so boyish right now it's disarming. He's usually so serious and solemn. I wonder when was the last time he had sex.

"Do you make all your conquests tell you you're the biggest and best?" I ask, rolling over on my side to poke him in the ribs.

"Nah, I just wanted you to say it." He side-eyes me. "It feels good to get a leg up on you because since the day we've met, I've felt like I can't catch up."

"Seriously?"

"Yes," he replies with a huff. "You argue about everything yet still get me to say yes to things I would normally never agree to…like a fucking mini horse in the barn."

"Don't think I haven't noticed you slipping carrots to Handsome," I deadpan, propping my hand on my hip. "You two are totally vibing."

"I'm not vibing with the mini horse." His brows furrow like I'm speaking nonsense, but I see a hint of a smile in the corner of his eyes. It's swoony.

But I can't be swooned right now. I have boundaries to set. "Well, I'm going to push another one of your many buttons."

"What?" he groans, shoving his hand through his short tresses.

"We need to establish some ground rules for this sexuationship."

"Sexuationship?" He repeats the word I just made up, and I have to laugh.

"Yes, this is officially a sexuationship," I reply, looking away because it's hard to think straight when he's shirtless. I did not think a hairy-chested man was my thing, but on Wyatt Fletcher…it just works. My voice is firm as I stare up at the natural wood beams that line the barn roof. "You can't just come in and get sex anytime you want. That does not work for me."

I feel him watching me, so I continue.

"If we're really going to keep doing this throughout the pregnancy, I think we should work something out like we did with our insemination nights. Maybe we do the sundown rule."

"Sundown every other night?" Wyatt asks, and I glance over to see a very pleased look in his eyes.

"Maybe not that much," I retort, wondering if my body could even sustain that much sex. I really need to call and ask the nurse about sex during pregnancy. "We can just do it when the mood strikes us, I guess."

"I will be in the mood every day," Wyatt deadpans.

"Jesus."

"Multiple times a day if you like."

"Okay—"

"A light breeze will get me in the mood with you."

"Whoa there, Mountain Man," I exclaim, and he looks positively tickled at my outburst. The ass. I sit up in bed, clutching the sheet to my chest to feel some semblance of control. I splay my hand out between us and say very firmly, "I need some boundaries honored here, or I am going to go insane."

"I don't like boundaries," Wyatt murmurs, and I see a flash of insecurity cross his face. "Boundaries feel like secrets."

"Well, they aren't," I argue, and my brows furrow at that bizarre take. "If anything, they're truths."

He sighs heavily and watches me for a moment. "What's this mean? I'm just at your beck and call? You call all the shots?"

"Since you seem to have the sex drive of a teenager, I'm afraid so," I reply firmly. "Now...about your brothers."

"What about my brothers?" Wyatt's mood takes a sharp nosedive.

"What is it with you and your brothers?" I ask, trying to make sense of this obvious shift in his demeanor. "You chose to live on this mountain together, right? Why are you so weird about them?"

"I'm not weird about them," he argues, his jaw taut. "I'm just weird about *you* with them." His eyes tighten as he glances at me. "My brothers and I have a strange history with women."

My brows shoot to the sky. "This sounds juicy."

"It's ancient history. It happened like ten years ago."

I wait for him to elaborate, but he doesn't. What does that mean? He's…jealous? Insecure? Of me hooking up with his brothers? The thought of that causes my veins to simmer with excitement. I don't enjoy torturing men for sport, but the fact that a strong, confident man like Wyatt Fletcher would think that I was some prize to win? That's like…totally going in my fictional girlie diary.

My eyes narrow as I gaze at a now grumpy-looking Wyatt. "So was there some love triangle or something?"

He frowns.

I tilt my head expectantly. "Oh, come on…you can't just drop a bomb like that and walk away. What was her name? Or was it multiple women? Did you guys fight over a girl?"

"I'm not going to talk about her," he snaps, and I can see that I've crossed a line he doesn't want me crossing, so I pull back instantly.

Just hearing him say "her" gives me a little flicker of jealousy. She must have been some type of woman to elicit this type of reaction. And she still has an effect on him…even a decade later.

I chew my lip for a moment and try to detach from the feelings that realization evokes. This is just sex. He's going to be a single dad with the baby growing inside me in a matter of months. Wyatt Fletcher is not boyfriend material, so why should I care if he's hung up on some girl from years ago.

I clear my throat and add firmly, "Well, I don't want your brothers to know anything about what's going on between you and me. I don't want anyone to know, frankly. If they found out about our sexuationship, it would make me feel like you're paying me for sex… which you're not."

"You'd be worth every penny."

"Not the point, Wyatt!"

He holds his hand up apologetically, and then a thought hits me. A thought that I really don't want to say out loud, but I must, or it will eat me alive. I swallow the lump in my throat and gird my loins. "And just because we're having sex doesn't mean anything with this"—I gesture to my belly—"changes."

He frowns, watching my hand hover over my stomach. "I don't follow."

"I'm a cow." I state my mantra out loud.

His face twists in confusion.

"I am an inseminated cow. A mere incubator. I'm not going to stick around after this baby is born, so don't, like…fall in love with me or something."

Silence descends over us, and I feel my face heat with mortification as he begins shaking with silent laughter. The act is so foreign to him I instantly regret my stupid fucking comment. God, I just should have stopped at the sundown rule. What an idiot! Of course this mountain man isn't going to fall for me.

He's him, and I'm…me.

"Okay, it's not that funny," I snap and feel my eyes prick with tears. I move to get off the bed, desperate to run away from this horrid feeling of rejection. I make my way to my closet to find some clothes because if there's one thing worse than being laughed at, it's being laughed at while naked.

As I aggressively rifle through my stuff, looking for something big and baggy to wear or a hole to crawl into, I feel Wyatt's big arms wrap around me.

"Don't." My voice cracks as I shake out of his embrace.

"Hey," he says in a concerned-dad voice. "What did I do?"

"You're laughing at me," I exclaim vehemently. I turn on my heel so he can see the full effect he's had on me, not hiding my tears. "I get that this is just sex, but the idea of you falling for me isn't that funny."

His face falls in horror. "That wasn't what I was laughing at."

"Then what was it?"

"I was laughing because you referred to yourself as an inseminated cow."

My head juts back as I consider his answer and try to decide whether he's full of shit or not. "I thought it was because you thought I was disgusting or something."

"Jesus, Lucky. You got fucking issues." He reaches out and cups my face, forcing me to look up at him as he eyes me seriously. "I've said this before, but I'll say it again. You're stunning. And if this baby is a girl and looks anything like you, I'm going to have to buy another shotgun to scare the guys away."

Pain that I did not expect sears through my chest at that comment. *If the baby is a girl and looks like me...*

I'm a cow. I'm a cow. I'm a cow. I'm a cow.

I pull back and force a laugh. "Just wait until I get a big ole pregnancy belly with stretch marks. Then we'll see if you still want to be in this sexuationship."

"I can't fucking wait for that," he says seriously, crossing his arms and propping himself on the doorframe. His eyes drift affectionately down my body as I gape at him.

Is he for real? Do men like this actually exist? Was my dad like this with my mom at the beginning, and then things just went to shit at the end?

He notices my confused expression and adds, "But if you need to hear it...you're beautiful pregnant, not pregnant, stretch marks, no stretch marks. If I passed you in a bar somewhere in Denver, I would definitely moo."

My smile is wobbly as my stomach flutters at that ridiculous compliment. A mooing mountain man—why is that so cute? Swallowing thickly, I turn and focus back on finding some clothes. I was sitting here worried about him falling for me...but if he keeps talking like that, it could very well be the other way around.

CHAPTER 32

WEEKS PREGNANT: 16
ANIMALS ON THE MOUNTAIN: WELL…

Trista

"I have to ask you something, Trista. And I want you to be honest."
I turn on my heel inside Handsome's pen, and a rush of heat hits
me as Wyatt's giant frame steps through the barn door.

My mouth goes dry as I drink him in. He's dressed in his standard faded jeans, Timberland boots, and T-shirt. He's traded in his
flannels due to the hot July sun. His skin is bronzed more than it was
when we first met, showing signs of how much he's been working in
the sun lately. It makes his blue eyes stand out even more.

I glance outside and see that we're at least thirty minutes away
from sundown, so he's early, but I'm not complaining.

I pull Handsome's halter off and pat his rear as I make my way out
of his stall, excited by the prospect of giving the animals another show.

"What is it?" I ask, cursing myself for wearing my stupid overalls.
They're going to be a bitch to get off quickly, especially because they're
getting tight on me, but I've ripped too many pairs of my jeans out
here, so I'm trying to stick with more sturdy fabric.

Wyatt's blue eyes are lasers, and I can't help but notice them drop
to my stomach before he asks a question I did not expect. "Where…
are…the fucking chickens?"

My lips part as goose bumps erupt all over my skin. "Chickens?" My voice sounds weak and guilty.

His nostrils flare as he tips his chin to the side to crack his neck. I haven't seen grumpy Wyatt in a while, and I'm only now just realizing I kind of missed him. He points back toward his house. "I just heard a rooster crow as I was walking down here, and Calder said he heard one the other morning, so I know they're here somewhere."

I hook my trembling thumbs into my coverall straps and stare down at my feet. "There's no…I didn't…maybe a neighboring property…"

As I ramble, he eliminates the space between us, reaches out, and presses my lips together with his calloused fingers, pinching them into a flat line. I close my eyes, relishing in his touch and his scent like a drug addict.

His voice is dark and threatening when he says, "Fess up, Lucky."

I like that nickname a lot better when we're naked.

"Oh, fine." I yank my face away from him and stomp my foot with a growl. "I put a chicken coop on the backside of the barn. It's a small one, though, and the previous owners swore there was no rooster in the flock," I flat-out lie. That damn bird is going to ruin this whole thing.

"There's a whole flock?" he exclaims, his voice higher-pitched than I've ever heard it. "How many are there?"

I cringe and drop my head. "Only seven."

"I fucking hate birds, Trista." He groans and turns away, pacing in the alleyway of the barn as he aggressively runs his hand over his hair. "They have beady eyes and eat weird things, and they're just…"

"They're not birds, they're chickens," I correct with enthusiasm. "And they're making eggs. I can make you breakfast for a change!"

I smile broadly, and he stops pacing, only to hit me with a flat, unimpressed look. This is our first real fight since our sexuationship started two weeks ago, and I was beginning to think we both had personality transplants. Apparently, mind-blowing, regular sex is a real mood booster, but I guess it can't last forever.

But he's right. He told me no chickens, and I explicitly broke that rule. Maybe if he knew they were going to be butchered because someone had them in their backyard and it was against their neighborhood HOA and a little girl who lived at the house had already named them, and while I love me some fried chicken, I don't love to eat it when it's named Heather...and Mallory...and Sasha...and...I forget the rest.

"Sooo," I coo, stepping closer and sliding my hands up his chest. "I could tell you the whole sob story about a six-year-old girl naming all the chickens and crying to me at the shelter about it...or you could let me make it up to you in other ways."

I comb my fingers through his hair, and he trembles slightly, his eyes fluttering closed briefly before he glances out the barn windows. "It's not sundown yet."

I smile. He's been very good about adhering to our sex schedule. Last week, he gave me a look in the barn one morning before we left for work that I know meant he wanted to break our rules...but he didn't make a move. I've been wondering who was going to cave first. Guess it will be me.

For the chickens.

"I must pay for my crime." I stand on my tiptoes and lightly press my lips to his.

A low growl vibrates in his chest at our contact, and without hesitation, he bends over and wraps his arms around me, capturing my mouth more fully as he thrusts his tongue deep into my mouth.

I've learned in the past two weeks that Wyatt isn't a light kisser. He doesn't do anything lightly. He gives it one hundred and ten percent... barn make-out session included, and I dare say I'm into it. I can't say any men in my bullpen have ever made me feel so *wanted*. It's going to be a tough feeling to let go of when this all ends.

His erection presses into my belly as he marches me backward and pushes me up against Reginald's pen. I let out a little moan when he reaches down and grabs my thigh, opening my legs so he can press himself against my center.

"Take me here, Wyatt," I beg, my hormones raging as lust ratchets through me. There's no way I'll be able to make it up the stairs to my bed right now anyway. I've been thinking about him all day.

And I must admit…there is something wildly magical about having sex in this barn. This place has been my sanctuary since the day I moved in, and it's only intensified since I got pregnant. Call it hormones or call it nature…I almost prefer it down here over my big fluffy bed upstairs.

He rips his lips away from mine as he struggles with the buckles on my overalls. They're tricky little bastards, so I attempt to help him. My breasts are finally free from their prison, and Wyatt's hands cup them greedily over my T-shirt, causing me to moan when I hear a voice call out, "Wyatt, you in there?"

We shoot apart from each other just as his brother Calder walks through the barn door. My nipples feel like they will break through my shirt as I watch Wyatt conceal his lower half behind the fence near Handsome's stall. I turn and shakily attempt to rebuckle my straps, and Reginald makes a noise as I stare down into his pen.

Don't judge me, Reg. You eat your own shit sometimes.

"Hey there, Momma Bear," Calder drawls cheerily. "How are you this fine Saturday evening?"

I swallow my sex fog down and turn to face him, my hands nervously going into my hair, wondering if it's a mess from Wyatt's fingers. "I'm good, Calder. Nice to see you again."

"You too." His eyes slide over to Wyatt, who's hunching over with his arms propped on the fence, but from my angle, the boner that Wyatt is sporting is still plain as day. "What are you doing, Papa Bear?"

"Chores, what do you think?" Wyatt growls, the veins in his neck looking angry. "What do you want?"

"Um…your help, obviously." Calder hooks his thumb to the door. "Max is on his way up the mountain, and the others are going to be here any minute, and I still can't find the cards or poker chips in your house."

Wyatt waves him off. "I'll be in in a minute."

I tilt my head curiously at that. Wyatt Fletcher is a twenty-minute man on his worst day. Forty-five is his average. It's not uncommon for him to put in a good hour. He side-eyes me knowingly.

Calder directs his attention back to me and waggles his brows suggestively. "You play poker, Momma Bear?"

I roll my eyes at that nickname that unfortunately seems to be sticking. "I've played before, yes."

"You should join us!" he says cheerily.

"It's usually just guys," Wyatt argues, looking irritated by his brother. He shakes his head and wrinkles his nose at me like I should definitely say no to poker night.

"Not tonight," Calder corrects. "Evie girl is coming. Probably our last poker night with her before she flies off to Ireland. Come on, join us. It'll be fun." Calder motions for me to follow him inside.

"She can't," Wyatt blurts out, looking completely awkward all hunched and red-faced and glued to the fence.

"I can't?" I ask, feeling a bit triggered by that controlling tone of his rearing its ugly head again. It's like he's taking my car keys all over again.

Wyatt's eyes widen knowingly at me. "It's almost sundown."

"And what…she'll turn into a vampire?" Calder laughs and glances over his shoulder when he sees an SUV pull up to Wyatt's cabin. "That's Max, and he's going to be pissy that we're not ready."

He marches over to Wyatt and presses his hands to his shoulders as he walks him toward the door. "Wyatt, let's go. Trista, come join us whenever you're free. We'll take you in your vampire or human form."

"I'll be there in thirty," I call to their backs. "I just need to take a nice hot shower first."

Wyatt shoots me one last scathing look that I know I'm going to pay for later. But no one tells me what to do. Not even grumpy-mountain-man Wyatt.

Wyatt

"Fuck my life," I murmur to myself as I watch Trista stride into my home almost an hour later, looking way too hot for how sexually frustrated I am right now.

"Trista!" Everly squeals, and her chair groans on the hardwood as she bolts toward the door to greet my lucky number thirteen.

She's a cow, she's a cow, she's a cow. I repeat Trista's mantra to myself to try to get control of my thoughts as she moves into the room, giving me a full view of her curves as she greets my niece.

My eyes drink her in as I clutch my poker cards so tight they start to bend. She's wearing this summery black dress with little straps that show off her tan. And her cleavage. Cleavage that I know intimately after the past couple of weeks. One breast has a beauty mark right by her nipple. It's the bigger of the two breasts, so it's become a favorite of mine.

She's still not showing in her abdomen, as far as I can tell. And the past couple of weeks, I've made a conscious effort not to discuss the pregnancy because it seems easier to live in this little vacuum of sex we have going. For now, at least.

"Sit by me," Everly says, dragging her over to the table. Our eyes meet as she lowers herself into the seat across from me.

Everly sets about introducing Trista to the whole crew here tonight. It's honestly a lot of Max's friends from Boulder, who have become my friends as well throughout the years. They all have kids and shit, but they seem to enjoy whatever it is my brothers and I represent to them...reliving their single days, maybe?

There's Dean, Max's financial adviser turned friend, then his friends Miles and Sam, who I know well because the two of them run Tire Depot in Boulder, and we do all our truck service work through there. And finally, there's Max's closest childhood friend, who I've known forever, Josh. These guys' wives are also super close, and they all have more kids than I can even keep track of these days.

"This one is a doctor," Everly adds, pointing at Josh.

"What kind of doctor are you?" Trista asks curiously.

"Family medicine," Josh adds with a polite smile. "I have a private practice with my wife in Boulder, who does more mental health stuff. We have three daughters as well, which means...I drink a lot of whiskey." He sips the amber liquid from his rocks glass and shakes his head.

Jesus. I'd forgotten Josh had a third kid. There is no way I could handle three kids. And three daughters? Forget it. I already struggle to say no to Everly. If I had three girls, it would be mass chaos on the mountain. Luckily, Trista is only pregnant with the one baby. That's all I'm interested in.

A thought strikes me that I hadn't considered before. My lawyer asked me about it during our first meeting, but I brushed it off, certain I was making the right decision. He asked if I decide someday that I want another kid, would I want Trista to be the surrogate again? Obviously, it'd be nice because then the babies would be full siblings, but I felt pretty certain that as a single father, one would be all I could handle.

But if I changed my mind, would she be up for it? Would we conceive the baby the old-fashioned way then? My dick stirs in my jeans at that thought.

"Dr. Richardson's niece Claire is one of my best friends," Everly says with a smile, ripping me out of my crazy mind. "She's a year younger than me though, so she won't graduate until next year. Maybe she'll join me in Ireland!"

"I'm afraid she's already decided she's going to University of Colorado Boulder like her auntie," Josh says with a wink.

"Wouldn't that be nice," Max interjects, shooting a flat look at his daughter.

Everly shoots me a sheepish smile, clearly looking for a lifeline, but I'm not going to be the one to save her. I'm just as miserable as Max over this Ireland move.

Everly's voice is soft when she replies, "At least it will be easy for me to visit her when I come home in the summers."

"And at Christmas," I press, my eyes narrowing on my niece.

"And any other holiday breaks they give you," Luke adds with a scowl.

Everly rolls her eyes. "We'll see how it goes. It's a long flight."

"Your dad can afford first class," I snap, my jaw clenching with irritation. This niece of mine seems far too eager to get out of Boulder, and I fucking hate it.

Everly smiles nervously and then directs her focus back to Trista. "Have you felt the baby kick yet?"

Trista's cheeks flush as she keeps her hands on the table, gripping the bottle of water she brought. "No, I haven't. The doctor said my placenta was on the top or something, so that can sometimes make it harder to feel movement until the baby gets bigger."

She finds my eyes and looks a little nervous, so I nod my head at her, silently telling her it's okay.

"Kate had that same thing with Tucker," Miles says with a nod to Trista, and her eyes light up, clearly grateful for someone else at this table to have some experience with that.

"We did not experience that with the twins," Sam says with a laugh. "It was like a jungle gym in Maggie's belly."

"Aw," Everly says, splaying her hand out on the table. "I hope I can feel the baby kick before I go."

"Everly," I chastise, my brows furrowing as I shake my head at her. "That's not appropriate."

"It's not?" Everly looks horrified and snaps her attention to Trista. "I'm so sorry. I felt my stepmom Cozy's tummy all the time when she was pregnant with Ethan. I didn't know it'd be weird."

"It's fine," Trista says and shoots me a scathing look like I came down on Everly too hard.

I'm just trying to protect her. This table is full of people with traditional families and traditional situations. Sure, maybe some of them got pregnant before marriage, but none of them got pregnant with someone they weren't in love with. And certainly none of them got pregnant with someone they were paying to have their baby. This group and my family can be a fucking lot. If you give them an inch, they will take ten miles. Everly doesn't need to be feeling Trista's stomach. Plus, if anyone is going to get to feel the baby move, it better be me.

"Are you going to find out the sex, Uncle Wyatt?" Everly asks, her blue eyes wide and animated like a Disney princess.

I lift my shoulders and grunt.

Everyone stares at me in dead silence, but it's Trista who answers, "That's a yes."

All eyes swerve from me back to Trista, and I have to admit, even I'm a little shocked she knows my answer. I haven't said the words out loud yet. I tilt my head and eye her curiously.

"You speak Wyatt?" Calder asks, gaping at her.

Trista laughs and leans back in her chair. "Oh yeah…I'm fluent in grunts, growls, and heavy sighs. So yes, totally fluent in Wyatt."

Luke's grave eyes hit me. "She has much knowledge."

This causes the whole table to burst out laughing, and Everly's eyes fill with tears that she gets every time something really excites her. It's a sight that makes me really happy, and it's at that moment that I realize I'm smiling like a loon. Things with Trista are going remarkably well…even with the addition of sex. Who would have thought?

Everly breaks up the laughter with an excited gasp. "Uncle Wyatt, can we do a gender reveal party when you find out? It can be a gender reveal and a baby shower. Oh my God, it will be so much fun. I'll do everything. You don't have to lift a finger."

I groan and shake my head. Gender reveal parties are so fucking extra. Plus, those kinds of parties are always more for women than men. Why would I want to sign up to make a spectacle of the gender of the baby I'm having with a woman I'm not even married to?

"It can be the last time we can all get together before I go." Everly begs and sticks her lip out. "Pretty please?"

"Fine," I grumble, hating myself for being so fucking weak.

She cheers, and I watch Trista force a smile that doesn't reach her eyes. So much for protecting her because there is no way in hell Everly won't demand Trista be there.

"Are we done talking about diapers now?" Calder whines, sounding like our nephew, Ethan. "I came here to play some cards and try to win back some of the money Everly has won off me basically her whole life."

"I learn from the best." She smirks proudly at me, and I watch Trista's eyes warm on Everly for a moment before we get back to our game.

"Damn, you have all the luck!" Dean says, tossing his cards down on the table as Trista shows pocket aces. "Seriously, you've had pocket aces twice tonight. Are you sure you're not hiding cards?"

"I am many things, but definitely not a cheater." Trista eyes Dean harshly as she leans across the table and drags the chips toward her ample bosom.

My eyes flash around to make sure no one is checking her out like I am. Luckily, everyone passes the test with flying colors, so I don't have to punch them in the face.

Whiskey was a bad choice tonight.

I've only had three, but they've only served to add fuel to the fire that is my desire for the lucky girl over there.

Trista stands up from the table. "I need to refill my water. Can I get anyone anything?"

"I'm good," Everly says as she collects all the cards and shuffles.

I watch Trista move through my house, and my cock twitches at the sight of her. The last time she was here in my home was our insemination nights. Now, I get to come inside her and not fucking ranch cups.

I get up from the table and follow her out to the kitchen. She stands in front of a bowl of popcorn, and I move beside her, my arm brushing hers, the skin-on-skin heat sending a jolt of need through my body.

"You still owe me for the chickens," I state quietly, my eyes glancing back to see if anyone is watching us. I'm pleased to see everyone's focus is on Calder as he shows off some new ink he got last week.

"That's some weird dirty talk, but I could be into it." She pops a kernel into her mouth as she turns around and presses her ass to my counter.

What I wouldn't give to just grab her by the thighs, hoist her up there, and have my way with her.

My cock throbs in my jeans.

She smirks and moves over to the island, opening the drawer to reveal the dressing cups still stored there. "Do you want to use one of these for old times' sake?"

"Fuck no." I move to the island with her like we're two magnets being pulled together.

She gets a conspiratorial glint in her eye. "The way we do it now works pretty good, I guess."

An image of her pretty pink pussy with my cum dripping out of her hits me like a ton of bricks, and I have to bite back my groan at just the memory of that.

Every other day isn't enough.

Her eyes narrow speculatively on me. "Why didn't you want me to come tonight?"

My brows furrow at her question. "You mean, besides the erection I'm currently having to fight off?"

"That's not the reason." She licks her lips and tilts her head at me. "It's the same reason you wanted them not to talk to me when I first moved up here. More than just them being wild mountain men."

My heart beats slower as her probing question nudges a bruise I like to pretend doesn't exist. A bruise that I've spent the past several years trying to push away.

"We're going to go show the guys the bench Calder made!" Everly calls out, and I look over to see everyone is up from the table and making their way out the door.

"What?" I ask, not sure I heard what my niece said because my mind was going down a very dark path.

"We're going to head out to Grandpa's bench. We'll be back in five…maybe ten minutes." Everly shoots me a strange look and then shoves Calder and Luke toward the door.

"I've already seen the bench," Luke whines.

"I made the fucker, and even I don't want to look at it," Calder adds.

"Just go," Everly snaps before closing the door behind her. Their voices fade in the distance, and I stand there frozen, unsure what to do with this coveted alone time.

"Do you want to go with them?" I ask, swallowing the knot in my throat. My question is loaded with the answer that I can't quite bring myself to give her.

"Why would I want to go with them?"

I shrug and look down at the counter, refusing to meet her eyes. Refusing to let myself see the interest that might be there for someone other than me. "Calder and Luke are a lot more fun than me. Younger, more talkative, less grumpy and controlling. Definitely less smothering."

My eyes lift to hers, unsure of what I will see. Will I see pity? Regret? Confusion? Intrigue? Any of those reactions to my fucked-up thoughts about my brothers are valid. My relationship with them is a confusing one that even I can't work out. I would kill for them. Literally kill. And there's no one else I want to spend time with. Like Max's friends are fine and all, but the ease and comfort I feel living near my brothers all the time gives me a sense of peace that I crave to feel right in this world. To stop worrying all the time.

But the comparison game I play in my head as a direct result of our past with women, one woman in particular, is something I still can't seem to get over, no matter how much wood I chop.

"I'm warming up to the smother." Trista's hand flattens over top of mine, and when she finally looks up at me, her eyes blazing with *that look*, the one that I have become painfully familiar with, the one that I picture with my hand around my cock on our off days…I don't think…I just do.

My lips crash into hers, my tongue thrusting deep into her mouth as my hands ravage her whole fucking body like I haven't touched her in years, not hours. I drag her down the hallway into my bedroom, sliding my hands up her dress to cup her full ass. My fingers squeeze greedily into the meat of her.

"We have to be quick." She gasps, pulling away for air as I back her up against my dresser and pull her panties down.

"I don't do quick," I growl, standing back up to help her undo my jeans and free my erection from the confines of my pants.

"It's quick, or it's nothing," she says, and my entire body stills when she wraps her delicate fingers around my length and hits me with a look that says she's not fucking around with this demand.

The desperation in her eyes has me fighting back a smile. She wants this. She wants me. Maybe just as bad as I want her, and that makes me feel more like a man than quite possibly anything I've ever done in my life.

"Whatever you say, Lucky." I peck her on the lips, nipping softly at her as I grab her by the legs and hoist her up on my dresser. The lamp and my loose change crash to the floor, but I don't bother picking them up because I'm already balls deep in her.

"Oh God," she moans loudly, and the prickle of need in my balls ratchets up to an all-new level as my bare shaft slides into her wetness. "Wyatt, holy shit—"

I take one of my hands to cover her mouth. "You have to be quiet," I rasp and hate myself for it because I love nothing more than making her scream. "If anyone outside hears you, it will fucking haunt me."

The ache in my gut over anyone hearing her this way makes me feel crazy inside, and before I have a second to unpack that fucked-up thought, I pull out and thrust back into her, driving my frustration into her like she's the magic pill that will heal me.

She whimpers against my palm and shakes her head like she can't possibly control her voice, so I look around my dresser for something to silence her, and an idea comes to mind.

"Do you trust me?"

She nods against my palm, so I release her and reach down to my jeans, which are hanging off my ass. The thwack of my belt echoes in my room as I slide it out and fist the strap in two hands in front of her.

"Bite," I command, my cock surging at the mental image of it alone.

She hesitates for a moment before her eyes flash with a fire I haven't seen before. When she parts her wet lips and lets me put it in her mouth, her teeth clenching down the way her pussy currently clenches around my cock, I feel myself begin to seep inside her already.

"When you need to scream, you just bite down on that...got it?"

She makes a sexy little noise and nods, looking so fucking hot with that strip of beat-up leather between her lips that I have to tell my own damn self to be quiet as I yank her to the edge of my dresser and pump deeper inside her.

Her cowboy boots dig into my back as she splays her hands out on the dresser for balance, holding on for dear life as the belt buckle jingles with every one of my thrusts. It's a heady combination. Seeing her all open and trusting...willing to do whatever I tell her.

Wanting me and only me.

I've had my fair share of experiences with women. But it's always pretty vanilla and brief. It scratches the itch good enough, but what I have with Trista…it's beyond satisfying. It's all-consuming. And the more we do it, the more I want it.

I realize that having sex this often creates the opportunity for feelings to come into play. But with Trista…it feels safe because there's literally a contract between us that guarantees this end date. That concrete fact gives me a sense of freedom I've never felt with a woman. For the next few months, I can just be me, and she can just be her, and when this is done, we both go our separate ways. End of.

A strangled sob murmurs from her lips as I feel her climax gripping me, milking me, begging for me to blow it inside her. And when she drops the belt from her mouth, I push into the hilt and let myself explode, my body shaking on top of hers as I press my head into her shoulder, inhaling her rosy scent like a drug I can't get enough of.

This is the best sex of my life. And I venture to guess the best of hers too, based on the teeth marks she left on my belt.

By the time everyone returns from outside, we're back in the kitchen, munching on popcorn like I didn't just fuck her like an animal in my room.

"You two playing still or what?" Max barks, taking his seat back at the table.

"We're coming," I snap back, and the smile that lights up my face over that double entendre is embarrassing.

We begin to walk over, and she inhales sharply and grabs my arm…her nose wrinkling as she hisses my name.

"What's wrong?" I ask, worried I might have hurt her in there. Fuck, could I have hurt the baby? She said she talked to the doctor about sex, and they said it was completely fine.

She stands on her tiptoes to murmur in my ear, "I forgot my panties in your room, and *it's* dripping down my leg."

It's, meaning…my cum.

I close my eyes in pain, my entire body radiating with an overwhelming desire to take her back into my room and fuck her again. It will take a miracle for me to make it through another hand of cards, let alone to the next sundown.

CHAPTER 33

WEEKS PREGNANT: 17
ANIMALS ON THE MOUNTAIN: 11

Wyatt

"**Y**ou have to call your woman," Calder shouts from across the house we're in the middle of hanging Sheetrock in. "Isn't she an expert in this shit?"

"She's not my woman," I murmur under my breath as I pull my gloves off and smack the drywall dust off my legs.

"You only have yourself to blame for that," Luke says with a smug tone. He props his hand on the wall and wipes the sweat off his brow.

It's balls hot today, and this house doesn't have central air installed yet, but we have to get the Sheetrock finished today because there's a delivery of tile coming tomorrow, and…fuck…we are behind schedule on this development.

Our dad would be riding our ass over this.

"You didn't offer Trista the 'D,' and now she's clearly getting it somewhere else because she looked very happy during poker the other night," Calder says in a chastising tone.

"Did she?" I ask, my voice high-pitched.

"Don't sound so cheery, man. This means you missed your window, and someone else climbed right in. And it wasn't me."

"Or me," Luke confirms like it needed to be said.

And a few weeks ago, before I had my way with her…I would have needed that confirmation. I would have pressed their necks up against the wall and made them swear they didn't touch her.

Now...I know better.

She's mine.

My head jerks back as I realize I'm reacting the wrong way to my brothers, who don't know the truth and can't know the truth per my promise to Trista. I should be mad. I should be sexually frustrated. I should be insecure over the fact that I'm not having mind-blowing sex every other day with a woman with curves that won't quit and a mouth that pisses me off quite regularly but I still want to kiss every time I see.

"Fuck you both," I grumble. "I'm not bothering Trista with this."

My eyes blink rapidly when a tiny black-and-white kitten is thrust in my face. Calder's voice is strained when he says, "I just caught it licking the nail gun, Wyatt. We need to call someone to pick this stray up, and if it isn't Momma Bear, it's going to be animal control."

"Don't call animal control," I growl harshly. "They'll probably kill it."

Calder and Luke eye each other for a moment and then look knowingly at me. "She's making you soft," Luke says smugly.

"The fuck she is."

Calder laughs. "Fletcher Mountain is one kitten away from being a petting zoo. Stop fooling yourself and call your lady so she can come save this fucking fuzzball."

As if on cue, the kitten's tongue begins licking Calder's beard at the exact moment he finishes that sentence. He fights back a smile and whispers, "Stop it, Fuzz. That tickles."

I roll my eyes and make the damn call, knowing full well this kitten isn't going to the rescue center, and I'm too weak to fight about it.

An hour later, Trista pulls up to our jobsite in her beat-up Honda, and I have to physically stop myself from touching her as she approaches me and my brothers, currently perched on the tailgate of my truck.

"Hello, Fletcher brothers," she says in a singsong voice. "I hear we have a new pet for the mountain!"

I fight a knowing smirk while Trista shoots me a wink that I feel in my balls as she moves over to Calder and holds her hands out for the kitten. Calder frowns and hands it over.

"And what do we have here?" She looks at the kitten's backside and says, "Congratulations, it's a girl!"

The smile on Calder's face is weird. He should be embarrassed.

"She seems really sweet," Trista says, holding the animal to her chest and petting its head. You can hear her purring plain as day. "Super tame. I'll need to make a call to animal control to make sure she doesn't already have an owner."

"She wasn't tame earlier in the week," Calder says with a scowl. "I tamed her. Fed her my lunch and gave her water every day."

Trista's brows shoot up. "Maybe you should keep her, then?"

Calder shakes his head and slides off the tailgate with a dirty smile spread across his face. "I don't need more puss—"

His voice is cut off as Trista swings back her cowboy boot and kicks him in the shin.

"Ouch!" he howls and holds his leg up, bouncing up and down as he does.

"Oh, shoot, sorry about that," she says, shaking her foot out like it was a nervous tic. "My leg just does that sometimes."

Calder gapes back at her, looking like he can't tell if she's serious or joking. He doesn't know her well enough to know that was definitely intentional. He rubs his leg and asks, "What's going to happen to her?"

Trista shrugs. "I'll probably bring her home for a few days, wait to make sure she doesn't have an owner posting in the pet groups about a missing kitty, and if all clear, then I'll bring her into the shelter to be adopted."

"Oh, like Handsome?" I ask knowingly. "Or Strudel? Aren't those two waiting to be adopted too?"

She narrows her eyes at me, and then her gaze drifts down my body for a moment and turn to liquid pools of heat. I'm covered in drywall dust and plaster and can't possibly be appealing, but I know that look well by now.

The only problem is, today is our off day. She should not be looking at me like that on our off day.

My dusty jeans suddenly feel tight.

"I'll take her back to the mountain and get her settled." Trista turns to leave and then glances over her shoulder. "Are you boys almost done for the day?"

I shake my head firmly. "We're behind schedule, so we've got a few more hours ahead of us tonight."

"We can't work too late. Luke and I have hockey practice tonight," Calder says with a pointed look at me. "It was on the family calendar."

"Hockey?" Trista asks curiously, holding the kitten to her neck.

Calder nods. "Yeah, we're in an old-man's league. It's basically a team full of guys pushing forty who had no chance to play pro but like to pretend they could have if they wanted to."

"We drink a shitload before we play, so we have an excuse for why we suck," Luke adds with a laugh.

"It can be pretty intense." Calder gets a distant look in his eyes as a memory hits him. "Last season, I experienced the hardest hit I've ever had in my hockey career, and it was me running into my own teammate."

"My neck is still fucked up, thank you very much," Luke says, tipping his head from side to side.

Trista bursts out laughing. "Oh, this I have to see."

"Our season doesn't start for a few more months, but we'll get you to a game if Papa Bear approves it." Calder eyes me curiously, but Trista tears my attention away from him.

"Wyatt, why don't you play?"

"I hate hockey," I reply with a frown. "Way too much failure."

"Wyatt is super fun at parties," Calder deadpans, and I cut him a menacing look.

"What time will you guys get home?" Trista asks, and I see that flicker of need in her eyes again.

My voice is strained when I reply, "It'll be after sundown for sure."

"After sundown," she mumbles. "I like after sundown." Her words are quiet, but I sure as hell heard them. Her lower lip juts out just slightly. "Okay. I'll see you later, then."

She gives us a friendly wave, and I watch for far longer than is appropriate, my mind reeling over the green light I'm pretty sure she was showing me. Does she want to break our rules? Because I sure as fuck would be just fine with that. But fucking hell, it'll be late when we get back after hockey.

I struggle for the next thirty minutes to get back to work, and when I nearly shoot a nail through my thumb, I call it.

"Fuck this," I growl, dropping the gun onto the ground and tossing my goggles off my face. I make my way to the door and call out to my brothers, "I, um…forgot about an appointment I have. I need to go."

"What?" Calder barks, tipping his goggles up on top of his head. His inked arms are covered in sawdust. "You're the one who's been bitching about us being behind all day long."

"I know, but this is important."

"This is important!" He points at the house. "And we drove here together. You can't just leave us."

"I'll be back to get you," I bark and remove my tool belt, dropping it on the floor as a sign of my promise. "It'll just take an hour. Ninety minutes, tops."

"Don't make us late for hockey!" Luke yells as I turn and tuck tail to bulldoze my way up to Fletcher Mountain because, well…I'm feeling lucky.

Trista

The sound of tires on gravel and a truck door slamming has my head popping up curiously. I'm currently on the floor in my bathroom with the newest addition to Fletcher Mountain, who is nibbling on some kibble I swiped from the rescue center. She seems quite content already. She's already used her new litter box, so we're off to a good start.

I stand to glance out my bathroom window and see Wyatt's truck parked in front of the barn. He said he wouldn't be home for a while, so I'm surprised to see him. Movement down by the barn draws my gaze, and I nearly fall through the window when I see that Wyatt is by the outdoor shower, stripping out of his work vest like a man on fire.

My hot breath fogs up the glass when I say out loud to myself, "Is he...oh my God, he is."

He wrenches off his damp T-shirt, revealing his chiseled, hairy chest, and I have to swallow the lump in my throat as he undoes his jeans, and...yep. He's naked. He's naked, and he's stepping under the water and aggressively scrubbing the dust off his skin with a sort of deranged look in his eye.

My body hums as he turns around on the concrete slab, coating himself in soap, giving me a full view of his front side, the pecs, the faint outline of abs, the deep vee that goes down each of his hip bones. What I wouldn't do to be those hands roaming over every ridge of him.

Hormones. It's the hormones. I'm not normally so possessed. *So easily aroused.* But my God, when a man puts on a show right outside my window, what does he expect me to do?

His tan hands slide down to his groin, and I splay my palms out on the window when I see him grip himself and stroke his length over and over. My nose flattens against the glass as he presses his other hand to the side of the barn, his head bowed, his back muscles sinewy as water sluices down his spine.

Pressing my forehead to the cool glass, I squeeze my legs together, the desire to touch myself at an all-time high. A second ago, I was congratulating a kitten on using the litter box for the first time. Now, I'm watching some sort of mountain-man porno that I can't click off.

And why should I click it off? I have sex with this man every other day. I've seen him naked countless times now. He's essentially...mine. *Mine.*

The spike of adrenaline that surges through me over that possessive word is alarming. Why does that feel so good to say?

Because a man like Wyatt has never been mine, not once in my life. A man like Wyatt has never even looked my way before. And if I listen to that quiet voice in my head, I know this man wouldn't either if I wasn't carrying his baby. He's told me he's attracted to me, and I hear him, but he's not attracted to *me*. To who I really am. He doesn't even know me. Not the real me. Not the fucked-up version that would terrify him if I ever told him the truth.

It's better to live in this fantasy with him for now. He might be *mine now*, but that is a very temporary state. A short-term arrangement only.

With a strange noise in my throat, I slide my hand over my leggings and tease my clit through the two layers of fabric, my body folding in on itself, desperate to feel his thickness inside me again. My panties are growing wet already, and I wonder briefly if I should just go down there and see if Wyatt can make me a believer in shower sex. I'm sure he'd be up for breaking our sundown rules. And his brothers must still be at the jobsite for him to be showering out in broad daylight like this. Stroking himself.

Yet...the voyeur in me doesn't want me to reveal my presence quite yet. This moment is hotter. Better. Naughtier. Watching him when he doesn't know it makes me feel a certain sense of power that I'm not sure I've ever felt before.

I stroke small circles over my clit, feeling fraught with need. How do I still want sex when I've literally never had more of it in my entire life? Is it truly just the hormones? Is it the sneaking around? Is it Wyatt?

It's all of it...all of it is a recipe for feral, uncontrollable lust, and I will mourn the loss of him when this all ends.

My heart leaps into my throat when Wyatt's head lifts, and he catches me gawking at him through the window. I squeal and drop down on the floor, horrified that I've just been caught peeping on him in the shower.

The kitten meows something that's obviously judgy before diving back into her food.

"I'm a pervert." I hit my head on the wall, cursing myself for being such a blatant idiot.

Moments later, I hear my apartment door open and cringe, cupping my hands over my face as his heavy footfalls across the floorboards grow near. He's going to give me so much shit for being a low-level creeper, and I deserve it.

When I look up, he's filling the doorway of my bathroom, looking giant and delicious dressed in gym shorts and no shirt, his furry, chiseled chest on full display but I barely notice over the captivating fire burning in his eyes. He steps inside and grabs my hand to pull me up while he kicks the bathroom door shut. Shoving me up against my bathroom sink, he commands, "Tell me everything on your mind as you watched me, Lucky. And don't you dare leave the good stuff out."

CHAPTER 34

WEEKS PREGNANT: 18
ANIMALS ON THE MOUNTAIN: ???

Wyatt

A scream rips me out of a deep sleep, and I sit up in my bed, heart racing. Rain pounds down on my roof, and flashes of lightning illuminate my house as I rush out of my bedroom to glance out the living room window. All the lights are on in the barn, and I glance at the clock to see it's three in the morning. What the hell is going on?

I rush back into my room and throw on jeans and a hoody, barely getting my feet into my boots before I'm jogging through the rain down to the barn. Terror vibrates through me as a million horrific scenarios play in my mind. The biggest horror I'm thinking about… is miscarriage.

Did Trista lose the baby?

Pregnancy loss isn't something I've let myself really think about since we got through the first trimester. But early labor can still happen, and the thought of seeing Trista experience a horror like that is something I can hardly stomach.

I'm soaked and out of breath by the time I step into the barn. I look around, expecting to find Trista, but she's nowhere. Millie, Reginald, and Handsome are all up and look visibly spooked by whatever is going on. Something definitely isn't right if Reginald is awake.

A strange noise echoes from the area where the chicken coop is, so I rush through the barn door that leads out to the pasture. I squint through the darkness as the deafening rain hammers down on the tin roof overhang. I turn the corner to where the chicken coop is located, and it's there that I find Trista hunched over what used to be her chicken enclosure. She's scantily dressed in her cowboy boots, a pair of shorts, and a baggy black T-shirt. My heart squeezes at the sight of her soaked to the bone and covered in mud.

"Are you okay?" I yell through the rain, and Trista's head snaps up, clearly surprised at my presence.

Her face is soaked with rain and tears as she wipes at her nose and points at the pile of rubble. "Coyotes ripped apart my chicken coop and attacked my chickens." A strangled sob erupts from her throat.

Relief hits me like a ton of bricks when I see she's okay, and the problem has nothing to do with her and everything to do with these damn chickens she's in love with. Guilt niggles as I move closer to her. She holds her hands up, shaking her head adamantly.

"They ran off when I screamed, but there's feathers and blood everywhere."

My eyes tighten as I look at the carnage, thanking fuck that none of this is from her.

She grips the sides of her soaked shirt and bites her lip, clearly deep in thought. "Some of them might have gotten away, so I'm going to look for a flashlight and see if any are still alive out there."

She moves to walk past me, and I step into her path, stopping her in her tracks. "Trista, no."

"Why not?" She stands under the tin roof and looks up at me, shock and defiance all over her face.

Every protective bone in my body roars to life as I glance out at the dark woods behind her. My fists clench at just the thought of her out there in this storm with coyotes nearby. I swallow the knot in my throat, and my voice is tight when I say, "It's lightning out. You could get seriously hurt."

"But this is my fault, Wyatt!" she cries, her eyes red-rimmed. "I'm the one who installed that stupid chicken coop. I knew it wasn't sturdy, but I thought it would be fine. This is on me. This is all on me! What if some are still alive and terrified out there? I have to look for them."

"Lucky," I urge, my hand flattening against her swollen stomach as she attempts to walk past me again. "I can't let you go out there."

"Don't tell me what to do, Wyatt!" she screeches, her voice venomous. Her eyes are fiery as she looks up at me, her hot breath dancing on my lips as moisture slides down her face and mixes with her tears.

"I am begging you," I croak, treading carefully because she is a live wire I'm desperate not to trip. "I'm just trying to keep you safe. It's not just you at stake here."

My hand twitches on her belly, and she instantly looks down at where I'm touching her as her chin trembles. I can see her mind whirling with this new information. Like she forgot she was pregnant for a moment.

She steps away from me, moving back into the rain as her own hands replace mine. She holds herself protectively for a moment as she looks up at the sky, the rain pounding down on her face like she's only now just realizing we're in the middle of a bad storm.

She never touches herself like this, and the sight of her embracing her belly with tears in her eyes, soaking wet in the rain, hair slicked down to her face, is soul crushing. I don't just want to protect the baby at this moment. I want to protect her. I want to comfort her. I want to hold her. I want to burn the world to the ground for making her hurt like this.

Her shoulders quake as she begins to cry. "I'm such a fuckup."

My chest concaves as I pull her back under the roof, my hand pushing the strands of hair stuck to her face. "No, you're not."

"Yes, I am," she bellows and jerks herself away from me. "I want to open my own animal sanctuary when I can't even keep chickens alive? What the fuck am I thinking?"

"Accidents happen," I reply firmly, my hands itching to hold her. "This isn't your fault."

She nods and bites her lip, sniffling loudly as she gazes out into the darkness. "I'm sure if any are still alive, the coyotes will have eaten them by now anyway." She kicks her mud-covered boot into the ground and shakes her head. "I'm going to bed."

She moves to head inside, and I call out to her. "Can I do anything? Do you want me to come up? Or I can carry Reggie upstairs for you if you want? Would that help?" I sound like an idiot, but I want to do something. I feel fucking awful she was out here dealing with this all on her own. I will literally do anything. I'll sleep on the damn floor with the pig if she wants.

She shakes her head, and her tone is resolute when she replies, "He's better off without me."

Trista

The following morning, I wake to a wet nose in my face. I peel my eyes open, feeling crusty and strung out as I cuddle the little kitten, who must have known I needed some extra love today.

"Good morning, Milkshake." I drop soft kisses on her black-and-white fur. Milkshake seemed like a fitting name for her after I saw how she brought all the boys to the yard on that jobsite last week. She had Calder wrapped around her finger for sure.

My chest aches as memories of last night hit me, and I glance at my phone to see it's after nine, and I have three missed calls from work. It's still raining outside, so maybe I can use the weather as an excuse. Mountain mudslide, perhaps? Seems a little dramatic, but it's worth a shot. Either way, it won't be the last time Earl threatens to fire me.

I hop out of bed and rifle through my clothes for something clean to wear. I showered after the chicken massacre last night, so I can skip that step this morning, but my hair is a disaster from falling asleep with it wet. I throw it up into a topknot and brush my teeth. No time for makeup today.

I quickly refill Milkshake's and Strudel's food and water bowls and clean out Strudel's cage. These two are not getting along, so I'm afraid the bunny has to be confined to his pen for now. I'll need to try to find a more permanent home for one of them sooner rather than later.

I open the door to leave and glance down to see a brown bag on the step. Even after a middle-of-the-night coyote attack, Wyatt still doesn't miss a breakfast. I glance inside, and my stomach rumbles when I spot a bagel and a yogurt. As I clomp down the wooden steps, I hear hammering outside of the barn and frown. Wyatt and his brothers should be long gone by now. Who's here?

I glance into the pens to see that Wyatt has fed and watered Handsome and Reginald. I pat Millie's head and make my way out to the pasture, where the banging seems to be coming from, but I stop dead in my tracks when I hear a familiar trill. I dart over to the stall on the end, taking in the chicken wire stapled up to the roof that was definitely not there yesterday, and look inside the pen.

"Holy shit, Heather?" I exclaim and drop my breakfast to the ground to frantically open the gate to close myself inside. Hunching over, I chase the three chickens around the pen for a few laps, trying to get my hands on one of them. "And Rooster!" I squeal, darting for him. Rooster jumps and attempts to fly away just as I get my hands around his wings. I press them down flat and hold his light body to my chest, eyeing the third chicken, who's been nameless since the day she got here. "How did you guys get here?" I cry, my eyes welling with tears. Honestly, I can't believe I have any tears left after crying myself to sleep last night.

"They were a bitch to catch," Wyatt rumbles, and I look up to find him standing at the fence watching me. His fingers are laced in the chicken wire and covered in mud.

"You caught them?" I croak, squeezing Rooster to my face as his little beak pecks at me.

Wyatt squints and wipes his brow with the back of his hand. He's wearing a tan Carhartt coat that's damp along the shoulders from rain. His hair is soaked as beads of water drip down his forehead. He looks like he's been up all night.

"The rain let up for a bit around four o'clock, and I couldn't sleep, so I decided to come back out and look around to see if any of them had wandered back. Sure enough, these three were pecking around the barn, eating worms, I suspect."

"Oh my God," I cry, my heart squeezing in my chest. "They came back?"

"Yeah, I managed to herd them into the barn, but they would *not* go into this stall. I had to chase them up and down the aisle for a good twenty minutes before I could wrangle them. I can't believe I didn't wake you up. Gave Millie and Handsome quite the show. Reggie snored the whole time."

A garbled laugh erupts from my throat, and I clutch Rooster tightly to my neck. His pecking turns a bit more aggressive, so I set him down. Heather would have been the better choice, but she's a fast bitch.

"I can't believe you did all of this."

He nods and exhales heavily. "I think it's just these three that survived. I found some feathers in the woods that don't look too promising for the rest."

My lips turn down at that, and he shoots me a sympathetic look. "These three should be fine in here until I fix the coop."

"You're fixing the chicken coop?" I gasp and make my way out of the stall. "Wyatt, you don't need to do that."

"I don't think your chicken coop was the problem," he says, making his way back out into the pasture. I follow him, the noise of the rain on the roof increasing in volume as we turn the corner, and he points at the area he's clearly put a lot of work into already. "We just need some electric fencing up to protect it from predators. I'm going to look for something in town today."

My eyes water as I look at the nearly fully repaired chicken coop. It's been reinforced with fresh lumber and looks a thousand times better than when I put it together. My chest aches at the gesture, but instead of telling him that, I elbow him playfully. "Don't you have a job to get to?"

"Don't you?" He quirks a brow at me, the corner of his mouth tugging up into a shy smile.

I shrug. "I'm always late."

"I'm early all other days."

Silence falls over us as we both stare out at the coop. I can't imagine what a horrid mess I was down here last night when he found me crying. And when I saw Wyatt, I'll admit, the weaker, more sensitive part of me wanted to fall into his arms and cry.

But I didn't because that's not what I do.

And now he's done this.

His voice is thick when he says, "I should have helped you build the coop before." His clear blue eyes find mine, looking stunning against the nature backdrop behind him. "I was a dick about the chickens, but you're not a failure, Trista. This is just a part of nature you can't control. It took me years of hard lessons out here to learn that sometimes…the mountain wins."

His sweet, reassuring words comfort me in ways I didn't even know I could be comforted, and I feel myself drawing closer to him, craving his embrace. His heat.

Today is an off day.

It's morning.

I'm late for work.

He's covered in mud.

He's been up most of the night…

…rescuing my chickens.

I've never wanted him more.

Without a word, I reach up and grab the collar of his damp jacket and pull him down to me. Our lips connect, and he makes a gruff, surprised sound before submitting to my will and kissing me back. He walks us backward, taking over the kiss as he presses his hands against the red barn, caging me in as his tongue thrusts deep into my mouth.

He pulls away for a second, his voice hoarse as he says, "I'm filthy."

"I don't care," I gasp, out of my mind with lust. I grab his neck and pull him back to me, desperation throbbing in my groin.

He moves his hands off the building and grabs my backside, squeezing me harshly and likely coating my ass with muddy handprints. The thought of it thrills me as I lift my leg and squeeze him into me, gasping into his kiss as the thick ridge of his erection presses into me. He grinds my ass into him, putting more pressure between us, and his denim catches on my clit, stoking the ache between my legs.

Maybe it's the hormones, maybe it's the sound of the rain on the tin roof, maybe it's the way the mountain seems so fresh and new after a storm. Or maybe it's this selfless, gruff, thoughtful man ravishing me as if I'm everything he wants and needs. But I'm raw and spent, and I want to chase this comforting feeling of hope he's blossomed back inside me.

Fuck our sundown rules.

Wyatt's hand slides up the side of my shirt, cupping my breast over my bra. He growls into my lips before tearing away from me to drop his head between my breasts. He yanks the cup down and squeezes my flesh before his lips wrap around my nipple and suck deeply.

"Wyatt," I scream his name, feeling unhinged being out here in the open like this with the rain pounding down above us.

I fork my fingers into his damp hair, squeezing the short tendrils for balance as I press him into my chest. The whiskers of his trim beard send a flurry of heat to my center, and I feel my panties dampen instantly.

"God, I can smell your arousal," he purrs into me, and I feel equal parts embarrassed and turned on.

No shame.

"I'm soaked for you," I cry out, my hips undulating on his thigh, desperate for more.

His voice is raw when he states, "I have to be inside you."

He yanks his coat off like a madman and drops it on top of a bale of straw next to the building. He turns back to me, and before he can say anything, I shove him down to a sitting position.

His pupils dilate as he watches me kick out of my boots, jeans, and panties until I'm left standing there, half-naked in the pasture enclosure, mountain trees and storm clouds swirling behind me.

Damp straw sticks to my feet as I climb onto his lap, fisting his silky, hard length in my hand and positioning him between my folds. Our foreheads press together, our breaths hot on each other's lips as I notch his tip at my center and sink down on top of him. I mewl like an animal as I take his fullness in as deep as I can while his fingers dig into my hips.

Once he's fully inside me, I arch back and ride him, relishing in the tightness, the fullness…the absolute maximum capacity this man's cock takes up inside me. It feels so good. I already dread his absence. If it were normal to walk around with him inside me all day, I probably would. I would get a mold of his cock and just hold him there for safekeeping because the pleasure he brings me when he touches my womb, my insides, when he thrusts up into the depths of my soul that is my innermost body…it is life-changing.

His hands slide under my shirt to rub over my chest, ribs, and belly as I move myself on top of him, gyrating my hips over and over. "Every part of you feels so good it hurts," he says with a groan before he grips my neck to pull me to his mouth. His tongue is aggressive and vengeful as his fingers slide around my throat to squeeze the roots of my hair at the nape, causing chills to cascade from my head to my toes.

"I'm going to fill you with my cum," he husks against my lips, and my whimper is inhuman. "Do you like that, Lucky? Do you like the thought of me fucking you like an animal outside in the dirt like this and spilling my seed into your greedy little cunt?"

"Yes," I cry out, his dark voice pushing my orgasm upward as I grind down on him.

"Do you know what it does to me to know you're carrying my baby inside you?" He bites his lip, his eyes reverent on me as his hands cascade over my stomach and tighten the shirt around my middle. His fingers tease the edges of my belly button. "You have a piece of me inside you, and I still want more of you. I can't get enough."

"Wyatt." I say his name like a prayer because he is a god to me right now. The hot air exchanging between us causes steam to rise up around us under this tin roof. "I'm going to come."

He moves his hand from my belly and slides it down between us, rubbing firm circles over my clit. I grip his shoulders harshly, holding on to him like I'm swinging on a rope over a canyon. With a sharp burst inside me, I freeze, my entire body going stiff as my muscles quake around his erection, my insides convulsing even more when I feel him empty himself inside me, his semen mixing with my own release like rain on the mountain. It's beautiful.

My heart thunders with the storm as I nuzzle my face into Wyatt's damp neck, breathing in the scent of sweat, nature, and him. Just him. God, he feels good.

Once he catches his breath, his hands skate softly up my back and pull some bits of straw out of my hair as his deep voice murmurs, "Imagine what I would have gotten if I saved all the chickens."

CHAPTER 35

WEEKS PREGNANT: 19
ANIMALS ON THE MOUNTAIN: 9

Trista

"This is a bad idea," Avery says with his arm shoulder-deep inside a ewe's ass.

"Better you than me," I murmur under my breath as I watch him do something ungodly inside this poor pregnant mother sheep's body. "I thought you had to feel inside to reposition the baby lamb."

"Not this." He pulls his arm out, and the shoulder-length plastic glove he's wearing is covered in stuff. "The part where you have sex with the guy who knocked you up."

I frown at the man who was literally just fisting a sheep. "It seems kind of logical to me."

"Tris, don't be dense. You're smarter than that." Avery eyes me sternly as he yanks the glove off and checks his hand for any remnants.

Gross.

He moves over to his clipboard on the corner of the pen and makes a quick note before putting on his stethoscope and walking back over to the ewe to listen to her heartbeat.

I wait for him to finish before I reply, "We have an end date," I say, pointing at my belly. "The boundaries couldn't be clearer."

"And what about feelings?" Avery asks, resting his hands on top of the sheep's back and staring over her at me.

"I'm a cow, baby!" I exclaim and gently mirror his pose, patting my farm animal compadre's back, who's taking this labor like a pro. I move over to her head and pet her wet nose before I add, "The fact that this guy's biggest dream in life is to become a dad is exactly why I know I won't catch feelings. I'm not about the family life. And I can detach with the best of them."

"But what if he catches feelings for you? I've seen how he looks at you."

The blood in my veins hums as a flash of Wyatt's smoldering eyes on my body outside the barn the other day hits me. Ever since the chicken coop fiasco, we've kind of fallen off the every-other-sundown routine. This past week, it's become a…whenever-the-mood-strikes sort of thing. And I can't even place the blame on him. It was me who attacked him that morning outside the barn. And the other morning, after I woke up from a sex dream, I knocked on his door at 6:00 a.m. to demand satisfaction.

He was so hot in his gym shorts, no shirt, and rumpled bed hair. We couldn't kiss because he hadn't brushed his teeth, and it was just this perfect kind of dirty, hot quickie that I was looking for. So much better than my vibrator.

His big dick has ruined me.

I clear my throat and shrug at Avery. "He's just weird like that. Possessive or something. But that's not like actual feelings. Guys like him don't fall for girls like me. They just randomly fuck girls like me."

"He chose you to have his baby," Avery says loudly, and I shush him because the farm owner is literally somewhere in this barn located outside of Littleton. He narrows his eyes and adds a bit more quietly, "He clearly liked you enough for that."

"But that's just because I'm a cow," I repeat, and as if on cue, the ewe's head swings over and butts me in the hip, clearly feeling left out of my barn animal analogy. "Once I have this baby, he'll be over me and busy being a single dad. This really is just sex."

"And a baby shower with his entire family," Avery huffs and shakes his head. "Look, Trista, I've known you a long time, and you don't let people get close to you. Anytime I try to ask about your past, you clam up tighter than Dolly's butthole on my arm."

"Nice." I frown sympathetically at my fellow farm animal.

He shrugs. "I just worry about you."

Avery's eyes soften on me, and I feel myself doing the butthole clam-up thing. Probably telling him about my sexuationship with Wyatt was a bad idea. But it's getting harder these days to just constantly live in my own head. I feel myself yearning for a bit more connection. Not enough to call my crazy sister, but I wouldn't mind a gal pal I could talk to about my life. My twenties up until this point have been boring, nose-to-the-grind work work work. What I'm doing on Fletcher Mountain…the surrogacy thing, the sex thing, the animals… it all feels so much heavier and important.

And while I appreciate Avery's concern, he really is off base. Wyatt and I are totally surface level. Our only true connection is sex and this baby. Next week is the anatomy scan, which will serve to refocus us back on what our relationship is. A surrogate and her intended parent.

"Okay, I think Dolly is ready to have this lamb," Avery says as the ewe begins shifting in the stall. "You ready to help?"

"I was born ready."

It's dark out by the time I park in front of the big red barn. I'm bone-tired and smell like a sheep and homemade pot roast the farm owners forced Avery and me to come in and eat after we delivered a healthy baby lamb. I need a shower in the worst way, and I'm even too tired to say good night to Reginald and Handsome.

Which is why I don't even notice Wyatt's brother Calder sitting at the bottom of my steps. "Oh my God!" I jump, my hands flying to my chest as I nearly step on top of him.

"Sorry," Calder exclaims, standing up and holding his hands out to steady me. "Are you okay? I was saying your name, but you didn't hear me."

"You were?" My chest heaves as my heart tries to reset itself back to a normal rhythm.

"Yeah, you must have been deep in your thoughts." He looks down at me with apprehension in his eye that seems unlikely for this Fletcher brother. Granted, I haven't spent a lot of time with him, but he doesn't strike me as someone who's overly concerned about the well-being of others. He grips the back of his neck and looks nervous for a moment before he stammers, "I was just wondering how, um...I was thinking maybe I could see Fuzz."

"Fuzz?" I frown curiously.

"The kitten?" His eyes widen. "Is she gone already? Did you already take her to the shelter?"

"Oh God, the cat." I sigh and shake my head. "Sorry, I've been calling her Milkshake."

"Milkshake?" Calder frowns.

"Black-and-white fur...her milkshake brought all the boys to the yard..." I sigh and shake my head. "I was tired when I came up with it."

A bemused smile lights up his face. "I like Milkshake."

I gesture up the steps. "Come on up. She's getting big."

"She is?" He looks like an excited puppy dog as he follows me into my apartment to reunite with his stray.

I watch him curiously as he drops down on the floor and plays with a frenzied Milkshake, who's pouncing on him like an old littermate. Calder gave me puppy dog eyes downstairs, but he's anything but a pup. He's nearly as tall as Wyatt but has a more severe, chiseled look to his face. And the ink scattered up his arms gives him more edge, making it his whole personality, whereas Wyatt's ink seems more strategic and intentional.

Calder exudes a bad-boy vibe. If I were to compare him to a dog, I'd probably call him a Rottweiler. Luke definitely has golden retriever energy, and Wyatt...that man is a German shepherd if I ever saw one. Striking, intimidating, protective, and strong. So strong.

My body trembles at the thought.

"Do you care if I hop in the shower?" I ask, taking off my shelter jacket and getting a whiff of my hair. "I've been literally at the ass end of a ewe for most of the night and feel disgusting."

"Oh, I can leave." Calder gets up to head out, but I stop him in his tracks.

"Please don't," I beg, sounding a bit desperate. "She's been alone all day and could use some attention, and I don't have the energy for a kitten tonight."

"Okay, that's cool," he says with a lopsided smile and drops back down to play with one of the cat toys I picked up for her the other day.

I wash the stench of barn off and come out twenty minutes later in my fluffy white robe, still towel drying my hair, to find him holding Milkshake on the sofa like a baby in his arms.

I stand over top of him and laugh. "Kittens. They are all kitty crazies one second and comatose the next."

"She's snoring," he whispers, trying not to wake her up. It's adorable.

"It's called purring," I correct with a wink. "And that means she likes you."

He shrugs, but the glint in his eye as he gazes down at her shows he's hopeful that's true.

I sit down on the sofa beside him, propping my elbow on the back of the couch so I'm facing him. "You should keep her."

"No, I shouldn't." He laughs and shakes his head.

"Why not?" I ask with a frown. "Cats are relatively low-maintenance. They don't need to be let out during the day like dogs. She's happy here, so I'm sure she'd be happy at your cabin."

He looks over to me nervously, his jaw muscle twitching under his trim beard. "I'm not as paternal as Wyatt. The minute he got that goat, he was obsessed. Did all sorts of research on it. He's definitely more qualified for caretaking than I am. I'm more of the fun, irresponsible-uncle type."

"I don't know about that," I reply with a smirk. "I think I see a little bit of a cat dad in you."

"What if you're wrong?" His brows furrow as he looks down and drags his finger along the cheek of the kitten. She purrs louder and presses into his touch while wrapping her little paws around his fingers like she was made for his big, inky arms.

"Why don't you keep her for a few days and see how it goes? I'll send you home tonight with all the stuff you need and give you my phone number so you can text me if you have questions. And if it doesn't work out, we'll find her a new home. No harm, no foul. And you'd honestly be doing me a favor. Strudel is not a fan of Milkshake. I've had to keep him in his cage since I brought her home. He's due for some stretching."

The corners of his mouth lift, and he gives a casual shrug. "I guess if you need help, I could do it."

I smile knowingly. This is a trick I use at the rescue shelter quite often. It's very rare for a family to ever return a pet they bring home. Animals are just too easy to fall in love with.

People, not so much.

While he snuggles Milkshake, I throw all the supplies he needs for a few days into a packing box, including her litter box, and type my number into his phone. The background photo is a picture of Everly and Ethan, and I have to roll my eyes. This guy has more dad vibes than he's giving himself credit for.

"Thank you, Trista. I'll try not to let you down," Calder says as I walk him to the door.

"You're going to be fine." I laugh at his nervous posture, holding the kitten like she's precious cargo. "Just text me if you need anything."

I swing open my door and am spooked for the second time tonight when I come face-to-face with Wyatt's chest. I glance up and see his steely eyes shooting daggers at his brother behind me.

"What the fuck are you doing up here, Calder?" He seethes, his voice low and more threatening than I've ever heard.

Calder's head snaps back. "What does it look like?"

Wyatt takes a big step into my apartment, pushing right past me. "Why don't you tell me?"

"Whoa," I exclaim, grabbing Wyatt's wrist as he barrels toward his brother. "What the hell, Wyatt!"

He turns accusatory eyes on me. "What the hell, Trista?"

My jaw drops. Is he actually accusing me of messing around with his brother right now? Based on the crazed look in his eyes, that sure seems like what he's thinking. Psycho, not sweet.

Calder clutches Milkshake, who's now wide awake, to his chest. "I just came up to see Fuzz."

"At almost ten o'clock at night." Wyatt says it like a statement, not a question.

"Trista needed a shower," Calder replies and then winces because that was not the right detail to share.

"And that involves you somehow?" Wyatt thunders, his temper boiling over as he butts chests with his brother.

"Stop!" I move to stand between the two of them, feeling small for quite possibly the only time in my life. I splay my hands out on their chests to back them away from each other before I turn to Calder. "Take Milkshake home, and let me know how she does for the night. I'll deal with this."

I shoot angry eyes at Wyatt, who stares Calder down as he makes his way out of my apartment. When I get the door closed, I turn my rage on the man whose baby lives inside me. "What the hell has gotten into you?"

Wyatt's lip curls up as he looks down at me, his face stony serious. "Why are you half-naked with my brother at night?"

"Because I needed a shower, and he wanted to see the cat."

"So you just showered with him in your place?" he bites back, his tone derogatory. "Don't you think that's kind of fucked up?"

"No, Wyatt," I exclaim, stomping my foot. "It's not like I left the door open for him to watch." I eye him pointedly, and his gaze flickers at that innuendo. "I just got back from delivering a lamb, and he wanted to see the cat. I wanted a break, so it sounded nice to have someone give her some attention that wasn't me for once."

Wyatt blinks back his annoyance as his eyes drop to my belly. "You're working too much."

"Not this again," I groan and turn to walk away from him. "Wyatt, I'm exhausted and don't have the energy for you. I just want to lie in bed and watch *Housewives* and maybe cry a little. My back and shoulders are killing me."

"Why do you want to cry?" he asks, his tone softening instantly. His face morphs from angry, overprotective, overbearing mountain-man asshole to that same puppy dog look that Calder sported a moment ago. Apparently, it runs in the family.

I shrug and feel my chin begin to tremble as I ponder how to explain to him that watching that lamb be born tonight messed with my head and that being pregnant means that my brain can't process everything because everything makes me tired. And being tired makes me feel sad. And feeling sad makes me want to cry. I answer, "Because I'm a cow."

He sighs heavily and, without warning, eliminates the space between us and wraps me into a giant bear hug. His body radiates heat as I bury my face in his chest and inhale his mountain scent. This hug is one of those hugs that feel so good it almost hurts because you know the instant it's over with, you'll miss the feel of it. He rubs my damp hair, and I can feel his lips and nose press against my head, inhaling deeply before he murmurs, "I like *Housewives*."

"What?" I ask, pulling away and swiping at my errant tears.

"And I have strong hands." He grabs my hand and walks us over to the bed before he kicks his boots off and hops under the covers. He positions his back against the headrest and opens his arms to me. "I've never given a girl a shoulder rub before, but I bet I'm pretty good at it. And no funny business, I promise."

I stare at the giant bearded mountain man sitting on my bed, offering me a back rub. I should say no. This is intimate and nice and crossing all the boundaries that I was just bragging to Avery about earlier tonight. And with how he almost went nuclear on his brother a few minutes ago for just seeing me in a bathrobe, I should be seeing this as a giant red flag.

But truth be told, I'd take a back rub from a homeless person right now.

I crawl into the bed and lay my back against his front and enjoy the moment of comfort. *He's so big. So warm.* But I'm not here for a cuddle, so I lean forward to let the brawny man rub my back. When I slip my robe off my shoulders and hold it across my chest so I can give him better access, I feel a point of pressure against my lower back.

"Wyatt…" I state with a warning tone.

His voice is deep and husky in my ear when he replies, "Just call it lumbar support."

Wyatt

"How does Meredith Marks's accent go from British to Boston in one angry rant?" I ask the back of Trista's head as we finish our second episode of *The Real Housewives of Salt Lake City*. "What is that accent called?"

"Oh, it's not an accent," Trista replies crisply, turning her head to glance over her shoulder at me. "It's an ancient language called Tequilish."

I huff knowingly. "I need subtitles with this show."

"Are you going to keep watching it after tonight?"

I shrug. "I feel kind of invested in the rummmmooors and nastiiiness now."

Trista's genuine giggle at my horrible impersonation is like a balm to my guilty soul, and I squeeze her tightly, grateful her mood has lifted a bit. I've learned that I cannot handle seeing tears in her eyes, and I would do just about anything to make them stop—like hike through the forest on my property in the rain, searching for fucking chickens.

Or offer up a back rub.

The back rub was far superior to the chicken quest. I rubbed her shoulders and back for the first episode and her feet for most of the second episode. And at some point, we shifted around and began to spoon.

Yes, spoon.

It's new to me, but I can't say I mind it. In fact, it feels pretty good.

She flips her laptop closed and turns around to face me in the bed. Her hair has dried into a frizzy, wild mess, and her makeup-free face makes her look young. She is young. A whole decade below me. It's crazy how easy it is for me to forget that sometimes. What she's doing for me is so mature and responsible. She's much more grown up than I was at her age.

"Are you going to have to apologize to your brother at work tomorrow?" she asks, her green eyes sparkling in the soft lamplight on the nightstand behind me.

"Apologize for what?" I ask, my body tensing in irritation again. It's like a reflex at this point.

Her brows shoot up into her hairline. "For nearly punching him while he was holding a sweet kitten."

"I wasn't going to punch him," I gruff and run my fingers over my beard. I don't think I was going to punch him. Honestly, I'm not sure what I was going to do. I just didn't like seeing him inside Trista's apartment. Especially when she was just in a bathrobe.

It activated me.

"Did you really think I'd fool around with your brother?" she asks, her fingers tracing the ink on my forearm.

I exhale heavily. "I don't know."

She yanks her hand away from me and rolls to her back to stare up at the ceiling. Her eyes blink rapidly as she says, "It kills me to know that you think so little of me that you could imagine I'd do that... sleep with two brothers while I'm carrying a baby for one. My God, you must think I'm total trash."

"I do not think you're trash," I state firmly and reach over to cup her face so she can see the sincerity of my words. The tears in her eyes devastate me all over again. On the surface, Trista is so strong, so confident, but as I've grown to know her, certain things seem to trigger this vulnerable side to her, and I hate myself for being the cause of it sometimes.

Especially when my defense for my actions tonight will require me to discuss my past with Trista. Baggage I'd prefer to leave packed away. But it's unfair for her to sit here and be hurt over my own fucked-up issues.

My voice is heavy and thick when I say, "It's definitely not you. It's Calder. And it's me. And it's even Luke."

Her glossy eyes swim with confusion as an old, familiar anxiety creeps in around me. I've gone so long not feeling it lately by living in a sort of fairy tale of my journey to becoming a dad. But one little misunderstanding with my brother, and I'm thrust right back into my old twenty-eight-year-old, insecure, bullheaded self.

My tone is grave when I say the next words out loud. "My brothers and I…we all sort of fell for the same girl about ten years ago."

"All three of you?" Trista's lips part as she deadpans, "*The Housewives of Salt Lake City* could have a field day with a storyline like this."

"No shit," I mumble and swallow the knot in my throat. "Her name was Robyn." I wince as her name still brings a sick feeling to my gut all these years later. "She was the one who lived up here in this apartment years ago. I'd been living on the mountain for a bit already, and we'd just finished construction on Calder's and Luke's cabins.

"Anyway, we were hanging out at the Merc constantly back then. Probably drinking way too much. My dad called us the Wild Boys a lot. We weren't exactly model employees for his business. He was constantly riding our asses about growing up, and he thought we were avoiding reality by living on the mountain. It was kind of a transitional time in our lives.

"When Robyn started working at the Mercantile, it was obvious we were all into her. She was fresh and shiny and brought some life into this sleepy, small town. And it became this game of chicken between me and my brothers for who was going to admit they liked her and who was going to back off. Keep in mind this happened almost ten years ago, so we were young and dumb. Cocky and competitive.

"Anyway…one night, Robyn was hanging out with us, and we were all drinking heavily. One thing led to another, and a bet was made on who could actually seal the deal with her…may the best man win."

"It's giving 'Boys will be boys vibes,'" Trista replies with her nose wrinkled. Her judgment stings, but I deserve it.

"You're right, but the thing is…Robyn was aware of everything.

She knew we were all competing for her, and she played into it. It was funny and lighthearted...until she moved up onto the mountain."

"Did all three of you...sleep with her?" Trista asks, her voice full of horror.

"Not like that," I exclaim defensively. "Not at the same fucking time or anything. Jesus Christ, no. And actually, part of the bet meant we had to promise not to sleep with her."

"So then what happened?"

My cheeks puff out as I blow out a long breath. "One by one, we all broke the promise."

"Ick," Trista groans and pinches the bridge of her nose. I hate that I have to tell her this. I hate that this is a part of my past. But I'd be lying if I didn't admit that it shaped a lot of who I am today.

"The worst part was we all kept it a secret from each other. All three of us hid it, so we never knew what was going on. The only person who knew the truth about all of it was Robyn. And that's because she had a bet of her own."

"Triple ick."

I nod slowly because she was fulfilling her own fantasy at the time, and we were all just falling for her. She was a spitfire, absolutely gorgeous, sassy, yet could be sweet, and hot in bed. And she knew it. *Used it.* I'm not sure Robyn ever truly cared about any of us.

"We all knew we were getting in too deep. We were sneaking around behind each other's backs. We were fighting on jobsites pretty regularly. It was bad. My brothers and I didn't speak for the months while this bet dragged on, and my dad knew something was up, but none of us were talking. It was that game of chicken again, but this time...it wasn't just flirty banter at the bar."

"Were you in love with her?" Trista asks, a rare glimpse of vulnerability on her face as she asks the question that I must begrudgingly nod to.

"I didn't want to fall for her. But we did a weekend away at this cabin of her friends, and I just thought...this is the girl of my dreams. The girl I could marry. No woman had ever affected me the way she did. But it was that same weekend that she told me she loved someone else. And I just knew…my gut told me it was one of my brothers. But no matter how much I asked, she wouldn't say."

"Ugh, this is painful," Trista says, shaking her shoulders. "This woman sounds like the absolute worst. Did she not care that she was likely ripping apart an entire family?"

"I guess not. But it was just as much our fault as hers. We were horrible to each other. Max wouldn't even let us see Everly until we got our shit together. I even considered selling the mountain because I couldn't stand it up here with them."

"Holy shit," Trista says, seeming even more shocked by that reveal than all the rest of the stuff. "This is all just so hard to wrap my head around because you're all so close now."

"It took some time and serious effort to get to where we are. We do an annual bonding thing every year to keep it that way. And I hate that I still struggle to trust my brothers, but I need you to know it has nothing to do with you…it's them. And it's her. And it's why I don't date. Trusting women in a romantic sense is just impossible for me."

Trista watches me for a long, quiet moment, and her voice is soft when she asks, "Is she the one who got away?"

"That's a hard question for me to answer," I reply with a cringe. "Usually 'the one who got away' is portrayed in films as these beautiful, heroic characters that a person loves until the end of time. Robyn is a very different situation. For me…Robyn is just pain."

I exhale heavily at that admission. In fairness, I'm not sure Robyn set out to hurt me. I think she was in such a dark place in her life that the attention of the three of us felt like a stimulant to feel better about herself.

I was plagued with self-doubt and self-hatred, but even though it was wrong, having all three of you want me did wonders for my nonexistent self-esteem. You and your brothers…healed me.

Not the sort of thing you want to read in a letter from the woman you thought you loved.

"Do you still talk to her?" Trista asks, and I see a wave of nerves pass over her eyes.

I shake my head. "Not really. She's called a few times throughout the years and showed up unannounced once. But Calder put goat shit in the back seat of her car, so I think she got the hint that she's not welcome up here."

The corner of Trista's mouth quirks up into a smirk as she drags her hand down my arm. "You sound like a country song. Brokenhearted mountain man living alone with his goat thinking about the one who got away."

I scoff. "Sounds like a terrible song. And I'm fine now. I'm not pining for her. It just took me a while to realize that I can still have a family without a wife. I mean, not physically, obviously. That's why I need you. But emotionally, financially, I can do this. I can be a good dad on my own. I don't need a partnership to have this."

The words feel harder to get out after revisiting old wounds. The memories of the torment the three of us went through are not something I like to think about. So much mistrust and hair-trigger reactions. An acute sense of betrayal from my closest friends. My brothers. It was awful. I loathed the sight of Calder and the ease with which he walked through life during all that. I hated watching Luke's confidence grow with Robyn's attention. It was sick how I let a woman draw me in so much I began to resent my own blood. Thinking about it shrouds me in shame. I'm the oldest of us three. I should have known better.

But time has healed our wounds. We're solid again like we were when we first moved onto the mountain. And our Dark Night tradition keeps us all in check. That's why I've chosen to never let another woman near my heart again. Yes, my parents had had an incredible marriage. And watching Max become sickeningly happy with Cozy and have another kid has been inspiring. But it's just not worth the risk of putting myself through that kind of stress again.

If all I have in life is this mountain, my brothers, and hopefully a child…then I will want for nothing.

Trista's hands move to her belly, a thing she doesn't do very often. My eyes shoot to hers. "Are you feeling the baby move?" I ask, hope laced in my voice. The doctor said it could take up to twenty-four weeks before she feels anything, but a lot of the books I've been reading say she could be feeling stuff by now.

She shakes her head sadly. "No. Still nothing. Sorry."

"Nothing to be sorry about," I soothe and splay my hand on her hip, my fingers itching to touch her stomach, to feel the rounded swelling that's starting to show, even if she refuses to admit it. But I stop myself, knowing it could make her feel weird. It's one thing to touch her in the middle of sex. She seems pretty open to any sort of touching and talking when it comes to all things sexual.

But touching her belly for the purpose of feeling the baby…watching my hand on her flesh as I caress her and having her watch me as I do it…that's a different experience. One I'm not sure she wants to have with me. Nor should I want to have with her.

I scrub my hand over my face, my own exhaustion setting in. "We have the big ultrasound next week, so I'll get to see plenty of the little taco then."

"Taco?" Trista laughs and rolls over, pressing her ass into my hip. "Is that the food comparison size for next week?"

"No…taco is this week," I answer, twisting back into the spooning position and letting my hand splay casually on her stomach, my fingers trembling nervously. "Next week, it's a can of cola."

"Definitely bigger than a goat turd," Trista murmurs around a yawn.

"What?"

"Oh, nothing."

I smile softly and let my eyes close as the smell of roses on her pillow envelops me like a warm cloud. I should go. I should get out of here and let her sleep. But I'm too tired to get up. I'm emotionally spent from revisiting a time in my life I try to forget. It makes me feel sick and regretful and ashamed.

But lucky number thirteen in my arms? In her bed? It feels like redemption.

CHAPTER 36

WEEKS PREGNANT: 20
ANIMALS ON THE MOUNTAIN: 9

Trista

"How hard is it not to look at that envelope?" I ask Wyatt as he pulls out of the hospital parking lot after finishing our big twenty-week appointment.

He shrugs and shoots me a look like he's as cool as a cucumber.

He's not.

I saw his hand trembling when the nurse gave him the sealed envelope with the gender written inside. I saw his face while the ultrasound tech printed out 4D pictures showing the baby's chubby little cheeks and button nose. I saw his eyes when he looked at them like they were the most incredible things he'd ever seen.

How did I feel about the scan?

I'm a cow.

But the way he looks right now with the window down and the setting sun slicing through his disheveled hair, his muscular forearms on full display as he drives the car in that tight white T-shirt…

It's a good look.

He's giving me lots of good looks lately.

Like how he looked when he woke up in my bed the other morning, still fully dressed from the night before. He just pressed a kiss to my temple and said he was going to make me breakfast, and that's what he did. He made eggs and toast in my kitchen, set it on my nightstand table, and headed off to work.

No sex.

No sundown promises.

Just this look that I didn't let myself see before.

And I have to admit, it caused my mind to wander. Like what if he were my boyfriend? What if we were just a normal couple and falling for each other and I didn't have to hate how good it felt for him to hold me all night long with no sexual advances whatsoever?

It's an interesting look.

"Hey, do you mind if we stop at Max's house?" Wyatt asks, his thick forearm perched on the steering wheel. "I need to give this to Everly. She has all this planning to do, I guess, and she said she'd be home today."

"Sure, that's fine."

He rolls his eyes like this is such a bother, but I spot the proud-dad smile on his face. He's dying to know the gender, but the shower isn't for another few weeks. Everly literally leaves for Ireland the next day, so I'm sure the girl is crazy busy getting all this done before she goes.

We pull up to Max's house, and Wyatt gestures for me to come inside with him. It's hot out, so I oblige, and we walk through the house and spot Everly and Cozy outside by the pool, reading in some lounge chairs.

"Uncle Wyatt!" Ethan bellows as we step onto the back deck. He's dressed in swim trunks with snorkel goggles on and comes sprinting toward us, barreling right into Wyatt and wrapping his arms around his legs.

Wyatt picks him up like he weighs nothing and holds him over his shoulder. "Ready to go for a swim?"

"Yes!" Ethan cheers, and I watch in horror as Wyatt walks to the deep end of the pool and launches Ethan into the water.

"Oh my God, Wyatt," I exclaim and glance over to see that Everly and Cozy look perfectly fine with this. "Can he swim?"

"Oh, he's fine." Cozy waves me off and then lowers her sunglasses. "Hey, how was the ultrasound?"

I take a moment to recover from the shock of the toss that surely must have given that kid a concussion, but Ethan emerges from the pool, looking unscathed.

"Again, Wyatt, again!" he yells, padding over to him, dripping wet.

Wyatt prepares him for another launch, so I turn on my heel and sit down on the patio chair next to Everly to collect my thoughts before another splash sounds off behind me. I wince and force a smile. "The ultrasound was great. All the growth stuff looks good, my fluid is normal. I still haven't felt the baby move, but the doctor says any day now. Do you remember what it feels like?"

"With Ethan, it was like bubbles at first. Little tiny pops inside me," Cozy says with a big smile. "Then when he got bigger, it was like… holy shit, there's a human doing backflips in there."

I nod slowly. "I think I've been feeling the tiny pops, but I always just assume it's digestion stuff. I'll have to pay closer attention, I guess."

"Did they see the gender?" Everly asks excitedly.

"They did." I gesture over to Wyatt. "He has the sealed envelope."

Everly smiles big and drops her book to run over to her uncle to retrieve the big intel.

"It will be a miracle if she keeps this a secret," Cozy says with a smile. "Oh, hey, I have something for you! Come inside with me. Wyatt, I'm stealing Trista for a bit."

He frowns curiously at me as Cozy wraps herself in a caftan and drags me onto the deck toward a second patio door farther down along the house. She leads me through a primary bedroom and attached bath and into a huge walk-in closet.

Good Lord, these people really are loaded.

"Would you be interested in any of my old maternity clothes?" Cozy asks as she pulls a huge tote off a shelf and cracks the lid open. "I know they're seven years old now, so some are a little dated, but I think there's still some good pieces in here." She begins to lay them out on the plush carpet flooring. "I just washed them, so they're clean. And if you don't want them, that's totally fine too. I just know I'm done with them and going to donate if you're not interested."

"I'm interested," I blurt out and kneel on the floor to examine the sizes and selection. The clothes are a little more colorful than I'm used to wearing, but I can look past that because I've yet to purchase one real maternity outfit. From what I can tell, maternity clothes are the devil, and plus-sized maternity clothes are the devil's bowel movements.

In fairness, I haven't done a lot of shopping yet. Mostly because I still don't think I even look pregnant. Since I'm tall, I think the goat turd is just sort of stretched out in there or something, which results in me just looking thick or bloated. Not really pregnant.

Super hot.

But I know my belly has changed because none of my jeans button anymore. The only maternity thing I did manage to buy was some belly-band thing you can wear over the top of your jeans, but I need to find something decent because jeans won't be nice enough for the baby shower in a couple of weeks.

"Can I pay you for them? My contract with Wyatt has a clothing stipend, so I can give you something for all this."

"God, no." Cozy waves me off. "I'm just glad someone can use them. Do you want to try some on to see how they fit? Maybe I can help you pick something out for the shower in a couple of weeks?"

Relief washes over me because I've been having serious anxiety about this shower ever since I got the fancy invitation in the mail. I actually called Everly to tell her that I didn't think it was necessary for me to be there. It's really an event for Wyatt, and since I'm not even obviously pregnant yet, it's not like I'd be some cute display item.

But that girl does not take no for an answer.

I even asked Wyatt if he could get me out of it on our way to the ultrasound appointment earlier today, and there was a flicker of disappointment in his eyes over the fact that I didn't want to come. And after everything he did for me and the chicken coop, I didn't want to let him down. I guess I'm going to the friggin' baby shower.

"I would love help picking out what to wear for the shower," I reply to Cozy. "I'm such a jeans-and-T-shirt girlie, and you guys all looked so nice at the graduation. I don't want to look frumpy."

"Oh my God, you couldn't look frumpy if you tried," Cozy chastises, her green eyes rolling to the ceiling. "And even if you did look frumpy, no one cares." She pauses and bites her lip. "Except maybe Wyatt's mom. That woman is sweet, but she loves to offer friendly feedback."

Her candid response makes me laugh and instantly like Cozy. She's more relatable than I expected her to be. Yes, she's living in a mansion with a pool and a guesthouse and has a closet bigger than my whole apartment in Denver, but I get the sense that she came from humble roots.

We get to work picking out some items for me to try on, and they all fit pretty decently. I'm impressed with how similarly sized Cozy and I are. That is not a common occurrence for a girl like me. And she clearly shops at places a bit nicer than JCPenney, so this stuff is probably worth more than my entire wardrobe.

"Okay, what do we think of this one?" I ask, exiting the closet in a yellow tie-dye maxi dress to find Cozy perched on the bathroom counter, waiting to see the next outfit. "It's much cheerier than I'm used to. Is yellow even my color? Do I look disgusting?"

Cozy sighs. "Disgustingly perfect."

"Really?" I ask, hope lifting my brows as I glance at myself in the giant vanity mirror.

Cozy slips off the counter and looks with me. "This honestly looks really beautiful on you."

"But don't I look really pregnant?" I ask, pressing the fabric to my stomach. "I swear these clothes do something weird. I didn't even think I was showing."

"Oh, you're showing." Cozy laughs. "But that's a good thing. You look luminous, Trista. You're super pretty."

I flinch at that comment and look over at her, expecting to see her laughing, but she's not. She's genuinely admiring me like a bride who just said yes to a wedding dress. It's kind of intense.

My sister wouldn't even compliment me the one time I saved up all my server tips and bought a dress for my first high school winter formal. I remember coming out in it, and she looked at me and cringed. She said it didn't complement my body type at all, and I better not try to have sex with anyone that night because she was leaving soon, and she wasn't going to stick around to help me raise a baby.

Thanks, sis.

Although, in her defense, I think I called her a cunt an hour before that for not letting me use the car for the night, so we weren't really vibing at the time.

"Well, these clothes are great because I was running out of things that fit," I state, turning to lean on the counter so I'm facing her. "Are you sure you're done with these, though? You're still young. What if you want more babies?"

"I would have been up for it, but Max is a bit older than me and felt kind of weird about being too old when his kid graduated from high school. And honestly, having Everly already made me feel like my cup runneth over."

I nod thoughtfully at that. "Was it weird being with a guy who had a kid already?"

Cozy's brows lift as a sly smile spreads across her face. "You know I was Everly's nanny before Max and I…"

"Um…no, I did not know this!" I exclaim and jerk my head back. "Holy shit, that's juicy."

She laughs and shyly plays with the strings on her caftan. "I know. It was pretty scandalous initially, and I didn't think it would turn into anything more than a fling. I thought he was just into me because I was convenient."

My brows twitch at that because the same thoughts cross my mind regarding Wyatt and me. I'm living right next door to him, pregnant with his kid, just…easy access.

"But then…it became more. So much more. And the fact that he had a kid who I loved at first sight…it just…worked. Instant family."

Instant family. I repeat the two words in my head, feeling a sense of dread because I've never yearned for a family. In fact, when I think of my own family, I just feel…angry.

"You loved Everly at first sight?" I ask, my tone almost a whisper as the question tumbles out.

"You've met her!" Cozy laughs affectionately. "She has that

effervescent spark, you know? That specialness that just pulls you in and makes you root for her. Ethan, I loved the minute I peed on that stick and found out that I was pregnant. God, he gave me such a gift growing inside me. The changes in my body, my heart…it literally felt like we had our own little secret. Our own little language of just existing together. Total happiness…even if he makes me crazy five out of seven days a week." I notice Cozy's eyes are filled with happy tears as she jerks back and waves her hand over her face. "Oh my God, I'm such a dick. I'm gushing about being pregnant, and you're…"

"Giving the baby up." I finish what she cannot, a sense of foreboding pressing down on me.

"Not giving it up. Giving it life. And giving it to someone who will love it until the end of time." Cozy steps toward me and rubs my shoulder. "It's an amazing gift you're giving my brother-in-law."

I nod thoughtfully. "So would you say you sacrificed your dream of a big family because of Max, then?"

Cozy's face twists in confusion. "Sacrifice seems like a strong word."

"Does it?" I ask curiously. "If you wanted more kids and he didn't, then you catered to him, right?"

"I didn't cater to him," Cozy replies, her brows furrowing at me. "It's called compromise."

"Right, but that's a huge life decision to compromise on, isn't it?" I feel my pulse increase as this conversation turns from light banter to intense discussion, but I'm not one to hold back when I'm curious about something. "It's sort of like dating someone with a different religion. At some point, someone will have to change who they are for the other person."

"But if that other person makes you happier than you've ever been, then the change isn't always a bad thing. Being in love with someone makes change feel exciting, not sacrificial."

I nod, trying to digest what she's said. My family wouldn't dream of sacrificing their own wants for something else. Especially not their own child.

"Can I ask why you decided to be a surrogate?" Cozy asks, ripping me out of my inner musings. "That's definitely a sacrifice to your body and your health. It must have been a big decision to say yes to Wyatt, right?"

My head is nodding as my mind races. "I'd be lying if I said a lot of it wasn't motivated by money." I chew my lip thoughtfully before adding something I never had the guts to tell Wyatt when he first interviewed me. "But the truth is, once I started researching it, I was fascinated by the idea of people out there being willing to shell out boatloads of money for a kid. Like…they want a baby no matter the cost. They jump through extraordinary hoops because a child is their ultimate dream." My eyes glaze over as I struggle to even remember my parents' faces. Do they even remember mine? Do they even still have a picture of me? "I think maybe by doing this, I'm trying to heal my own inner child because the people in my life…my parents…they had kids by default. They didn't try for them, didn't struggle for them. They certainly didn't dream about them. They just got them. Which made throwing them away so damn easy."

The silence is thick in the bathroom when I realize what I've just said, and I look up to see Cozy's eyes filled with tears as she stares at me, lips parted, nose running, cheeks red.

Fuck.

I just spilled my guts to a basic stranger, and I should be embarrassed. Or sorry.

But today…I'm not.

I'm bitter.

I'm bitter at how easy it seems for this family to love and care about each other when mine couldn't find a single fuck to give about me.

CHAPTER 37

WEEKS PREGNANT: 20
ANIMALS ON THE MOUNTAIN: 9

Wyatt

Every head turns to stare when Calder, Luke, Trista, and I walk into the Mercantile. It's Saturday night, and my brothers wanted to go to town for a beer and some food. We were heading there in the truck, and I saw the light on above the barn, and something in me felt compelled to stop and invite her. We've been seeing each other most nights anyway, unless she's busy with Avery, so it felt weird not to have her come along.

And part of me wants this night to be an opportunity to show her that I'm okay with her talking to my brothers and even spending time with them. Her asking me if I thought she was trash the other night really hit me hard. If anything, she's too good for us.

Judy sets three beers in front of us and a Shirley Temple in front of Trista. Her eyes drop to Trista's belly, but she says nothing. Just tips her chin and leaves us be.

My own eyes can't seem to stay away from Trista's belly either. She looks good tonight. Tight black top and a pair of shiny black leggings. She's showing more every day, and the urge I have to constantly touch her is honestly becoming an issue.

"Can you guys explain to me the real reason you all thought it would be a good idea to live as neighbors on a mountain? Like…

forever?" Trista deadpans, causing Calder to chuckle around a mouthful of beer.

"What? Is that not normal?" Luke asks with a playful smile.

"No, it's not normal!" Trista says, her eyes glittering in the dim
bar lighting. "I haven't seen my sister in a decade, and you guys are
neighbors, coworkers, and brothers who carpool to work every day."

I smile and lean back in my chair, casually draping my arm on the
back of hers. I'm going to let my brothers field this inquiry.

Calder smiles cockily and leans across the table to start counting off the reasons. "Well, for starters, Wyatt let us build on his land
for free."

Trista shoots me an impressed look, and I shrug.

"The views are fucking spectacular." He ticks off another reason.
"And we already work together every day, so who gives a fuck where we
sleep at night? Might as well be somewhere with a great fucking view."

"And we had to help him develop the land, so he owed us big."
Luke shoots a pointed look at me, and I nod knowingly. They worked
their asses off helping me make the land livable before I could even
start building. It became a bit of an obsession for us all.

"And we're best friends." Calder slams his hands on the table before thrusting a finger right at my face. "Even if this fucker doesn't want
to call me his best friend."

Trista frowns at me, and I just shrug. "I don't like labels."

"He loves me, even when he wants to punch me." Calder gets up
and moves around the table to grab my face, planting a big, sloppy
kiss on my cheek. I shove him off me, and just as he moves to sit back
down, I kick his chair out from under him, causing Calder to fall to
the ground laughing. I fight back my own laughter as I watch Luke
help him up.

Luke smiles over at Trista. "They're best friends who fight a lot."

Calder drops down into his seat and glares knowingly at me. "The
truth is, Wyatt is the loneliest loner you'll ever meet."

I growl under my breath and sip my beer, turning my attention
away from the table.

"He likes to be alone, but not too alone."

Luke interjects, "He actually doesn't like to be alone at all. He's just particular about who he spends time with. He has zero tolerance for people he doesn't like."

"I keep a small circle. There's nothing wrong with that." I shrug dismissively and turn to face Trista before I ask, "Why aren't you close with your sister?"

Trista's head jerks back, clearly not expecting the change in conversation, but she opened a door, and I'm sure as hell going to step through it.

"Well, because she's not a potbellied pig, most likely." She shrugs like she's completely serious, and I half think she might be.

Calder and Luke laugh.

"And because she's kind of a raging bitch who bailed on me when I was sixteen, and she was all I had." She sips her drink loudly.

"Where were your parents?" Luke asks.

"They dipped for good when I was fourteen."

"Both of them?"

"Yep."

"Did you live with a grandparent or something?" Calder asks.

"Nope," Trista replies cheerily. "Just my sister, who was eighteen at the time and my technical legal guardian. That is until she met a guy and moved to Hawaii with him right before my sixteenth birthday."

"Jesus, so who did you live with then?" Luke asks, concern evident all over his face.

"Myself." Trista shrugs like it's completely normal for her to live on her own at barely sixteen. That's two years younger than Everly, and I am inwardly seething that her parents could do that to her. *She was a child. Someone who needed parents.* "I literally lived in my family's same income-based apartment until I moved up onto the mountain with you guys."

How the hell did she pay rent? Feed herself? Buy school shit? Pay utilities?

The three of us all blink back at her, our minds reeling with this new information.

"That's fucked up, right?" Luke's angry voice perfectly portrays the rage I'm feeling right now but am unable to say it out loud.

Trista's nose wrinkles. "I mean, I was almost an adult, so it was fine. I had a job and finished high school. One of my friends had me over to her house all the time, so I wasn't always alone."

Calder's tone is scary serious when he asks, "Do you ever hear from your parents? Where did they go?"

"Alaska that time." Trista looks thoughtful as she seemingly works toward recalling the whereabouts of her parents. "They joined some cult, but then they were kicked out and living in Canada illegally for a while. That was five years ago when my mom called and told me that. I haven't heard from them directly since then, but I think my sister said they were in Maine at one point. I don't fully recall." Trista looks stiff and detached as she forces a bright smile that literally hurts my guts. "They weren't model parents to begin with growing up, always leaving for these religious retreats, so I'm probably better off without them, but yeah...no idea where they are now."

The table grows silent as the three of us stew over what these kinds of parents must be like, especially when we had parents who would walk through fire for us. I'd walk through fire for Trista now, and I've only known her a handful of months. I want to burn every home their parents ever lived in to the ground and make them watch.

Calder breaks the tension when he asks, "I bet you wish you could drink right now, huh?"

Trista bursts out laughing, and we all smile along with her, but it feels sad. She literally has no family looking out for her. Everyone who should have cared about her left her.

It makes me want to hurt someone.

Trista

Jesus, I really need to get a grip these days.

Can I blame the pregnancy hormones on oversharing? Because

two days ago, I spilled my guts to Cozy, and now, I have three mountain men all looking at me like I'm a lost puppy dog. Not the vibe I want for the first night out I've had in ages, especially since I've been feeling really good about my life lately.

There's a weird thing that happens up on the mountain. You seem to lose track of reality a bit. Yes, I go to the shelter every day and beg Earl not to fire me when I'm late. But when I return to Fletcher Mountain, all the noise just sort of goes away. Time just sort of ceases to exist in the magnificence of it all. It's like this little sanctuary that makes the stresses of the real world disappear.

It's magical.

When coyotes aren't eating my chickens, at least.

Calder and Luke are up at the bar, talking to some locals, and I can feel Wyatt's eyes burrowing in on me. He's looking at me differently since I opened my big mouth, and I'm pissed at myself for being so stupid. I wish I was drinking alcohol to have something to blame.

"You have to stop," I state firmly, turning severe eyes on him.

"What?" he says, his eyes soft as they sweep over my whole face.

"Stop looking at me with pity."

"I'm not looking at you with pity," he says, brows furrowed.

"Yes, you are."

"I'm looking at you because you're beautiful."

"Okay, now I know you're lying," I harrumph and grab a french fry off my plate.

"You are beautiful, you know," he says firmly, turning so his legs are on either side of my chair. I glance over to see if his brothers are watching because this is certainly a more intimate way to sit next to someone who's not supposed to be having sex with me.

"And you're strong," he adds with piercing eyes. "I could tell that from the first time I met you."

I lick my lips and nod. "Thanks."

"I mean it, Lucky," he says with urgency in his voice. "I can't imagine what it was like losing your parents that way. Mourning the loss of someone who's not even dead. That has to be a mindfuck. I'm still not over my own dad's loss, and there was never a day he wasn't there for me. Never a day I doubted how much he loved me."

His words cut deep into a part of my soul I don't like to access, so I shake him off. "It's honestly fine. When you grow up in a dysfunctional environment, you don't know it's dysfunctional because it's all you've ever seen."

I chew my lip thoughtfully, thinking back to the memories of what it was like every day. The verbal, sometimes physical abuse. The erratic behavior. The coming and going without even checking in on me. The nights I would go without anyone cooking a meal or asking if I ate. It sucked that I thought that was all normal.

"But now that I'm grown, I take care of myself in ways my parents never did. Like when I was little, all I wanted was a dog or a cat…hell, I even begged for a stupid betta fish. And it was always no. And look at me now. I have a pig and a horse and a bunny and chickens and a cat…well, not a cat anymore, but if I want one, I'll get one. Because I'm doing all the things for myself that no one ever did for me—that no one ever even encouraged me to dream for."

I take a sip of my drink and avoid Wyatt's probing eyes.

"And as hard as I know an animal sanctuary is going to be to open, I'm going to fucking do it. I've been researching how it can be financially sustainable to leverage donations and sponsorships, as I discussed with Max. Land acquisition will be hard, but I have a real estate agent looking for properties that could double as housing for me too, so I'm making moves. I'll show them—my sister, my parents, the world—that even though I was left behind, I still found my way out."

Anger simmers in my veins as I white-knuckle grip my glass until Wyatt's hand reaches out and folds over mine, silently urging me to release the drink. I do, and when I turn to look at him, his hand moves up to touch my face. His thumb caresses my jawline in a tender way that sends shivers down my spine as he whispers, "Fuck yes, you'll show them."

There's something about the whisper that makes it so much more meaningful. Like it's a secret he's been in on with me the whole time.

Like he's always known I'd do what I said I would do. That kind of validation feels so fucking good.

I tilt into his touch, relishing in the texture of his calloused palm against my cheek. His hand is warm and dry, like the perfect kind of comfort after off-loading a lifetime's worth of trauma.

His eyes drop to my mouth, and I feel myself drawing toward him, desperate to feel the certainty his lips just uttered with my own. Maybe if I taste them, I'll believe them too.

He moves in to close the space, and just before our lips touch, a loud crash sounds off behind us.

Wyatt swerves around, and we see Calder and Luke face-to-face with two guys I've never met. Calder shoves his guy and pulls back to take a swing. His fist connects with the other guy's jaw at the same time Luke takes a punch to the stomach. Wyatt's chair crashes onto the floor as he rushes over there, grabbing the guy off Luke. He grips him by the arms long enough for Luke to take a swing and connect with the guy's gut.

Someone jumps Wyatt from behind, twisting his arms into a full nelson, and I gasp as Calder's guy moves to take a swing at Wyatt. Just before Wyatt gets punched in the ribs, he manages to bend over, lifting the guy behind him off the ground and flipping him over his shoulders before he thuds onto the floor.

Judy hollers for them to take it outside as several other patrons jump in to break up the brawl. The three guys are dragged out the back toward the beer garden while Wyatt, Calder, and Luke are shoved out the front.

Heart racing, I grab my purse and follow them out, desperate to find out what the hell happened.

When I come outside, Wyatt is screaming at both of them. "What the fuck got into you two?" he hollers, giving big daddy energy that I definitely find attractive.

"Nothing! We handled it!" Calder exclaims, wiping the blood dribbling down his lip with the collar of his flannel shirt.

"The fuck you did. I handled it," Wyatt booms.

"I fucking had him," Luke bellows defensively.

"Tell me what was said."

Calder's eyes flash nervously to me as he responds, "It's not important."

"Tell me," Wyatt thunders.

"No."

"Just tell him," I exclaim, stepping between them, desperate for this madness to stop.

Calder and Luke exhale heavily as they struggle with what to say to me, but Luke finally answers. "They said the whole town is saying you don't know whose baby you're carrying."

I inhale sharply.

"They said it could be any of ours," he adds, pointing at the three of them.

"They're calling you our concubine." Calder's eyes are harsh and menacing like he wants to march right back in there and finish the job he started. "Everyone thinks you're fucking all three of us, and we're paying you to do it. They're calling you a whore, Trista."

Wyatt's face looks positively murderous as he growls and turns to storm back into the bar. I grab him by the arm and stop him in his tracks. "Wyatt, stop. It's not worth it."

"The hell it's not," Wyatt thunders.

Calder takes my breath away when he steps in close and grabs my shoulders instead of Wyatt's. His eyes are grave and serious as he says, "We won't let anyone besmirch your good name, Trista."

"Besmirch my good name?" I repeat, my lips parted in complete shock and confusion. Is this a joke?

"You're family now," Luke adds with a heavy breath, no signs of humor on his face whatsoever. "Your reputation won't be tarnished over this."

I step back and blink rapidly, my mind processing the words coming out of their mouths. These two got into a bar fight because of me?

Tears burn in my eyes, and I feel pissed off at the traitorous, salty assholes as they fall down my cheeks and turn all these angry mountain men into puddles of goo right before me.

The knot in my throat is thick as I struggle with what to say to that. What do you say to three grown men who just got into a fight to defend your honor?

What do you say to someone who's only known you for a handful of months and has done more for you than your entire family ever has?

What do you do when the world shows you it's not as broken as you always thought it was?

"Trista, please don't cry. We will fix—"

Calder is cut off when I reach up and pull him down for a hug, my arms cinching tightly around his neck, my shoulders shaking with silent sobs as I reach for Luke behind him and pull him into the hug as well. I watch Wyatt stare at me open-mouthed as I hug his brothers as tight as I possibly can, muffling my sobs into Calder's shoulder as I squeeze the life out of him and Luke for somehow putting life back inside me with one punch.

Okay, maybe a few punches.

And a flippy thing that Wyatt did that was really impressive.

I reach my hand out to my mountain man, and he moves in, wrapping his arms around all three of us, completing this concubine group hug. I don't give a shit what the town says about me. I don't even know any of them. But I care what these three Fletcher brothers think of me. And to know they'd go to these lengths to protect me feels better than I ever would have imagined.

"Let's go home," I murmur, pulling away from them to wipe my nose.

They nod and help me to the car, watching over me like I might fall apart into a million pieces. And something tells me these three would spend the night putting me back together if that happened.

When we return to the mountain, my emotions are fried, and I don't even argue when Wyatt slides out of the truck and makes his way into the barn with me. I glance at his brothers, worried we'll give ourselves away, but Wyatt just dutifully follows me upstairs.

I let him inside, and he moves straight for my dishwasher. "What are you doing?"

His voice is tired when he replies, "I'm going to empty your dishwasher."

"Why?"

He hits me with a devastating look. "For the same reason I got you a new bed, and bring you breakfast, and hired you a cleaning lady. I like to do things for you, Lucky. And tonight, I want to just do what I want for you."

He bends over and gets back to work but pauses to add, "And tomorrow, I'm going to vacuum out your car, and I don't want to hear a fucking peep about it, okay? Now, go crawl into bed. I'll join you when I'm done."

And just like that...the mountain man unloads my dishwasher.

CHAPTER 38

WEEKS PREGNANT: 20
ANIMALS ON THE MOUNTAIN: 9

Wyatt

I wake the following morning to beams of sunlight on my face, and when my eyes crack open and the barn ceiling comes into focus, I remember where I am. I turn my head and see that Trista is rolled away from me, curled into a little ball, sleeping soundly. I gaze back up at the ceiling, and memories of when I lived up here years ago start replaying in my head.

Dad thought I was fucking nuts for buying this mountain. He thought I was double nuts when he saw I was living in a dilapidated barn, where you could literally hear the mice crawling around at night.

I was crazy back then.

I was brave too.

I miss feeling brave.

The bullshit with my brothers and Robyn fucked with my head so much it took years for me to even feel remotely safe enough to take chances again.

And strangely, last night, when I brawled at the bar with my brothers…I felt like I was getting parts of my old self back again. It felt like we were this united front, and I moved with renewed purpose. I was fighting for something bigger than me.

I was fighting for my family.

Family Trista clearly never experienced after everything she revealed to us last night. She honestly believed she wasn't worth our loyalty. Her fucking parents and sister showed her that. And now all I want to do is beat that thought out of her and show her what I see plain as day. *She's one of the bravest, kindhearted people I know.*

Trista makes a noise and rolls onto her back, kicking the covers off her body as she does. I look over, and her baggy T-shirt rides up, exposing her belly. It's still so small. It's crazy to me that what I saw on the ultrasound machine last week is living inside her. It doesn't seem humanly possible.

I roll over, and my hand hovers over her abdomen, the heat of her sleeping body radiating on my palm, itching for me to touch her. When I softly press my palm onto her flesh, a feeling of possessiveness roars through me.

She is mine.

Not just this baby but this woman. I want to protect and take care of them both. I'd do anything for them, and the heaviness that settles in my gut over that realization is terrifying and exciting.

She begins to stir awake, so I deftly slide my hand down her waist and slip into her panties, my fingers trailing over her smooth mound before teasing the lips of her cunt.

She moans and twists, her arms lifting into a stretch as her pelvis greedily pulses up into my palm.

"Morning, Lucky," I croak, my voice deep and raspy from sleep.

Her eyes flutter open and then widen when I sink one long finger inside her, groaning softly when I find her soaking wet for me.

We didn't have sex last night, which means that the two nights I've slept over are also the two nights we didn't fuck—probably not exactly sexuationship behavior, but I'm happily breaking all the damn rules for her.

Her eyes close as she moves her hands to her groin. She grabs my hand and holds me to her, thrusting her hips up onto my finger, fucking me like I'm hers to fuck.

I am.

I am all hers.

She rolls onto her side and slips her hands under the covers to find my rock-hard erection, which has been there since the second I woke up. Her fingers slip into my boxer briefs and wrap around my length, stroking me up and down as she presses her face into my chest.

I inhale the intoxicating aroma of her rose-scented hair, my pelvis thrusting into her grip as my fingers work hard on her center, her leg bent upward to give me full access.

Our breaths are hot, our bodies growing sticky as we fuck each other with our hands like two teenagers just figuring out how sex parts work. My fingers are soaked as I slip out and rub her arousal on her clit in hard, circular motions.

Her whimper is loud in the quietness of the barn, and I want to say something to urge her to be louder, but I don't want to break this spell we're both under. It's a quiet, secretive session we're having, and it feels more intimate because of that.

I audibly growl when she releases my shaft to grip my balls and tease my taint. The friction she's creating in that area drives me fucking mad.

I fight the urge to climb on top and slam my cock inside her for some relief. This edging we're both doing to each other is the sweetest form of torture I've ever experienced. My dick grows sticky as she slides the precum around me, gripping me firmly and pushing me to the brink.

I curl my two fingers up and rub along her G-spot, and in seconds, she cries out, the grip of her hand on my cock like a vise as she comes on my fingers without warning. Her body tenses as she throws her head back, her chest heaving upward as she breathes through her climax. I curse her T-shirt for covering what I know to be a beautiful sight of her soft breasts, but honestly, I don't need to see her for what we're doing right now. This encounter is all about sensations beyond visuals. It's erotic in ways I'd never expect.

When she comes down from her orgasm, she turns back to me, stroking me softly. Her voice is hoarse when she says, "I want you to come on my belly, Wyatt. I want to watch you."

Her words are like pressing an easy button on my cock, so without pause, I throw the covers off and climb over her.

She pulls her shirt up above her breasts and uses her arms to press her lush tits together in a way that I would love to bury my cock between. She continues stroking me with one hand, and my eyes close as I feel my climax cresting.

With a shudder, my jaw drops as I expel myself over top of her. She angles my cock in various ways as I spurt over her breasts, her belly, and her mound, my pearly semen decorating her body like a piece of art. I sit back on my heels, blinking rapidly for my vision to come back into focus so I can enjoy the view of my woman covered in my seed.

My woman.

Never did I think I'd crave those two words again. I never thought I'd risk my heart again. But Trista…she's so much more than just the woman I'm fucking. She's strong, vulnerable, wise…*selfless*. And if my heart can be trusted right now, she is mine. Her body, her baby, her mind…and maybe *her* heart.

I want it all to be mine.

With a wicked look, I rub my cum onto her belly, using the sexual moment as an excuse to feel her body to my fill.

"You are beautiful," I state huskily, and the Neanderthal in me wishes she'd always leave this on her skin so the whole world knows who she belongs to.

"Because I'm covered in your jizz? Okay, perv." She laughs, and her light tone causes a sleepy smile to pull at my lips.

"No, you're just…beautiful," I reply simply, staring down at every inch of her flesh on display for me. I lightly circle her nipple and watch it pebble beneath my touch. "Everything about you."

I glance up and see her brows furrow, and the smile on her face twitches. It's at that moment that I state the words that were on the tip of my tongue last night but was interrupted before I had a chance to say them. "You know, you could stay on the mountain longer than the one-year-lease thing in our contract."

"What do you mean?" she asks as I stroke her thighs on either side of me.

"If you want to stay on the mountain another year or two, you should."

She sits up on her elbows, her face the picture of confusion. "What about the baby?"

I shrug. "It won't know who you are for at least the first year of its life. Probably even two years. I just don't want you to think you have to be looking for a new place to live before you've even given birth. Just focus on growing the baby in that beautiful body of yours and stay here for as long as you like."

Her face looks sad for a brief second before she steels herself to reply, "You'd charge me rent, obviously."

I frown. "It's not really necessary."

"For the animals too," she adds urgently, pulling her legs up and away from me as she scoots to the head of the bed and pulls her shirt down to cover herself. "I'd need to rent barn space. Fair market value."

I frown over at her, not really enjoying the discussion of semantics when I'm still naked in her bed. "We can work something out if that's important to you."

"It is." She licks her lips, her eyes alive with something dangerously close to anger. "I don't want a pity apartment, Wyatt."

"It's not pity," I state seriously. "It's just…logical."

"Logical, totally," she chirps as she shifts to get off the bed.

"Where are you going?" I ask, feeling whiplash at the change in temperature in the room right now.

"I have to head out."

"Head out?" I ask as she bends over to check her phone on the nightstand.

"I'm meeting Avery this morning for coffee."

My hands turn to fists instantly. Every time she's spoken of Avery, it's only been for work things. Now she's seeing him socially?

"Are you supposed to drink coffee?" I bark, my tone more judgmental than I intended.

Her brows lift as she pauses at the foot of the bed. "Was there a coffee clause in our contract that I missed?"

Her reply hits me like a ton of bricks.

My teeth clench as I narrow my eyes on her. "No, but I'm pretty sure caffeine isn't good for the baby."

She waves me off and pads barefoot over to her closet. "I know it's not. I just do decaf. Don't stress, Papa Bear."

My lips curl at that nickname. She's never called me that before, and something about the way she said it feels…intentional. Distant. I walk over to her closet and lean on the door behind her as she rifles through her stuff.

"Are we good?" I ask, my voice sounding more uncertain than I like.

"We're great!" She pats me on the chest and shoots me a wink. "That was a really good offer, and I'll seriously consider it. But right now, I need to clean myself up."

She moves past me, and I watch her walk away, feeling awkward as fuck for some maddening reason. Shaking off my irritation, I grab my jeans off the floor and say, "I'll fix you breakfast."

"Don't bother," she calls out from the bathroom. "I'm going to eat at the coffee shop. I'll just see you later!"

She closes the door to the bathroom, and I'm left with an odd, familiar feeling that I haven't felt in ten years. Like something—*some-one*—important is slipping through my fingers. Something too valuable to lose.

And this time, it feels far more terrifying.

CHAPTER 39

WEEKS PREGNANT: 21
ANIMALS ON THE MOUNTAIN: 9

Wyatt

"**M**orning, Papa Bear," Calder yells out his truck window as he pulls up in front of my house on Monday morning for work.

I bristle at that label as I get up from my deck chair, coffee thermos in hand. My eyes move to the barn for the hundredth time this morning, irritation prickling in my veins. For the past few months, I have been delivering breakfast to Trista's front door at six o'clock every day because I've never seen her leave the mountain before six fifteen. Today, she was gone before I came out, and the irrational rage I feel over the fact that I didn't get to feed her is something I'm failing to get control over.

"You look especially broody this morning," Luke huffs as I slide into the back seat.

I grunt my wordless reply.

"So it's going to be one of those days," Calder groans as he traverses down the mountain.

I fight the urge to text Trista to make sure she's okay. There's something about giving her breakfast every day that made me feel like it was our daily check-in. If I saw she took the food, then I knew she was good. The fact that she most likely didn't eat this morning is making me fucking crazy.

"I have something that will cheer you up," Calder says brightly, turning his neck to glance back at me. "I've figured out what we'll do for our Dark Night."

My brows lift. Our Dark Night is a thing the three of us do around Labor Day every year because it was around this time that we almost ruined our whole family.

All over a girl.

My mind flashes back to when we all discovered we were secretly dating Robyn. It was like this slow-motion explosion of realization after realization that all three of us were getting played. I can't help but wonder how long she would have kept stringing us along... if it weren't for the baby.

"I want you all to keep an open mind, okay?" Calder says, his tone light and bouncy. "We did Luke's stupid lumberjack competition last year. The year before that, you made us go fishing in Canada, Wyatt. Super thrilling, by the way. Talk about an adrenaline rush."

I growl at the back of Calder's head. Our Dark Night has been a variety of things throughout the past decade, so we've had to get creative to come up with new activities. The point of it really is just to help the three of us reconnect and remind us of what we almost lost when we let a girl come between us. One year, Calder made us fucking skydive, and while I was not happy about that selected activity, I do admit that afterward, I felt a newfound connection with my brothers over experiencing that together. Our Dark Night is important, and as much as I like to complain about it, I still look forward to it every year.

"I have two words for you guys," Calder says, eyeing me and Luke with raised brows. "Sex. Club."

"What?" Luke's eyes nearly bulge out of his head.

"Sex club!" Calder repeats with confidence.

"Calder, that's your thing, not mine," Luke argues, and I feel grateful he's saying this for both of us.

"That's because you've never tried it," Calder says with a laugh. "Seriously, you guys...this will be an experience like you've never had before. And with Wyatt due to have a baby in a few months, this is his last chance to really do something crazy before he goes into full-time Papa Bear mode. It's like a bachelor party for a soon-to-be single dad."

"What do we do there exactly?" Luke asks, and my hands turn into fists when I hear his tone change from denial to intrigue. That didn't take much convincing.

"Whatever tickles your pickle," Calder says with a dirty smile. "You have a kink? There's a room for that. People at these sex clubs are down for all sorts of fucked-up things. Last year, I watched a guy fuck a girl wearing a horse tail butt plug."

"Jesus," Luke says with a disbelieving look at me. "Okay, I'm kind of interested in seeing that."

"What the fuck is wrong with you two?" I snap, my tone visceral. "Why would you want to go get off with your brothers at a sex club?"

"We're not getting off together," Calder argues. "We won't even be in the same rooms. We can separate easily. The place is huge."

I shake my head adamantly and can feel Calder's eyes on me in the rearview mirror.

"This is my year, Papa Bear. And a pact is a pact." My eyes snap to his, and he looks back at me with defiance all over his face. "Do you think I wanted to go fucking fishing in Canada last year? Fuck no. That was lame as shit."

I scowl at him.

"But I did it because this night is important," Calder says, staring seriously at me. "This night pushes our boundaries and our comfort zones so we can walk out of it with a new experience, feeling changed...together."

Luke turns back to look at me. "He's right, Wyatt. We agreed years ago never to argue with whatever the choice was. It's why we all take turns picking every year."

My teeth clench as images of Trista naked in her bed fill my mind. No way will this go over well with her. But a sick part of me is desperate to see how she reacts when I tell her.

Trista

I nearly step on Wyatt the following morning when I find him outside my door, setting a brown breakfast bag on my step.

"Oh my God, you scared the shit out of me," I exclaim, pressing my hand to my chest. "Wyatt, it's not even six."

He stands and runs a hand through his hair. "I know. You left early yesterday, so I didn't want to miss you today."

It's dark out still, and I haven't even woken up completely. I don't have time for mountain-man pity glances.

"Well, thank you," I say with a forced smile as I take the bag from him.

I move to make my way down the stairs and can feel him following close as he says, "Hey, um…I need to talk to you about something."

"Can I feed the animals while we talk?" I ask, not taking my eyes off my task at hand.

"Sure."

Wyatt follows me around, rambling on and on about some Dark Night tradition he does with his brothers. He starts telling me about things they've done in the past and the reasons and meanings behind why they do it. Honestly, those are the most words I think I've ever heard him speak in one breath, and I start to wonder if he even slept last night.

"Anyway, Calder wants us to go to this sex club in Denver."

"Come again?" I state from the middle of Reginald's pen. Reggie is out cold, and not even a sex club mention would stir him.

But it stirred me.

"Those places actually exist?" I ask, feeling kind of dumb.

"I guess so," Wyatt replies with a pained look in his eye. "It's Calder's thing, not mine. But he wants us all to check it out."

My nose wrinkles. "Seems like a weird brother activity, but you Fletcher boys play by your own rules."

"I won't sleep with anyone," Wyatt says as I step out of Reggie's pen and turn to re-hook his gate. My back is turned to him, and I feel my shoulders lift as my entire body tenses with the realization of what this conversation is really about.

I swallow the lump in my throat and school my voice to sound calm and collected. "You can if you want."

With a sharp inhale, I turn on my heel to face him, and he looks… bothered. His brows furrow as his eyes drift down to my lips. "I can?"

I shrug casually. "This is just a sexuationship. We didn't really talk about exclusivity."

"The hell we didn't," Wyatt thunders, pressing his hand to the gate beside me, caging me in. "You haven't slept with anyone else, have you?"

"Oh, in all my free time?" I laugh, but it sounds weird and hyenic.

"If you had free time, you would have?" His tone is full of rage, and his body seems to grow a few inches taller as he bows over me, blanketing me in his scent.

Or maybe I'm just shrinking in his presence, begging the world to swallow me whole so I can get out of having this conversation.

"I don't know, Wyatt," I reply with a huff and duck under his arm to go tend to Handsome.

I feel him watching me as I move through Handsome's stall, trying desperately to figure out what to say next to a man clearly looking for something from me.

"Did I do something to hurt you?" Wyatt asks, his tone soft and uncertain.

There's something horrifyingly painful about weakening a strong man. Especially one who has only ever been good to me.

My eyes soften on him. "No, Wyatt. You're perfect. You're the perfect man." *Just not perfect for me.*

"Then tell me not to go," Wyatt croaks, his Adam's apple bobbing in his thick neck. "Tell me to tell Calder to fuck off. Tell me that it would make you fucking crazy to think about me seeing another woman's body because it makes me want to violently hurt someone when I think about you just having coffee with Avery."

"That's insane!"

"That's me," he thunders unapologetically. "Am I going to hurt him?

No. Am I going to stop you from going? No. But are the feelings I have for you real? Fuck yes, they are."

"Wyatt, we need to calm things down here," I state firmly, my throat feeling tight as I step out of Handsome's pen.

"Calm things down?"

"Yes. This is all moving too fast."

"What do you mean fast? I think it's moving fucking slow."

I laugh as I recall him in my bed the other morning, telling me I could stay in the barn another year or two if I wanted.

Stay in the barn.

Like an animal.

Like a concubine.

Like a whore.

Fast…slow. It doesn't matter. This whole thing is moving in a direction I do not like, and I need to get control of the wheel.

He stops me in the alleyway of the barn, his hand braced on Millie's pen as his eyes bore into my soul. "Are you really trying to act like you don't have feelings for me, Trista?"

"What difference does it make?" I ask with a shrug. "What you and I have has an end date anyway. And if I'm being honest, Wyatt, I don't think you even really like me. You just have a pregnancy fetish or a breeding fetish or a big-girl fetish. You want a thing about me…you don't want me. This baby inside me is just confusing your mountain-man brain."

His eyes blink rapidly as he steps back, lips parted, face full of betrayal. "How could you think that?"

"Because you don't even know me," I snap, my temper boiling over at the whipped-puppy-dog look he's giving me right now. "You think you have real feelings for me because of what I shared with you and your brothers? That was only a glimpse of it. You offered for me to live in this barn for another year, having no idea that this place…a fucking apartment above a barn where animals shit…is ten times nicer than anything I've ever stepped foot in."

"I don't care about that—"

"Do you know that I used to stand on a street corner with my

mother, holding a sign that said, 'Need money for diapers.' I was mortified because I was eight and clearly not wearing diapers anymore,
but my mom forced me to stand there with her to get sympathy cash."

"Trista, I—" He reaches for me, and I hold my hands out, cutting him off.

"I didn't want to tell you how pathetic my life was...is...because
this is just sex. I didn't want to tell you that I never left my parents'
shitty apartment for fourteen fucking years because a sick part of me
hoped they would come back! But now you're forcing me to lay it all
out here. You're forcing me to remind you that I am giving up a baby
from my body for money at the end of all of this because of how much
I struggle. I'm more like my shitty parents than I ever realized. And
you're weaponizing my greatest weaknesses against me by offering me
this apartment."

"That's not what I was trying to do."

"What were you trying to do, then?" I snap, my hands trembling
at my sides as my chest aches with the pain of that offer. "You didn't
tell me you had feelings for me then. You just offered me the one thing
you know I value more than anything because of my animals."

"Then I take it back!" he thunders, his neck veins bulging angrily.
Desperately. "I take it all back. Let's just go back to how we were because nothing you've just shared with me changes how I feel about
you." His voice cracks as he steps into me, the warmth of him like a
drug I would do anything to take a hit of again. "I'd want you even
without this baby."

"Well, I don't want you because of this baby." The words spill out
of my mouth, and I fight the urge to hold my stomach. To apologize
to the baby inside me. To the thing that forces me every single day to
remind myself that I am a mere cow. An animal. An incubator of sto-
len goods. This baby isn't mine. It's his. It's always been his, and the
reason I probably haven't felt it kick yet isn't because of the location
of my stupid placenta. It's because I don't deserve that experience the
same way my parents never deserved to have children of their own. I
am not worthy of this baby.

"You're fucking lying," Wyatt grinds, his voice aching in a way that sounds almost inhuman. Like the cry a dog makes when it gets hit by a car. "Why can't you just admit that you want more?"

Because I can't have more.

Because I'm a cow.

I'm a cow.

I'm a cow.

"Wyatt." I close my eyes and feel the burn of hot tears threaten to slide down my face. I take a slow, deep breath before speaking because I know if I open my mouth too soon, I will cry. And I hate myself for that too. When I've regained control, I say the words that will hopefully end this conversation for good. "This is just a job for me."

CHAPTER 40

WEEKS PREGNANT: 22
ANIMALS ON THE MOUNTAIN: 10

Trista

"**W**hat the hell is that?" Luke asks, appearing from the other side of the livestock trailer just as Avery pulls away.

I wave Avery off before offering a weak smile to Luke. "That is a miniature Highland cow."

"Like from Scotland?" Luke asks as he stands beside me and rests his arms on the pasture fence. It's always jarring to me how similar the mannerisms are between the brothers. They all look so different, but they have the same sort of swagger.

"Historically from Scotland, yes," I reply, squinting out at the auburn-colored heifer, who's licking her pink nose while Millie sniffs her butt and Reginald roots at something in the ground, completely uninterested. Handsome has already dragged his flaccid tongue all along the new cow's side, making for a very up-close-and-personal introduction. The sight of the four of them out there lightens my sullen mood. Animals are so much easier than people. I know what to expect from them, even with their weird, floppy tongues and affection for butt sniffing. "This particular calf came from Breckenridge. Many of these people who buy acreages and want to start hobby farms don't always understand the work that goes into caring for them. She was surrendered to a rescue center, and Avery thought she could live up here for a while. Her name is Butterscotch."

Luke's brows lift. "Does Wyatt know yet?"

Just the mention of his name causes my chest to squeeze, so I do my best to steel my expression as I shake my head.

Luke laughs. "Well, maybe this calf will improve his shitty mood. I think he actually likes these critters you got filling up his barn."

My brows furrow at that. "Has Wyatt been grumpier than usual recently?" I chance a glance over at Luke, trying not to look overly interested.

"Oh yes." Luke blows out a breath and turns to face me. "I don't know what his deal is, but he's been a bear at work all damn week. Barking orders, demanding we stay late to get caught up. He hasn't acted like this in years...not since..." He stops talking and shakes his head.

"Not since what?" I urge, hating myself for still caring.

Luke's lips form a thin line as his expression hardens. "She's ancient history."

"Are you talking about Robyn?" My hands grip the fence nervously in front of me.

Luke turns to gape at me. "You know about Robyn?"

I shrug. "It came up once."

"Robyn came up?" Luke asks, clearly not convinced. "Wyatt actually told you about her? About...all of us?"

"Sorry, I shouldn't have said anything."

"No, it's fine," Luke says, reaching out to touch my arm. "I'm just shocked. He doesn't talk about her...ever. None of us do, really, but Wyatt especially never talks about her. But I suppose with the baby coming, it brings up old wounds, maybe."

"Old wounds?" I ask, trying to be subtle.

Luke lifts his shoulders. "I mean...just the fact that Wyatt thought he was going to have a baby with Robyn, and it blew up in his face."

My lips part as Luke reveals a hell of a lot more to the story than Wyatt ever did. She was pregnant? My mind races with this new information. Apparently, we've both been editing our backstories. I school my response to be casual so I don't give myself away. "That had to be hard on him."

"No shit, especially because she told him it was his and gave no inkling that anyone else was even in the picture. It wasn't until I told him that the baby could be mine, too, that we realized how much she was playing all of us...even Calder."

My mind whirs as I picture a young twentysomething Wyatt finding out from his brother that the baby might be his. It's heartbreaking.

"Whatever happened with the baby?" I ask as an odd ringing in my ears begins. "Wyatt never said."

"Lives with its dad, I suspect." Luke shrugs casually. "Thank God we asked for a paternity test. That's when we found out that she was still married. Had a whole-ass family back in Colorado Springs that she abandoned. She must have found out she was pregnant a month or so after arriving in Jamestown but never said a word. I don't like to hate many people, but I will hate that woman until the day I die. Wyatt was especially devastated by it all. He always wanted to be a dad, even back then. He would have married Robyn and tried to make a go of it, which is why I think she chose him instead of me or Calder. He was a safe bet to her."

A peculiar feeling of jealousy slices through me. It was one thing to find out that Wyatt was in love with her and she broke his heart. It's another to find out they almost had a baby together and he might have married her. It makes whatever the hell we have feel less significant somehow.

Robyn isn't just the one who got away...

She's the family he probably always wanted.

A sick sensation roils through me as my mouth goes dry, and I picture Wyatt as a father with another woman. What if he meets someone after this baby? What if she becomes the mother to this baby inside me? My heart starts racing, my body having a physical reaction to the idea of this baby having another mother. Probably a mother who knows how to stick around and actually take care of it. A woman who isn't screwed up in the head like me.

Luke starts calling out to Butterscotch as the ringing in my ears shifts to a buzzing sound. I try to focus on the calf as she makes her way over to us, but it's difficult because little stars start poking in on my vision. I blink my eyes to focus on the Highland cow when a sudden warmth rushes up my neck and into my face.

"Trista, are you okay? You don't look so good," Luke says, and I can see his face, but I have to squint to focus on him as black creeps in around the edges like a lens closing. I nod and try to say something, but no words come out, and the last thing I see is Luke lunging for me.

The sound of a galloping horse fills the room as I close my eyes, fighting back tears as my heart tries to explode out of my chest.

"Calm down, Mom. Your heart rate is going a mile a minute," the ER nurse says, touching my shoulder in a comforting way. "Everything is sounding good in there."

The word *Mom* stings coming from her lips, but I don't fault the woman for it. She has no idea who I am or that the baby I'm carrying will never call me Mama. The OB-GYN clinic has that information readily available, but this triage nurse doesn't have a clue.

Luke clears his throat from beside me. "Is that the baby's heart rate or hers?"

The nurse moves the Doppler microphone around my small, swollen belly and smiles. "That's all baby right there, but Mama here is apparently trying to race with it. Do you guys know the gender yet?"

Luke looks bashful and rubs the back of his neck. "I'm not the father."

"Oh, I'm sorry. I just assumed."

I chew my lip nervously as I stare at the monitor wrapped around my belly to check for contractions. "Will we get an ultrasound to see the baby too? Make sure I didn't hurt anything in there? I'd really love an ultrasound."

"The doctor will decide that, but based on your blood pressure, I'm guessing this was just a run-of-the-mill fainting spell. When was the last time you ate?"

I wince at that question because it's nearing four o'clock, and I still haven't eaten today. I just…wasn't hungry. My mood has been in the dumps for the past week, and every time I have depressive episodes, food is the last thing I want to touch. I've never fainted from it before, though. I've also never had a baby inside me depending on me for nourishment. How could I be so irresponsible?

"No need to stress," the nurse says, rubbing my arm affectionately. "The doctor will be in soon to examine you, and we'll get all our questions answered."

Thirty minutes later, the ER doctor gives me a laundry list of reasons I could have fainted, ranging from low blood sugar to low blood pressure, hormone changes, and possible anemia. He orders some blood work to double-check things but doesn't feel the need to order an ultrasound. Relief washes over me as he says his goodbyes, and when he opens the door to walk out, a familiar voice roars down the hallway.

"Where the fuck is she?" Wyatt thunders, and goose bumps erupt all over my skin.

My wide eyes shoot to Luke. "Did you call Wyatt?"

"Fuck yes, I did. You were unconscious for most of the drive into Boulder. I was losing my shit." Luke runs a trembling hand through his shaggy hair, and it's only then I realize how terrified he looks. I was so focused on the baby that I didn't even notice how he handled all of this.

"Luke, I'm so sorry—"

The door to my exam room swings open, cutting me off, and I look over to find Wyatt's terrified expression as he sees me lying in bed in a hospital gown, hooked up to an IV and a monitor around my belly that watches for contractions that I thankfully have had none of. But the haunted look in Wyatt's eyes…definitely causes a squeeze inside me somewhere.

"Trista." His voice cracks as he rushes over, grabbing my hands and fighting for breath as he hovers over me. "Are you okay?"

"The baby is fine," I reply quickly, trying to calm him down with the most important fact. I have two giant mountain men losing their shit in my room, and if I don't get control of this situation, they'll need their heart rates checked too.

"Are *you* okay?" Wyatt asks, repeating his earlier question but in a soft, strangled whisper. A whisper that cuts me right to the core, like it always does when he murmurs to my soul like that.

When his eyes lock on mine, my vision blurs with tears, and I begin shaking uncontrollably, the past week of emotions all coming to a head.

"Oh, baby," he croaks and, without hesitating, crawls into the bed beside me, taking me in his arms as I cry into his chest, aching over the fact that I haven't smelled him in a week. Now that he's here, I don't know how I'll find the strength to let him go again.

Luke's voice clears from beside us, and I faintly hear him say, "I'll be in the waiting room."

I feel Wyatt's head nodding above me. "Mom's waiting out there too."

And that little remark only makes me cry more. Luke didn't say he was going home. He said he was going to the waiting room, even before knowing his mother was out there. They'll both wait in the waiting room for who knows how long. This family gives and gives so easily, and I'm just the big, dumb idiot who doesn't know how to take it.

Wyatt holds me for I don't know how long. It feels like seconds and hours all at the same time, but I know his shirt is soaked with my tears by the time the phlebotomist comes in to take some blood.

"I'm an asshole," I say, touching the Band-Aid on the crook of my arm as the tech wheels her cart out of the room.

"You're not an asshole." Wyatt dips his head down to kiss my arm where the needle was. He does it so casually, so effortlessly. Like affection is natural for him.

"I didn't eat, and that's why I fainted. The doctor pretty much confirmed it." I sniff and pull back from him, wiping my nose with the back of my hand. He uses his flannel sleeve that smells like sawdust and wipes my nose for me. It's weird and even more intimate than kissing my arm, which only hurts my heart more. "I'm so sorry."

"What do you have to be sorry for?"

"For being a bitch about your breakfasts. I've been leaving them on the step every day."

His jaw muscle slides under his beard. "I noticed."

I shake my head. "I just can't get too close to you, Wyatt."

"Why not?"

"Because this isn't my baby," I reply honestly, my throat burning with that admission. "Because I need to be more responsible. Because I'm getting paid to take care of myself, and I let the stuff with you and me get in the way of all of that. I have a plan, Wyatt, and none of this is a part of my plan."

Wyatt's brows twitch knowingly. "I love plans just as much as the next person, but plans can change, Lucky."

"Not mine," I reply firmly, my nose wrinkling as I try to harden my emotions by sheer force of will. "I don't connect with people the way others do. I'm fundamentally flawed. I always push people away. I've done it my whole life because I know it's for the best. Everyone in the world has another language they use that I've never understood. Animals, though…they always hear me. They give me what I need. That's why my plan is so important."

"That's funny because I feel like you hear me better than anyone I've ever spoken to," Wyatt says, his voice soft.

I shake my head adamantly. "But there's still so much you don't say to me."

"Like what?"

"Like why didn't you tell me Robyn was pregnant?" I glance up and see the confusion in his eyes as his body stills.

"Who told you about the baby?"

"Does it matter?"

His lips thin. "I don't like to remember that part of my life."

"But don't you see? She's your 'one who got away,' even if what she did was messed up. You wanted a family with her. How on earth would I ever feel secure enough to have feelings for you when I know I'm just second choice? Hell, technically, I'm not even the second choice. I'm the thirteenth choice. There is nothing lucky about that."

"Trista—"

"We have to end this…for both our sakes and, most of all, the baby's. I am not built to be part of a family. We don't speak the same language. We need to go back to this just being a business deal. I'll go to this baby shower and play the part of the hired surrogate because that's the job, but after that, we have to create some distance."

Wyatt's chest heaves as he shakes his head sadly and stares at his hands. "You're playing defense for something that isn't even a game." He swallows and turns to look at me. "This is real life."

I look up at him and imprint the feel of his warm arms around me and his soft blue eyes upon me because I know I'll never have him this close again. I can't. I'm not strong enough to push him away again.

My voice is soft and resigned when I reply, "Life is a game."

CHAPTER 41

WEEKS PREGNANT: 23
ANIMALS ON THE MOUNTAIN: 10

Wyatt

Silence.

I used to like it.

I used to crave it.

I needed it to survive.

I needed it to sort through the voices of worry in my head about the what-ifs. What if I can't survive on the mountain on my own? What if sustainable living doesn't fucking matter because the world is fucked anyway? What if I fight with Calder and Luke again? What if I can't keep my dad's business afloat? What if my mom dies suddenly too? What if Everly moves overseas for good? What if living on my own for the rest of my life isn't the best idea?

What if…what if…what if…

That's why a plan is a beautiful thing. My dad always said if a man has a plan, he can be content in his life. And he was right because being content quiets my mind. And damn, do I love the sound of nothing. I'd do just about anything for it…

Like hire a woman I felt an immediate connection with to have a baby for me because no matter what I've done with my life, I've never been able to quiet the voice of wanting to be a father. Try as I might.

"No one told me we were drinking," Calder booms from behind

me, and I swerve around to spot him and Luke walking toward where I'm seated on our father's memorial bench.

I grumble my wordless reply, keeping my gaze fixed on the mountain sunset before me. September is approaching, and the leaves are threatening to change. Autumn is normally my favorite season up here, but right now... I'm not looking forward to it.

I hold up my six-pack with four beers left, and they each take one.

"A drink for Dad," Calder says, leaning on a large oak tree as he pours some beer onto the ground.

Luke sits down beside me and takes a drink of his beer. The pensive look on his face as he stares down the mountain can't be ignored.

I elbow him gently. "You okay after yesterday?"

His head jerks back defensively. "Yeah, why?"

I say nothing, just silently stare back at him because he knows why I'm asking. He was the one who found Dad collapsed on a jobsite. He was the one who issued CPR while dialing 911. He was the one who decided it would be faster to carry our six-foot-three, two-hundred-and-fifty-pound father to his truck and drive him to the hospital rather than wait for an ambulance.

Luke made a lot of decisions that day that I know haunt him. And him being the one with Trista yesterday when she collapsed couldn't have been easy. I'm not sure he's stepped foot in a hospital since then.

"He's fine," Calder jeers, taking a long drink of his beer and staring out at the mountains.

My lips thin. Calder tends to avoid hard topics. We all do, but him more than anyone. He'd barely even acknowledged our dad's death, and then suddenly, this memorial bench appeared out of nowhere, showing signs that he does, in fact, have a heart. We didn't even know he was working on it. He made one for our mother, too, that sits in their backyard, overlooking the garden our dad fussed over for years and has now turned to weeds. I should really help her with that.

"Are you okay after yesterday?" Luke asks, propping his arm on the back of the bench and rubbing his finger over the engraved saying.

I shrug. "Baby is okay, so I guess I'm okay."

"What about you and Trista?"

"What do you mean?" I ask, feeling both my brothers' eyes boring into me expectantly.

"We know you two are hooking up," Calder says with a laugh. "You gave yourself away on poker night, bro, staring murderously at any of us who dared lay eyes on her. God, you're about as subtle as that stupid horse's tongue."

"I don't know what you're talking about," I offer noncommittally, refusing to break my promise to Trista. She didn't want me to tell anyone, and I won't, even if things between us are over.

Luke clears his throat, and I wince as I recall crawling into the bed with Trista at the hospital yesterday while he was still in the room. It was probably pretty obvious at that point, but when I saw her in that bed, looking pale and depleted, I thought my heart was going to rip out of my chest. Even when I got the call from Luke that she was passed out in his truck, I thought I was going to have a heart attack of my own as I drove a hundred miles per hour from the jobsite.

And when her eyes filled with tears, I couldn't help but hold her. I'd never wanted to comfort someone more in my entire life. Even when my mom was sobbing on her kitchen floor six months after Dad had passed, I didn't feel the same sense of desperation. I would have blown up the whole world to make Trista's pain go away yesterday.

And the hits just kept on coming when she told me she wanted space.

Definitely a cause for day drinking.

I feel their eyes on me and reply defensively, "You guys are the ones who told me to hook up with her."

"Didn't tell you to fall in love with her," Calder huffs.

My brows furrow. "I haven't fallen in love with her."

"You sure about that?" Luke quirks a brow.

I exhale and run my hand through my hair, irritation prickling in my veins because this isn't what I need to worry about right now. "It doesn't matter because it's over."

"She's only halfway through her pregnancy?" Calder says it like a question.

"And?"

"And...how could it be over?"

"Because it is," I snap back.

Calder smiles. "Great, then you can come with us to the sex club."

"I'm not fucking going there with you," I bite, my hand tight on my beer bottle, as the idea of touching another woman makes me violently ill.

"Because you're in love with her," Calder volleys. "Just admit it."

I growl in frustration, fighting the urge to punch my brother in his smug face.

He laughs like he can read my mind. "For someone who's always thinking five steps ahead, I don't know how you didn't see this coming, Wyatt."

I shake my head as the severity of this situation weighs heavily on me. Before Trista, I thought I had my life all figured out. I had my land, my family, my home, my goat. I wanted for nothing in life. Except maybe to be a father. Now...I don't know what I want anymore.

"Our pact was made for a reason," I reply, my voice quiet. "To protect this." I gesture to the mountain. "To protect us." I gesture to the three of us. "This is for the best. I don't want to go through the same hell I went through with Robyn."

"Robyn isn't even close to the woman Trista is," Luke argues.

"You think I don't know that?" My voice cracks in my throat. "You think I didn't realize that the moment I met her? God, she's fucking incredible. But even if I do love her, even if I admit that she has lit up my whole fucking life these past few months in ways that have nothing to do with my baby inside her...she doesn't want any part of this. She doesn't want a family. She doesn't want a kid. She doesn't want me."

Luke makes a noise in his throat. "I don't think she knows how to admit what she wants. She's too busy expecting the worst because that's what the world has given her."

I frown at my baby brother, and he shrugs knowingly at me.

"She didn't grow up like us. She didn't have a family who prioritized her. Hell, our pact requires us all to be fucking loners for life because we care so much about each other."

"Then what are we even talking about?" I cry, pain searing through me at the finality of this discussion.

"I'm saying she deserves to feel that level of devotion as much as you do," Luke urges, his eyes softening. "She deserves to be a part of a family who actually cares. She deserves to be a part of our family if that's what you want. Fuck our pact. We didn't agree to it so it would never be broken. We agreed to it so *we* wouldn't be broken. And losing Trista when this is all over will break you even worse than before, Wyatt. Fuck your contract, and fuck our pact."

My lips turn down as I fight back the emotion swelling in my chest over the thought of her leaving this mountain when this is all over. It will kill me. If there is one very glaring fact that having Trista here—sleeping with her, *caring for her*—has shown me, it's that Robyn isn't the one who got away. My feelings for her were nothing. All I was experiencing back then was lust and competition. It was for sport.

But my brothers are right. Trista leaving will fundamentally change me. Will I even be a good dad anymore if I lose her? Can I live my life without her?

I stare at my two brothers, watching me with so much care and concern in their eyes it guts me. "I thought this surrogacy thing was so smart because I could avoid the heartache I watched Mom go through after losing Dad. I could avoid the shared-custody thing that Max has to endure. I wouldn't have to deal with a Robyn situation ever. I genuinely thought my dream was to become a single dad, and a contract could keep me safe from all of that. But now, I have different dreams. I want Trista to want all of this with me. I want her to want the baby, you guys, this mountain. Me. I want it all, even at the risk of life-changing pain."

"Then what are you going to do about it?" Calder asks, his eyes piercing. "What would Dad tell you?"

I lift my brows and shrug. "He'd tell me to come up with a plan to win her over."

Calder nods. "Then that's what we'll do."

CHAPTER 42

WEEKS PREGNANT: 23
ANIMALS ON THE MOUNTAIN: 10

Trista

"**D**on't look at me like that, Sir Reginald," I say, squatting down in the fresh straw I just laid out in his mucked-out pen. "You're still my favorite animal on the mountain."

Reggie snorts his reply and moves over to rub his coarse fur along my jean-clad legs. The pressure from him causes me to sit back on my butt as I laugh and submit to his affection. He rests his head on my thigh, and I rub behind his ears, causing him to moan with pleasure.

"I know there are lots of new animals around here, but don't worry. You'll always be my number one."

My phone vibrates in my pocket, and Reggie's head pops up, his face showing me he's clearly irritated by the disruption of his snuggle time. I pull it out to see my sister's name on the screen. If I was smart, I wouldn't answer it. I'm already in a sour enough mood—I don't really need to have her add fuel to the fire. But a strange part of me longs to hear an old voice from my previous life. Something familiar, dysfunctional as it might be.

"Hey, Vada," I answer, stretching my legs out so Reggie can rest his head on me again.

"Are you knocked up yet?" she blurts into the line with a laugh. "Or has the mountain man cast you aside for someone else already?"

I sigh heavily. "Do you really want to know?"

"Of course. That's why I called!"

I lick my lips and gird my loins as I hit her with the news. "I'm currently twenty-three weeks pregnant."

"Holy shit!" she exclaims so loudly I have to pull the phone away. "Why didn't you call me?"

I shrug to myself. "I've been busy."

"I'd say!" she says, still sounding shocked. "So, to be clear. This is for the mountain-man guy, not an accident? Like you're getting paid for this?"

"Yep," I reply, ignoring the sick feeling that rolls through my belly every time I think about that lately.

"Holy cow, this is wild. You really did it. How do you feel?"

I pinch the bridge of my nose and continue with the honesty. "I'm emotionally fucked, but physically, I feel pretty good. Other than I still haven't felt the baby move, which is apparently weird, but everything checks out okay."

"Why are you feeling emotional? Do you not want to give up the baby or something? Can you even do that?"

A knot forms in my throat as I consider those questions. "I mean... there are clauses in my contract that protect me and what I want, so ultimately, I do have some choices. But the baby is his. It belongs to him. And it will be way better off with him than with me anyway, so it doesn't really matter."

"Why do you say that?"

I bark out a laugh. "Because I'm completely fucked up."

"In what ways?"

"In all the ways, Vada!" I exclaim, irritated that she's acting like this is news. The older I've gotten, the more I've learned that having parents leave their children home alone for weeks on end isn't typical. Not even close. "I don't know what it's like to be a part of a normal family, let alone start one of my own. I don't even know how to be in a relationship. How you got married to someone is beyond me. You must be way less fucked up than I am."

"Oh, trust me, I'm fucked up. Mom and Dad did a number on

me, leaving me to take care of you when I was just a kid. And clearly, I sucked at it because I left you just like they left me."

My jaw drops as she says those words out loud. Words we've never spoken to each other. Honestly, my whole life, Vada made it seem normal for her to move away and start a new life. She acted like the fact that I was only sixteen was irrelevant. And I sort of believed that myself. When you have parents who are absent a lot, you grow up real quick, so figuring out my last couple of years of high school without Vada or my parents was just something I had to do.

"But girl, I had to go. I was no good to you the way I was. We fought all the time, and I was so nasty to you. I left because I was chasing something that could heal my anger. And Kai was it for me. He showed me more love in the first month I knew him than Mom and Dad did our whole lives. They were irresponsible and selfish and crazy and kept thinking they'd find the meaning of life in religion. And maybe they did. I haven't heard from them in years, so maybe that means they're happy. I don't really give a fuck, though, because I'm happy. I found the meaning of life with Kai. And maybe with food too." She laughs casually. "You should see my pantry. It is full of all the snacks we used to drool over at the grocery store and could never afford."

My chin wobbles as my sister reveals more of herself to me in one phone call than she has in the ten years she's been gone. I glance down at Reginald snoring on my lap and look out at all the other animals, tucked safely in their pens. A horse, a heifer, a goat, a bunny, chickens, a pig. I want all of them forever and so many more.

"I cope with animals," I state softly, my eyes welling with tears.

"But are animals really enough?" she asks seriously. "Seems kind of lonely to me."

"Animals can't disappoint me the way humans can," I reply honestly.

"Well, preferring loneliness over rejection or disappointment won't work forever. You're hurting yourself under the guise of protection, but it makes no sense because all you're doing is literally hurting yourself. It's a pointless cycle. And you're missing out on life, girl. Being human. Having human experiences and splashes of pain. I never went to therapy for this. Probably should have. I could word all this shit better, but Jesus, Trista, we didn't go through our shitty lives just to turn into scared little pussies. If you want more, you have to take it because no one will give it to you."

Tears spill down my cheeks as I think of the exception to that comment. Wyatt has given me so much—a home, a bed, daily break-fasts...himself. He's constantly giving, and I've been begrudgingly tak-ing because of how utterly broken I am inside. And now he wants to give more of himself to me, and I just keep pushing him away to save myself from future pain. But being away from him, all I feel is pain. *How did that happen? These feelings?* And why did I lie to him and say this was only a job?

I hold my stomach, allowing myself to consider the possibility of more at the end of all this, and my thoughts are thwarted when a strange sensation rumbles through my belly. I inhale sharply and drop my phone as a tumbling sort of ripple that's foreign and unnatural vi-brates inside me. When I move my hands lower to follow the stirring, I realize what's happening.

I move Reginald off my lap, ignoring my sister calling out to ask if I'm still there. Heart racing, I pull my shirt up to look down at my flesh, swollen more obviously now, and I nearly squeal when I see the vibrations reflecting on the surface of my skin.

"Holy shit...is that you, Goat Turd?" I gasp, awestruck as the mo-tion stops briefly. When it picks back up, I can't help but place my hands over it, savoring every second of it like my life has been in black and white until this very moment when I've been hit with a burst of color.

The flip-flopping is insane as this baby has what feels like a party inside me. It's as if someone is rolling a textured ball over my belly but from the inside. The magical sensation causes a warmth to spread through me.

"You definitely feel bigger than a goat turd now," I croak, the tears falling freely over my smiling lips. This feels like the most perfect gift. Like a private, wonderful experience that only I get to have. I could want for nothing for my entire life just for having experienced this miraculous thing.

I sniff loudly and say without thinking, "I can't wait for your dad to feel this." And that one sentence spoken out loud hits me like a ton of goat turds.

CHAPTER 43

WEEKS PREGNANT: 24
ANIMALS ON THE MOUNTAIN: 10

Wyatt

"Calder wanted to parachute out of a plane and release a smoke bomb over the mountain to reveal the gender," Everly says, squinting under the hot August sun as she sets a gender-neutral sheet cake on the picnic table.

"Yes!" Ethan cheers, swiping his finger into the frosting. "I want to go on the plane with Uncle Caldy!"

"My man." Calder thrusts a finger at our nephew and then closes his hand for a fist bump that Ethan obliges.

"I said a low-impact reveal with a zero percent chance of damage to a person or property." I pinch the bridge of my nose, already hating all the fuss happening outside of my home.

"Relax, Papa Bear," Calder says, patting me on the back. "The reveal will be very chill, very calm, very boring...very...you."

I exhale a small breath of relief but then glance around because this shower setup doesn't look chill. Red checkered picnic tables are scattered in front of my cabin, with rustic wood slab centerpieces that I had to chop for Everly. She set Mason jars with baby's breath on top of them and hung jars and floating lanterns from the nearby trees. A caterer delivering enough barbecue to feed all of Jamestown just left, and now I see a frickin' acoustic guitar player setting up on my upper-level deck.

"Everly, is that a children's inflatable playhouse?"

"Yes, but it's totally chill!"

"You stuck to my guest list, right? Just our immediate family coming? Is that giant thing all for Ethan?"

She winces slightly. "Well…I invited a few more people."

"What's a few?" I seethe.

She counts off on her fingers. "Judy from the Mercantile is coming and a few of the townies, plus some of Max's friends—that way, there are other kids here for Ethan to play with. And my friend Claire is coming with Josh and Lynsey, so their three girls are coming too."

"Fuck me," I grind out, hoping like hell the townies she invited don't include the assholes we brawled with a couple of weeks ago. I already apologized to Judy about the fight, and she assured me the whole town was not wondering who the father was. But she did ask for permission to tell everyone about the surrogacy situation to try to tamp down the rumors. It's small-town bullshit, but I said yes because I don't want to give Trista any more reasons not to want to stay here on the mountain.

My plan is simple…I'm playing the long game with her. We're only halfway through this pregnancy, so I'm going to use these next few months to show her that what we had was more than a sexuationship. I'm going to show her what being part of a family looks like. I'll continue to show up for her with my daily breakfast drops. I'm even going to embrace the new fucking cow that suddenly showed up in my barn when we got back from the hospital last week. Honestly, if she wants to bring more animals up on the mountain, I'm game. I'll take a flock of chickens if she needs that to feel safe with me. With us. I'm going to be her friend because I don't give a shit what was in her past. I give a shit about what is in her future.

And in the end, if she still decides motherhood and family life are not what she wants, I'll accept that. It will crush me. But I'll have a baby I need to be strong for, and my family will be there for all the support I'll need.

But damn, do I miss the hell out of her already. I miss watching her sleep and waking up in a stressed-out rush because she's late for work. I miss counting the beauty marks on her face. I miss her excited eyes when she sees what breakfast I brought for her. I even miss her narrating what Reginald's responses would be to all the questions she asks him while doing chores.

And I especially miss the way she touches her belly when she thinks I'm not looking.

I probably miss that the most.

"Do you think Trista will let the little ones ride Handsome?" Everly asks, jerking me out of my thoughts. "I texted her, but she hasn't replied yet."

"No pony rides, Ev," I growl and turn on my heel to storm into the house to get ready. I need to hurry up so I have time to go down to the barn and warn Trista of today's spectacle. It sounds like half of Boulder and most of Jamestown are on their way up to Fletcher Mountain, and I know that's not what she expected. Maybe I can help her escape up onto the mountain on Handsome's back. She can ride off into the sunset with his tongue flopping the whole way. It'd be a hell of a lot more fun than what this shit show is turning out to be.

When I emerge twenty minutes later, my jaw drops at the number of people spread out over my lawn and more cars driving up the lane. Kids are running wild, and Max's friends don't seem to be watching any of them. Cozy's friend Dakota shoots daggers at Calder. Luke flirts with the guitarist up on the deck, and Max, Cozy, and my mom fuss over a pile of presents that have already started collecting on a gift table.

This is my fucking nightmare.

I spot Trista standing by the cake table, dressed in a yellow summer dress and looking like a dream as she holds a cup of what looks like some kind of punch. Everly chats her ear off about God knows what, and she looks wildly uncomfortable.

This is not a good start.

I make my way over, and Trista's head turns as she senses my approach. Her eyes drink me in, giving me a look I haven't seen from her in a while. A look that says, *I've seen you naked and want to see you naked again.*

Maybe my long game will be a short game after all.

"I'm sorry about the crowd," I rush out and reach out to take Trista's hand but stop myself, determined to give her the space she requested. "Are you okay with all of this?"

She shrugs casually, her coppery-green eyes glittering in the setting sun. "Why wouldn't I be?"

"This is a lot more people than I gave permission for. I should have warned you. Are you up for this? Are you feeling okay?"

"I had a nice big breakfast, so I'm feeling great," she says and shoots me a tiny wink that I feel right in my gut.

I move to stand closer to her, but my pain-in-the-ass niece steps between us. "Trista, can I show you to your special chair?" Everly asks eagerly, causing me to frown at the back of her head.

"Special chair?" Trista shoots me a dubious look, and I shrug, feeling just as clueless as she is when Everly drags her away from me. I can't help but follow because I have no idea what the fuck is happening.

I spot Calder standing next to the large oak tree in front of my home. Mason jars hang from the low-slung branches, and he leans on something covered beneath one of my mother's quilts. As we approach, he pulls it off to reveal a stunning cedar chair.

"It's a thank-you for the cat." He grips the back of his neck and points back at his cabin. "I really appreciate all your help with her."

"This is for me?" Trista asks, pointing at the chair. "Like...to keep?"

"Of course it's for you." Everly laughs.

"Here, try it out," Calder says, guiding Trista by the crook of her arm into the seat like she's forty weeks pregnant and breakable. My chest contracts at the sight of it because I know how much work he puts into his custom furniture, so for him to gift her something like this means he put in some serious time on it this past week.

"I tried to make the chair nice and tall because I read that pregnant chicks don't like to sit too low to the ground."

"I'm not really a fan of it when I'm not pregnant either," Trista murmurs and sits down, her face nodding with approval. "Shouldn't this be for your brother, though? It's his shower. He should have the special chair."

"We'll get to him," my mom says from behind me, and I swerve around to see her, Max, Luke, and Cozy all standing there with gifts in their arms. "But we wanted to do a little something just for you, too, before the party started."

Panic descends over me as they set the presents down one by one next to a shocked-looking Trista. This was not a part of my plan. This is the exact opposite of my plan.

"You guys, if this is baby stuff, I really don't want to open it." Trista's chin trembles, and I open my mouth to agree with her but am cut off by my sister-in-law.

"Just open the gifts, Trista," Cozy urges with a laugh and grabs a gift bag off the ground. "Start with mine."

Trista nervously pulls out a bunch of tissue paper to reveal a plethora of facial care stuff, including cleansers, creams, some fancy jade roller thing for her face, and some masks.

"Oh my God, this is amazing." Trista smiles brightly up at Cozy. "And a T-shirt?" Trista holds up a tee that says, "Animals Always Put Me in a Better Mood."

"My friend Dakota owns a custom tee shop. I saw that and had to get it for you. Maybe the three of us can do a girls' night sometime soon and use those face masks."

"Oh, that sounds like so much fun," Trista says sincerely.

Calder clears his throat loudly and coughs into his fist, "Beware of Dakota."

"Calder!" Cozy shoots a warning glare at my brother, who rolls his eyes and holds his hands up in defeat.

Trista looks puzzled, but the subject is dropped when Luke hands her a box. "This one is from me."

With a bit more confidence, Trista rips open the paper to reveal a weird made-for-TV foot-warming-pillow thing. He nods excitedly as he says, "You put the beads in the microwave and then stick your feet in them."

Trista's lips turn down. "Wow, I didn't know that was a thing."

"I have one…it's really nice, especially in the winter."

She giggles softly and thanks Luke before opening my mom's gift next. It's two gift certificates for a full spa day at a place in downtown Denver. My mom smiles warmly. "You can use one now and one after the baby is born if you like."

Trista blinks back her shock. "This is so generous."

"And I'm working on a new quilt for you too, but that'll be for delivery day," my mom says, wiping a tear out of her eye.

She turns to gently rub my back, and I feel myself leaning into her. My family is way too fucking much most days, but some days, they're just enough.

"Mine is sort of a future gift," Max says, handing Trista an envelope.

She frowns as she pulls out a check with several zeros on it.

"I heard you were looking at properties for your rescue center, and I figured you might need a down payment sooner rather than later." He shrugs and pushes his hands into his pockets. "I discussed it with Wyatt and my corporate accountant, and we all decided it would be fine to allocate a good chunk of our charitable budget your way. Just need the name of your 501(c)(3) once you have it, and we'll make that donation official."

"Are you kidding me?" Trista releases a garbled noise, then shakes her head back and forth. "I'm not even in business yet."

Max shrugs. "I know a good bet when I see one."

My face twists as emotion overcomes me, and I fight back the tears I feel burning my eyes.

"Mine last," Everly says with a big smile as she hands Trista a large canvas with a bow on it. She turns it around to reveal a professional photo of Reginald. "I had a secret photo shoot with Reggie one day when you were at work and blew up my favorite one into a large canvas print. I took pictures of all the animals. Maybe they can be artwork for your future shelter or just hung up in your home? Or used for firewood if you hate them." Everly laughs nervously and glances at me. "Wait until you see the photo of Millie, Uncle Wyatt. It's so good it makes my stomach hurt."

The lump in my throat feels permanent as I glance at all my family members, who went totally rogue on me today. But it's clear as day they didn't do this for me. They did this for Trista. And this is exactly what I want for her. A family who just...gets her.

Trista's watery eyes move from Everly to my mom and everyone else before settling on me for a long moment. Her chin trembles, and before I have a chance to say anything, she sets the portrait down and gets up out of her chair, pushing past me to run down the mountain toward the barn.

"Fuck," my brothers, Everly, and I all say in unison.

"Everly," my mom chastises. "I expect it out of them but not you."

"Sorry, Grandma." Everly shoots me an apologetic look. "And I'm sorry, Uncle Wyatt. This was all my idea. I thought she'd love it."

"It's not your fault, kid," I reply with a heavy sigh. "It's mine."

I head swiftly toward the barn, my heart thundering in my chest because this big gesture from my family could seriously screw things up for me. She needs time to wrap her brain around all this, not be force-fed love from my whole family.

I walk through the barn door and find Trista walking back and forth in front of Reginald's pen, both hands resting firmly on her hips. I swallow thickly and plead my case. "Trista, I'm so sorry. I didn't know they were going to do all that. I would have told them it was too much and you hate gifts."

"I fucking love gifts," she snaps, her voice manic and untethered as she continues pacing, barely sparing me a glance.

"You do?"

"Yes!" she exclaims and stomps her foot, turning her wide, red eyes on me. "I love every single one of those gifts. Especially the foot-warmer thing. Did you tell Luke my feet are always cold?"

"No. I never said a word."

"That's so weird he just knew that, right?"

"I guess."

"But damn, I love those gifts. And I love the things you do for me. The breakfasts, the car vacuuming, the random topping off of gas. It's so nice, and I'm so tired of pretending I don't like them," she says, her voice cracking at the end. "I'm tired of thinking I can do everything on my own. I can't pretend anymore, Wyatt."

"Then don't," I beg, wanting nothing more than for her to accept whatever is happening between us.

"Watching your family these past several months…it's intense. You guys just give unconditional love by default. You forgive each other so easily. You defend each other without question. It's unreal. You are so fucking lucky, Wyatt."

"I know," I state, a heaviness pressing down on my chest.

"No wonder you felt brave enough to be a single dad. You have a literal army out there who will drop whatever they're doing to support you and this baby."

"I know." I feel sad watching her work through this. I'm upset that no one in her life has helped her feel brave.

She gasps, and her hands squeeze tightly to her stomach. "Wyatt, come here."

"Shit, are you okay? Did something happen? Are you cramping?" I rush over, my heart in my chest at the fear rushing through me that something could be wrong with Trista or the baby. Our baby. Fuck, this shower was too much for her after she fainted last week. She's too fragile for all this. She's the most breakable, strong person I know.

She grabs my hand and spreads it out on her stomach, so I hold myself there, waiting for her to tell me what's going on.

"Just wait," she says with a sniff.

"Is the baby—" My voice is cut off when I feel a little bump against my palm. "Holy shit, is that—?"

Another bump, followed by a series of swoops.

"Holy fuck."

"I know, right?" Trista replies with a garbled laugh. "I've been feeling them for a few days now but didn't want to tell you until I could show you."

The baby moves again, and I drop to my knees in the barn and splay my other hand out on her belly too, not wanting to miss a single kick. Honestly, it will be hard to get me off her now that she's opened this door because this feeling is incredible.

That's our baby in there.

"This is amazing," I state, and without thinking, I press my lips to Trista's belly, kissing her as much as the baby. "Hey, little Pop-Tart. I'm your dad, and I'm so excited to meet you. And I'm so proud of the woman who helped me make you. You'll be a force of nature, kid."

Trista's belly shakes under my hands, and I look up to see that she's full-on crying. Fuck, the Fletcher family is the king of taking things too far, me included. I stand and cup her face in my hands, swiping her tears away with my thumbs. "Lucky, I'm sorry. I got carried away. There's no need to cry."

"Yes, there is."

"Why?"

"Because I want to amend our contract. I want contact with the baby. I want to see her. I want to see you being a dad to her. I don't know if I can fully give her up anymore."

"Her?"

Her eyes widen in horror. "Shit. It's a girl. I'm sorry. The tech asked me if I wanted to know privately. Fuck, I screwed up the reveal. Everly will be so mad at me."

"We're having a girl?"

"Wyatt, yes, but are you listening to me? I'm telling you I want to change the contract. I've been thinking about it this past week. Honestly, I've probably been thinking about it since I delivered a lamb with Avery a few weeks back. I watched this ewe lick the afterbirth off the baby, and it's totally disgusting, but I had this weird intrusive thought where I was like…would I lick this baby inside me clean if I had to? If that was societally normal, you know? And my answer was yes! I might even do those placenta pills I've read about, and I didn't know that I'd ever feel that way. I really didn't. I thought I was like my parents, but I'm not. You know how you only love Millie and you hate Reginald?"

"I don't hate Reginald."

"You kind of do." She shrugs dismissively. "But you love your own pet, and I think that's me with babies—which I guess means I'm not a sociopath after all—because I love this baby. Our baby. Can I even say that? Do I even have a right to? Probably not. I know the deal I signed, and this baby is yours. But we just need to call our lawyer to discuss terms—"

I pinch her lips together to stop her from talking. "I don't want to amend the contract, Trista."

"You don't?" she murmurs through my fingers, her eyes wide with fear. When I release her, she inhales a shaky breath and nods, her face hardening. "I understand I probably ruined my chance with you. But I want you to remember that you told me once that you're a 'five minutes from now' person, always stressing about the future. And remember, I'm a 'five minutes late' person because I've been constantly stuck in the past. But what if, together, we're right on time? What if we help each other be in the present every day? Doesn't that sound good, Wyatt?"

I can't fight my smile as I grab her cheeks and press my forehead to her. "I don't want to amend our contract, Trista. I want to tear it up."

"You do?" she sobs, blowing soft hair on my lips.

"I'm in love with you, lucky number thirteen. You're not my second choice or thirteenth choice. You're my only choice."

"Are you sure?" she asks, pulling away to look up into my eyes. "Did you hear what I just said about licking our baby after delivery?"

"Yes, but I'm kind of hoping I can talk you out of that."

"I'd be fine with that," she says, rubbing my arms weirdly. "'Cause I think I might be in love with you too."

I move in to kiss her, but a loud pop goes off in the distance, and we both look out through the barn door to see what happened. My eyes move up to a cloud of neon pink smoke floating in the air, and when I follow the trail it's coming from, I see Calder standing beneath it, covered in the colorful dust.

"My eyes!" he screams, holding the tube cannon outward as he reaches for something to wipe his face.

"What did you do?" Everly wails.

Luke and Max laugh from the side of the table as my mom rushes over to help Calder.

"Uncle Calder, you ruined the reveal," Everly screams again and looks around for Trista and me, but we're safely tucked away in the shadows of the barn. "Help me, Dad and Uncle Luke. Maybe they didn't see it, and we can clean this up before they get back."

I gaze back at Trista, rubbing her cheeks softly as I ask, "Are you sure you want to be a part of this circus?"

She laughs, and more tears fall down her face. "I'm sure I want to be a family with you."

My chest rises with pride at the sexiest words I've ever heard this woman say out loud. I wrap my arms around her and kiss her fiercely, pulling away when I remember, "We're having a girl, Lucky."

She laughs against my lips. "We're having a girl, Mr. Mountain Man."

CHAPTER 44

WEEKS PREGNANT: 24
ANIMALS ON THE MOUNTAIN: 10

Everly

"Calder, you have to let her go," my dad says, gripping his brother's shoulder outside the Denver airport passenger drop-off area. "We're going to miss our flight."

My eyes are welled with tears as Calder pulls back and rubs the heel of his hand into his eyes. "I'm going to miss you, shithead."

"I'm going to miss you too, dumb fuck," I deadpan.

"Everly!" Grandma gasps. "We're in public!"

My whole family bursts out laughing, except me. Nothing feels funny about this moment. Uncle Luke moves in for a hug next, and I feel more tears flood my vision. I'd never tell anyone this, but I will miss him and our talks the most.

He pulls back and chucks my chin. "Hit me up when you need to talk. Don't let the time difference stop you."

My lips quiver as he says the words I most needed to hear. "No one else I'd rather call."

Sniffing loudly, I turn and look at Uncle Wyatt, whose face is stone serious. He hasn't said a word since we all loaded up in my dad's SUV this morning to drive me to the airport. It's a little dramatic to have eight people see you off, and security has come by and yelled at us twice, but my family is nothing if not over the top.

I offer a weak smile to my grumpy uncle. "You gonna miss me, Uncle Wyatt?" I prop my hands on my hips.

"Millie might," Wyatt grunts, and for some ridiculous reason, a soft sob shakes through my chest as pain slices through me.

"Don't let Millie forget about me, promise?"

"Oh hell," Wyatt grumbles and moves in, binding his arm around my neck as he pulls me in for a gruff hug.

I cry into his arms for a moment, relishing in the mountain smell on his flannel. I'm going to miss it like crazy. I'm going to miss all my uncles like crazy. I've lived most of my life seeing the three of them on a weekly basis. They treated me like a daughter, a friend, a sibling, a concert buddy. I've felt so loved and supported and protected by them I don't know what it will be like without their constant presence. It's terrifying.

But I have to find my identity beyond my family. It's time.

Out of the corner of my eye, I see Trista holding her belly and pull away from my uncle to point accusingly at her. "Weekly belly pics. I mean it."

"Yes, ma'am." She salutes and steps up beside Wyatt, whose hand instantly threads into hers just like it did yesterday when they walked out of the barn. "I'll send you pictures of the animals too. And all the new ones that come to live on Fletcher Mountain while you're away."

My eyes flash to my scowling uncle. "More animals?"

Wyatt turns his scowl to the pregnant woman beside him, but his eyes are soft and crinkly around the edges, revealing his true feelings. He looked at her like that all day yesterday while everyone's heads basically imploded with shock.

Except for mine.

I saw this coming a mile away.

I beamed with pride as I watched my uncle dote on Trista during the rest of the baby shower. His eyes and hands rarely left her, and while I could tell she was overwhelmed by the people and the nosy questions, she seemed happy too. There was a twinkle in her eye that I didn't see when I first met her. They're both totally in love, and it's all because of me. Winning!

And while I don't know what their future holds, I feel relieved
that they're trying because there are a million ways to make a family.
I'm a great example of that. I have three moms, three uncles, and a
dad who I consider my primary caregivers. Who cares if they started
this whole journey as a surrogate and a single guy? They're ending it
happy, and that's all most of us want out of life.

Trista leans her head on Wyatt's arm as I glance down at her belly.
"Is she kicking yet?"

Trista presses her hands to her stomach and shakes her head sadly.
All day at the shower, I kept trying to feel the baby move, and every
time I'd put my hand there, she'd stop. I felt Ethan move in Cozy's
belly all the time, and I really wanted to feel one little kick before I left.
Especially because I won't be back before this baby is born.

Trista tsks, "Sorry, kid. She must be taking a nap in there."

"A Fletcher girl needs her beauty sleep." I feel the tears return as
I glance back at Wyatt. "You're having a little girl."

Wyatt's hand moves to touch Trista's belly as he presses a kiss into
her hair. They look so content, like they've been together for weeks,
not just a day. At least I got to see this before I flew across an ocean.

I say goodbye to my grandma and my little brother, who's teary
as well. Uncle Calder flings Ethan onto his shoulders to help cheer
him up, and I give everyone a big wave before I head into the airport
with my dad and Cozy, who are flying out with me to get me settled.

As we make our way to the baggage check, Trista calls out behind
me. "Everly, wait!"

I turn on my heel to see her jog over to me as my parents watch us
curiously. Trista grabs my hand and presses it to her belly, and instantly,
I feel a light drumming on the palm of my hand. My eyes widen as a
huge smile spreads across my face. "Aw, that's my girl!"

"A parting gift." Trista laughs, and I can't help but notice her eyes
filling with tears. She sniffs and waves her hand in front of her face.
"It's not lost on me that I wouldn't be here without you, kid."

My own eyes fill with tears at her saying that. A chance meeting
on a Denver street corner and a door in the face, and now...she's making a family with my uncle. Life is wild, and I can't help but feel my

grandpa's presence wrapping me up in his own hug at this very moment. I know he had a hand in all of this too.

Trista moves in to give me a hug, and I croak into her shoulder, "I still can't believe my plan actually worked."

"What plan?" Trista pulls away and eyes me curiously.

"You and my uncle." I glance past her at Wyatt, who's waiting at the door for her, watching us with so much love and affection I feel ready to burst.

"Huh?"

I waggle my brows at my soon-to-be auntie. "I knew you two would hit it off. It's why I asked you to interview for the job."

"You didn't know." Trista scoffs and gives me a playful shove.

I shrug and begin to walk backward away from her confused expression.

"How could you have possibly known?" she asks, still puzzling over this bomb I just dropped.

I shoot her a coy wink. "I told you I was a mastermind."

CHAPTER 45

WEEKS PREGNANT: 37
ANIMALS ON THE MOUNTAIN: 12

Trista

A few months later

"Jo, your son won't stop gawking at me," I say into the phone as I stand at the kitchen counter, preparing myself a very hard-earned snack.

"Tell him he has a baby room to get completed," Johanna snaps firmly.

I lift my brows knowingly. "Your mom is on my side."

"What else is new?" Wyatt's shoulders shake with silent laughter as he stares at the bread in my hand. "I'm just trying to figure out how much more peanut butter you're going to pile onto that struggling piece of toast."

I point my table knife at the hot mountain man currently bothering me. "What you don't understand, boyfriend, is that this bread is merely a vehicle of transport for the peanut butter."

"I just skip the bread and use a spoon straight out of the jar," Johanna chimes into my ear. "One perk of living alone, I suppose."

The corners of my mouth lift into a small smile at Wyatt's mother's casual reply that didn't contain an ounce of emotion. We've grown close over the past several months, and she's added me to her weekly lunch delivery rotations in Denver. It's been good for both of us, I think.

She sits and watches me eat, and I pick her brain about motherhood because Lord knows I never had a good example of it growing up. I need all the help I can get, and she likes feeling needed. We're healing each other in completely unexpected ways. And I'm the only one she lets call her Jo, so she obviously loves me.

And damn, does it feel good to be loved by these Fletchers.

Wyatt bends over and boldly takes a bite of my toast. "Is this as serious as that time you cried at the restaurant because I ate your favorite-*looking* french fry?"

I cut a sharp look at the man treading on very thin ice. "Jo, I'm going to need to call you back. Your son clearly woke up today and chose violence."

"Let me know if I need to come up there," she states in her utterly perfect mom voice.

We hang up, and I set my knife down to pinch the bridge of my nose. "I know you had no way of knowing I was saving that particular french fry, but it felt personal at the time, okay?"

The way he fights back his smile is so goddamn hot it makes my stomach hurt, and I forget why I'm mad at him. Or maybe those damn Braxton Hicks contractions are at it again. Those motherfuckers are wearing on my last nerve. Along with these leggings that are trying to kill me.

I set my toast down to drag the maternity panel down to the base of my belly. "God, I miss my jeans," I groan as I brace myself on the counter and exhale heavily.

Wyatt angles his head and stares at my backside as he moves in closer. "These leggings are putting in a good shift for you, though," he husks as he presses in behind me, kissing the area below my ear and groping my belly like it belongs to him.

Which these days, I suppose it does.

I moved in with the man, and I'm hardly recognizable anymore. I'm besties with his mom, and I'm hanging out with Cozy like she's my sister-in-law already. I'm calling him boyfriend like a pompous asshole and demanding breakfast in bed because my ankles are just the tiniest bit swollen. I even ask him to fill my gas tank now. No hesitation. I've

let having a man and a family who enjoy taking care of me go straight
to my head, and I am now completely insufferable.

And happier than I've ever been.

I turn on my heel to face my acts-of-service lover so I can drink
in his scent. My hands slide up his arms and grip the edges of his in-
sulated vest. "Listen, you have to take off this Carhartt vest."

He frowns and pulls back, adjusting his vest. "What's wrong with
it?"

"Nothing. You just look so ridiculously hot in it that I want you
to get me pregnant again, and that ain't possible, *and* I really should
be mad at you for tormenting me about my peanut butter obsession."

Wyatt's brows lift as he leans in and presses a tender kiss to my
lips. He moves down my jaw and neck, his trim beard causing shivers to
erupt over every inch of my body. His voice is deep and sensual on my
flesh when he replies, "I don't mind practicing for the next one, though."

"Okay, Mr. Next One," I snap and push him away, already feeling
the effects of our canoodling squarely between my legs. "You know the
plan. Baby first, a healthy maternity leave, then the rescue center…
then we can discuss the possibility of more children. Get your breeding kink under control, man."

He laughs and grabs my neck to pull me in for a deep, drugging
kiss that consistently makes me wonder if I need to do this rescue
center at all or if I'm better off just letting this man breed me until
the end of days.

Oh hell…now I'm getting a breeding kink. It's the damn Carhartt
vest! Gray sweatpants never did it for me. It's just too sloppy of a look.
Not masculine enough. But Wyatt right now, with a little extra winter facial hair and this oak-brown-vest situation over his blue flannel
that brings out his eyes? Stick a fork in me, I'm done. Seriously, the
man could hit me with his truck in this vest, and I would jump up
and tell him I'm sorry.

But then he removes the vest, and I regain control of my thoughts
and remember that I have ambitions outside of my loins. I cashed that
donation from Max as soon as my nonprofit was approved, and that
money has already been put to good use feeding the extra critters I

have populating Wyatt's barn. If only he had a bigger barn, I wouldn't have to continue searching for my own property, which is proving to be much more expensive than I originally expected.

This is why Wyatt and I are still arguing over what to do with the surrogacy fund. He wanted to donate the full amount to the rescue center, but I refused because there are still some gifts I cannot accept. And he's already given me so much more than I ever dreamed of for my life. He's given me a chance at a real family.

I break our kiss, which is quickly headed into the bedroom, because I have too much to do today. "We need to finish this nursery before you plan for more babies, Papa Bear."

He laughs and licks his lips. "Well, I've made progress on your to-do list, Momma Bear, so come upstairs and see for yourself."

My heart picks up speed as I follow him up the stairs that he's already installed baby gates at the top and bottom of even though I told him we had months before we needed to worry about that, but he's a "five minutes from now" man, and I've learned to just let him do what he needs to do to feel content.

When we round the corner into the baby room, my heart sighs happily. He's put the white oak custom crib and rocker that Calder made for us directly under the large window that overlooks the backside of the mountain. He's hung the mossy-green curtains I bought on clearance at my favorite JCPenney. And he mounted the quilt his mother made of all of his father's old shirts on the open wall opposite the changing table and dresser. It's not the girliest of rooms, but something tells me this kid of ours will care more about playing in the mud than playing with dolls.

I move over to rub my fingers along the quilted stitching. "This looks so perfect here."

Wyatt shoves his hands into his pockets and nods as he looks at it. "My mom is going to lose it when she sees this."

"What about you?" I ask, watching him closely.

His lips thin. "Feels right in here. Like my dad will be front row center for her whole life."

My eyes well with tears. Damn hormones. I join him in the

doorway to admire his hard work. "I never had my own room growing up."

Wyatt wraps his arms around me and holds me from behind. I've been doing this a lot lately. Confessing my past traumas. I'm not sure what it means, but it feels good to get them out. Growing up a kid in a struggling household is a very early experience of shame, and acknowledging some of the things I endured instead of bottling it all up seems to be healing in more ways than one.

And Wyatt is an incredible listener. One of the instances when the whole strong, silent type works well for us.

I pat his hands on my belly. "This kid is so lucky."

"Yeah, she is," Wyatt says, rubbing my belly affectionately. "Because she'll have you for a mom."

Mom.

I love when he says that.

I swipe at my errant tears and shake off the emotions weighing down on me. "So I've been thinking about names."

"Not this again." Wyatt groans and releases me to lean on the wall and hit me with another one of his infamous glowers. "I am running out of vetoes and am terrified we're going to end up naming our daughter some insane barn animal name like Trumpet or Manwich."

"Don't come for Trumpet and Manwich!" I snap defensively. "Those two alpacas came from very troubled homes and can't help what they're named."

"Okay, but you keep suggesting these fancy names, and our daughter will need something strong if she's going to be a mountain kid, you know? Did you know that your name means noise?"

"Mine?"

"Yes, the name Trista literally means noisy."

"You're lying. I need to google that. Go downstairs and grab my phone."

"Fact-check me for the rest of our lives, baby." He kisses me on the lips and smirks. "Because when I read that, I figured that's why we're so perfect together. I've been quiet my whole life because the only voice I wanted to hear was yours."

I roll my eyes at his cheesiness. "Well, now I can't fact-check you because you managed to turn an insult into a compliment."

He beams proudly, and I cross my arms and glance back over at the quilt when a thought strikes me. "What if we name her after your dad?"

"Steven is kind of an odd name for a girl, isn't it?"

"Not if we call her Stevie."

Wyatt's head pulls back as he considers this, his eyes turning to stare at the quilt with me. "Stevie?"

I bite my lip and nod. "Stevie Everly Fletcher sounds pretty perfect, don't you think?"

Wyatt turns to look at me, concern etched in his brows. "These are all my family names."

"No, they're not." I poke him in the ribs, my heart warming in my chest as I say the next part out loud. "It's my family too."

His eyes soften as he moves in and wraps me in a big bear hug, my giant belly making it a bit awkward but no less life-changing.

CHAPTER 46

ANIMALS ON THE MOUNTAIN: 14
BABIES COMING TO THE MOUNTAIN: 1

Wyatt

1 Month Later

Everly breaks down bawling the minute she steps into our post-partum hospital suite, causing everyone to erupt with laughter. Max moves to stand beside her, helping her remain on her feet as she continues to lose it the closer and closer she gets to our baby girl.

Baby girl.

I'm a dad.

"Hey, kid," Trista says with a knowing smirk from her hospital bed as she holds our daughter, looking more beautiful than I've ever seen her. The woman was a beast during the entire delivery. She didn't want any drugs and didn't even scream once. Just made this weird, satanic humming noise that might haunt me for a few months, but I'll get over it because…I'm a dad.

"Want to hold your cousin?" Trista asks as Everly stands beside her.

Everly nods, and I watch nervously as she passes our baby over. My protective instinct over this kid might be an issue for me. If I'm this bad when she's a tiny, helpless baby, how bad will I be when she's running around the mountain exploring? Or worse yet, turning into a teenager like Everly and making decisions on her own? This will be hard for me. Luckily, I have Trista to help me through all of this.

"You ruined my baby pool guess at the Mercantile, you know," Calder says with a huff. "I didn't even know you could be pregnant for longer than your due date or whatever."

"How much money was in the pool?" Trista asks.

"Seven hundred and fifty bucks," Luke replies with a laugh. "I think the whole damn town is in on it. But I don't even know who won it?"

"It was me," Everly says, not taking her eyes off the baby. "I knew this little one would hold out for me to come home for the holidays." She smiles and drags her finger gently over our daughter's little button nose. "So what did you name her? I'm dying to know. You know I can't stand secrets."

I reach for Trista's hand and smile at my whole family. We were waiting to tell them all once Everly arrived, so here goes nothing. "We decided to name her Stevie Everly Fletcher."

"After two very important people in her life," Trista adds with a smile as she looks over at my mom nervously.

The waterworks on Everly begin again, and I rush over, holding my hands out to take the baby because she is scaring the shit out of me with her hysterics.

My mom sniffles softly from her chair, grabbing a handkerchief out of her purse as she nods solemnly. "That's a really good name."

I smile at Trista, whose eyes are also filled with tears as she watches my mom. Their bond was clear as day when my mom walked in the door today to meet her new grandchild, only to bypass her and check in on Trista first. She pushed my girlfriend's hair out of her face and asked her how she felt, wanting every little detail before she even gave herself a moment to meet the baby.

They cried tears of joy in each other's arms, and I thanked my lucky stars that my family gets it. Trista doesn't have anyone showing up to check on her today. No mom or dad was calling to get the latest ultrasound pictures or ask what kind of casseroles she wanted in the freezer for her maternity leave. Her sister didn't put money in the Jamestown bar baby pool, where they guessed the height, weight, and delivery date.

My mom understood what today would be like for Trista better than I could have ever imagined. Cozy has easily become the sister Trista deserved because of their genuine connection. And if my dad was still here...he'd be right beside her, checking on both my girls.

This is Trista's found family. And I'm a lucky man. I'll be even luckier if she marries me someday.

But that's tomorrow's problem. Today...I'm just going to live in the moment and enjoy being a family with my girls.

I wake early our first morning back at the mountain as a family of three to find Trista standing in my living room. The fire crackles as she stares out the floor-to-ceiling windows, watching fresh snow fall on the mountain as the sun sheds tiny rays of light on the red barn down below. My eyes drink in her tall wool socks and big, baggy T-shirt. It will be a long six weeks, that's for sure, but with views like this, I have no problem waiting.

She's swaying back and forth with our daughter in her arms, humming a Taylor Swift song I'll never admit to knowing. I make my way over to them and wrap my arms around the two of them to join in their movement.

"I didn't even hear her wake up," I whisper, staring down at our little one, who's now fast asleep. Stevie has a light dusting of brown hair on her head and the sweetest little lips, with the top one just slightly bigger than the bottom. Just like her momma.

"She didn't cry," Trista says with a happy sigh. "I just didn't want her to miss her first mountain sunrise."

My heart tightens at that comment. The way Trista loves it up here feels so good. Like she was always meant to be here with me.

The sun peaks over the mountain crest, shining a ray of light on the three of us. "It is a pretty good view," I offer.

"You're not even looking at it," Trista says, gesturing to the window.

"The mountain pales in comparison to you two," I say, and without hesitating, I reach around Trista and set a small velvet box on top of our daughter's swaddled belly.

"What is that?" Trista asks, stopping her swaying instantly.

"I wanted to get Reggie or Millie to help me with this, but I was too afraid they'd eat the ring."

"So you're using our baby instead?" she deadpans, her lips parted in shock.

"Hell yes, I am." Releasing her, I kneel beside her, taking her hand in mine as she uses her other one to hold Stevie. "You made me promise not to talk to you about marriage until after Stevie came. Well, it's after."

"Literally two days after," she says with a garbled laugh.

"I'm feeling lucky." I wink up at her and try to remember the speech I've been building up in my head for the past several weeks. "Trista, I read in one of my parenting books—"

"There is no way this was in one of your parenting books!"

I tilt my head and eye her sternly. "Are you going to let me finish?"

"Yes, sorry." The teasing glint in her eyes warms me from the inside out.

"I read that one of the most important things a father can do for his child is to love its mother."

My voice cracks at the end, and her smile falls instantly. Her chin trembles with the same emotion swelling inside my chest. I fight the urge to stand and kiss the fresh tears falling down her cheeks, but I have an important question to get out.

"I love you, Lucky. More than I even thought possible. This mountain was once my escape from the world, my quiet sanctuary to get away from my thoughts. But I love the noise you bring into my life. You turned my house into a home, and I want to continue our life up here forever...whether that be with more babies or more animals or more of both, I'm all in. I love you, past, present, and future, and I want to spend the rest of my life with you. Will you marry me?"

She beams through her tears as she clutches our daughter close to her cheek. "What do you think, Mountain Man?"

EPILOGUE

ANIMALS ON THE MOUNTAIN: 16
FAMILY MEMBERS GOING TO MEXICO: 10
PLUS-ONES GOING TO MEXICO: ???

Trista

"**W**yatt, look at me!" I call out while trudging up the snow-worn path toward the wood-chopping station behind his house. Our house. It's *our* house.

My soon-to-be husband sets his ax down and turns on his heel, looking delectable with the snowy mountaintop background. Even hotter than usual with that baby monitor strapped around his chest. Stevie is currently down for a nap, and this overbearing, overprotective dad demands to take that big-screen monitor with him everywhere he goes—even though the app sends notifications to our phones.

What can I say? He's an obsessed father.

I've caught him mindlessly petting Millie while watching the monitor in the barn more times than I can count, and our baby is barely two months old. I can't imagine what he'll be like when she's a teenager.

Sweet or psycho? Who can tell?

Wyatt's eyes turn to liquid pools of heat as he rakes his gaze over my body. "What am I looking at specifically because I like it all."

My God, this man. I'm still postpartum, softer and squishier than ever, way too fat for a surrogacy agency, and he still wants me all the time.

But here's a big truth bomb: that six-week postpartum break was rough on me too. As it turns out, I've grown accustomed to regular dickin'…especially when it comes from someone who looks at me like *him*.

I prop my hands on my hips and smile. "Do you hear that?"

He frowns as the sound finally hits his ears. "What is that?"

"I'm a cow!" I nearly squeal with excitement.

His face falls. "Baby, aren't we well past the cow stage?"

I lift my shirt to showcase the breast-pumping contraption that you can barely tell is operating. "It's completely mobile, no plug. This will be perfect for our wedding in Mexico next month!"

"Oh God!" Luke bellows, and my eyes widen as I look past my fiancé and spot his two brothers currently making their way down the hill from their cabins toward us.

"Avert your eyes!" Wyatt thunders, stomping over to me to yank my shirt down. His nostrils flare, and he's breathing heavily as he growls, "Seriously, Trista?"

"How was I supposed to know your brothers would come over?" I huff back. "Besides, all they're seeing is stretch marks and mostly covered nipples."

"All my favorite parts," he grumbles and turns protectively to block me from his brothers' views, even though I'm fully covered now.

"What the hell were those horrible things attached to your titties?" Calder has the nerve to ask. He's brave for that one.

"Stop looking at my wife's breasts." Wyatt thrusts a finger at both of his brothers as they stand by the woodpile, and I struggle not to swoon. I love when he calls me his wife. Premature, yes, but it feels so glorious all the same.

"Kind of hard when she's flashing the whole mountain," Calder jeers, his nose wrinkling. "And besides, there's nothing sexual about whatever is going on under there."

"My wife making milk for our daughter is extremely sexy." Wyatt is out of control with his rage. It's so cute.

"It's so I can pump milk for Stevie and still hang by the pool in Mexico!"

Wyatt turns to look at me, his brows raised. "So does that mean you're coming around to the idea of us getting married so quickly?"

I exhale heavily. Originally, the plan was to wait a while before we got hitched. Let us adjust to parenthood a bit. Get used to the idea of being a family of three. We're in no rush, right?

But when Max told the whole family he won a week's stay at a fancy private Mexican villa complete with butlers and staff and that it was over Everly's Easter break from university and he wanted all of us to come, things got a little carried away.

It was New Year's Eve, and the whole family was hanging out at Max's. I was tipsy on my first drink since getting knocked up and in love with my husband and baby and this newfound family I won the lottery with. The words *"We should get married while we're there"* just kind of tumbled out of my mouth.

I blame Cozy. That bitch has a heavy pour.

Of course, everyone loved the idea. Everly immediately went into party-planning mode. Johanna said she would be Stevie's nanny while we're all down there because she knows I could never leave Stevie so soon. And Wyatt?

The man had happy tears in his eyes over my declaration.

It made me realize that it was my turn to show him how much I love him and his whole crazy family. So here I am.

"I applied for my passport and have been dress shopping with Cozy already, so yes, Mr. Mountain Man. I'm ready to marry you."

He hits me with the most panty-dropping smile as he leans in and wraps his arms around me, crushing me to his chest. His lips begin to devour me whole, and the whiskers from his beard make my body hum with desire. I lose myself in the moment, relishing in the light snowflakes dropping over us as we kiss in this snow with his brothers watching like the lovable creeps they are most days.

Until I feel something wet on my chest. "What the…"

I break our kiss and pull away to see that my breast pumps have somehow detached, and I've leaked milk all over my shirt.

"I'm going to be sick," Calder groans and turns away.

Luke gives an apologetic smile. "We were going to see if we get plus-ones for this big wedding, but we'll, um…let you guys deal with that."

They walk away, and I flinch at that request because Mountain Man Matchmaker Everly has been in my ear with big plans for Calder and Cozy's best friend, Dakota, who is, in fact, coming with us to Mexico. She's taking photos at Everly's demand. I'm not sure how she'll take the news that her uncle wants to bring a date that I'm pretty sure won't be Dakota.

Mountain-man drama!

I attempt to save whatever ounces of milk are still in the containers and struggle with my damp shirt under my coat. "This stuff is liquid gold, you know."

"I'll help you make more." Wyatt waggles his dirty, filthy eyebrows at me, and I hate that I can't help but smile back at him.

"I'm mad at you for spilling my milk," I snap.

He points at my lips. "But you're smiling, so that comment feels very confusing."

"I know!" I growl, and the sound of Stevie's cry breaks through our moment of flirting.

Wyatt grips my shoulders and leans in to brush his lips to my forehead. "I got her, Momma," he murmurs before moving past me toward the house.

My heart contracts with that term of endearment, and I realize I can't wait to hear those words come out of our daughter's mouth someday. I cross my arms and sigh as I watch my fiancé walk away and thank my lucky stars that I stuck around for all this. Hell yes, I'm ready to get married to this man. Bring on Mexico.

The End

Ready for Calder and Dakota's story? Get ready for this one-bed, tropical Fletcher getaway, complete with laughs, steam, and all sorts of Fletcher family shenanigans! Find details for *Seven Year Itch* at amydawsauthor.com.

And grab the bonus epilogue for Wyatt and Trista at https://bookhip.com/HBBHAWT…you'll never guess how many animals are on Fletcher Mountain now!

MORE BOOKS BY
AMY DAWS

The London Lovers Series:
Becoming Us: Finley's Story Part 1
A Broken Us: Finley's Story Part 2
London Bound: Leslie's Story
Not the One: Reyna's Story

A London Lovers/Harris Brothers Crossover Novel:
Strength: Vi Harris & Hayden's Story

The Harris Brothers Series:
Challenge: Camden's Story
Endurance: Tanner's Story
Keeper: Booker's Story
Surrender & Dominate: Gareth's Duet

Payback: A Harris Brother Spin-off Standalone
Blindsided: A Harris Brother Spin-off Standalone
Replay: A Harris Brother Spin-off Standalone
Sweeper: A Secret Harris Brother Standalone

The Wait With Me Series:
Wait With Me: A Tire Shop Rom-Com
Next in Line: A Bait Shop Rom-Com
One Moment Please: A Hospital Cafeteria Rom-Com
Take A Number: A Bakery Rom-Com
Last on the List: A Nanny Rom-Com

Mountain Men Matchmaker Series:
Nine Month Contract: Wyatt's story
Seven Year Itch: Calder's story, coming soon
Six Ways Til Sunday: Luke's Story, coming soon
All in Good Time: Everly's story, coming soon

Pointe of Breaking: A College Dance Standalone by Amy Daws &
Sarah J. Pepper

Chasing Hope: A Mother's *True* Story of Loss, Heartbreak,
and the Miracle of Hope

For all retailer purchase links, visit:
www.amydawsauthor.com

MORE ABOUT THE AUTHOR

Number 1 Amazon Bestselling author Amy Daws writes spicy love stories that take place in America, as well as across the pond. She's most known for her footy-playing Harris Brothers and writing in a tire shop waiting room. When Amy is not writing, she's likely making charcuterie boards from her home in South Dakota where she lives with her daughter and husband.

For more of Amy's work, visit: www.amydawsauthor.com or check out the links below.

www.facebook.com/amydawsauthor
www.tiktok.com/@amydawsauthor
www.twitter.com/amydawsauthor
www.instagram.com/amydawsauthor

Made in United States
North Haven, CT
26 May 2024

52063183R00214